A LITTLE BIT OF EVERYTHING

ALSO BY RICHARD REZENDES

Ground of the Devil Book One
Ground of the Devil Book Two
Ground of the Devil Book Three
The Revelation of Emma Grace
A Haunting in Mattapoisett
Hell Under the United States
Windy Outbreaks

A Little Bit of Everything

RICHARD REZENDES

Sandra
from
Richard Rezendes
8/9/25

A Little Bit of Everything
Copyright © 2025 Richard Rezendes

Visit our website at
www.StillwaterPress.com
for more information.

First Stillwater River Publications Edition.

ISBN: 978-1-965733-45-5

Library of Congress Control Number: 2025903270

1 2 3 4 5 6 7 8 9 10
Written by Richard Rezendes.
Published by Stillwater River Publications,
West Warwick, RI, USA.

Publisher's Cataloging-in-Publication
(Provided by Cassidy Cataloguing Services, Inc.)
Names: Rezendes, Richard, author.
Title: A little bit of everything / Richard Rezendes.
Description: First Stillwater River Publications edition. |
West Warwick, RI, USA : Stillwater River Publications, [2025]
Identifiers: LCCN: 2025903270 | ISBN: 9781965733455
Subjects: LCSH: Rezendes, Richard. | Life change events. |
Sports. | Discotheques. | Parties. | Providence (R.I.) |
LCGFT: Short stories. | Essays. | Humor.
Classification: LCC: PS3618.E985 L58 2025 |
DCC: 818/.6--dc23

A LITTLE BIT OF

EVERYTHING

CONTENTS

A Little Bit of Everything

SECTION I

BROWN OF THE DEMONS
A STORY OF HOPE

PART 1

I had a lot of mean bosses when I worked at Brown University, and I ended up getting fired because of them! It's called the union against management! In 1973, I applied for a custodian job at Brown University. At the time, I was a dishwasher at the Hospital Trust Bank and a janitor with Allied Maintenance in the evening. I was working two jobs, and between shifts, I would go up to Brown University to play basketball in their gyms, lay in the sun, and talk to the girls. Every time a job posting went up, I applied until I got in.

One day, I went to Sayles Gym to play basketball, and I heard what sounded like someone bowling downstairs. Curious, I went to the main office and met a lady named Janet Lutz. I said to her, "You have a bowling alley downstairs!"

"Yes, we do," she said.

I asked her, "Can I go take a look?"

She said, "Yes."

So, I went down to see the bowling alley. There were two

lanes with gutters, a ball return, and various types of bowling pins—tenpins, duckpins, and candlepins. There were small balls and big balls, and you had to set up your own pins. I came up with a plan: if I could bowl here, I might have a chance to make a career out of it. I ran upstairs and asked Mrs. Lutz if I could bowl there.

She said, "You have to be a Brown student."

I said, "I'm not a Brown student, but I am waiting to get a job here. I've been trying every day."

Meanwhile, TJ, a Brown security guard and a friend of mine, came in. We were friends because my younger brother, Tom, worked at the Mobil station nearby.

TJ asked, "Is he giving you any trouble?" He joked with Mrs. Lutz, then said, "He's a good guy—he plays basketball every day across campus!"

Mrs. Lutz said, "You can use the bowling alley."

I was so happy that I forgot about basketball. I went bowling every day at Sayles Gym. One day, I went to Lang's Bowl-o-rama, and they gave me free bowling pins because they had gotten new ones. I tied two boxes with 40 pins to my bike and rode from Lang's in Cranston, Rhode Island, all the way up the hill on the East Side of Providence. The pins held up until I got in front of the police and security. Suddenly, they fell off my bike, rolling down Waterman Street.

There were bowling pins everywhere! Traffic was stopped for half an hour while the police helped me pick them up, repack, and bring them to Sayles Gym. The cop put half of them in the trunk of his car. TJ never laughed so much watching the whole scene. Since then, we've been very good friends.

With four sets of pins, my own ball, and shoes, I bowled regularly. Mrs. Lutz told me I had to leave when TJ came to lock up. Then, I bowled so much that my black rubber ball left marks on the lanes. Mrs. Lutz eventually said, "You can't bowl here anymore."

When I finally got hired at Brown, I could bowl again under certain conditions: I had to clean the black marks I left on the lanes. I bought a can of lane conditioning oil from East Providence Lanes for $15.00, which lasted a year. I kept those lanes looking good, and this is how my bowling career started.

Before I was hired at Brown, I worked for Bayside Apartments in Warwick as a porter/maintenance cleaner. It took six months for Brown to reach me, and it happened by chance: I was home sick that day! I had two interviews with a man named Phil Andrews and was hired on Monday, December 3, 1979.

The Saturday before starting, I attended a party in South Wayland. While there, I went to the men's room and saw that the sink had been ripped out of the wall and the basement was flooded. I thought, "Oh my God!" That night, I rode my bike from Edgewood in Cranston to the East Side, went to the party, and rode back home at two o'clock in the morning.

By Sunday, I decided to move closer to work. I borrowed $206.00 from my dad to help pay for an apartment at 257 Gano Street. I paid him back by the end of the week and moved into my new place—a one-bedroom efficiency with high ceilings. It had a living room, bedroom, bathroom, and kitchenette. I set it up with a small table, two chairs, a leather couch that folded into a twin bed, a TV, a stereo, and a bureau for my clothes.

The day I started at Brown was one of the worst. My assigned building was South Wayland's Delta Tau fraternity—the same building where I had attended the party. The basement was flooded with a foot of water, and I had to clean it up using several wet vacs and squeegees.

My daily tasks included:

- Cleaning offices and buffing floors every morning.
- Cleaning bathrooms and the lounge after the morning break.

- Cleaning hallways from the fourth floor to the basement, sweeping stairs, and removing trash after lunch.

Later in the week, as the work got easier, I became friendly with the fraternity members. They started inviting me to their parties. One of the students, Russel Setterpain, was my allergy doctor, and his roommate Stenny was a bit of a nutcase. The fraternity housed many football players, who gave me tickets to their games.

At the time, I was in my late 20s and looked like Elvis Costello. The fraternity brothers nicknamed me "Elvis." They even swore me into the fraternity and put me in the 1980 yearbook. Whenever they had a party, I could join by paying $3.00 and drinking all night with them.

As part of my initiation, they made me drink four shots of Jack Daniels and chug a 16-ounce beer. I warned them, "If I puke, you're going to clean it up!" Sure enough, I did, and they cleaned it up. That was the easy part.

Next, they sent me to Delta Phi Omega, another fraternity, and told me to dance with a girl there. I arrived at 10:40 p.m., but the party hadn't started yet. They then told me to go to the Engine Company nightclub in downtown Providence, grab, and kiss as many girls as I could while they waited across the street.

Fueled by adrenaline (and probably too much alcohol), I went into the Engine Company nightclub as part of my initiation. A band was playing, and I wasted no time getting to work. I danced with every girl I could, grabbing them and even French kissing most of them! The crowd at the bar thought it was hilarious, laughing at my antics.

However, not everyone was entertained. Someone threw a beer bottle at my head. Luckily, I didn't feel it—it just bounced off my head and hit a girl, knocking her drink out of her hand.

The irony? This was the same girl I'd been all over earlier in the night.

That's when things escalated. Two bouncers grabbed me and threw me out of the club headfirst. My head hit the pavement so hard that I bounced upright. But instead of sulking, I ran back up the East Side to the Delta Tau fraternity in a hurry, sober in an instant.

When I got back to the Delt house, I told the brothers what had happened. They were furious and decided to take matters into their own hands. A group of football players marched down to the Engine Company and tore the place apart. They broke things, got into fights, and caused significant damage.

The fallout was serious. The fraternity was thrown off campus because of the brawl. Meanwhile, my initiation continued—though it was far less dramatic.

After the chaos at the nightclub, I was told to return to Delta Phi Omega to find a girl to dance with. By the time I arrived—around 2:40 a.m.—the party was already over, and there was no one there. Frustrated and exhausted, I finally went home and slept all day.

The next morning, I woke up with a pounding headache and a big bump on my head. But I was now a confirmed member of Delta Tau.

Despite the chaos of my initiation, I became a full-fledged member of the Delta Tau fraternity, and life with the Delt brothers was a mix of camaraderie, parties, and unforgettable moments. Among my favorite memories were the massive stereo speakers in the Delt house lounge—speakers I absolutely fell in love with. They were powerful, sleek, and perfect for my music obsession.

One day, I worked up the courage to ask the brothers about them.

"Boy, I'd love to have those. I could make a nice disco with them," I said.

The response was typical Delt humor.

"I'm sure you would, Elvis," one of them joked. "Those are the main speakers for the lounge. But hey, you can come by and listen to them whenever you want."

I accepted that offer, showing up on Sunday and Thursday nights to enjoy the speakers with the guys. But then something unexpected happened.

Two weeks after my initiation, the brothers called me to the Delt house. The leader, John Woodring, a football player known for his leadership and sense of humor, had surprising news. "Elvis," he said, "take these speakers!"

At first, I thought it was a prank. Woodring was a legendary jokester, and I didn't want to get my hopes up. So, I double-checked with the other brothers to see if he was serious. To my shock, they confirmed it—it was real. The speakers were mine.

Ecstatic, I took the speakers home. I already had plans brewing for my very own disco, and these speakers were the perfect centerpiece. Around the same time, the fraternity was deconstructing their basement bar as part of clearing out the house following their expulsion. This gave me another idea.

I asked, "Can I take this wood home to build something?"

"Be my guest, Elvis. Take whatever you want," they said.

So, I loaded my car with 4x4 poles, plywood, and paneling from the dismantled bar. It was a treasure trove of materials for the disco I envisioned.

Back at my apartment at 257 Gano Street, my landlord, Irwin Greenberg, noticed the pile of wood. "What the hell are you going to do with all that wood?" he asked, clearly amused.

I grinned and said, "I'm going to build a disco in my apartment."

He burst out laughing. "A disco? In here? Good luck with that!"

With the speakers from Delta Tau and a pile of reclaimed wood, I got to work turning my one-bedroom apartment into a full-fledged disco. It wasn't just an idea anymore—it was a mission.

I started by using the 4x4 poles and plywood panels to create a structure in the living room. I nailed the poles securely to flat panels at the base for stability and then attached additional panels to the top. The frame stood a solid 10 feet high. I drove spikes into the wood floor to hold it all in place.

To create a nightclub feel, I wrapped the poles with Reynolds Wrap aluminum foil, giving them a reflective, futuristic look. Then I strung 300 blinking Christmas lights around the poles to make them pop.

I added two mirror disco balls, one 12 inches and one 4 inches, hanging from the ceiling. Next, I installed two lamps—one with a green bulb and the other with a red bulb—to bathe the room in dynamic color. For the finishing touch, I hung a framed picture of a window overlooking the ocean with a red curtain, adding a quirky "VIP lounge" vibe.

The stereo speakers from Delta Tau were the crown jewels of my setup. To power them, I went to Angel Street Stereo, where I bought a radio receiver, a small mixer, two turntables, and a tape deck. I carefully wired the speakers, stapling the cables along the walls and out of sight. With the DJ system in my bedroom and the speakers blasting in the living room, the sound was phenomenal.

At that time, CDs didn't exist yet, so everything was vinyl. I stocked up on disco records, scouring local stores in downtown Providence to build my collection.

The final piece of the puzzle was the dance floor. My brother Tom and I constructed a lighted dance floor using panels, mirrors, and even more blinking Christmas lights. The floor was a 6x4 platform, covered with Plexiglass squares to protect the lights while creating a glowing effect beneath the dancers.

By the time I finished, my disco was ready for its debut. I christened it Eastgate 80, inspired by the black iron gates outside my building, my move to the East Side, and the turn of the decade. Then I made a bold move:

I put up a sign that said, "Party at Eastgate 80, Saturday Night – BYOB."

That Saturday, the crowd was beyond anything I expected. At first, only a handful of people arrived. But by 11 p.m., there was a line stretching down Waterman Street and up Gano Street, with hundreds of students waiting to get in.

Inside, the place was packed with over 120 people dancing, laughing, and enjoying the disco vibe. My speakers blasted the latest disco hits, the blinking lights set the mood, and the lighted dance floor dazzled everyone.

The next day, I woke up to a refrigerator full of leftover beer and wine—enough to last a year. But the party hadn't gone unnoticed. My landlord called me, clearly exasperated.

"Ricky," he said, "you can't put a red light at the front door! People driving by will think this place is a whorehouse. And you can't have that many people here. The building might collapse!"

He laid down a strict rule: No more than 10 people at a time.

After the overwhelming success of Eastgate 80's first party, I knew I couldn't stop there. My landlord's warning about keeping parties small forced me to get creative. I started hosting smaller gatherings, but that only fueled my ambition to upgrade the disco.

In 1982, I took Eastgate to the next level. My brother Tom helped me build a larger, more impressive lighted dance floor. This one was a 4x6 platform but featured an intricate system of blinking white Christmas lights and mirrors, all covered by clear Plexiglass squares.

The effect was mesmerizing. When the lights blinked, the mirrors below created a kaleidoscopic illusion. Dancers felt like they were on the floor of Studio 54!

The debut of Eastgate 82 was a party for a church youth group. The crowd was smaller but lively, and the mood was electric. A few of the young women were dancing on the lighted floor, and someone joked that you could see their underwear through the mirrored tiles. Everyone, including the women, laughed hysterically.

It was at this party that I met my new girlfriend, who would become a regular at Eastgate.

By 1983, Eastgate had evolved into Eastgate Palace—a true masterpiece. I added another pole, more panels, and hundreds of blinking Christmas lights wrapped around the structure. This time, I also built a second, larger lighted dance floor that measured 3x15 feet and spanned one side of the room.

The new floor featured an even more advanced lighting system, with white lights blinking in synchronized patterns under clear Plexiglass. The room was wrapped in tin foil and mirrors, making the entire apartment shimmer. It was a full sensory experience.

The last major party at Eastgate Palace was an end-of-the-year blowout for the Delta Tau brothers and their girlfriends. By now, I had stopped inviting random crowds and stuck to smaller groups of close friends.

This party, however, got out of control. Someone found my stash of pot and started passing it around. The music was pumping, and people were jumping up and down on the lighted dance floor. I had to yell at everyone to stop before the floor collapsed.

The night ended with the police showing up. Neighbors had called in a noise complaint. When the officers came inside, they searched the entire apartment for drugs, opening drawers and cabinets. Somehow, they missed the most incriminating evidence—two bowls of pot plants I was growing on the windowsills, covered by closed curtains.

Had they found those, I might have spent 29 years in jail instead of 29 years working at Brown University.

By the next year, the Eastgate parties were over. The Delta Tau brothers had graduated, and I was focusing more on my DJing gigs around town. The disco remained, but it was used more for personal enjoyment than public events.

PART 2

I had some demon bosses and some big rats! After working for four years, things began to change. My first boss was nice, Phil Andrews. He's the one who hired me: 7 a.m. until 3:30 p.m. Then Louie DeDenardo took over. He was a good boss until I started talking to the girls. For three years, I worked in South Wayland House, Delta Tau fraternity. Then, I was placed in the support group as a floater, and you go everywhere. That was more fun. I never missed a day, never took a sick day, and never was late or got into trouble, other than talking with the girls.

One day, working during the summer in Emery Willy Hall on the Pembroke campus, a rat by the name of Frank kept harassing and telling the lead man/HBC (head building custodian) that I wasn't doing my share of work, and that I was working more than he was. It was not equal, so I challenged Frank. Things got personal, and he punched me. We both got suspended for fighting. I got three days off because I didn't retaliate, and he got five days for punching me. When we came back to work, Louie put us to work together again. When we got to know each other better, we became best friends, and he let me work with him for the rest of the summer.

After I came back and Frank was out, I had to go move tables.

This redheaded guy I was working with dropped the table, and it slipped from my grip and crushed his finger. He was very upset. I told him I was sorry—the table was too heavy for me to move, so I had to keep working with him moving furniture. He was a union steward, and he did not like me. He knew if I made one more mistake, I'd be fired. He told the big boss I left early and took long breaks, but I didn't disobey the rule. He couldn't prove it, though, so I filed a grievance against him with the head of the union, and he never bothered me again.

Then, in the fall, things changed. All the support group was shipped to Bob Fallow at Robertson Hall, and Matt Barros was the big boss. I was in Metcalf Research Center, and this Bob Fallow kept checking up on me every half hour to make sure I was working. He changed his clothes several times so I wouldn't recognize him, but just by the way he walked and his appearance, I knew it was him. I challenged him, and he got mad. So, I told him to get my union steward, and he didn't. I turned him into Matt Barros, and then filed a grievance against him for harassment after my shift. He came in 23 times that day, and by the third day, he left me alone.

The following summer, I was back at work, and things seemed to be going smoothly. But then came a new challenge: the building was being renovated, and the schedule was all over the place. Bob Fallow was still my boss, and even though I had filed grievances against him, he continued to keep an eye on me. He would come by every hour, checking to see if I was doing my work. It felt like he was trying to make me look bad. Every time he showed up, I just went back to work, never giving him any excuse to criticize me.

One day, I got into an argument with one of the workers in the crew. He was being lazy and tried to blame me for the work not getting done. I calmly explained that we needed to divide the tasks better. He got upset and started yelling, but I just walked away and kept working. Louie, who had returned as the supervisor, saw the whole thing and gave me a nod of approval. He knew I was working hard, and that I wasn't the problem.

The next incident happened when I was working with Frank again. Even though we had become friends after the suspension, he still had a tendency to get under my skin. One day, he asked me to help him move some heavy equipment. I agreed, but the moment I lifted the object, I could feel my back give out. I ended up injuring myself, and when I tried to report it, Frank tried to downplay it. I told him firmly that I was in pain, and I insisted on going to the doctor. I filed an injury report, and Louie was supportive, making sure everything was handled correctly. Thankfully, the injury wasn't severe, but it still caused me to miss a few days of work.

As time went on, I started to realize that working in this environment wasn't the most sustainable for me. While I loved the team and appreciated the friendships I had made, the constant tension with certain coworkers, especially Bob Fallow and Frank, started to wear me down. I decided to look for something more stable and less stressful. I was ready for a change.

Then, after two weeks, the chemicals in Metcalf were making me sick, and I wanted a transfer. He said, "No, go see a doctor."

I said, "Okay! I'll go see my steward." I filed a grievance against Matt Barros, and I saw a doctor, and I got my transfer. I moved to the BioMed Building and other buildings, working for Leroy Halloway. We hit it off at first, but then it went bad. When I had a problem, he wouldn't tell me about it until it was too late. One day, I saw a union paper, and I put something nasty on it, thinking it was about a lady worker at East Providence Lanes.

I wrote, "You can do a big black Spanish ----." He's black, and his wife is Spanish. I put it in my bag. Leroy came in the morning, read my sports page, and questioned me about it.

At first, I denied writing it. Someone told him I had written the nasty note, so I admitted it. I didn't know it was a union person. I got suspended for five days, and I filed a grievance against him for going through my bag without my permission. Since then, we have been enemies. I ended up getting my five days paid back, and I brought him up on harassment charges. I also asked for a transfer. Bob Lavine, not the lawyer but a big boss, was involved. I filed a grievance against Leroy, Bob Lavine, and his boss for a transfer. I told them that if the union didn't help me, I would get my own lawyer. I showed these bosses that I wasn't afraid of anybody.

I said to Leroy, "You have two weeks to give me my transfer, or I will come after you with my own lawyer. I got rid of one boss, and I will do anything in my power to get you fired." Leroy and the two upper bosses knew I wasn't fooling around. The following day, I got my transfer.

I'm not supposed to be in the dorms because I like girls too much, but what happens? I'm right back in the dorms. Then, I went to the Grad Center in Tower C because the previous worker got fired. I worked for another black boss, and he was the nicest person you could work for. The manager was Germaine, and she started a student work program. My new boss, Omar Hazel, a great guy, gave me five student workers—all good kids. One kid did the vacuuming, the second swept and washed the stairs, the third removed all the trash/recyclables, the fourth cleaned the laundry and kitchens, and the fifth cleaned the windows. All I had to do was clean the bathrooms (six floors, no elevators). Each student had two hours to clean the building every day, and if one finished early, they'd help me.

Omar came to me and asked, "Why are you cleaning the windows? There's a lot of work to be done in here." I replied, "Five students, Omar. A lot of work got done. Go check it out." The boss couldn't believe how clean the building was. He would come down and read books with me at the end of the day. He was cool. He'd check up on me once a week, so I had plenty of downtime to write Ground of the Devil.

Then Dorothy took over, and she was a bitch. She took away the student help, and Omar retired. I got stuck with Bob Fallow again, checking up on me two to four times a day. He always caught me working, and he gave me a good evaluation because he knew I wouldn't take his shit. He got sick and retired, and he was better with me the second time.

Then, Dan Crawley came in. He was a mean man, harassing me every day until we had shouting matches. Everybody hated this guy, and he thought he was going to get me. He was so bad, I was filing grievances on him daily. I found out that if he got one more grievance, he would be fired. So, I was the one who was going to make it happen.

Finally, after several months of dealing with Dan Crawley, I knew I had to do something about it. He was an absolute nightmare—constantly belittling me and trying to undermine my work. His behavior made everyone miserable. Every day, he found something new to harass me about. The tension was unbearable, and I decided I wouldn't tolerate it anymore.

One morning, after an especially heated argument, I went straight to the union office. I filed yet another grievance, but this time, I made it clear to them that Dan Crawley was pushing me to my breaking point. He was making my work life so miserable that it was affecting my health and my performance. I told the union I wasn't going to just sit back and take it anymore. I knew Crawley had a reputation for being difficult, but I wasn't about to let him bully me out of my job.

The union was on my side, and soon after, they launched an investigation into his behavior. I found out that if he accumulated one more grievance, he would be fired. I knew it was my chance to finally end the reign of terror he had over me and the rest of the team. I kept documenting every interaction with him, and sure enough, a few weeks later, I was the one who made it happen. Dan Crawley was fired.

It felt like a huge weight had been lifted off my shoulders. The office felt quieter, more peaceful, and everyone seemed to breathe easier without him around. With him gone, I thought maybe things would settle down. But that's when the next challenge arrived.

I ended up working with Janet, who had just started in the department. She seemed nice at first, but over time, I started to notice a few things that didn't sit right with me. She was constantly talking behind people's backs and undermining the work of others. She'd find ways to take credit for things that weren't hers, and she'd never give anyone else the credit they deserved.

At first, I tried to stay out of it, but eventually, I had enough. I couldn't stand watching her treat my coworkers so badly. One day, during a staff meeting, Janet made a rude comment about a colleague's work. I immediately stood up for the person, and that's when Janet turned on me. She accused me of being disruptive and disrespectful, even though I had only been defending my coworker.

I knew I had to handle it professionally. I reported her behavior to my supervisor, and after some investigation, it turned out I wasn't the only one who felt this way. Other colleagues spoke up, and Janet was given a warning. I felt good about standing up for what was right, but I also knew that sometimes, it wasn't enough to just speak up—you had to take action when the time came.

After the drama with Janet, things calmed down again. For the first time in a while, I felt like I could actually focus on my work without all the distractions. But, as always, I stayed alert. I had learned the hard way that things could change quickly, and you had to be prepared for whatever came next.

Over time, I started to realize that working at this place was becoming more about survival than actually enjoying my job. I had gone through so many conflicts and power struggles with bosses and coworkers that it was starting to feel like a game of chess. But at the end of the day, it was my livelihood, and I had to keep pushing forward.

After the Janet situation, things seemed to settle down a bit. For a while, I actually enjoyed my work again. I could focus on the tasks at hand without worrying about people undermining me or creating unnecessary drama. But I knew better than to let my guard down completely.

One day, I got a call from Matt Barros, asking me to meet him in his office. My heart dropped. I hadn't heard from him in a while, and I wasn't sure what to expect. When I walked into his office, he didn't waste any time. He told me there had been a complaint about my behavior from one of the new workers.

I was immediately on edge. What now? I hadn't done anything wrong. Matt went on to explain that the new worker was having trouble adjusting to the pace and had blamed me for making the work harder than it needed to be. I couldn't believe it. I had always been someone who helped others, especially the new guys, to get settled in.

I stayed calm and explained that I had done my best to help this person, but it seemed like they weren't putting in the effort themselves. Matt Barros listened, but he didn't seem convinced. He told me he was going to keep an eye on things and that I should be more mindful of how I interact with others.

I was frustrated, but I didn't let it show. I knew this was just another test. I had dealt with worse, and I wasn't about to let one disgruntled coworker derail my progress.

After that meeting, I made it a point to double down on my efforts to help the new employees, to make sure there were no misunderstandings. But Matt kept his distance, and it felt like he was just waiting for me to slip up. I knew I couldn't afford to make any more mistakes.

In the meantime, the department was undergoing some major changes. There were more new faces, and a lot of the old crew had moved on to different jobs. While this meant less conflict for me, it also meant I had to build new relationships with people who didn't know me as well. Some of them were fine, but others made it clear that they weren't thrilled to work with someone who had such a "colorful" history.

The new atmosphere was strange. For once, it wasn't just the old bosses I had to watch out for—it was my peers too. I realized I had to navigate this new dynamic carefully. People could be nice to your face, but that didn't mean they weren't talking about you behind your back.

One of the new supervisors, Ellen, was particularly difficult to deal with. She liked to micromanage and had a tendency to take credit for work that wasn't hers. She was very meticulous, but it wasn't in a good way. It became clear to me that she wanted to be the "star" of the department, and if you weren't careful, she'd make sure you stayed in the shadows.

I didn't like the way she operated, but I kept my distance and did my job. I didn't want to make any waves, but I also wasn't going to let her walk all over me. I kept my head down, worked hard, and focused on the tasks I was given. Eventually, she got frustrated with me because I wouldn't play her game. I wasn't the type to suck up to anyone, and I made that clear.

After a few months, things took another turn. Ellen was reassigned, and a new supervisor came in. His name was Steve, and he was the total opposite of Ellen. Steve was laid-back, fair, and treated everyone with respect. I could tell right away that I was going to get along with him.

We hit it off immediately. For the first time in a long time, I felt like I had a supervisor who had my back. I was able to focus on my work without constantly worrying about whether or not

I was being watched or judged. I could actually relax and do my job the way I knew I could.

With Steve in charge, the atmosphere improved drastically. The whole team seemed to get along better, and there was less tension overall. Even the new workers were happier, and productivity went up. It felt like a breath of fresh air.

But just as I was starting to feel comfortable again, another curveball was thrown my way.

Every day, he was waiting for me in my custodian's room, trying to catch me coming back late from lunch. One day, I came back 20 minutes late, and he wrote me up, but I didn't sign it. He wrote me up again, but I still wouldn't sign, and he couldn't prove I came back late. First, I went to lunch late, and second, I was upstairs working. I filed two grievances against Dan Crawley, and he got fired. The workers asked me, "How did you get him fired?"

"Easy. Just come back a little late from lunch."

Everyone had to be in the place their boss told them to be after lunch or break time. Then, Dan (not the same boss as before), a Black boss from Foxwoods Casino, took over, and he was a good boss. Then came Claudette Alves, and she was tough; I had to watch out for her. A short time later, Scott Oakland took over, and he was a great boss. I was working in B Tower by myself— all six floors. Scott was there for about six to eight years, and we got along great. I would go to the trades during the summer months, then back to Claudette Alves, and we had to work our butts off and help clean up buildings when people were out. Claudette was covering two areas. I filed some grievances against her when she said I wasn't doing my work because I was helping others. I won every grievance.

Then came John Guglemetti, and he was the worst of them all. He came off second shift, and he was a disaster. I had been at Brown for nineteen years, and he was going to make sure that

I didn't make it to twenty. He was a big man, and he thought he was going to bully me around. He wasn't going to quit until he finally put me down. But little did he know, he was in for a big fight. He thought he was going to get me, and I almost let him do it!

I had a personal key to enter my building. One day, Ollie, a Black guy I worked with, ratted on me. The big boss, Dorothy Renihan, told me to bring the key, and she questioned me because I denied what Ollie said. He claimed, "Richard Rezendes let me in the building with his own personal key." My previous bosses, Claudette and Scott Oakland, knew I had this key, but Dorothy said it wasn't a Brown key. At a later meeting, they were going to decide if I was going to get fired.

So, I had a plan. I went to see my doctor and went out on stress leave until December 3rd, 1999. I stayed out until January. When I came back to work, I didn't even say "good morning." I just said to John in a high voice, "I made my twenty years!" He said nothing. I grabbed my keys and went to work in B Tower.

One day, he said, "I want you to get all the old cleaning materials that aren't being used and bring them to the trash room." My leg was all puffed up from moving the heavy chemicals and cinder block bricks, and he asked me, "How many bathrooms did you get done?"

I said, "Five," and then he had a fit. I asked him, "How much do you expect me to do? Look at my leg, I can't do any more. Get me my steward."

He said, "No." Then he told me, "Go to B building, the new dorm, and do some vacuuming. The day's almost done!"

Meanwhile, I filed a grievance at the end of the day, got my pay, and came in on Friday because John was out. Then, a month later, there was a fire in the trash room, and I was blamed because Ollie said I did it. So, I filed a grievance against both of them. I had to go for a hearing at the Brown police interrogation room with two officers who asked me all kinds of questions. I told them, "If you're blaming me for lighting this fire, and I'm telling you the truth that I had nothing to do with it, I will sue Brown and this police department. I will win, and you both will get fired."

Finally, they let me go, and I challenged John. "It was you or Ollie who said I did this, and if I get fired for something I didn't do, I'm going to take you to court with my own lawyer. You're not dealing with Brown or the union; you're dealing with me. I have two brothers and an uncle who's bigger than you, and I'm sure you don't want to tangle with them."

"Are you threatening me?" he asked.

I walked away.

Then there was a fire in B building's new dorm custodian room, and it was flooded. He told me to clean it, but I said, "There are fumes from chemicals there, so I'm going home. Here are eleven cigarette butts I found in there. I'm going to show them to my lawyer, and I'll see you on Monday. I'm taking a sick day."

I saw my doctor to get a week off for stress. I filed five grievances against John that day. It was a warm March day, so I went to the beach for the day. When I came back, we had a grievance meeting about the issue. The firemen were there, and they told me there were no cigarette butts in there.

I said, "No shit, there they are, all eleven. Do your job, or I'm going to get you fired because I'm going to the health department when I leave today."

Then, I was blamed for hiding beer to take home, and I filed grievances by the dozens. He told me I was being suspended with pay for five days. I said, "Five days without you? I'd be delighted."

He won that one. I had to use vacation time. In the summer, I fixed him. I used all six sick days after seeing my doctor.

Then, there was another fire in the trash room, and when John came in, he said, "Another fire, Richard?"

I told him, "I don't work Saturdays." All the custodians laughed. Then, a few days later, the same two cops from the Brown police station caught a student who flunked out setting fires in a kitchen in Pembroke, leaving me off the hook. Then, I went to the Brown Science Library building for easier work after winning the swollen leg grievance.

John harassed me there. I was blamed for sexual harassment, but he couldn't prove it, so I was suspended for the rest of the summer. When I came back, all the workers were called into a meeting with John Wilson, another jerk. He was the big boss, and Donna Butler was John G's boss. I won that grievance, then I transferred to Keeney Quad with Claudette Alves, now Santos. I believe I was out for six months due to a leg injury, but John tried to fire me three times. Later, he was upgraded to a manager position, and I saw him walking. He said, "Good morning, Richard."

I said, "I'm back April 2nd, 2002." I went back to work after being out for six or seven weeks due to stress, but I forgot what it was. So, I went to John Hay Library and worked there with Claudette Santos and George for a while. Then, in October 2002, I was voted into the union meet for at least two years, and I caught Claudette doing wrong things, so I had to file grievances against her based on complaints from workers. Most of the workers filed with Vickey, another union steward. Then, two years later, when I was voted out, Claudette started harassing me, picking on small things. I asked for a transfer to Pembroke to work with Ronny Alves, and I was there for two years with no problems. Now, I have twenty-seven years of service. I need one more year to get what I was hoping for: the Rule of 80 and a full pension, and I got it with good behavior. Twenty-eight years at 53 years old.

I worked in Leeds Theatre, and I liked it there, but the workload was terrible. The union changed from AFL-CIO Local 134 to a weaker union, USAWRI (United Service Allied Workers of Rhode Island). I was trapped by a big rat who filed a sexual harassment charge against me. Me and one of the female workers used to tell dirty jokes together while working during the summer. Meanwhile, her friend Pat had something going with her, and a girl named Denise was working with us. She asked me, "How long do you think Chris and I will be married?"

I said, "Six weeks or less." Sure enough, in five and a half weeks, Denise and Chris were divorced. She did not like that prediction very much. She also ratted on me. The head of the union told me a sexual harassment charge had been filed against me, and I had to be removed from campus. Then, I went out on stress for seven weeks, and I was told to go back to Claudette when I returned. If I didn't come back by January 7, 2009, I would be fired.

Before that, I had a meeting at the sexual harassment office, and the meeting did not last more than two minutes. The sexual harassment officer asked me a few questions, and with my answers, he said, "This is not sexual harassment. The university will do what they have to do." Then, I went out on stress so I could get twenty-nine years.

Every year, since I was going for twenty years on my anniversary date, they would try to find ways to fire me. But there was hope at the end of the tunnel. I filed a lawsuit against Brown to change termination to voluntary leave, collect unemployment, sick time, vacation pay, and to keep my COBRA until I found another job. I was asked to take a settlement in place of arbitration, but that could take two years. Brown accepted the settlement, so I had a nice year-long vacation, finishing my TDI for stress and unemployment. Then, I got a job cleaning the schools in Lincoln for three weeks. A week later, I got a job with the East Greenwich school department, and I was well-liked from the first day. Everyone enjoyed working with me, and I got good ratings from the principals at all six schools in East Greenwich. I was well-liked. My goal was to work until I turned sixty-two. They laid me off for the summer on May 20th, 2015. I took my social security and lived on unemployment over the summer. Since October of 2015, I haven't worked. I got what I was hoping for.

The only thing that set me down was when Obamacare came out, and East Greenwich cut my hours. That ended up working in my favor because I was paying $600 a month for COBRA versus $295 a month for Obamacare. So, I worked two days at East Greenwich schools and one day a week for North Attleborough schools. My plans worked in my favor when I lost my job at Brown with a full pension. Shortly after I was terminated, more than two hundred custodians and maintenance workers were terminated or forced out at sixty years old because the university wanted to get rid of the Rule of 80 pension. A new company took over management, and they were the worst group to work for. They did me a favor!

Two years after I was let go, I was told that if I had waited for arbitration, I would have won, but in the meantime, I would have had to wait two years with no money. My lawyer said to take the settlement, and Brown had to pay my lawyer five thousand dollars instead of going to court. I believe in God when there is hope at the end.

SECTION 2

IN A DARK TIME

On March 9th, 2020, I was in Newport, Rhode Island, scouting a baseball game between Johnson & Wales and Salve Regina. A thought came to me, like a dark voice, saying, "Enjoy this game because it's the last one you will be watching!" I didn't feel right about this thought, so I started saying prayers. Then, a bunch of army men arrived with big guns, surrounding the field on both sides. I didn't think much of it at first. I assumed the Salve Regina ROTC was practicing because they have a strong military program there.

The game lasted three and a half hours, ending in a 9-9 tie. My wife watched from my car because she's handicapped. There were no issues during the game, and when it was over, everyone left. Afterward, I took my wife out to dinner, and we had a nice time in Newport that day.

The next day, I heard a warning on the news about the Coronavirus outbreak—Covid-19. Then I heard the NCAA basketball tournament was canceled, along with all my local sports teams. The baseball season was canceled too! I thought to myself, "You've got to be kidding!" Coaches started telling me the season was canceled due to the pandemic outbreak.

Then all I heard was, "Get tested," and this pandemic was

killing people. I had a good laugh at first, thinking, "This virus is no worse than the flu." But then people started dying in big numbers, and I began to think that this was for real.

Soon, I couldn't go to the park or the beach, etc. I asked, "What's going on?" There were police on loudspeakers telling everyone to go home! Stay home. Then everyone had to wear a mask. We couldn't go to the doctor or even go food shopping unless we wore a mask. We couldn't even go to church!

I started thinking, my mind racing at 360 miles per hour, "What's next?" Are we at war? Is another attack coming? An EMP (electromagnetic pulse) or nuclear war? I began to fear the worst. Are we at the mark of the beast, or is the rapture coming? The Bible talks about the mark of the beast, the 666 mark, saying that you have to be tested and vaccinated against Covid-19 or you can't work, eat, or do anything! Many people refused to take the shots because of the side effects, but the government was forcing everyone to get vaccinated. Is this the mark of the beast? We don't know. The Bible says if you take the mark, you will go straight to hell. I hope that's not the case with Covid-19.

Everything shut down—no schools, everyone was at home, self-learning through Zoom, etc. The casinos closed, no work for weeks. Then, when we were finally allowed to leave the house to go to testing sites, I saw tents everywhere, military trucks driving by, and roads being closed off. I thought, "This is getting bad!"

RICKY R. GREEN BASKETBALL COMEDY

SECTION 1
RESTORING THE BOSTON CELTICS

The Celtics have not been much more than a .500 team during the 2021 season. Players are not getting along with one another, often fighting, calling each other names, and Brad Stevens is unhappy with their behavior. The Celtics managed to make the playoffs but lost to the Milwaukee Bucks in the first round.

Later, Danny Ainge and Brad Stevens had a meeting with the players before the offseason began.

"Everyone, let's all get together before we clean out our lockers. A 145-144 loss in game seven after four overtimes is a heartbreaker to the Bucks. Falling short hurts, but it is what it is! We did not protect the ball the way we should have—too many turnovers, sloppy play, shooting too many three-pointers, throwing up bricks, and lacking defense until this game. We have too good a team to lose this way.

This year was supposed to be a championship season because we have the talent, but we did not play that way. Inconsistent play led to an eighth-seed finish, and we were lucky to make the playoffs. We did play well against the No. 1 seed Milwaukee Bucks, except in game two, when we lost 165-122. That game was disgusting—we could have been beaten by anyone that night! Games like that are not acceptable in this organization!

Starting next year, I will be bringing in some big men, and the game is going to be different. We will become a championship team again. I also hate to inform you that Brad Stevens is resigning as the Boston Celtics coach, and Joe Pesci will be the coach next season. Brad Stevens is taking over as head coach of the Toronto Raptors.

I want everyone to have a nice summer, stay safe, and be ready to hear from me soon about who's staying and who's going." said Danny Ainge.

The Celtics went home for the summer after finishing the 2021 season. Danny Ainge went to work during the offseason.

"Joe, welcome to the Boston Celtics organization. I know you're big in show business, you've been in a lot of movies, and you've played a mobster in many of them! But what do you know about basketball?" asked Danny Ainge.

"Well, before I got into show business, I was brought up around the game of basketball in New York. My kids played basketball at St. Patrick's High School in New Jersey, a Garden State superpower, and they played their college ball at Essex County in New Jersey. I was an assistant coach at Princeton University, and I played for the Venice Express pro team in Italy," Joe replied.

"What kind of professional experience do you have in coaching?" asked Danny Ainge.

"Well, I just told you—I was a player and bench coach for the Venice Express before I got the assistant coaching job at Princeton. I had a pretty good track record in this game before getting into show business," said Joe.

"Joe, you're a smart man. When you get hired, how are you going to run this team?" asked Danny Ainge.

"We're going to score a lot of points—like the way I used to play!"

"What do you mean, Joe? Scoring a lot of points? How are you going to do that? Shoot three-pointers all day? What's your style?" pressed Ainge.

"No! Some three-pointers, but not too many. My style is the Michigan Fast Break—the way Johnny Most likes it. The old-school Celtics way, back when Larry Bird, Kevin McHale, and Robert Parish were playing. Just like that!"

"What style of defense is in your plans?" asked Danny.

"Just like Larry Bird—steal the ball and run. Pressure defense, man-to-man matchups, blocking as many shots as possible to set up the fast break. Play trap zones in the back and frontcourt, force turnovers with ball pressure, draw fouls under the basket, and fight for loose balls. I'm also in favor of enforcing the five-second violation."

"That's what I like to hear, Mr. Pesci! Welcome aboard. Our first game of the 2021-22 season will be against the Tampa Bay Stars, a new NBA team in Tampa, Florida. Next week, we'll be flying to Dublin, Ireland, and heading to Shamrock Celtic City to meet a man by the name of Donald F. Fitzgerald."

"He's a very good recruiter for the NBA," said Danny Ainge.

The plane to Ireland left Logan Airport bound for Dublin. Joe Pesci and Danny Ainge boarded a bus to Shamrock Celtic City, checked into a hotel, and arranged to meet Donald Fitzgerald the next day.

At the Celtic Alexandra Restaurant, Joe Pesci and Danny Ainge were greeted by a man dressed in green with yellow shoes.

"You must be Mr. Donald Fitzgerald," Joe said.

"Yes, sir, gentlemen," replied Donald with a smile.

"I'm Danny Ainge, director of basketball operations for the

Boston Celtics in the NBA, and my partner here, Joe Pesci, will be
the coach replacing Brad Stevens next season. We're here to dis-
cuss a trade for the tallest African basketball players in the world.
I'd like to hear about these players and evaluate their potential for
a $30-million guaranteed deal over five years," said Danny Ainge.

"I have two of the greatest international basketball players who will team up exceptionally well with Tacko Fall. First,
Kareem Abdul Shabazz, who played for the Sudan Hyenas. He's
a 7-foot-4 shot blocker, averaging 34 points, 30 rebounds, and
20 to 30 blocks per game. At 280 pounds, he's unstoppable! He
would make Wilt Chamberlain look ordinary. He's a black African player who dominates the game.

The second player is Karim Kappa Jebba Jabore, also a black
African player from Dakar, Senegal—the same place Tacko Fall
is from. He plays for the African National Pro Team and is the
tallest basketball player in the world, standing at 8 feet 9 inches.
He's a 131-pound beanpole, but he's a formidable shot blocker
and a powerhouse in the paint! He's also a surprisingly good
free throw shooter and can make three-pointers, most of them
from half-court.

This boy can play ball. His diet is unique—he eats grass,
shamrocks, clovers, peanut butter and jelly sandwiches, hot
dogs, and beans every day.

Give me a copy of your roster, and then we'll head to the
Celtic City Gym so you can see these guys in action," said Donald Fitzgerald.

Later, Danny Ainge, Joe Pesci, and Donald Fitzgerald watched
game films of the Boston Celtics before heading to watch a live
game.

"There they are, both playing for the African National Team
with 4:15 left to play before halftime. They're beating my Celtic
Shamrocks 51-3," said Donald Fitzgerald.

"Look at that block by the 8-foot-9 player! Rebounded by

Kareem Abdul Shabazz for the fast break—53 to 3! They crushed us 125 to 13 the last time we played them. The African National Team wins by 80 or 100 points all the time. Their biggest victory was a 326-15 rout over the Polish Sea Robins in 2019," explained Fitzgerald.

"Oh my God! I didn't think basketball was this strong here!" said Joe Pesci.

"We stink here in Ireland. All the powerhouses are in Africa. Poland has some good teams, and our Shamrocks aren't bad— we have a winning record. But this team we're playing is overpowering," said Donald Fitzgerald.

"Wow! These guys are incredible!" said Danny Ainge.

At halftime, the score was 63-7 in favor of Africa. The final score was: The African National Team 135, Celtic Shamrocks 24.

After the game, Donald Fitzgerald, the Irish recruiter, along with Danny Ainge and Joe Pesci, reviewed the Boston Celtics roster. They were ready to negotiate a deal, preparing to meet with both teams to finalize arrangements.

"Okay, Danny, you and I have been doing business for the last 30 years, but we've never been able to get something finalized. For $30 million over five years, I want three first-round draft picks, a second rounder, and a good chunk of your roster," said Donald Fitzgerald.

"In addition, I want Daniel Theis, Marcus Smart, Kemba Walker, Tristan Thompson, and Javonte Green," he added.

"You have a deal," said Danny Ainge.

"Good. Your team is invited to the Irish Summer League in August, where you'll have a chance to play against our Shamrocks team and the never-beaten African National Pro Team," said Donald Fitzgerald.

Next, the two towering stars met with Danny Ainge and Joe Pesci. Together, they watched film of the Boston Celtics and were amazed by the championship banners the Celtics had won over the years.

Later, Danny Ainge and Joe Pesci flew back to Boston, ready to prepare for the new season.

SECTION 2
PUTTING THE NEW ROSTER TOGETHER

When Danny Ainge and Joe Pesci returned to Boston to deliver the news, the players who were traded were very upset. They received their notices via email, and their reactions were anything but pleasant.

Marcus Smart wrote back to Danny Ainge with some harsh words before heading to Africa to join the National Team.

Next, Daniel Theis received his email. He responded angrily, telling Danny Ainge where to go, and decided to play for the Celtic Shamrocks team in Ireland.

Kemba Walker, upon receiving his email, had his own choice words for Ainge before also choosing to play for the African National Team.

Tristan Thompson's response was curt. He said, "Good riddance," and likewise joined the African National Team.

Finally, Javonte Green reacted with fury. He called Danny Ainge every name in the book before hanging up the phone. He, too, joined the African National Team.

With the trades finalized, the Celtics roster now looks like this:

Starting Five:
- #7 Jaylen Brown – Small Forward
- #0 Jayson Tatum – Guard/Small Forward
- #42 Carsen Edwards – Point Guard

- #2 Kareem Abdul Shabazz – Power Forward
- #67 Karim Kappa Jebba Jabore – Center (8-foot-9 shot blocker and rebounder)

The team's new lineup features a mix of familiar faces and towering new talent, set to usher in a bold new era for the Celtics.

Second Team:
- Sixth Man: Payton Pritchard – Point Guard
- Aaron Nesmith – Forward
- Robert Williams – Power Forward
- Tacko Fall – 7-foot-6 Center
- Tremont Waters – Point Guard

Third Team (Reserves):
- Grant Williams – Small Forward
- Jeff Teague – Point Guard
- Semi Ojeleye – Forward
- Romeo Langford – Forward

This completed the Boston Celtics roster for the 2021-22 season.

The players who remained on the team had mixed feelings about the changes. While some expressed disappointment, others felt optimistic about the new direction. Meanwhile, the traded players were upset but also relieved to move on.

Later, the Celtics traveled to Ireland for an eight-team, round-robin summer tournament. In the quarterfinals, the Celtics faced the Ukraine Dunkers, a team known for its tall players.

The game was a complete blowout:
- Jayson Tatum scored 35 points.
- Jaylen Brown added 29 points.

- Karim Kappa Jebba Jabore dominated with 38 points.
- Kareem Abdul Shabazz contributed 29 points.
- Carsen Edwards chipped in with 10 points.
- Sixth man Payton Pritchard scored an impressive 34 points off the bench.
- The rest of the Celtics bench combined for 18 points.

The final score: Boston Celtics 193, Ukraine Dunkers 39.

The Celtics' performance was a strong statement, showcasing their revamped roster's potential and dominance.

After the game, Danny Ainge said, "We almost scored 200 points tonight because Karim Kappa Jebba Jabore had 80 rebounds. If we play like this at home, we could go undefeated! We definitely have a championship team here now that we got rid of all the troublemakers! We will be playing the trouble-makers tomorrow night—the African National Team, who just finished last season with a 110-0 record. They had a better team than the Harlem Globetrotters, who won 229 straight games. This team had Karim Kappa Jebba Jabore and Kareem Abdul Shabazz during that run. Now let's see how they'll do tomorrow night with Marcus Smart and company."

A brief meeting with Danny Ainge and Joe Pesci was held to prepare for tomorrow's game.

Next up: The African National Team vs. the Boston Celtics in the semifinals of the Shamrock Celtic Summer Classic of Ireland.

For the African National Team:
- Former Celtics player Javonte Green scored 10 points.
- Marcus Smart had 9 points.
- Tristan Thompson scored 15.
- Kemba Walker had 6 points.
- The rest of the team contributed 100 points, bringing the total to 140 points.

- For the Boston Celtics:
- Karim Kappa Jebba Jabore was held to 18 points.
- Kareem Abdul Shabazz scored 22 points.
- Jayson Tatum had 22 points.
- Jaylen Brown had 23 points.
- Robert Williams contributed 14 points.
- Payton Pritchard added 16 points.
- The rest of the team scored 33 points for a total of 148 points.

Final Score:

Boston 148, African National Team 140.

This was the first-ever loss for the African National Team.

Instead of handshakes at the end of the game, a fight broke out.

The Celtics went on to beat the Celtic City Shamrocks and won the Irish Summer Tournament Championship: Boston 144, Celtic City Ireland 81.

The Celtics' victory cemented their place as the dominant team in the tournament, showcasing their new roster's strength.

SECTION 3
THE REGULAR SEASON

"Good evening, ladies and gentlemen. Welcome to the Tampa Bay Bubble, home of the new Tampa Bay Stars, entertaining the Boston Celtics on opening night. Welcome, Tampa Bay Stars, to the NBA. Here is tonight's starting five for the Boston Celtics: #7 at forward, standing at 6-foot 6-inches, Jaylen Brown; #0 at forward, standing at 6-foot 8-inches, Jayson Tatum; at guard, #42, standing at 6-feet, Carsen Edwards; #2 at power forward, standing at 7-feet 4-inches, Kareem Abdul Shabazz; and finally, at center, standing at 8-feet, 9-inches tall, Karim Kappa Jebba Jabore, the tallest basketball player in the world!

Now for your Tampa Bay Stars: Starting at guard, standing at 6-feet, 4-inches, Denny De Jesus; next, at guard, standing at 6-foot 5-inches, #0, Michael St. Patrick; next, at center, #00, Sylvester Cliffhanger, standing at 7-feet even; at forward, #33, standing at 6-foot 8-inches, Larry Loydd; and finally, #54, standing at 6-foot 9-inches, forward, Nickolous Nickolina!!!" said the Tampa Bay announcer. The National Anthem was sung, and then it's game time. Denny De Jesus was putting on his jersey, wearing uniform #4.

"Good evening, this is DJ Brown along with Jonny Most, Junior on NESN, broadcasting this game live from Tampa Bay, Florida. The tip-off. Karim Kappa Jebba Jabore controls the tap, and Carsen Edwards scores with a dunk. We will call the 9-footer KKJJ. The shot is blocked by Kareem Abdul Shabazz, fast break to Jayson Tatum, passes off to Jaylen Brown for the three-pointer, it's good, and the Celtics lead 5-0 in the first minute of play. Denny De Jesus of Tampa Bay drives to the hoop, and he's stuffed by the 9-footer, picked up by Jaylen Brown, passes off to Jayson Tatum for three, and he misses the shot, and KKJJ, the 9-footer, jams it home and he's fouled. He leans halfway over the key, under hands the free throw, and it's good, 8-0 Boston. Denny De Jesus is charged with the foul. Sylvester Cliffhanger challenges Kareem Abdul Shabazz at the other end for Tampa Bay, and KKJJ, the 9-footer, stuffs him, knocking the ball loose. Carsen Edwards sets up the fast break to Jayson Tatum driving underneath the basket, passes to Jaylen Brown for three! And he buries it! 11-0 Boston. Robert Williams enters the game for the Celtics, steals the inbound pass, hands the ball to Kareem Shabazz for the jam, and he's fouled! He makes the free throw, making the score 14-0 Boston. The Tampa Bay fast break downcourt is deflected by KKJJ, and he picks it off in flight, passes to Jayson Tatum for the three-pointer, swish! We have a time out here at the Tampa Bay Bubble, and the Celtics lead the new Tampa Bay Stars 17-0. This is Jonny Most, Junior on NESN, and we will be right back."

The Celtics lead 40-4 after the first quarter, 81-16 at the half.

The Tampa Bay coach said to his players, "We don't deserve to be in the NBA getting beat like this! We had better go out and play a lot better. We need to stay away from the 8- and 9-footers and make our shots because we are a better team than this. Let's make it respectable, I don't want to lose by 100! Let's go!"

The Celtics lead 122-32 after the third quarter, and the final score was 156-55, the most lopsided game in the NBA!

Then the Celtics went 75-7, the #1 seed, with the best record ever for 82 games. The Celts beat Philly at home in the next game 152-114, then they beat the Lakers 127-77, without LeBron James, his son James Junior, and another James all playing for the LA Lakers. They beat the Knicks in New York 140-60. Karim Kappa Jebba Jabore, the 9-footer, scored 99 points in that game. They beat the Nets by one hundred points. They beat the Bucks by 90! They beat the Raptors by 80! They beat the Miami Heat by 60 and beat Tampa Bay again by only 50 points: 181-131. The 9-footer scored 111 points, beating all the odds in the NBA for an 8-foot, 9-inch beanpole toothpick!

SECTION 4
THE NBA PLAYOFFS

The Celtics were on a roll with their formidable twin towers, but now they're in a tough series against the Los Angeles Lakers. The momentum is palpable as Boston dominates the early games, but the Lakers, determined to fight back, bring the series to a tense moment in Game 4.

In the first round, the Celtics beat the living you-know-what out of the Atlanta Hawks, four games to none! Then they beat Cleveland four games to one because the 9-footer fouled out, along with Kareem Abdul Shabazz, in the game they lost. Then they beat the Milwaukee Bucks four games to two. The Bucks found a way to control the two big monsters, getting them to foul out early. The 9-foot beanpole picked up three early fouls in the two losses in the Bucks series. Then it was the NBA Finals against the Lakers, opening in Boston.

"Ladies and Gentlemen, welcome to the TD Bank Garden for Game 1 of the 2022 NBA Championship, for the first time since the 2010 season, with the Celtics looking for their 18th World Championship with the world's tallest basketball player. Welcome Karim Kappa Jebba Jabore, 8-foot 9-inches tall, averaging thirty-eight points a game, thirty-five rebounds a game, and twenty-eight blocked shots per game. If Bill Russell could see this…, ARE YOU READY TO RUMBLE? LET'S GO CELTICS!" said the announcer.

Then the game started and KKJJ won the tap ten feet over Anthony Davis, and Jaylen Brown raced downcourt, giving the ball to the 9-footer for the dunk and the foul to open up the game. The Celtics trashed the Lakers 154-108 in Game 1. Karim Kappa Jebba Jabore scored twenty-four points in the first quarter, twenty-nine in the second, thirty points in the third quarter, and fourteen points in the fourth quarter for a total of 97 points. The team kept feeding him the ball all night, scoring over everyone!

In Game 2 the Lakers shut down the 9-footer, and it was Kareem Abdul Shabazz's turn with seventy points. The Celtics bury the Lakers again 152-125.

Game 3 is in LA at the Staples Center. It was 118-118 with 0.3 seconds remaining. The Celtics inbound the alley-oop to the 9-footer with five fouls for the dunk and the win, and the floor at the Staples Center erupted in green, giving the Celtics a 3-0 lead in the series.

Lakers coach Jack Nicholson Jr. was ripping mad, and the Staples Center was echoing with boos. The Celtics won, 120-118. Jack Jr. said to his players in the locker room after the game, "We had them! We had them, and we let it get away! We had a five-point lead with 3:20 to go, and we let it slip away! How can we beat a team with a 9-foot flamingo bigfoot and two grizzly bears? We need to score 170 points to beat this team. We lost 121-118 during the regular season. But tonight's 49 points from LeBron James, his son Dick with 18, and Anthony Davis' 40 rebounds was not enough. The rest of our games are elimination games, and we need to find a way to beat this team. We can't break the flamingos' legs because we have a couple of Grizzly bears coming after us! Let's sleep tonight, and tomorrow we have to come up with a plan and take this series back to Boston, because I like their Italian Sausage at the Hay Market," said Jack Jr.

The next night was Game 4 at the quiet Staples Center. The Lakers won in triple overtime 155-152, getting the twin towers to foul out and holding the 9-footer to 9 points and 56 rebounds! The series goes back to Boston with the Celtics leading 3 games to 1. Lakers coach Jack Nicholson Jr. bought 13 Italian Sausage sandwiches at the Hay Market, brought them back to the hotel, and put twelve of them in the refrigerator because he ate one!

Game 5 at TD Bank Garden: The Lakers won again, 119-118, getting the twin towers to foul out once more! Now the series shifts back to the Staples Center, and the place was going crazy. The 9-footer got hurt in the first half and had to leave the game. The Staples Center erupted. Now the Lakers have a chance to steal the next two games.

Finally, the Lakers seemed to have figured out the Celtics in a tie game, and Kareem Abdul Shabazz went on a tear, scoring 66 points. He tied the game at 119, sending it into overtime. He scored 8 more points in overtime! He tied the game with a three-pointer, bringing his total to 74 points, sending the game into a second overtime tied at 133.

Continuing Game 6 in Los Angeles: Kareem Abdul Shabazz took over, scoring 9 more points in the second overtime, but the Celtics held strong and won by six points, 150-144. He sank 9 free throws in the second OT, finishing with 83 points overall. Once again, the Staples Center floor was filled with green, celebrating the Celtics' 2022 NBA Championship! The Lakers fans filled the Staples Center with boos.

The Celtics celebrated their 18th NBA Title, pouring champagne all over the players and coaches. The players were using foul language during the celebration, and Danny Ainge said, "Gentlemen, please cut down on the bad language. Coach Joe Pesci doesn't like swearing; he's a Christian man!"

A few days later, the Parade in Boston took place, during a thunderstorm and pouring rain. Danny Ainge said, "Congratulations Boston Celtics! The 2022 NBA Champions!"

Kareem Abdul Shabazz threw the Championship Trophy from a duck boat in downtown Boston out to a boat in the Charles River, and Kiram Kappa Jebber Jabore caught it in midair, just like Tom Brady to Gronk during the Tampa Bay Super Bowl celebrations.

This story is only a dream. The Celtics did make it to the NBA Finals but lost to the Golden State Warriors in 2022. So, we will have to back up and push this dream story forward to 2023 or 2024. The Celtics still need to find that 8-foot center, not a beanpole or a telephone pole, but a true center.

Days after the loss to Golden State, the Celtics had to watch film about what went wrong in that series and then listen to Jonny Most's recordings:

"The Celtics came so close this year, but it's clear that they're missing that dominant presence in the paint, the kind of center that can change the game both offensively and defensively. The dream of having

that 8-foot player was closer than ever, but the reality is they still need to find that next great center to push them over the top."

The journey isn't over yet for the Celtics, and the dream of an 8-foot center continues as the future unfolds in 2023 or 2024.

"Havlicek stole the ball! Havlicek stole the ball!! Havlicek stole the ball!!!! Havlicek stole the ball!!!!!!!! Celtics win !!!!"

"Kevin McHale is at the line shooting two, he dips, shoots, gets it! He will have another, dips, shoots, swish!"

"Bird elbowed Bill Laimbeer and knocked him out of bounds! I don't believe it! The refs called the foul on Bird!"

"The garden is very quiet right now. Detroit is rebounding the ball under the Celtics basket with one second to go trying to steal game five and move on to Detroit. Here we go! Bird steals the ball, passes to DJ and he lays it in! And the Celtics Won!"

"Tempers are flaring, the 76ers keep pushing and shoving and something's going to happen. There they go! Bird and Dr. J going at it! Dr. J is grabbing Larry Bird by the throat! Now Moses Malone and Robert Parish are going at it and now it's an all-out brawl! The Philadelphia 76ers are a dirty team! They're trying to kill Bird!" "We have a time out at the Boston Garden and the Celtics are leading 88 to 80. Larry Bird just sank an 8-point field goal, but it doesn't count.

"Jo Jo White on the break and he's fouled! Golden State grabbed him and almost pulled his shorts down!"

"Dave Cowens grabs the rebound and he's knocking people over. Time out here at the Garden."

"Celtics win tonight in overtime and the next game will be at the snake pit tomorrow night against the 76ers."

"Time out here at Madison Square Garden, the Knicks lead the Celtics 91 to 86. Glen Ordway along with Jonny Most. We will be right back."

"It's not Madison Square Garden, it's Madison Square Zoo!"

"Rebound by Bird, pass to Cedric Maxwell, over to McHale under the basket to Parish and he dunked it, and he's fouled!"

"Larry Bird at the free throw stripe shooting one and one. He dips, shoots, and swishes! He'll have another. His second free throw, bang! He got it!"

Jonny Most was one announcer to listen to on the radio and television when the Celtics were playing. He would make you laugh, he loved his Celtics and hated everybody else! He hated the 76ers, the Knicks, the Lakers, and the Detroit Pistons are his worst enemy!

In 2008 the Celtics won the NBA Championship for the first time since the Larry Bird era. They won 19 in a row in 2009, and they hit the injury bug during the playoffs. When the Celtics got Kevin Garnet and Ray Allen to team up with Paul Pierce they began the dynasty. In 2010 they lost to the Los Angeles Lakers in the finals because Kendrick Perkins went down, killing their chances for winning another one. Ray Allen had a bad game in game 7. Then, for the next several years, when Kendrick Perkins and Rachon Rondo were traded, the Celtics hit the skids and were not much of a threat. Since the 2009 season the Celtics began to get lazy throwing up too many threes and missing shots, free throws, and turnovers. These Celtics are not the same dynasty anymore because the game has changed.

The Celtics went out to get Brad Stevens to coach and build this team back into champions again. Danny Ainge could not put a team together until Stevens took over his position and in the 2021-22 season the Celtics made it to the NBA finals losing to the Golden State. The two seed Celtics took out Milwaukee, the defending champions, in 7 games then beat the Miami Heat in 7 games. After sweeping the Nets in the first round, they were up 2 to 1 in the NBA Finals then fell apart losing the next three games. Jaylen Brown and Jayson Tatum kept turning the ball over and they had a terrible series. It was hard to watch! This team has been inconsistent for the last 14 years including the 2022-23 season, dreaming of getting it done.

The Celtics had many chances to reach the Eastern Conference Finals about three times under coach Brad Stevens but
couldn't get over the hump, until the 2022 season. This Celtics
team plays like a college team, it's been that way for years, it's not
going to work in the NBA. They have the group to win the NBA
Finals, but they have to change their bad habits from firing up
too many 3 pointers and turning the ball over, taking bad shots
and going to the basket more, and drawing fouls. When Larry
Bird took a shot, that ball was going in, unless it was blocked.
Robert Parish and Kevin McHale made their shots in the paint
using the square on the backboard and when they were fouled,
they always made their free throws, seldom ever missing. As soon
as the ball left their hands, it was going in the basket. The old
Celtics always protected their home court, which is why they
won so many championships. Three out of five in the Bird era
and Bill Ressel won 11 NBA Championships. The game is not
the same today.

Will the Celtics win their 18 banner in 2023? Sure, they will
or was it a dream again!

Here we go again! The Celtics meet the Denver Nuggets in the
2023 NBA Championship.

Announcer Kendrick Perkins pushes Celtics coach Joe Mazzulla around teaching him the fundamentals of the game.

"Coach, we barely got by Miami and Milwaukee, and we
shouldn't have beaten Cleveland, but we got lucky against the
Cavs to make it to the NBA Finals. Our problem is, we are still
shooting up too many threes and turning the ball over and taking bad shots. Defensive breakdowns and lazy, sloppy play. We
look like a bunch of idiots out there! We are not protecting our
home court, giving up big leads and blowing games in the 4th
quarter and overtime. We lost 12 overtime games this year, 7 of
them at home. That should not be happening. We lost 5 overtime
games to Cleveland. We were down three games to one against

Cleveland and finally we pulled our heads out of our butts and played like a team to get the wins in the last three games.

In game five in Cleveland, we were up 33 points with 10:12 to go in the third quarter 73 to 40. We collapsed and had to settle for overtime before pulling away in the second overtime or we would have been out of it! We played very well the last three games with the Cavs until this collapse before Jayson Tatum got hot scoring 72 points. We got away with our inconsistent play during the last three series because we had the home court advantage but now, we go to Denver to open up the NBA Finals.

We're in the same boat we were in last year traveling to Golden State. We have to go to the basket right out of the gate and draw fouls and not turn the ball over! Denver leads the league in forcing turnovers, rebounding, assists and scoring in the paint. They play inside as well, shooting the 3 just like the Golden State Worriers. We can do the same, but we have to play our game and not choke up like last year. If we go to the finals playing catch up, Coach, we may not win. Good luck and let's get it done! I have to go take a leak!" said Kendrick Perkins.

Game one, the Celtics lost! In Game two the Celtics got blown out! Down 2-0 quickly!

"Guys, we have our backs against the wall! We have to win in Boston, or we go home. We lost 133 to 99 in game two, that can't happen! We have to play better!" said coach Joe Mazzulla.

Game three, the Celtics won by one point 176 to 175 in 4 overtimes! "We are going to be exhausted by the time this series is over!" said the coach.

Game 4, the Celtics lost in overtime 100 to 99 in Boston. "We are in trouble, down 3 games to one. Now we have to take one at a time. We must win in Denver tonight to stay alive! We win or go home," said Joe Mazzulla.

Game 5 the, The Celtics won, 113 to 110! Jayson Tatum put up the game winning 3 with hands covering his face, avoiding overtime again! The ball went in, all net! And the Celtics celebrated like they won the thing! Game 6 in Boston, the Celtics won in triple overtime 157 to 154 when Payton Prichard ran down the court and laid it in, and he got fouled making the free throw! The crowd poured out on the court to celebrate! In Game 7, the Celtics beat the Denver Nuggets in Denver by 15 points and won the 2023 NBA Championship!

Days later they had a big parade in downtown Boston in late June 2023. It rained all day with thunder and lightning, and everyone was soaking wet. Duck boats, bands, and millions of people crowded together following the duck boats, with the Celtics players holding the championship trophy! People were drinking, smoking pot, and having parties everywhere, cheering; "Let's go Celtics!"

Red Sox players, the Patriots, and the Bruins players celebrated with the Celtics pouring champagne on all the Celtics players! Jayson Tatum drank a whole 6 pack of champagne bottles then he passed out! The crowd cheered, "MVP! MVP! MVP! MVP! MVP!"

Then a bolt of lightning struck the Celtics' duck boat setting it on fire! Everybody jumped off in time, and the drunken Jayson Tatum was thrown into the crowd. Hundreds of bottles of champagne were thrown off the burning duck boat into the crowd! The burning duck boat crashed into the Charles River. Will this happen or is it a dream? It was a dream! Denver won. Celtics finally won in 2024.

SECTION 4

FRIDAY NIGHT LIGHTS/FIGHTS

A new semi-pro football team, formed in Rhode Island as part of the new NFL G League, has their home field at Brown Stadium. The team is called the Providence Steam Rollers, named after the original NFL team from the 1920s. In the fall of 2023, they scheduled their inaugural season and found an opponent in the Wyatt Detention Drag Queens from the Wyatt Detention Center in Central Falls. The game took place on a Friday night at Macomber Stadium.

The Steam Rollers' cheerleaders arrived first, decked out in red, white, and blue, reminiscent of the New England Patriots. The cheerleaders from the Wyatt Detention Facility, on the other hand, were a unique sight—dressed in leopard print speedos.

Next came the spectators, followed by the players from both teams, all of whom were ready for a game that would be anything but ordinary.

Here's a revised version of the coach's speech for clarity, flow, and tone:

"Alright, everyone, listen up. We've got a game against a prison team, but don't be fooled. Yes, we're a professional football team, and they're a group of amateurs, but this team is good enough to play us—that's why we're here. All I've heard in practice is, 'We're going to kick their ass!' But this is no ordinary game. There are no rules here. We play our game and obey the refs. But Wyatt Detention Center has their own set of rules. They're going to play dirty and look for trouble. Prison teams aren't here to win—they're here to get their frustrations out, and they don't care if they hurt someone. We're here to score touchdowns; they're here for blood.

Let's keep our heads, play clean, and avoid trouble as much as we can. If you start a fight, their whole team will jump on you like a pack of lions! Now, break, and let's get out there!"

The Rhode Island National Guard Band took the field to perform the national anthem, and then the game kicked off. Wyatt received the ball first at their own 25-yard line and quickly marched down the field, moving the chains and securing first downs. They scored a touchdown in the first seven minutes, taking an early lead.

The Steam Rollers responded when they got the ball. On their first possession, a Wyatt player leveled a vicious hit, drilling his helmet into the runner's gut and knocking him over—no call from the refs. Undeterred, the Steam Rollers moved the ball downfield with a series of big passes, eventually tying the game 7-7 by the end of the first quarter.

Wyatt scored again, aided by an interception and a recovered fumble, and the Steam Rollers found themselves down 28-7 by halftime after a field goal attempt was blocked. The teams headed to the locker rooms, with the military band playing and the cheerleaders dancing. It had been a hard-fought first half, but the Drag Queens were dominating, proving their point by running all over the Steam Rollers.

"Who's getting their ass kicked now?" the coach said in frustration. "This is what happens when you get overconfident. I think we're a better team when we run the ball and get to the sidelines.

We need to run the ball more and blitz harder on defense in the second half if we're going to get back into this game."

As the third quarter began, the Steam Rollers kicked off and ran it back for a touchdown, with an extra point bringing the score to 28-14. On the following kickoff, the Steam Rollers went for the onside kick and successfully recovered it. There was some pushing and shoving, but no punches were thrown—yet. On the very next play, a 58-yard touchdown bomb, followed by the extra point, brought the Steam Rollers within 7, 28-21.

On the next kickoff, a Wyatt player was hit so hard it forced a fumble. The red-hot Steam Rollers scooped up the ball and scored again, tying the game at 28-28!

While the play was going on, instead of the Wyatt team tackling the runner, a big fight broke out, and the Wyatt team was penalized. One man took his helmet off and struck a Steam Roller in the face, causing an all-out brawl—pushing, punching, and kicking! It was a karate match instead of a football game!

The Wyatt team had fourth down kicking from their own 9-yard line. The kick was blocked, and the Steam Rollers scooped it up for another touchdown. Then, another brawl erupted! The runner was hit after scoring the touchdown, picked up and thrown over a trash can. The Steam Rollers went for two after the brawl, swinging the run to the left side of the field and scoring easily, making the score 36-28 Providence Steam Rollers.

The two-point runner also took a hit, being bowled out of bounds, triggering another brawl! The Wyatt Drag Queens were penalized repeatedly. Will this game even finish? At the start of the 4th quarter, the Steam Rollers kept blitzing and hitting hard, and Wyatt couldn't move the ball, triggering a brawl on every down until kicking off to the Steam Rollers. The runner was hit so hard that both of his legs were broken! He was carried off the field and taken to medical rescue. On the next play, a Steam

Roller player took a helmet to the head, breaking his neck! He was carried away in a rescue.

Cumberland, Pawtucket, Providence, and Lincoln emergency response teams arrived to help scoop up all the injuries from the brawls in this game. On the next play, a Wyatt player grabbed a Steam Roller player's horse collar, holding him in place until another Wyatt player bowled him out of bounds, pushing the Steam Roller player over a bench, setting off a bench-clearing brawl between football players and spectators. Now things are out of control!

After the violent brawl, police and the coaching staff had to cool down all the violence, and several penalties led to a Steam Rollers field goal, making the score 39-28 for the Steam Rollers. After the field goal kick, a Wyatt player charged over the line and punched the field goal kicker in the face, knocked him down, and sparked another bench-clearing brawl! Another player stepped on his head, driving his cleats into his face. Both teams were punching and kicking one another, and then the crowd poured onto the field to join the fight!

"By the time this game's over, everyone is going to wind up in jail!" With 12:34 left in the 4th quarter, this game may not finish if the fighting doesn't stop! Then the Steam Rollers kicked off to the Wyatt Drag Queens and hit the guy hard, flattening him until he fumbled the ball, and the Steam Rollers scooped it up for a touchdown, 45-28!

The whole Wyatt team piled on him in the end zone, punching him, stepping on him, and kicking him like a soccer ball until he was unconscious! The Steam Roller spectators poured onto the field, attacking the Wyatt team with knives and sticks. They were throwing rocks at them until the football team had to run back to the jail for safety! Then the Wyatt spectators fought back, setting the Steam Rollers' bus on fire and throwing rocks at one another. A crowd arrived, armed with baseball bats, beating on the Steam Roller players and smashing car windows. Even the policemen were getting beaten up until a SWAT team arrived to pepper spray the crowd!

The Steam Roller players who survived the brawl were escorted away from the crowd when the SWAT team began using pepper spray. Then gunshots were heard! The announcers kept telling the crowd and the players to stop the violence or everyone would go to jail! But it didn't work. Arrests were being made, and people were taken to jail so they could fight as much as they wanted behind bars until everyone was left dead!

The jail was full of blood, with Steam Roller spectators fighting with the Wyatt prisoners in the jail. The coaches and refs left the game, and the Steam Rollers won 45 to 28. The game was stopped with 12 minutes left. The rest of the Steam Rollers football team was escorted to another bus and taken back to Brown University. The crowd and all the spectators ended up in jail. Half the team made it back, and the other half was injured or killed!

Meeting in the locker room at Brown Stadium with the coach:

"We had 72 players when we left here for Macomber Stadium, only 40 returned. Three are dead, and 37 of our players are in the hospital! This will be the last time we play a prison team ever again! We have three more prison teams on our schedule, and I will be canceling those games. We play the Southern New England Admirals next week at home. We don't have lights here at Brown Stadium, so we will be playing this game at Moses Brown Academy next Friday night at 7 p.m."

"If we have another night like we had tonight against the Admirals next week, I'm pulling the plug on the season! Tonight was unacceptable! We have three dead players from the brawl and 37 more in the hospital. The Wyatt team caused all this, and their team is now banned from the NFL G League. We do not know if this league will fold because of the riots in Central Falls. Right now, we are concentrating on next week. Let's take our showers, put our equipment away, and get out of here!" said the coach.

The News: "Good evening, we have breaking news on WJAR TV 10. Five people are dead and over one hundred injured during a football game brawl in Central Falls tonight. The teams exchanged blows until the crowd got out of control, leaving the dead and injured before the R.I. State Police were called in with SWAT teams using pepper spray and gunshots to break up the brawl.

Thousands of people were arrested and taken to jail along with the Wyatt Detention Facility football team! Buses and cars were set on fire, tipped over, and destroyed. The Providence Steam Rollers of the new NFL G League won the game 45 to 28! Channel 10 news reporting." The new G League canceled the season because of the brawl. The Southern N.E. Admirals were laughing at them!

SECTION 5

50 SHADES OF COMPASS ROSE

Claire and Stanley, from Worcester, Massachusetts, were getting ready to go to the beach and were looking for dog-friendly beaches online because they have two dogs: a German Shepherd and a Doberman.

"Stanley, here's a good beach: Compass Rose Beach, located at Quonset Point in North Kingstown, Rhode Island. Take Route 146 to Route 295 South. That brings you to Route 95 South to Rhode Island Route 4. Then take the Quonset exit straight, and Compass Rose is to the right of the airport, before the Martha's Vineyard Ferry. It's one hour and 10 minutes from Main Street, Worcester. Let's go!" said Claire.

Claire put the dogs in the car and turned on the AC until Stanley finished packing the trunk with beach towels, chairs, and a cooler full of drinks and food. Then off they went! When they got to Compass Rose Beach, they saw a sign reading: "COMPASS ROSE 50 SHADES FASHION SHOW!"

Stanley pulled up to the gate. A military guard was there.

"Good afternoon, sir. Welcome to the 50 Shades Fashion Show! The admission fee is $160 to get in," said the guard. "Say what! I'm not paying $160 to go to the beach. Fuck you!" said Stanley.

"Sir, we have a private festival here today. There are other beaches here in Quonset. Go back where you came in, about four or five lights ago, and take a left onto Circuit Drive, and there's Blue Beach. And if you take the Davisville exit, that will take you to Allen's Harbor, and Sphinx Neck Beach is over there!" said the guard.

"Forget this, Claire! We're going home! We're not going to drive around and get lost. In fact, look at the sky, a thunderstorm is coming! Let's get the hell out of here!!!" said Stanley. For those who paid to get in, they got a real treat! Stanley peeled out, screeching his tires, and dust and pebbles flew everywhere. He pulled out of the parking lot and onto the road, storming through red lights because he was so pissed! "Here's Circuit Drive, we will go to Blue Beach, wherever the hell that is!" said Stanley.

They got lost and Stanley was so pissed off he was out of control! Then it started to rain heavily and thunder and lightning! Finally, he lost it! He stormed up Circuit Drive running over a few Canadian Geese right in front of the Blue Beach parking lot and he drove up Circuit Drive like a bat out of hell. He just missed hitting another car and a motorcycle and he drove back to Worcester! He never saw the Blue Beach sign.

After the brief thunderstorm stages were set up on the beach at Compass Rose, getting ready for the X-rated festival. Four stages were set up, side by side. Jason Tatum from the Boston Celtics performed on the first stage. Next was a dancing stripper dressed in a string bikini showing off her sexual moves wrapped around a pole. She had a pair of tits the size of basketballs! On stage three were the Compass Rose fashion dancers stripping their clothes off and chucking moons at the crowd. The men dancers wore speedos, and the women wore cups to cover their breast and private parts. 10 were on stage three, 5 women and 5 men dancing and exchanging sex acts! On stage four there was a giant beach ball and four beach chairs with naked women sitting in them! One lady was black, one was white with long hair down past her ass! There was also an Asian girl and an Indian girl with who was a naked belly dancer.

Between the four stages there were food vendors and tents set up where drinks were served. People were enjoying the funny fashion shows, drinking and having sex on the beach and in the water. Fights broke out when the wrong crowd got involved with the wrong people. By dusk it was a big orgy and hundreds of people were fucking everywhere! Everybody was naked, screwing anybody they can; clothes and bathing suits were tossed aside while everyone was running around naked! Prostitutes were there trying to get people to pay for sex in return for drugs! Boats were coming into the beach looking for a free show and free sex, but the national guard was chasing them away with big guns!

One married couple were laying on the beach enjoying the sights when suddenly a naked black man with a dong 15 inches long tried shoving it in the woman's mouth. The husband got up, grabbing the black man's leg then kicked him in the balls and again in the head. Then he grabbed the man in a head lock twisting his head and breaking his neck. He left him dead on the beach. The event got out of hand when the fights broke out! Hundreds of people were arrested because of the violence.

Women with women, men with men; threesomes, foursomes, train sex, you name it! Strait sex, oral sex, anal sex, etc.... Every hole they can find, a stiff one is going in it!

"Ladies and gentlemen, you must stop the fighting and violence. Stop all sexual activities and put your clothes back on, or the second show will be canceled, and I will ask you all to leave. My name is Lt. Rex Thomas from the Rhode Island National Guard. Our first act on stage #1 is Jayson Tatum from the Boston Celtics. He will demonstrate his ball-handling skills, and then he will be signing autographs. You must be fully clothed to approach the stage. Thank you."

Next, we have the Mary Swinger strip show. Dancing with a pole swing. You may place a dollar in her G-string but no touching. Next, we have the Compass Rose fashion dancers. If you're good you may get a lap dance, otherwise they will moon in front of you. Stay at a distance and watch please," said the guard.

One man grabbed one of the girl's dress and pulled it off her. He was beaten with a Billy club, arrested and taken away by North Kingstown Police officers. Another man showed his private parts and he was arrested too! A third man stuck his head up one of the lady's dresses and he was beaten by police and arrested too!

"Ladies and gentlemen let's behave please! Next, we have the naked girls beach ball show. Review their naked show of art as they show off their talents from lips to bush and their sexy legs. Sit back and enjoy. These ladies are available after the show but it's going to cost you!!!" said the guard.

About 9 men were beating their meat watching the naked girls preform. They were all arrested and taken away. Security gathered around the stages to keep the girls safe and keep the crazy men away who were arrested and taken away by police. Eighty percent of the cock happy men were from Cranston!

After the show was over military security and police guarded the four stages to keep the girls safe. People leaving the beach area looking for places to have private sex running around naked, were arrested by police. People having sex parties on the beach were told to stop because the festival is over! Violators were arrested. "Fuck You!"

"Oh! Yeah!"

Off to the police station they went!

The food vendors and drink tents closed right after the show and the police and national guard troops escorted everyone off the beach. Some who were resting in sleeping bags and tents refused to leave and were arrested. Some sex hogs had to be pepper sprayed and tasered to wake them the fuck up and get off the beach! The police and the national guard were not fucking around, when you're told to leave, you have to leave or get arrested and pay a big fine! At 11:02pm the 50 Shades of Compass Rose festival was over.

12:02am people were getting arrested, still fucking and eating out each other! At 1:02am strict force was being made by police and national guard troops. At 2:02am things were getting nasty up and down the beach with naked people getting teased and pepper sprayed, and final arrests. At 3:02am the beach was clear and police and the military stayed there all night in case people re-entered. At 4:02am a couple of boats pulled up on the beach and people putting blankets down were chased off the beach by police.

At 5:02am a couple made it onto the beach to do their thing and just when they finished the police came to tell them. "You better not be doing anything like I think you're doing or you're going to jail!"

"No officers, we came down here to sleep because we have no AC at home and it's cooler here," said the man.

"Well, you can't stay here, you have to leave."

"Yes sir, officers," said the girl.

The couple picked up their sleeping bag and were escorted out by the police.

At 6:02am people started coming to the beach to walk their dogs, but the police and the national guard troops were watching people having sex!

SECTION 6

VACATIONING RHODE ISLAND

There are many sites to visit in Newport, Rhode Island. Known as the Ocean State, Rhode Island is famous for its beautiful beaches and views. Misquamicut Beach in Westerly and Charlestown Beach are among the most beautiful beaches in the state. Narragansett Town Beach is the most popular beach and is nice and clean year-round. The Coast Guard House is the most popular restaurant in Narragansett, and Scarborough Beach is another popular beach in Narragansett. You can take the ferry from Point Judith to Block Island, another vacation destination in the state.

In Oakland Beach in Warwick, there's Iggy's Chowder House and Clam Cakes, one of the best seafood restaurants in the country, open year-round with record crowds daily, even in the winter.

Rhode Island is also home to several ten-pin bowling alleys, the most popular of which is Lang's Bowl-O-Rama in Cranston. Roger Williams Park in Providence and the Roger Williams Zoo are also top places to visit.

PPAC—The Providence Performing Arts Center—is similar to Radio City Music Hall in New York City, where the best plays in the country are performed. The Dunkin' Donuts Center in Providence is where basketball and hockey games are played. The Providence College Friars is Rhode Island's favorite basketball team. We also have the best hotels and restaurants in downtown Providence.

WaterFire on Saturday nights along the Providence River looks like Little Italy. Then there's Federal Hill, home to some of the best Italian restaurants in the United States. Rhode Island boasts some of the best restaurants on the East Coast, including Camille's and The Old Canteen, which are among the most popular restaurants on Federal Hill.

Bally's Twin River Lincoln and Bally's Tiverton Casino are popular destinations if you want to gamble. Bally's Twin River has a live band every Saturday night at the Light House Bar, located in the middle of the casino. They have slot machines, table games, and sports gambling at both Bally's Twin River and Tiverton.

Lincoln Woods is a popular walking park, and there's a beach with a freshwater pond that's nice and clean. Rhode Island also offers many walking trails and parks. Chase Farm on Rt. 123 in Lincoln is a large open field with plenty of trees and walking trails where you can spend the day and view all kinds of wildlife. Then, you have the Blackstone River Bike Path, located down the road on Front Street. It runs from Lincoln to Woonsocket. The ride or walk is about ten miles with water on both sides—a great place for deer watching—and there are bridges where people can go fishing. Brenton Park in Newport is a nice place to visit with a view of the ocean.

Popular events in Rhode Island include the Scituate Art Festival, the Washington County Fair, and the Burrillville Art Festival, all during the fall season. The Providence Convention Center hosts year-round events. Another place you must visit is Wickford Village and Boat Marina. The East Greenwich waterfront has The Harborside Nordic and Blu on the Water, the best places for nightlife and great restaurants in East Greenwich.

One beach I love in Quonset Point is Blue Beach. When you

get on the base, turn right at the first light onto Circle Drive, follow it to the end of the buildings, and you'll see a small parking area. There's a walking path with trees on both sides for about a quarter of a mile, and then a beautiful beach with Caribbean-like white sand and clean water. On a sunny day, the water looks blue, and most of the time, there's a sea breeze. It's a free beach and not many people go there—my favorite! There are three more beaches in Quonset Point: Sphinx Neck Fishing Port, where you can walk out a mile and a half at low tide; Compass Rose, which is a little rocky but offers a beautiful view of the Jamestown Bridge. The Quonset beaches are all dog-friendly.

Popular towns to visit include Barrington and Bristol. Every year, the Bristol 4th of July Parade is a must-see. I may not have provided all the addresses for these places, but you can easily find them on Google Maps. Another place to visit is Wright's Farm Restaurant in Burrillville, Rhode Island, where they serve family-style chicken, salad, ziti, French fries, and ice cream. I've lived in Rhode Island for 67 years, and I still haven't seen it all. There's so much to explore in little Rhody!

MUSICAL ASSEMBLY CHURCH

"RICKY, YOU HAD A NICE CLEAN BOOK GOING UNTIL YOU FUCKED UP IN THE LAST STORY; YOU BETTER GO TO CHURCH!"

Sunday morning at" Kings Musical Assembly Church." Port Charlotte Florida.

"Good morning my dear brothers and sisters. Welcome back to church. We were destroyed in a lightning storm, then again by a tornado and now by hurricane Ian, the worst storm ever in this part of Florida and here we are rebuilt again in a brand-new Christian church, KMAC, Kings Musical Assembly Church. This church was formed by a west coast radio news station.

The worldwide radio station out of Oregon built this church with Christian music across the world. Now they play the best of the 70's to today's music. Welcome our band. "The Klue Maxx American Cover band." They play Christian rock music with four electric guitars, a twenty-three-piece drum set, 15 horns, trumpets, a cello, three keyboards, an organ, a piano, seven saxophones, bongos, trombone, and a woodwind section in this orchestra.

In today's sermon I want to talk about the end times beginning with the human body. One day our bodies are going to break down as we get older. First of all, let's talk about the holes in our body. One day our ears will close and no more will you hear on God's green earth! Next our eyes will close and no more will you see on God's green earth! Then our nose holes will close and no more will you smell on God's green earth! When your mouth hole closes, no more will you eat on God's green earth! If your hands get weak, no more will you grab, if your legs stop working, no more will you walk on God's green earth. When your private area hole closes, no more will you pee on God's green earth! There's a bigger day coming! When your rectum hole closes, no more will you crap on God's green earth! Amen!

"Everyone, please stand and come to the altar and praise God! Use your voices and instruments! Praise God! Praise God! Praise God!!! Talk to Him—the almighty Jesus Christ! Praise Him! Praise Him, with the almighty GOD! Tell Him how much you love Him! Scream to the Heavens and invite God into your hearts! Praise God! Praise God! Praise God!!!" said the pastor.

Then, everyone in the church stood in front of the altar, praising God. The noise was overwhelming as they used all kinds of instruments—cowbells, whistles, sticks banging together, foghorns, and air horns. The band pounded the drums, clashed cymbals, and played Christian rock music, all while the crowd continued to praise God with passion.

The pastor then poured holy oil on everyone's foreheads, said prayers, and the congregation continued to dance and praise God as the band played Christian rock 'n' roll style.

The pastor spoke again: "Everyone, please be seated. Our God must know our feelings, both when things are good and when things are bad. The devil will tempt us to turn away from God, which is why we praise Him, celebrate with Him, and believe in Him. For the past five years, the devil has been attacking our church and the town of Port Charlotte. First, the COVID-19 pandemic hit. Then, we were struck by lightning, burning down our church, which was already struggling from the pandemic. We quickly rebuilt, and as soon as we were organized, a tornado struck, destroying our church once again. After rebuilding for a third time, hurricane Ian came and destroyed our church for the fourth time. And now, with the help of God, we are rebuilding yet again for the fifth time. Years ago, our church first burned down in a fire."

It was a different Christian church back then. You see, the devil has a way of destroying God's faith when these bad things happen, and with your help rebuilding and praising God, that means we have to pray harder from being destroyed a sixth time! Or move to another area. You see, we the people are the church, not the building; the building is simply a place to pray to God. Do I believe the devil is trying to destroy us? Yes! When things get bad, we have to pray harder and keep rebuilding! Amen!" said the pastor.

When the service was over, a meal was prepared in the church hall. After the service, brunch was served. Hundreds of people gathered, and the pastor said grace, then everyone was able to eat. Ham, eggs, omelets, oven-baked potatoes, sausage, muffins, orange juice, and coffee were served.

SECTION 8

THE 12 HOUR BIGAMIST

A man visiting Las Vegas from El Salvador decided to marry two beautiful women; one at noon and the other at midnight.

Mary Martha and Martha Mary's conversation at the Paris Hotel: "Miss Mary Martha or are you Mrs. Mary Martha from Costa Rica? Do you remember me, Rex Mountain, your former lover? I am really surprised to see you here in Las Vegas, we had a good friendship together when we were in Costa Rica. Then I moved to Metapan, El Salvador, and we never saw each other again! Are you married or single?" said Rex.

"No, I'm single, working as a casino host and table dealer here at the Paris Hotel."

"Oh! That's nice! I am still an airline pilot flying back and forth from Las Vegas to Central America, seven days a week, from midnight till noon just like before. I Only have twelve hours of social time, I'm lucky to get 6 hours sleep a night. I really like my job and I always like flying and meeting new people."

"Oh, that's great Rex. I have been a casino host and table dealer for the last eighteen years here at the Paris Hotel and was at The MGM for 6 years. I have been here in Las Vegas for the last 25 years. I once was a prostitute for a while, but I have been strait for the last 6 years. I went both ways with other women and men.

Sometimes I wish I had a tool about eight or nine inches long, so I have to use a twelve-inch-long dildo to satisfy myself; I'm still a horny bastard just like before! I can't go more than six hours without getting laid or sucking all day. I need to fuck until I die. I can't go too long without a physical pounding at least once a day. I work hard then I want to get laid!" said Mary.

The couple had a nice time with each other; maybe they got laid and had sex all day. Who knows? But they hit it off for fifteen hours just bull shitting about their lives.

"Hay Honey, if you are that good in the sack, let's go downtown and get married, then we can screw ourselves to death here in Las Vegas, it's that easy!" said Rex.

Then they got so drunk they staggered to the altar to get married. After getting married in a Las Vegas chapel, Mary had to work while Rex kept drinking and gambling before crashing at the hotel room. Rex is a high stakes big-time gambler at the tables and lives on his winnings and comps and sleeps where he wants at any hotel and eats and drinks for free! He's still an airline pilot, part time, not 12 hours a day like he told Mary.

At 11:02 p.m. Rex wakes up and he goes to the New York-New York casino from the Paris Hotel where he and Mary are staying. He goes to the high limit crap tables, and he meets a beautiful girl. Her name tag says "Martha Mary" and he throws the dice, 7-7-7 seven times in a row. The two of them are winning thousands of dollars, cleaning up the crap tables!

"Martha, we're doing pretty well cleaning up the cash playing craps. I get a kick out of your name tag, Martha Mary. Rex Mountain, it's a pleasure to meet you."

"Pleased to meet you, sir."

"Do you know Mary Martha, a casino host here in Las Vegas?" said Rex.

"No. Never heard of her!" She said.

The two of them celebrated all night sharing the winnings

together and went for an early morning walk and Rex decided to marry her in a Las Vegas chapel.

"Just for the hell of it, let's stop here and get married!"

"Okay! Let's do it!!" said Martha.

They got married at 7am, then they went back to the New York-New York Hotel for some hot nookie and some shut eye. At 11:30 a.m. Rex said, "Martha I have to go to work at the airport, I will meet you here tonight at midnight and we'll do it all over again."

Then Rex took a quick shower, brought a Boston Red Sox baseball hat on the strip, and went back to the Paris Hotel to meet his other wife, Mary, at noon, for brunch then went to the hotel room for a day of nookie and bed rest.

After the nap they went gambling all day, drinking then going to dinner. Then they went to a show in the evening and spent the rest of the night in the casino. Then just before midnight, Rex had the same excuse!

"I have to go to work at the airport. I will meet you at noon when you get out of work. Good night!"

Then Rex got the airport shuttle at 11:52pm to meet Martha at New York-New York at exactly midnight! Now it's round two with Martha. They went gambling at the Mandalay Bay Casino until 3am.

They had an early 4am breakfast then they got a room there and it was baboom, baboom, baboom again for the rest of the night!

11am Rex got up to take a shower and he has the same excuse again! "I have to go to work at the airport. Where do you want me to meet you at midnight?"

"Right here honey, I'll be somewhere in the casino. Maybe we can go see a late show." she said.

"Ahhhhh! A taxi! Maybe I can get to the Paris hotel in time

to meet Mary at Noon." Rex said to himself. Rex contacted Mary on his cell phone. "Mary where are you?"

"I am out in the pool."

"It's hot outside! Okay I'll meet you there."

They went swimming in the pool today with hugs and kisses all day. Then they went gambling, then went for a nap in the hotel room, getting some action, then slept for a few hours. They got up, went to dinner and danced, and then Rex has to go to work again! He took the airport shuttle from the Paris Hotel to meet Martha at Mandalay Bay at midnight. He has to keep track on both women on their whereabouts on his phone to keep these double dipping marriages together!

The shuttle arrived 10 minutes late and at midnight Martha met Rex at Mandalay Bay and they went to a Las Vegas show. Meanwhile, Mary had a meeting to go there, and she walked right by Rex and his other wife going to the show, but she didn't see them and Rex and Martha didn't see her! The show had all naked ladies running around.

"I bet you're enjoying this Rex!"

"I didn't expect the show to be like this but it's funny."

Martha and Rex went out into the casino to gamble and get snacks and drinks before going to bed. Did they fuck again? Who knows! While in bed, Martha said. "Rex why do we see each other 12 hours a day during the night until noon every day. Something don't add up here!"

"Because that's my work schedule. I fly planes and helicopters, then I run the airport making sure the air traffic control towers are doing their jobs, monitoring baggage claim and flight control counters. Without me; Las Vegas Airport shuts down, it's a 12-hour day, 7 days a week."

"Can't you take a sick day!?" said Martha.

"My sick time and vacation are over until next year, I used all my time, including my personal days. We have only thirty percent of a work staff that's why I have a 12-hour day, 7 days a week. I hope that someday things will get better when the airport gets more help. You know how it is, even the casinos are lacking staff," said Rex. {THAT'S ALL BULLSHIT!!!!!} Then they rolled over and went to sleep.

11:02am Rex got up to take a shower and he's off to work to see Mary! He met her at the crap tables where she was dealing. Later in the day they went to dinner and had a few drinks. "How was work last night Rex?"

"It was busy like always, a lot of flights coming in and going out. I have to fly to Reno tonight and I'll be back by morning. It's a tough life spending little time with each other, you work during the daytime, and I work nights 12 hours a day, 7 days a week, being the manager of the airport and flying planes."

"I know Rex, it's hard but I am glad we got married because we had been going out for a while in Costa Rica. Then it was bedtime, bang, bang, bang! Then it's time to get up, it's 11:11pm.

Rex took a quick shower, then he's off to work to see Martha. (It's the same bullshit all over again!) He took the shuttle to the MGM to meet Martha there. The shuttle arrived. Rex looked at his watch and the time was 12:02am. He met Martha in the casino. Then they went to the blackjack tables to play. While Rex went to the bathroom a man said, "Martha, is that man your husband?'

"Yes, he is!"

"He looks like a man who married someone else at the wedding chapel a few days ago near downtown. He has the same shirt on, and he looks like the same man, but I could be wrong."

Martha gave him a dirty look and she left the blackjack table to meet Rex. "She said, "Rex, do you know that man over there in the red shirt?"

"No, never saw him before." The man got a good look at Rex and then they disappeared. Martha kept her mouth shut. After drinking and dinner. It's bedtime! Fun under the sheets! Then they got up for brunch and went back to the casino in the MGM. Then Rex is off to work to see Mary back at the Paris Hotel. Meanwhile Martha contacted the airport.

"Good afternoon, Las Vegas International Airport."

"Hi this is Martha Mary from the New York- New York. Does Mr. Rex Mountain work there, he's my new husband and I need to talk to him?"

"Hold on," she paused, "I've heard about him he flies planes but he's not in the airport right now."

"Thank you, sir," said Martha. Then Martha ignored the red flags, and she did what she had to do until she meets Rex at midnight.

Later, Rex met his first wife at the Paris Hotel and went to the pool, then they went to the Mirage to play. A dealer at the blackjack table was giving Mary a hug and a little kiss in the ear while Rex was talking to people waiting to get a table. Rex saw him and he grabbed him by the throat and he said, "Keep your fuckin hands off my wife or I will kill you!" Then Rex and Mary went to the craps table to avoid more trouble. It was a losing day for both of them, they lost thousands of dollars together. Later Rex took Mary for a helicopter ride, lifting off from a helicopter port on a roof at one of the hotels. Then they went to dinner at the Top of the World restaurant at the Stratosphere Hotel, looking over Las Vegas and the mountains. Blue sky on one view from the rotating restaurant and flashes of lightning over the mountains on the other. Then Rex saw Martha walking into the restaurant at a distance with three other girls, then they were gone!

Quickly Rex got up! "I will be right back I need to go to the restroom, bad!" Rex didn't come back for more than a half hour. He said to himself, *If she saw me, my beautiful marriages maybe over.*

"Oh my God, Rex, what took you so long, the food is getting cold."

"I had to go bad!"

Then the lightning was getting bad, bright light flashing through the restaurant and the rain pounding on the windows.

"Mary let's finish eating and get the hell out of here! I don't like thunderstorms!" Rex put $150 on the table and he grabbed Mary by the hand and they left in a hurry! The time was 9:02pm. Martha never saw Rex at the restaurant. Then with not much of a conversation Rex and Mary took a shuttle bus back to the Paris Hotel.

"Rex you're acting really strange tonight! Are you alright!?"

"I don't feel that great with not much rest and I have to fly to Los Angeles tonight and back here by morning bringing high limit gamblers from California, then shuttle them to the Mirage before I see you in the morning. It's 9:30 so let's get a little bed rest before I go to the airport," said Rex.

Then he's off to work to see his second wife Martha. He's telling the truth tonight; he's going to the airport! Rex was acting strange fearing he was going to run into his second wife at the Stratosphere. Then he met Martha at Monte Carlo Hotel. "So, Rex! When are you taking me for an airplane ride?" She said.

"I am flying out to Los Angeles, LAX to pick up some gamblers on a private jet at 1:17am. Get your stuff and let's go!" Martha went with Rex on a brief flight to LA. Meanwhile Mary woke up and she looked at the alarm clock and the time was 2:02am. She called the airport. Now Mary is checking up on him.

"Las Vegas International Airport, Janice Springboard speaking."

"Hi, did Rex Mountain's non-stop flight to Los Angeles leave yet?"

"Hold on!"

"Come on lady! I'm pregnant and my water's bursting, how long do I have to hold on for?" Mary said to herself.

Nine minutes later. "Are you still there?'

"Yes! Finally!"

"Rex Mountain's plane left about 1:30," said Janice Spring-board the airport receptionist.

"Thank You!" said Mary and she hung up and she went back to bed. Now she can sleep tonight.

"Good evening, ladies and gentlemen gamblers, I hope you all won today. Welcome aboard my aircraft. My name is Rex Mountain, aboard with my beautiful wife Martha. We just left Las Vegas at 1:17am pacific time and we will arrive at LAX some-time around 2:30am. The weather is nice, and we should have a smooth flight. Sit back with seat belts fastened and enjoy your flight."

Rex's jet arrived just after 2:30am PT. The passengers aboard were high stakes gamblers and then more boarded the plane for Las Vegas about 45 minutes later. The plane left LAX about 3:30am, right away! The jet arrived in Las Vegas around 5am. The co-pilot, Martha, slept through the round-trip flight. A shut-tle waited before the jet departed at 5:30am and arrived at the Mirage before 7am and the high stakes gamblers were let off. Then the shuttle took Rex and Martha back to the Monte Carlo Hotel around 7:30am and it was nap time for a few hours before Rex had to see Mary at noon.

"Where are you going now?" said Martha.

"I have to go back to the Mirage to line up the high limit room and set up the buffet. Have a nice day at work and I'll see you later tonight". Kiss, kiss! Hug, Hug! And goodbye! I think Rex just fucked up! He's going back to the Mirage! Rex left Monte Carlo to meet Mary at the Paris Hotel.

"Mary let's get something to eat and hit the sack before you go to work because I had a busy night last night flying. We'll go to the Excalibur for dinner and a show. They fucked like rabbits for an hour then they went to sleep. The sex was so intense you'd have to call 911 to get them apart! Meanwhile, while they slept, Martha goes to the Mirage to check on the high limit players.

"The high limit players arrived from Los Angeles, but we have no buffet here, everyone is on their own. There are no set ups for the high limit," said casino hosts at the Mirage.

"Mr. Rex Mountain had a crew from LAX, he was working with," said Martha.

"I have no clue!" said casino staff at the Mirage.

Martha stormed out of the Mirage casino calling Rex on his phone, but he has his fuckin phone turned off! She's pissed, and she thinks something wrong is going on! Martha went from casino to casino looking for Rex before returning back to work in New York-New York.

After Mary's work shift was over, she and Rex went to Excalibur for dinner and a show then went drinking and gambling. Then Rex is off to work to see Martha at midnight at the New York-New York Hotel right across the street.

"Rex, why are you going to New York-New York?" said Mary.

"Because the shuttle stops there before going to the airport." Kiss, kiss, hug, hug! And he's off! The shuttle gets to New York-New York and Martha meets Rex getting off the shuttle.

She said. "Come inside, I have a bone to pick with you!"

"What's the matter!" said Rex.

"You take me for a nice flight to LA, then you leave me at noon to set up high limit rooms and a buffet at the Mirage. I went there about 1:30 and the casino hotel managers told me there's no such event."

"That's correct, Martha, because they were canceled."

"Something is going on and I will find out! Where did you go after?"

"I got a room there to get some sleep then play the tables before I came to see you at midnight."

"Rex, meet me at the wine bar we've got to talk!" Martha's fuckin pissed!!!

Meanwhile Mary walked from the Excalibur to New York-New York to do some gambling at the blackjack tables while Rex and Martha were drinking at the wine bar and arguing. An hour later, a fight broke out at the blackjack tables and the table area was closed off, so Mary went to the wine bar. Mary ordered a glass of wine at the bar, and she looked to the right and there was Rex and Martha mugging it up, hugging, kissing and rubbing each other!

Mary went over to them and she threw her wine drink in Rex's face, and she grabbed a glass of water and she thew it in Martha's face! "Now I know why I see you only 12 hours a day! We just got married a week ago and you're already cheating on me! This is why we broke up before when we were in Costa Rica," Mary cried.

"Who the fuck are you!"

"He's my husband!"

Then Mary tipped the table over spilling all the drinks and food on Rex then the two of them were pulling each other's hair and beating on each other! A cat fight at the wine bar! Rex got up covered in the food and drinks that had been poured all over him and he ran away into the casino while Mary and Martha were beating the shit out of each other!

Martha picked up a chair pushing Mary into a corner while Mary kept punching Martha in the face and kicking her! Martha picked up a flower vase and she smashed it over Mary's head knocking her out! The two of them were full of blood; they looked like they were attacked by a wild animal!

Then restaurant staff with casino staff ran to help break up the fight. Mary was taken to the hospital, she had pieces of glass sticking in her head while Martha lost several teeth from the beating, and she was taken to the hospital. The two ladies were arrested and charged with assault and property damage. Rex was long gone! He got the shuttle, and he went back to the Paris Hotel where he and Mary were staying and he packed up and he went to the airport and flew his private jet back to Metapan, El Salvador, where he's from.

He will learn a lesson if he ever gets married again! About a month later Rex received divorce papers from Mary, then days after he received divorce papers from Martha and lawyers' fees. Then he was banned from Las Vegas and entering the United States because he only had a green card. Mary Martha and Martha Mary became friends later and married each other in Las Vegas!

The two of them spent 24 hours a day with no issues. They work together, eat, drink and gamble together and they have a good sex life. They enjoy a good dike marriage in the bedroom. The gay couple remained in Las Vegas.

SECTION 9

FREE ONE-WAY TICKET TO MARS!

Lucatana Prison in Yorker, Spain.

August 2029. A meeting was held after dinner in the mess hall, where the prisoners eat.

"Good evening, my name is Lenny Bowser. I just got a message from Pope Peter De Dinardo allowing all death row prisoners out of jail, but there's a catch. We have the biggest prison in the world here, trapped between two active volcanoes and fenced off from the ocean on all sides. No one's breaking out of here! We are five hundred times bigger than Alcatraz! We have fifty thousand prisoners on death row here. Pope De Dinardo allowed these killers to go free as of today, August 5, 2029, to free up space in prisons worldwide. It's not fair to the rest of the inmates. The catch is, all death row inmates have a free one-way ticket to Mars; you heard right, a one-way ticket to Mars! You will be boarding a laser-powered jet from Fox Air Force Base that carries five thousand passengers to the red planet. The flight takes six weeks! We have twenty of these jets at that location. When you get to the planet Mars, you're on your own, free, if the planes make it there!

The planes have three big engines on each wing and three on the tail end. There are no pilots or flight crew. Everything is run by autopilot from a computer. The plane runs on jet fuel and travels at the same speed as a regular jet airliner. When reaching the stratosphere, the lasers turn on, saving jet fuel when landing on Mars. The plane will fly at laser speed, six million miles per hour, until reaching Mars' atmosphere, and it will land at the equator, the warmest area on Mars. The average temperature is thirty-four point eight degrees, seventy degrees during the day, but at night the temperature plummets to zero! Your home will be the plane you're traveling on. You will have heat for about a year on these planes, enough food if you share it together, for at least a year. Two small meals a day, and you're golden. You have warm clothing, circulated water from waste, pure enough to drink and bathe in."

The most educated death row inmates will be running the show. If you want to fight and kill each other, it's not a good way to go free and enjoy the cosmos. There are no rules; once that plane leaves Fox Air Force Base, you're on your own! These planes have eight decks, like a cruise ship, plenty of room to move around, and the seats fold into beds like a recliner. Keep seat belts fastened until you get into the stratosphere. The planes have several restrooms and kitchens, like an underground military bunker. Men will travel with men and women will travel with women. Remember, you're still on death row, you're not free until your flight lands on Mars. Buses will leave the prison, taking you to the planes with guards on board. If you mess up, you will be shot, and your bodies will be dumped in the volcanoes." said Lenny Bowser, Prison Officer.

The first plane carrying five thousand death-row passengers never made it! Maybe an asteroid hit it! Who the hell knows! The second plane got lost in space! The third plane made it to Mars! Planes four through twenty were never heard from again; did they get lost too, or did some make it? The third plane slowed down in Mars' atmosphere, the gas engines turned on, and the plane landed safely in a dirt field and came to rest near a mountain.

The wind was blowing dust around, and the temperature was 33 degrees below zero. All the prisoners had to use oxygen to breathe.

Ladies and gentlemen, we did not land on the equator. Before exiting this aircraft, we need to put on space suits and walk with a rope because there's no atmosphere here. If we don't stay together, roped together, we may get lost in space! Don't exit the aircraft until the weather warms up when daylight arrives, or you will freeze to death!" said one of the head prisoners.

The next day, at about noon Mars time, prisoners began exiting the plane, exploring the red planet. One man said, "Follow me!" The man forgot to rope up and he disappeared into Mars' atmosphere, floating away, and he was dead hours later, floating into space.

"Goodbye, Howard!" said the crew.

"Ladies and gentlemen, you have to pay attention while exiting this plane. We have only 100 space suits aboard this plane. Only 10 passengers at a time should exit the plane, holding on to the chain rope, and don't let go. You saw what just happened, now we've lost a guy! Howard Brown tried to be Superman! Hold on, there's no atmosphere on Mars, and it's very cold and windy!

Chain up together and lock on to the rope. We only have an hour of air to use in the spacesuits; use your own judgment. Many spacecraft have been here, but we are the first humans arriving on Mars, and so far, nothing has been found but dust and rocks. Life may have been here at one time. Be careful exiting the aircraft because it's very cold and windy," said one of the head prisoners in charge.

One man went out first, and the wind was blowing so hard he was bouncing against the aircraft, holding on for his dear life. Other prisoners were able to pull him back into the plane, and the plane doors slammed shut, knocking people down. "Everyone just stay put. We still have at least 10 months to get some fresh air! The wind is way too strong. Tomorrow's another day. Remove your spacesuits until we can go out," said the head prisoner.

One man was checking out the plane and looking at the control panels. He asked, "Can we just take off and go somewhere else?"

The head leader said, "This plane is run by a computer from Earth; we're not going anywhere! We are here to stay."

The prisoners on death row did what they do all day long: sleeping, having sex with one another, fighting, and killing each other! The dead bodies were thrown out a door at the tail end of the plane and taken away in Mars' wind and dust! There was no cell phone service other than communications from Earth that kept the plane heated and air circulated. The plane is operated like an underground military bunker with plenty of food, water, bedding, and warm clothing.

Ten days later, the wind wasn't that bad, with dusty sunshine and a temperature around fifteen degrees.

"May I have your attention? You may start exiting the aircraft, only ten at a time, and hold on. You have thirty minutes, then the next ten can suit up to explore the red planet," said the head prisoner.

Ten prisoners went out, walking the rope, and all they saw was rocks and dirt. Scooping up rocks, they found nothing. The same for the next ten, and the next ten, and the next ten! But no change. Finally, one man broke loose to explore on his own and walked for miles but found nothing—just dirt and rocks. Then his air ran out, and he dropped dead.

"We lost Brian Richi. Don't wander off on your own; everyone must stay together. We're not on Earth anymore! Three hundred and twenty people have died in the last few days. It's not safe here. I understand we're all up here to die, but we all have to make the best of it while it lasts. If we can't find life here on Mars, we have to stay aboard this aircraft until the air runs out. About 40 people have explored Mars so far, and nothing has been found but rocks and dirt," said the head prisoner.

Two days later, a major haboob with three-hundred-mile-per-hour winds buried the plane under fifty feet of dirt and dust. Blowing rocks smashed windows, blowing dust and dirt inside the plane until everyone suffocated and died within a few minutes. About a month later, all the bodies had rotted to bones and were buried in Mars' dust. Human bones drowned in hell on Mars. Not a good idea sending death row prisoners to Mars! Nobody survived on Mars.

The first plane hit space debris and burst into flames just after leaving Earth's atmosphere, killing everyone aboard! The second plane got lost in space. The third plane made it to Mars, but no one survived! The fourth crashed into the Moon—Boom! The fifth plane crashed into the ocean on takeoff! Prisoners trying to swim to shore were eaten by sharks. The sixth plane made it to Mars, but it crashed and burned. The seventh and eighth planes collided in the stratosphere and exploded! The ninth plane never left the ground, and the prisoners were escorted back to Lucatana Prison. The tenth plane was hijacked and crashed in Iraq. The eleventh plane crashed into space debris, then— Boom! That plane disappeared! The twelfth plane made it into Mars' atmosphere but broke apart, and three thousand death row prisoners froze to death! The thirteenth plane got lost in space. The fourteenth plane almost made it to Mars, but it got lost too. The fifteenth plane made it to Mars but was blown away in a dust storm and disappeared! The sixteenth plane got caught in a thunderstorm over the Indian Ocean and crashed, killing everyone aboard. The seventeenth plane made it to Mars but crashed into a mountain and exploded from strong winds. The eighteenth plane lost control in the stratosphere and broke apart! The same thing happened to the nineteenth plane! The last plane was struck by a meteor, and it went puff! None of the twenty planes survived their journey, and most didn't even get out of Earth's atmosphere!

SECTION 10

THE TOCKWOTTON VOLCANO

The Tockwotton Volcano is a strip joint and private nightclub under the Narragansett Brewery in Providence, Rhode Island.

People driving on Route 195 east saw a sign: "Tockwotton Volcano under the Gano Street exit, help wanted." The sign attracted a crowd, including police. Traffic jams caused by people looking for the volcano alerted officers, who went to investigate the Narragansett Brewery. The Providence Police entered the brewery looking for the manager.

"Can I help you, officers?"

"Yes, did you hear about a volcano somewhere here in India Point? It's tying up a lot of traffic on 195 east. It's posted on a sign under the Gano Street exit."

"Yes, we have a private club under the brewery called the 'Tockwotton Volcano,' for special events," said the manager.

"Can we see this private club?"

"Sure, come this way, officers."

The manager led the police officers to a trap door covered by a large oriental rug. A ladder descended thirty feet to get into this underground palace. The club had several dancing stages where strippers strutted their stuff. A large bar stretched across the club, with disco balls hanging everywhere and colorful lights to match the music.

The dance floors lit up, and the name of the club, Tockwotton Volcano, was prominently displayed. After the tour, the policemen said, "You have a nice club here, but you're running an illegal operation with no windows or exits. Suppose you have a fire; you could be sued big time! There's only one way out—climbing a thirty-foot ladder to get out!"

"We have a good sprinkler system down here, coming from the ceiling and spraying out of the walls and floors. We may be underground, but we're not the Station Nightclub. If a fire breaks out, this place will flood like Niagara Falls, giving everyone a chance to get out. We have a high-tech computerized system here, and we also have a loading dock area with a freight elevator leading to a garage in the main brewery, in case of a massive evacuation," said the manager.

"Okay, so you do have another exit in case of an emergency. You need to remove the signs hanging above Route 195 and the Gano Street exit. Due to people looking for a volcano here in Providence that isn't actually here, it's causing a traffic issue."

"Okay, officers!"

The police left, and strippers were being hired for summer jobs. Most of them were students from Brown University, RISD, and Johnson & Wales University.

"Good afternoon. May I speak to the person in charge?" one girl said.

"Sure, have a seat, and I'll bring the manager over to see you," said a brewery worker.

"Hi, I'm Vincent McShawn, owner of Narragansett Brewery."

"My name is Mary Martha from Brown University, and I'm looking for a job at the Tockwotton Volcano. I was told to come here."

"Come into my office, and we'll talk. Martha, I am looking for dancers and strippers for the volcano club."

"Where is this volcano club?"

"Come and I will show you the facility." The owner pulled the oriental rug away and opened a trap door to lead her down to the club. "Be careful we have to climb down a thirty-foot step ladder to get into the club. I will go first and you follow. Take your time," said the owner.

The girl looked around the club and saw girls dancing naked, lights flickering and techno music playing. "You have quite a club here, but I do not want to dance naked, this is not my thing. If you want a waitress or bartender or a DJ I'm interested but, I do not want to be a stripper or prostitute. If that's what you're looking for, please show me the door and let me out of here!"

The owner was standing there with his zipper open and a boner about a foot long! He said. "I need dancers and strippers, and I pay $50 an hour!"

"No thank you," said Mary. She climbed out of the club and left the brewery. Later, more college students came looking for jobs and became strippers and prostitutes. They danced naked and worked in private sex rooms, meeting pimps. The police, doctors, lawyers, and businessmen come here for sex, hiding from their wives. * I'M JUST GOING TO THE BREWERY FOR A COUPLE OF BEERS AND A COUPLE OF HOURS" * The Resmini's come here, the Bottaro's, the Calvino's, The Cunha's, the Iannotti's, the Rhode Island State Police, Providence Police.

The fire department and rescue come here for a piece of ass or a blowjob! A pimp had a meeting with a bunch of girls from Brown University. "Ladies, my name is Corey Spinxneck. I will be your instructor if you want to work with me. I am a pimp out of New York City. My job is working with dancers and strippers. If you just want to be a dancer and not be a stripper, you're on your own. You make your own tips and you're your own boss, but if you want to make big money, you have to be a stripper and a prostitute, that's what I am here for. I will send you to someone for a lay or a BJ and collect the money and you get a percentage. You meet the man here and you dance on stage naked, and I set you up with him for a date. You do your thing here behind closed doors. Do not leave this club or you will be fired. You must get at least $300 for a lay and $200 for a BJ. I get half of the profit. You may have four or five partners a day and you can make a quick grand a week. If you can't make the money I am asking, you will be removed and you will have to do it on your own. Remember you do not leave the club. Are there any questions?"

"Yes Mr. Spinxneck. Can I make more money screwing on my own?" said one girl.

"Yes, you can, just set your price. However, you don't know who you're messing with! Working with me you will be having sex with clean people, like lawyers, doctors, police officers, high class businessmen, and military men etc....," said Corey Spinxneck.

"Sir: Are you going to beat me up if I don't make the money you want like most pimps do?" said one girl.

"Like I said before, if you don't make the profit, you will be replaced—terminated. I am not a violent person like most pimps from New York."

"What happens if I get arrested for prostitution?" said another girl."

"You have to hide what you're doing and don't get caught," said Corey.

While the pimp Corey Spinxneck was lining up his broads, policemen and firemen were coming in to pick up prostitutes to get laid and placing dollar bills in the girl's G-string while they were dancing. One girl dropped her drawers doing it in the club in public and Corey Came over to them and said, "You two will need to go to one of the private rooms, you can't be doing that here!" The man was finished, and he was thrown out from the club.

The bartenders were mixing drinks and bringing them to the strippers. Fake volcanoes were erupting at both ends of the bar with music playing and lights flashing and people dancing at this private club. The national guard arrived in 5 armored vehicles with about twenty troops. They came into Narragansett Brewery and were escorted to the trap entrance to the Tockwotton volcano strip club to get laid and get their rocks off!

Meanwhile a thunderstorm was brewing, and the power went out. The only lights were the fake volcanoes at each end of the bar. Police were walking around with flashlights so the strippers could put their clothes back on. I hope the national guard troops got laid before the power went out. Then water came in, flooding the club from the heavy rain outside. The strippers had to dress up on the dance stages or on top of the bar. The crowded club had to climb the 30-foot single ladder to get out of the club. The sex rooms were filled because they got to get their nookie first before exiting the flooded dark club. The strippers used their phones to give light so they could see what they're doing!

Everyone walked through two feet of water to get out of the club. Don't worry, the police, firemen, national guard, lawyers, and doctors all got laid before the mishap happened. Part of the floor in the club collapsed and buckled causing a wall to crack and the water rushed in like a river. Then everyone got out of the club safely but soaking wet. They were hanging around in the brewery buying food and drinking beer. The power was still out, and the pimp had a meeting with some of his girls.

"Ladies our private club has been damaged from this storm going on outside. Until further notice I have to find a place for you girls to do your work. #1 one at a time in my office. #2, you may have to do it in your car, #3 go to your home or his home,

#4 you may have to do it in a park or out in the woods in some area where you can't be seen. Finally, #5, pick anywhere away from public places. Do it at a beach when no one is around, etc.... I set up the date with the man you will be with, and the man has to pay me my share before going with you. Or you can go out on your own and take your chances. If you choose to do that, you don't need to see me anymore. If you want to make big money, stay with me," said Corey Spinxneck, the pimp.

RICKY'S SPORTS STORIES

BE NICE RICKY AND KEEP IT CLEAN WILL YOU!

On April 18, 1981, I had plans to go see the Pawtucket Red Sox, but I had to go to church for Easter, and after that, I was going to my sister Charlene's house for my niece Kelly's first Easter egg party. I couldn't miss that! So, I decided to go to the Brown-Cornell baseball doubleheader. Brown won both games. Then, I went home to eat dinner.

I was living on the East Side of Providence at the time. After dinner, I went to the Easter mass at St. Paul's Church in Cranston. The service lasted two hours and forty minutes. Then, I went to my sister's house for about three hours.

I called McCoy Stadium around 11:00 p.m.

"Who won the game?"

"One to one after eleven innings," said the clerk at McCoy Stadium.

I called again just after midnight.

"Who won the game?"

"One to one after sixteen innings."

"I said to my sister, "Boy, I should have gone to that game."

IT'S NOT OVER YET! I went home around 1:00 a.m., smoked a joint, grabbed a beer, and put music on. At 1:15 a.m., I called McCoy Stadium again.

"Who won the game?"

"Two to two going into the twenty-second inning."

"Wow! I thought they would call the game after 1:00 a.m."

"We're going for the International League record—twenty-three innings," said the clerk.

I quickly put down my beer, got into my car, and drove to McCoy Stadium, only ten minutes away. I got there at the start of the twenty-third inning, and I laughed and laughed! I sat and watched ten innings, and nobody scored. I got there at 1:30 a.m. and stayed until 4:07 a.m., when the game was stopped after thirty-two innings because it was getting bright, and the sun was about to rise.

I said, yelling from the stands, "Oh, come on, let's finish the game!"

There were only twenty people left to witness the longest baseball game ever! On my way home, a PawSox player waved, and I waved back. When I got home, I called Charlene. "The game's over, a two-to-two tie after thirty-two innings!" The next day, I went to my parents' house in Cranston for Easter dinner. I threw my ham dinner down as fast as I could so I could be back at McCoy for 2:00 p.m. to catch the thirty-third inning. They decided to finish the longest game when the Rochester Red Wings returned on June 23rd, 1981. Everyone at the packed ballpark was booing! They decided to play a regular game, and the PawSox won that game, seven to six in ten innings. It was a long wait for that big night. Then, I went to see the thirty-third inning, and it lasted one inning on June 23rd. Rochester went one-two-three, and the PawSox got a hit, then a double, and a walk until Dave Koza got a base hit to win the game in the bottom of the thirty-third inning.

The place had the biggest crowd ever, with sports scouts from all over the world. And that's my story on the longest game, eight and a half hours total.

Back to that night: a PawSox player was out all night the night before this game, and his wife was pissed. She said, "If you do this again, you're out of this house!" The next night, his wife didn't believe a baseball game would be played all night, and she threw him out of the house! Later, she saw it all on the news, and the PawSox player was able to go back home.

Six weeks after the longest game, I had a fight with my girl-friend Kathy Noonan about a cookout at the beach, but she wanted to go to the PawSox game. So, to cool her down, we went to McCoy because she likes baseball. After eight and a half innings in less than two hours, I said to her, "Well, Kathy, I guess we'll have that cookout anyway because Pawtucket's going to lose, one to nothing!"

She said, "Think positive, Richard! We're going to win. The PawSox tied the game, one-to-one in the bottom of the ninth."

I said to her, "You might be right!"

The game went twenty innings, and the PawSox lost to the Richmond Braves, four to two. The PawSox' only home run was the first pitch at the bottom of the twentieth. That game started at 2:00 PM and didn't get over until 8:30 PM—six and a half hours, and we stayed for the whole game.

About a couple of years later, the PawSox beat the Syracuse Chiefs, two to one in twenty-seven innings, in a game that lasted nine hours because of rain delays. For all that, the Pawtucket Red Sox weren't much of a team back then, fifth place, maybe.

BRYANT UNIVERSITY BASEBALL GAME

From 2012 to 2021, the Bryant University baseball team won nine division titles in a row. The 2020 season was canceled because of the pandemic. About a few years ago, maybe during the 2017 or 2018 season, Bryant's streak might have been over if I hadn't been there!

Bryant was playing a weak team, Mount Saint Mary's or FDU. Bryant was losing 6–5 with two outs in the bottom of the ninth, and I, with my big mouth, helped them! Matt Mangini was coming to bat, and I yelled, "Come on, Mangini, you gotta get a hit here so the next batter can blast a homerun so we can get the hell out of here because it's too cold!"

Matt Mangini hit a single right up the middle. I said, "That's the way, Mangini! Next batter up, one crack of the bat and let's get it over with!" The next batter blasted a homerun into the stratosphere! Then, a massive celebration because of my big mouth! If I hadn't been there, Bryant may have lost, finishing second instead of first! Over 100 spectators yelled, "He called it!"

One more baseball story. Cranston East was playing a rare, weak La Salle team, winning 14–2, I believe, and I kept yelling at the La Salle catcher, who was having a bad game because of about 10 passed balls, and for the fun of it, I kept yelling, "Error, error, error, error!" When the game was over, the La Salle baseball team chased me out of Cranston Stadium with baseball bats, and I ran like a bat out of hell all the way down Park Ave. until they disappeared!

They couldn't catch me because I was too fast! Had that been a week later, this story would have been different. One week later, I was playing all by myself in the locked Cranston stadium, hitting baseballs, running the bases, and sliding into second base. I tore my knee open and ended up in Cranston General Hospital. I was laid up all that summer, and still today, it was my worst summer ever. I crawled out of the same hole in the fence that I crawled into, and the people living in the house called the rescue to help me get out of the hole in the fence. The accident happened on June 23rd, 1973. Had this accident not happened, I may have played in the major leagues or professional baseball somewhere. I did make it in the PBA bowling with the pros. I can write a book about all the baseball games I went to since the early 1970's. My dad always told me, "RICKY KEEP YOUR GD MOUTH SHUT AND WATCH THE GAME!"

BRYANT UNIVERSITY FOOTBALL

About 10 years ago or more, I was watching last-place Bryant against Sacred Heart. Bryant was losing 24–7 with 4:58 to play. Everyone left the stadium except me and my big mouth, helping the Bulldogs after Sacred Heart scored the dagger touchdown. Now it was my last chance to cheer. I kept yelling, "Throw the ball, throw the ball, throw the ball!" leading to pass interference penalties, until Bryant scored, missing the extra point, 24–13.

Then I yelled, "Squib kick, squib kick, squib kick!!!" Bryant did it! Sacred Heart never went after the ball, and Bryant recovered. I yelled, "Throw the ball!" over and over, leading to another pass interference penalty, until Bryant scored again, missing the two-point try, 24–19.

Then, with three seconds to play, there were offsetting penalties and a dead-ball foul against Sacred Heart, forcing them to punt. I yelled, "Kick it to Jordan Brown so he can run it back 75 yards for the win!" That's exactly what happened! When Jordan Brown caught the ball, Bryant set up a wall on the left side of the field, and Jordan Brown ran it back for the win, 25–24.

The cheerleaders and the dance team tackled me in celebration, with boobs and butts smothered in my face! I got the biggest laugh, and the football team was laughing hysterically!

THE NEW ENGLAND PATRIOTS SUPER BOWL VICTORY OVER THE SEATTLE SEA-HAWKS IN 2016

I was at Fred & Steve's restaurant eating dinner, and I kept saying, "Interception and the Patriots win!" The waiters kept saying, "From your mouth to God's ears!" Then, with 18 seconds to play, Seattle called a timeout, and I kept saying, "The game can't end without my interception! I know what's going to happen: the ball's going to Marshawn Lynch to run it in for the win for Seattle." The QB dropped back to pass, and Malcolm Butler picked it off in the end zone, and he was tackled at the one-yard line, and the Patriots won!

I was only kidding about the interception, but it happened! Then, once again, I was tackled in celebration by a bunch of girls on the Lighthouse Bar floor, with boobs and butts rubbing me in my face like the Bryant-Sacred Heart game.

The year of champions 2024 extends:
The Newport Gulls wins the 2024 NECBL baseball title in August, winning back-to-back championships.

TIVERTON-CLASSICAL HIGH SCHOOL GAME IN 1980

Chapter 1

December 1980. I was going to the game, but before I made a sign predicting the score of the game: Tiverton 59, Classical 57, double overtime, and the scoreboard would break down seconds before the game ended. Arthur Guimond scored 25 points with two free throws for the win, and it happened exactly as the sign had read before the game started. The coaches, the refs, and the spectators could not believe it! Channels 6, 10, and 12 news were called to the Classical High gym to witness my sign, and it was the headline of the news that night.

I told Arthur Guimond he was going to score 25 points tonight with two free throws in the 2nd overtime for the win."

He told me, "I never scored more than 13 points in a game."

I said, "Just shoot the ball and drive to the basket because tonight's your night." And he did! When I was 17, Arthur's father called me to bring him down to the Tiverton Recreation Center to show him how to play basketball. Arthur was only 5 years old, and I told him, "You're going to win me a state championship when you go to the high school."

Sure enough, that dream came true because Tiverton won the Class C state championship that season with a 54-43 victory over Ponaganset High School.

Getting back to the sign. Before the game started, I showed the sign going over to the Classical side, and the fans threw water cups at me, booing me. Then I went over to the Tiverton side, and their fans erupted in celebration!

"I lived in Tiverton most of my life when I was a kid, and I learned how to play sports just like teaching Arthur. My favorite sports are football, basketball, and baseball, in that order."

Chapter 2
My Sports History in Tiverton

In 1969, Tiverton had an undefeated baseball team playing La Salle in the state championship, and I wanted to go to the game on the bus, but my mother said it was too much money. $2.00 was a lot of money back then. Good thing I didn't go: Tiverton lost 7 to 3. I liked watching college basketball on TV and PC before I began to like baseball. I played in a few basketball leagues in Tiverton. I was a special needs person when I was a kid in room 258 at the high school for three years, and only two other kids and I were able to take high school classes. I got my GED at Cranston East High School in 1978.

In 1970, I went to my first-ever baseball game behind Pocasset School. Tiverton beat Barrington 4 to 3 in 12 innings. Even today, that was the best Tiverton High baseball game I ever saw. Best game I ever saw! Tiverton High has been in the state finals four times but only won once, in 1982, when they beat Westerly 2 to 1 in 10 innings. In 1980, Tiverton was unbeaten in their conference but lost to East Greenwich, 9 to 3. I saw that game. Then I mentioned before when they lost to La Salle in 1969. In basketball, they won five Division Three state championships and lost three. In 2011, they had their best team ever but got nothing for it. St. Ray's out of Pawtucket beat them for the Rhode Island State Title, 58 to 47. I was there. They beat La Salle, Bishop Hendricken, and Central, back-to-back before running out of gas in the final. They finished second in Division 2 that year. Tiverton won 4 out of 9 state football championships, 3 in Division 4 and their first in Division 3, and lost 4 in Division 4 and one in Division 3. And that's my Tiverton sports history! I only went to the football, basketball, and baseball games at Tiverton High.

SECTION 12

THE DIRTY CUSTODIAN

PART 1

Rocky Hockey was a custodian cleaning 71, 122, 161, and 376 Benefit Street apartment buildings, and he was a lazy bastard! The landlord was his boss, and his name was Rick Salve.

Interview

Rocky went to the office at 161 Benefit in a coffee shop inside the building.

"Good morning. I am looking for Mr. Rick Salve."

"Right here, sir."

"Hi, my name is Rocky Hockey, and I'm looking for the custodian job advertised in the *Brown Daily Herald* last week."

"Yes, sir. Come into my office. Grab yourself a cup of coffee and have a seat."

"Thank you," said Rocky.

"What kind of experience do you have in general cleaning?" said Rick Salve, the property manager.

"I used to clean apartments at Royal Crest Apartments in Marlboro, Mass., when I was living there."

"Okay, what we have here are four apartment buildings, all on Benefit Street here in Providence, R.I., and it's a 20-hour-a-week job cleaning hallways and laundry rooms, sweeping entranceways and parking lots, picking up trash, and removing trash from laundry rooms, washing floors, stairs, etc... We have mostly RISD and Brown students living in these apartment buildings. You do not clean the apartments, we have a maintenance crew that cleans, removes debris, and fixes damage, such as broken windows, holes in the walls, etc... You may have some rugs to vacuum in the halls. Come with me, and I will show you the properties."

"We're at 161 Benefit Street. We have three floors and wide hallways. These buildings get very dusty. The stairways get very dirty, and don't touch anything in the halls that may belong to the students. Use your own judgment. Anything like this—furniture and trash left in the halls—you report it to the office. Remove the trash.

Come downstairs, and I will show you the laundry room. In here, you sweep the floor, wash down the machines, move the trash, and wash the floor. You have a mop bucket by the sink and cleaning materials in the closet. There's Johnson & Johnson cleaning products for washing walls, floors, and sanitizing sprays, etc....

Next, we'll go to 122 Benefit Street. At this property, there are two parking lots: one in front of the property and a lower parking lot. The laundry room is located at the back of this building off the lower lot. There are three floors and a tight rotating stairwell and hallway in the front and back of this building. Here, you sweep and wash the halls, clean the laundry room, sweep the parking lot, and pick up and empty trash into the dumpster in the back of the building. Take a walk through, then meet me in the front of the building, and we'll go to 71 Benefit Street," said the boss, Rick Salve.

Rocky Hockey, the custodian, walked through the property at 122 Benefit Street, met his boss, and went to the next property.

"Rocky, 122 Benefit Street was built in 1822, and residents reported ghosts there, but I don't believe in that stuff!"

Welcome to 71 Benefit Street built in 1836. The front door enters a wide hallway going up three floors with two apartments on each side on each floor for a total of 12. There are 24 apartments in this building, front and back. The back of the building is smaller with tighter hallways. All landings are tile, and the stairs are made from wood. This property is bigger than it looks. We have a big parking lot with two dumpsters and recycling bins here. The building at the end of the parking lot is where the laundry room is: There are six washers and six dryers in here and a custodian room and storage space. Here you sweep and wash halls, the laundry room, and sweep up sand and pebbles in the parking lot and sweep around the dumpsters and keep the area clean. Pick up trash along the property. Now let's go to our final destination.

Any questions?" "These buildings are very old Rick! Providence is an old city and there's a lot of old buildings and mansions here on the east side of this city."

Marlboro, Massachusetts is much nicer!" said Rocky.

"That's right! City life is very different. Let's take a ride and I will show you 376 Benefit Street. Here's another old building much like 122 Benefit Street. We have 16 apartments here going up four floors with wooden halls and stairs. One apartment on each side and 8 in the front and back entrance. This building has a basement where the laundry room and storage areas are located. You have two washers and dryers here and the hallways are small at the front and back of the building. The apartments here are very large. Outside you have a large parking lot, two dumpsters and recycling bins.

All cleaning instructions are the same for all properties. Sweep the halls/stairs, clean the laundry rooms, and damp mop all wood floors and stairs. Scrub tile if necessary. Do not put a lot of water on wood floors or stairs. Wash tile floors in the laundry rooms. Wash dirt or soap out of washers with a bucket of water and wash down the machines. When you finish in the buildings, concentrate on sweeping the parking lot and trash sites. Pick up trash along the properties in a trash bag and throw it in the dumpsters.

Once again, you will be working 20 hours a week with no benefits. You'll be cleaning properties on Benefit Street only. On Mondays and Tuesdays, you will be cleaning the property at 161 Benefit Street, from 10 am to 2 pm, including the coffee shop. On Wednesdays, 122 Benefit Street gets cleaned from 10 am to 2 pm. On Thursdays, 71 Benefit Street gets cleaned from 10 am to 2 pm. And on Fridays, you will clean 376 Benefit Street from 10 am to 2 pm. When a holiday falls on a Monday, you will spend 8 hours at 161 Benefit Street on Tuesday. You clean these properties on the days scheduled. Do not mix properties and do not start cleaning or enter before 10 am. Leave the property by 2 pm. Here's the itinerary instruction sheet. Go over it, and pick up your keys Monday morning," said Rick Salve, property manager.

Two weeks later, Rocky was doing his job, keeping the properties clean, and he was good at following instructions. Then, before Christmas, Rick Salve went to Florida for the winter until March. Before he left, he said, "Rocky, this is Ruby Pleasure. He will be looking after you at least once a week. If you have any problems, see him. I am going to Florida, and I will be back in March. You're doing a good job so far. Just keep up the good work and have a Merry Christmas and a Happy New Year!" Rick Salve, the property manager, was gone.

WHILE THE BOSSES ARE GONE THE MOUSE WILL PLAY!'

PART 2

Right after Christmas, Rocky started fucking up, taking advantage of the college students going home for Christmas break and winter vacation; but tenants that live here year-round, are still here. Rocky was talking and texting on his cell phone, the buildings were not getting cleaned and he's bothering the tenants, racking up complaints in Rick Salves office.

He said to a girl in the coffee shop at 161 Benefit Street. "I like the way you dance! You have sexy legs. Can I get a hug! You have beautiful hair, and I would like to go out with you!"

"Go fuck yourself!" She said.

The next day, Rocky was outside emptying trash at 161. The garbage truck arrived to empty the dumpsters. A man started yelling at him. "Hey, fruitcake!" Rocky kept throwing bags of trash into the dumpsters. The man yelled again. "Hey, fruitcake!" Then again, "Hey, fruitcake!"

"He might be inside or the truck emptying the dumpsters," said Rocky.

The man yelled again, "Hey you! Fruitcake!"

"Are you talking to me?" asked Rocky.

"Yeah, you!!! What gives you the right to give my wife compliments, dance with her, tell her about her sexy legs, and ask her for hugs? Are you trying to pick her up?"

"I don't know what you're talking about, buddy!" said Rocky. "This is my wife!"

"I'm sorry, sir, but I didn't know she was married."

The man grabbed Rocky by the shirt, picked him up, and pinned him against the dumpster.

The woman said, "Eric, don't hit him! There are people out here!"

The man still had Rocky pinned up against the dumpster, and

he said, "If you ever say anything to my wife again, I will fuck you up! You got that!"

"I'm sorry!" Rocky cried. The man let him go and Rocky ran to the office crying like a baby! Ruby was in the office, and he said to Rocky. "Mr. Hockey, what's going on outside between you and Eric Stillwater?"

"I gave compliments to his wife, and he threaten to beat me up really bad!" Rocky cried.

"I heard about the issue. You need to do your work and keep your mouth shut. You can't be bothering the tenants. You can lose your job, and I can get into trouble defending you! We can't have that here! Rocky we have a few complaints here in the office. The buildings are not getting cleaned.

Tenants are complaining about you talking and texting on the phone all day and disappearing for hours and telling a parking attendant to go fuck himself! That can't be happening; that's grounds for termination. This does not look good when Rick comes back. You need to do your job and leave people alone," said Ruby Pleasure.

Weeks later the complaints kept piling up on Rocky Hockey--the dirty custodian! "Rocky, There's more complaints about your job. You have to do your job. A lot of the college kids went home for Christmas break, and you will be working with the maintenance men, cleaning apartments and shoveling snow.

First you will be shoveling snow and salting stairs with Adam and Steve, the maintenance workers. First you will shovel snow at all properties beginning here at 161 Benefit Street," said Ruby Pleasure.

"Yup, okay!" said Rocky.

"Then you will salt all the properties."

"Yup, okay!"

"Then next thing, you will be moving debris in all the hallways."

"Yup, okay!"

"Then you will clean out apartments, where students left."

"Yup Okay, ah ha!"

"Then you will clean the apartments after all the debris is moved out."

"Yup, Okay, ah ha!"

"Then you will help Adam and Steve, paint the apartments."

"Yip, Okay! Ah ha! Ah ha!"

"Then you will wash floors and shampoo rugs, before leaving the apartments; vacuuming if needed, etc..."

"Yip! Okay!! Ah! Ha!!"

"Then you help the maintenance men fix damages and repairs."

"Yip, Yup! Okay! Okay! Ah! Ha!!!"

"Then you go back to your job cleaning halls and laundry rooms when your done working with Adam and Steve."

"Yup, yip Okay! Ah Ha!"

When Rocky was working with Adam and Steve, Rocky kept fucking up!

"Rocky, you got to work with us and stop going off on your own. You need to work with me and Adam shoveling snow and salting together," said Steve.

"Yup! Okay! Ah! Ha!"

"Never mind Yup Okay ah ha! Just do your God Damn Job. Now go in the van with Adam to move the snow at 122 while I finish salting the stairs," said Steve.

"Rocky, lift the snow in the shovel and throw it over the edge. Don't push it down the stairs," Steve added again.

At 122 Benefit Street, Adam and Rocky were shoveling the stairs and entrance ways and Rocky threw a shovel load of snow on someone walking by.

"Hay you fuckin asshole! Watch where you're throwing that snow," said the girl walking by.

"Oh! I'm sorry!" said Rocky.

"You fuckin dick!!" she said.

"Rocky! What are you doing? You have to watch where you're throwing the snow, there's a lot of foot traffic here! You have to look first before throwing snow. Rocky, salt the stairs and sidewalks while I run the snow blower," said Adam.

"Yup! Okay! Ah ha!" He said.

After the crew went to 71 and 376 Benefit Street to finish shoveling snow and salting. Rocky was breaking up ice with an ice breaker and he almost chopped Adams foot off!

"Hey, you asshole!! Chop the ice, not my feet! Go to the back entrance and break the ice over there! I will take care of here; now get lost!" said Adam.

Rocky did not do a God Damn thing after the maintenance men were through with him. "Rocky, just go do your work cleaning; we do not want to lose any limbs from your ice pick and snow shovel," said Steve.

Rocky went into hiding until Rick Salve got back from winter vacation. Rocky was found sleeping in the laundry room, hanging around hiding behind a dumpster where he was caught when someone was throwing a trash bag in the dumpster. Trash was left in the hallways, halls and stairs were not getting swept or cleaned. He's hanging around, talking and texting on his cell phone and not doing his work, disappearing and not seen for days. The laundry rooms are a mess and trash cans are not getting emptied.

The trash was overflowing on the floor and laundry containers leaking and the floors are a mess in all the buildings and hundreds of complaints are coming into Ruby Pleasure's office at 161 Benefit Street. Dust balls the size of bowling balls left in the hallways, some of them look like rats rolling around, trash left in the halls, water bottles laying around in the halls, sand dirt and dust all over the halls and stairs, bottles and beer cans leaking. The halls and stairs were covered with salt, dirt and sand from the snow. Stairs and walkways were covered in ice and snow and people are falling on their ass! Railings and banisters were never dusted.

Rats the size of dogs were running around the properties getting into the trash and spreading it all over the parking lots and in and around the dumpsters. Mice and field rats were running around inside the buildings, scaring the living shit out of the tenants! Puke was left in the hallways at 161 and there was a dead cat laying in the hallway and the mice were feeding on it. The walls and apartment doors were filthy! There were naked pictures on the doors. Ceiling tiles were hanging down, paint chipping off the walls, lights out, light fixtures hanging down and bare wires showing! Even the maintenance workers are fucking up; but the custodian is not reporting damages in the buildings!

Papers of Rocky Hockey's complaints piled up about a foot high on Rick Salves desk waiting for him to get back; it may take months for him to go through all the complaints. March 16th Rick Salve returned from winter vacation and met with Ruby Pleasure in his office.

"Welcome back Tricky Ricky!" said Ruby.

"What the hell is all this on my desk!?" said Rick.

"These notes are all Rocky's complaints from the last three and a half months while you were gone. It will probably take a year to go through them all!" said Ruby.

"Let's take a walk through the buildings." Rick and Ruby were checking out Rocky's work and saw the disaster at 161 Benefit Street. Rick Salve went off! "Look at this place, it's a fuckin disaster! These stairs are filthy! Jesus H fuckin Christ! Didn't Rocky do anything while I was gone! It looks like a tornado went through here! I have to hire a cleaning company to clean my properties before my buildings fall down! Look, there's dust balls bigger than rats, and mice running around, and the halls smell like the dead! Trash everywhere! Mud and dirt and scuff marks all over the place!"

"Look here Rick, under a pile of trash, a dead cat!" said Ruby. Rick Salve threw up in a waste basket! He said, "Where is he working now?"

"He may be working at 122 or 71, if he's working, hiding or he disappeared somewhere!" said Ruby.

"Go find that little prick and bring him to the office!" Rick continued checking Rocky's dirty custodian work at 161 Benefit Street. Ruby went looking for Rocky and found him at 71 Benefit Street.

A big man had Rocky pinned up against the wall when Ruby spotted him. He was grabbing Rocky's throat in the hallway on the second floor, and he said, "If you bother my wife one more time, I will kill you! Do you understand!?"

"Yup! Okay! I'm Sorry! I won't do it again!" Rocky cried. The man dropped Rocky to the floor as he cried like a whining baby.

"Oh my God! Rocky, what kind of trouble are you getting into now!? Rick is back and he wants to see you back at the office. Let's go!" said Ruby.

Back at 161, *MEETING WITH THE BOSS*

"Rocky, I am very disappointed in you! You did not do a God Damm thing since I left for winter vacation. You are the dirtiest custodian I have ever seen in the 43 years I owned this property! I can't believe you left these buildings in this bad shape, and I hope I don't have to knock some of them down. It's a good thing I have insurance to cover these properties. I have to send an email to the Guinness Book of World Records because of all your complaints! You are the most disgusting custodian I ever witnessed! Turn in your keys and you're out of here!" said Rick Salve.

"Ruby, I know you don't want to bother me while I am on

vacation, but you should have contacted me for something like this. It's not safe here now because of someone like Rocky being here. Now I have to hire a wrecking crew and a cleaning company to go through my buildings. Mr. Hockey left these buildings in such bad shape; I don't know if I can keep up with them now! The maintenance workers were also slacking on their jobs. Wires hanging down, light fixtures ready to fall down in the hallways. Look at these complaints: Residents falling down breaking bones because stairs and sidewalks were not getting shoveled, salted, and sand and ice everywhere! Rocky kept harassing the tenants, hanging around, stalking people, breaking into apartments, and stealing money. I may have to file a lawsuit against Rocky because he left so much damage!

We have dead animals and the buildings stink to the high heavens and there is puke in the hallways. Trash was left everywhere and there were rats running around the size of dogs. I don't know how long it's going to take to go through all Mr. Hockey's complaints!" said Rick Salve. Later a wrecking crew knocked down 161 Benefit Street and an outside cleaning company came in to take care of the rest of the buildings. Rick Salve fired his crew.

SECTION 13

DEATH OF MY WIFE

I started writing this book while my wife was dying in hospice care. My wife, Ruth A. Rezendes, passed away on May 27th at 11:06 p.m. I was watching the Celtics game, and Derrick White made that great shot to win the game—that's when Ruth took her last breath. I saw that she was not breathing and called Hospice, and the nurse came, declaring her dead at 12:06 a.m. Sunday morning. The nurse had just been there forty-five minutes before she died, and she said Ruth would pass within twenty-four hours, but no more than two days; she was ready to go anytime. The same nurse had been at the apartment three times that day. She died here at home. The undertakers arrived at 1:30 a.m. Sunday morning to remove the body, zipping her up in a body bag. Hospice arrived about noontime to remove the hospital bed. She was cremated, and her service was held at the Bethany Church of the Nazarene on June 3rd, 2023. It was a nice service, and the church had the reception downstairs in the church hall. There was plenty of food to feed one hundred eighty-eight people, including myself. I took home plenty of food that lasted three days.

My stepdaughter and her daughter prepared the arrangements online to save me a lot of money! Ruth had no life insurance, and neither did I, that's why I had her cremated. Ruth's daughter, Shirley, took the ashes to be buried with her first husband at my request; she was very helpful.

Ruth was married before me to Arthur Andrews for thirty-four years, and she had three kids with Arthur Sr. One died. I was married for twenty-nine and a half years to Ruth and with her a year before we got married. She was not only my wife but also a mother and best friend, and we helped one another throughout our marriage until she died. Ruth was widowed before we got married, and I was never married until I met her. I had family, church, and counseling support while she was dying and afterward to help me with my grief.

The grieving period started as soon as she went into hospice. It was worse than before she died because I knew she was going to die. Ruth had Parkinson's disease, Neuropathy, Sciatica, Stenosis, and Scoliosis of the spine. She suffered pain in her back, hips, legs, and feet for years! She died from Parkinson's disease. If Ruth had never met me, things may have gone the wrong way. She had serious health allergies. She had heart stent surgery in January 2016 to help her breathe, and she fell on ice, breaking her hip in January 2014. Soon after that, she was in a wheelchair. I was her caretaker from that point on. Back to home hospice— when she went on Palliative care, they told me she was going to go quickly once hospice took over. The hospice team told me she had no more than three to six months to live. When hospice took over, she was taking strong medicine for pain, along with her pain medicine from her doctor. Ruth was on Lorazepam and Morphine to kill her pain and calm her down. When hospice increased the medicine, she went into a coma and died a week later. Ruth was in hospice for three and a half months, beginning in February 2023. Then she kept falling because she could hardly move until she stopped moving altogether, and I couldn't handle her, so hospice brought in a hospital bed and told me she had about two weeks to live. I had hospice nurses and CANs come in to take care of her. Two days after she fell three times, she was in that bed for good. May 19th, 2023 was her last day at the adult day care, and she was good that day. I helped her get up, dressed her, fed her, and took her to get her ride to the daycare. The next day, things started to go downhill.

I met Ruth at the Top of the Court singles dance in November 1992, and we married a year later. We went on trips together, including to Hawaii, Florida, and the Caribbean islands. She was a great cook, and she cared for me like a mother, because my mom was dying. My mother could not believe I was getting married and came out of the hospital to attend my wedding. Ruth went to all the basketball games with me, even while she was sick, and she liked the casino and the Garfield restaurant. Ruth was a great wife. She will be missed because I loved her very much!

SECTION 14

ROSEANN THE MAFIA'S GIRL FRIEND

A Short Marrage and a Quick Divorce—One Slip of the Tongue—and You're in Deep Shit!

Rex and Roseann met at a wake after her best friend died in a fire. Rex knew her best friend and supported Roseann at the funeral home.

"Miss, she was only twenty-three years old. Her name was Marsha Bayside, and she died in a house fire at Greenville Gardens here in Whoreville, Connecticut outside of New Haven. She was one of my best friends. I work at Greenville Gardens as a maintenance man. My name is Rex Neckpoint."

"Pleased to meet you. My name is Roseann Ziti. Marsha was my best friend, we used to live together in Brookdale, Connecticut. Can you take me to Greenville Gardens to see the damage to her house? Before we go there, could you follow me down Booster Road to Landmark Commons so I can drop my dad's car off and then we can ride in your car to Greenville Gardens. Please?" said Roseann.

Rex followed Roseann out of the funeral home parking lot on to Booster Road, he almost got into a fuckin accident because he is so excited over this girl. The man in the car he almost hit yelled. "You fuckin asshole!" Rex made it to Landmark to pick up Roseann and went to Greenville Gardens to where the house fire was. She was writing notes and taking pictures.

She said, "I work for the New Haven Newsletter."

"Oh! Cool!" said Rex. A man who pulled up in another car was the manager of Greenville Gardens.

"Excuse Me miss. May I ask what you're doing here? And why are you here Mr. Neckpoint?"

"My name is Roseann Ziti, and I work for the New Haven Newsletter."

"She's my friend, Mr. Porthanger."

"Rex, you need to leave! You're not supposed to be here after working hours without a uniform on."

"Yes sir, Mr. Porthanger, she's with me," said Rex.

"Rose, I wonder why you're crossing yellow police tape in a restricted area. News reporters have been here already!" said Mr. Porthanger.

"I'm just doing what I'm told by the newspaper. We are leaving now," said Roseann.

The manager waited for Roseann and Rex to leave, then he drove away.

"Roseann, do you want to go to East Beach?" said Rex.

"Yes, but let's drive by my boyfriend John's house first to see if he's home." She said.

I guess I will not get laid today if he's home, Rex thought.

Then it started raining, then thunder and lightning, so the beach was out! Rex drove by John's house near the beach in the pouring rain and he was not home. "Do you want to go to my place and have a couple of drinks and we can have some fun together," said Rex.

"Okay!" She said. Rex was driving on Beach Road. "Here comes John! Duck! Roseann yelled!

"I can't duck, I'm driving! I almost hit the guy!"

"Rex, turn around and drop me off at the top of his street! Call me tomorrow," said Roseann and she kissed Rex in the ear!

"Roseann just go before you get me in trouble!" Then Rex pealed out, turned his car around, left Beach Road, and went home to jerk off! *I guess I'm not fucking this broad!*

Rex never called her, but she called Rex weeks later after exchanging cell phone numbers at the Funeral Home when they met. *Meeting someone in a funeral home; was she a ghost? You're better off meeting someone in a nursing home!*

One night Rex was sleeping with a chubby black girl with big tits. His cell phone rang in the middle of the night.

"Rex Neckpoint, it's Rosanne, you need to come to my apartment at 166 Leroy Road, apartment 008 in the basement located in East Haven."

"It's three o'clock in the morning and I'm with someone!"

"Okay Rex call me later."

Later Rex called Roseann after the black chubby girl went home.

"Hello!"

"Hi Roseann, it's Rex, What's up!"

"I need you to come over because I want to check up on John."

"I'm sorry, but that's your problem!" He said.

The next day Roseann invited Rex over and another man was there.

"Who's this! Are you trying to get me in trouble Roseann!?"

"No Rex, he's my friend Carl. He's a nice guy!" Rex and Carl started talking, Roseann opened a bottle of white wine and served Knockwurst, sauerkraut and au gratin potatoes for dinner. "Rex, Carl's German."

"The meat looks like a giant hot dog to me!"

After dinner, Carl joked: "Rex, let's have a threesome!"

"No, I don't do threesomes."

Rex went home and Roseann called him the next day. "Rex come on over and will watch the Yankees game on TV with my two kids. Rex came over to Roseann's place to watch the game. "Rex this is my son Billy, and my daughter Carrie."

"Roseann, we have to talk! When I come over to see you, I don't want to see another man here; it's either me and you or go find someone else! It's okay if your kids are here but I am not a fan of threesomes. When I come over, I want to see you and only you. If you want to get serious, I can't be going through your friends to start a relationship."

"Okay Rex!" She said.

Later that evening they had a conversation trying to get to know each other. "Tell me Roseann, are you married?"

"Separated but allowed to date and start a relationship."

"Are you sure it's not more complicated, because every time I come to see you it seems you have a different man in your life, or you want me to check up on. Can we get a relationship going or are you trying to get me in trouble!?" said Rex.

"Yes, Rex it's okay, we can get a relationship together and I will get rid of my men. My former boyfriend John, I have been trying to get rid of for a long time but he keeps coming around. He's not my separated husband. My separated husband's name is Eric, and I left him in Florida because he does not want to leave Florida; he's far away! He won't bother us," said Roseann.

"The bottom line is you can't be bringing your friends around when I am here! It's one on one or we are done!" said Rex.

Every time Roseann and Rex went out her husband Eric was taking pictures from a car or from inside a building or store or hiding where he couldn't be seen. Rex does not know he's playing with fire because Roseann is trying to trap him to get into the mafia with her. Eric has been monitoring Roseann and Rex for months, that's part of the trap. Eric put cameras in Roseann's apartment in every room, in the lights, inside closets, in the bathroom and bedrooms even in the cracks in the hardwood floors. Every time Roseann and Rex have sex, shower, or sleeps together Eric is watching the camera video from his truck/ house etc.... Eric and Roseann are in the Mafia, and they are still married. Eric was watching a video with Rex pounding Roseann doggy style in the kitchen; Roseann was laying over the kitchen table and Rex was fucking her from behind, moaning like a wild animals!

Eric said to himself. *I am going to kill both of them-mother fuckers!* Roseann and Rex had a good relationship together for about five months. Roseann was good to Rex and no men were coming around and Roseann had her cell phone off all the time while she was with Rex, but when she was alone she would talk to all her boyfriends and meet them for sex at private locations, and she was even prostituting to mobsters on the side.

Eric had Rex followed to his place or when he went to see Roseann. When Rex went over to see Roseann, she fixed dinner for him and watched TV with her children and her husband was watching every move they made on video. Around midnight the kids were in bed sleeping on a Saturday night and Roseann and Rex were having oral sex in the shower, then more sex in the bedroom. The next day Roseann went to church and Eric met her there and they went to their favorite restaurant for brunch after church.

He was very friendly and loving, but Roseann had no idea about what he's doing. They both had westerns at the restaurant. "Tell me Roseann. Who's this Rex guy, you've been hanging around with?"

"He's a book writer and I buy books from him, and we meet for coffee once in a while. He's just a friend, nothing serious." She spoke.

"Okay Rose, I can deal with that," said Eric.

"Will you excuse me; I have to run to the restroom."

When Roseann got up to go to the restroom, she saw Eric spiking her coffee and putting something in her western omelet from a reflection in a mirror in the restaurant. When she came back Eric encouraged her to eat.

"I'm not hungry! I have to go!" Then Roseann walked out of the restaurant quickly!

Eric yelled, "Wait! I want to talk to you!"

Roseann got in her car and drove off as fast as she could. Then she drove to the police station and filed a police report about Eric putting drugs in her food, then she went home, and she grabbed a gun in case Eric came to threaten her. She put a restraining order on him at the police station and the police so the police will be waiting for him when he comes.

Sure enough Eric arrived ringing her door buzzer and banging on the door yelling; "Roseann let me in! We have to talk!"

"Hold it there buddy! Put your hands over your head," said the police.

The police were pointing a gun at him. A second cop hand cuffed him and he said. "You are to remain silent, any words you say can be used against you in a court of law. You may hire a lawyer, and if you don't have one, we will provide one for you. Do you understand these rights?"

"Yes sir, officers."

"May I have your name?" said the cop.

"Mr. Eric- fuckin- Ziti!!"

Another police officer went to get Roseann to bring her outside while police were reading Eric's rights, holding him at gun point, hand cuffed to a flagpole.

Roseann said. "What did you put in my food!?"

"I did not put anything in your food, sweetheart! Can you tell me what's going on here!?"

"I saw you put something in my food and coffee through a reflection from a mirror in the restaurant. I want a divorce! I will be seeing my lawyer tomorrow to file for divorce and I will bring the divorce papers to jail and you will sign them and we are done!!!" said Roseann.

"Rose I don't know what you're talking about!"

"You know God damn well what you did, This is the third time you tried to poison me!"

Officers, I want to press charges against him and take him to jail tonight, because if he breaks into my apartment I will pull out my .44 and blow his fuckin head off!" said Roseann.

The police took Eric into custody! Later that night Rex called. "Roseann how are you tonight, I would like to come over and spend the night with you!"

"Not tonight, Rex, I had a very bad day. Call me in a couple of days."

"Please Roseann I am horny like a firecracker!"

She hung up and turned off her phone! Rex kept calling her and he kept getting: "Please leave a message." The next day Roseann went to see her lawyer to file for divorce. Later she took the divorce papers to jail at the police station for her husband to sign. After Eric signed the papers, she said. "Remember, I have a restraining order against you and if you come to my house you will be shot! Do you understand!"

"Yes, Roseann," said Eric. A few days later Eric was released, and he was still up to his tricks stalking her, like he always does, watching videos from the cameras in Roseann's apartment. The police were checking on Roseann's address when Eric comes by. The police know this cock sucker is in the mafia!

Before he was released the police men said to him. "If I ever catch you going on Roseann's property for any reason, you will be arrested and taking straight to jail. Do you understand Mr. Ziti."

"Yes sir." He said.

A few days later Rex came over and Roseann showed Rex the divorce papers. She told Rex about her separated husband poisoning her food leading up to the divorce. Then she gave Rex a blow job and swallowing his load while he was sitting on the toilet having a shit!

"Mommy, Mommy! I want some orange juice."

"Just a minute Carrie I am busy!"

When she came out of the bathroom, Billy said to her. "Mom how come you have milk dripping from your mouth?"

"Do I? I will clean my face!"

After the kids were in bed Rex went to bed with Mommy Roseann. The next day Billy was going to school and Eric tried to kidnap him and Billy threw a big rock at Eric's head, and he broke free. The school is close by, and the kids walk to school. Billy called his mother from the school and the police came right away but Eric was nowhere to be found despite a nice crack in his bleeding head. It was a rainy day, and all the blood washed away so Eric made a quick get away!

Things were quiet for a few months and Rex, Roseann and the kids went on short trips together, taking walks on the beach, going to parks, going to movies, bowling, and going to school plays for the kids: Rex is a good dirty old man! Around Christmas Roseann's kids went on a school trip to Disney World in Florida for a week while Rex and Roseann went to Las Vegas and got married in a Las Vegas chapel. Rose and Rex had fun partying, gambling, going to shows and night clubs and took a bus trip to the Hoover Dam.

Where did Roseann get all this money! From her boyfriends of course! Eric sent one of his fellow mobsters to Las Vegas to monitor Roseann and Rex. Eric and Rose are not divorced yet, they still have to go to court to finalize it. They have no idea that Eric has connections in Las Vegas. Eric knows his wife is a fuckin prostitute! When they returned, Eric knew they got married in Las Vegas. Roseann was shot in the head and between her legs and Rex was gunned down dead, right in front of Roseann's apartment execution style. Rex fucked up!

SECTION 15

THE 83-YEAR-OLD SUGAR DADDY AT NICK-A-NEES

Nick-A-Nees is a very popular bar in the jewelry district in downtown Providence, Rhode Island. The bar has a history of great music and looks like a jewelry shop with barred windows that look like a jail.

"BEFORE WE GET INTO THIS STORY. RICKY YOU WROTE A NICE STORY ABOUT THE PASSING OF YOUR WIFE RUTH IN SECTION 13, UNTIL YOU FUCKED UP IN THE NEXT SECTION, "ROSEANN: THE MAFIA'S GIRLFRIEND."

YOU'RE NOT 83 YEARS OLD, BUT YOU BETTER BEHAVE AT NICK-A-NEES!

Nick-A-Nees has great music: They offer jazz, blues, and bluegrass on Wednesday nights, rock music, punk rock, country rock, southern rock, and solo bands. There's a band every night of the week at this place. Starting at 4 p.m. on Sunday afternoons, a jazz or blues band plays, and sometimes solo bands perform during the day and evening. There's a band playing every night, beginning at 8:30 p.m. On Tuesday afternoons, around 5:30 p.m., a jazz band plays, and it's "Taco Tuesdays." There's even a band playing on Saturday afternoons. There are ten bands performing here every week, and sometimes more—good bands too!

Nick-A-Nees is the place to go to hear music; this bar is the music capital of Providence!

There is a man by the name of Dick Boil. He's eighty-three years old, stands six feet, four inches tall, weighs about 180 pounds, has a tool about eight-and-a-half inches-long, and he's a Sugar Daddy! He goes by the name Big Dick, and he's well known here at Nick-A-Nees. He's a nice man but he does have a dark side. He met a young twenty-one-year-old lady named Nancy Name. Big Dick is here every night buying drinks for this young chick, smoking pot, doing hash, and using her as a sex tool. One Wednesday night on Blue Grass night Big Dick was buying this young chick so many drinks she passed out at the bar when the band was taking a break. Big Dick bought her shots of Jack Daniels, Southern Comfort, whiskey, then a White Russian before she puked on the bar and passed out!

"I think I have to take her home!" said Big Dick.

"I think you better!" said the manager.

Then Big Dick picked up the girl and carried her out of Nick-A-Nees and to his BMW to take her to his apartment just like Michael Myers carrying his victims in the movie Halloween. Nancy gave Big Dick a blowjob in his car then he took her to his place to spend the night. All hell breaks out after that!

Nancy woke up in the morning and she was surprised to see where she was. The big titty twenty-one-year-old was naked. She got out of the old man's bed because he was snoring like a bear!

"Hey Dick! I have to go to work, Wake up! Hey Dick, wake up! Come on Dick, wake up! I have to go to work, It's 7:30!" Then Nancy had to shake Big Dick Boil to wake his ass up! "Get up! You have to take me to work. Please!"

"Oh!!! I'm sorry, give me a few minutes to dress up and we can go." He said.

Big Dick took Nancy to work and later met her at Nick-A-Nees to start all over again! It's Thursday night and a blues band is playing.

"Good evening, welcome to Nick-A-Nees, we are the Red Headed Sluts! Playing the best blues and punk rock Music. Sit back and enjoy!" said the leader of the band.

"Nancy, would you like a shot of fireball followed by an Irish Whiskey on the rocks?" Asked the old man.

"Okay!" She said.

Twenty minutes later he said, "Nancy, would you like a shot of Hennessy and Jack Daniels?"

"Okay, Big Dick!"

Twenty minutes later he said, "Nancy would you like a Mudslide?"

"Okay!"

Twenty minutes later. "Nancy, do you want a rum and coke?"

"Okay!" She said.

The old man drank seventeen shots, twelve beers and eight mixed drinks. The couple still got up to dance after drinking all those drinks! Forty-five minutes later he asked, "Nancy would you like to go outside and smoke a joint with me?"

"You bet, Big Dick!" Later Dick Boil and Nancy Name staggered back inside to get more drinks at the bar. Twenty minutes later, Nancy passed out! The old man was downing mixed drinks before they left Nick-A-Nees. Twenty minutes later, Nancy unzipped the old man's pants. She wanted to blow him right there at the bar inside Nick-A-Nees.

"Hey, Nancy you can't be doing that in here!" said the manager and bartender. The old man paid the Five-hundred-dollar tab. Nancy puked on a dog while leaving. Twenty minutes later the old man almost got into an accident, he was so drunk and high! Twenty minutes later, Nancy puked in Dick's car. Forty-five minutes later, the sugar daddy and the young lady were home in bed.

They woke up on Monday morning and Nancy went to work.

Her boss said to her. "Nancy, what happened to you yesterday? Why didn't you show up for work?"

"Arlene, I do not work on Sundays."

"Nancy, today's Tuesday. You look glassy eyed; are you okay?"

"Yeah, I'm Fine. I thought today was Monday."

"You need to keep track on your drunken weekends and come to work on Monday morning, It's the third time you have not shown up on a Monday. If it happens one more time, you will be terminated. Now go to work!" said Arlene, her boss.

Later that day Big Dick arrived at Nick-A-Nees to start all over again! At 4:02pm he arrived but the door was locked. He was banging on the door, calling, "Let me in!" The bar usually opens at 4pm but the owner was a little late opening up. A jazz band was warming up inside and it was" TACO TUESDAY."

The owner said. "Have patience Dick, the bar's open!"

Big Dick sat down, downing shots and beers until Nancy arrived. At 5:02pm Nancy arrived, and she and Dick had tacos and drank shots, beers, and mixed drinks until closing time.

At 12:02am the owner comes over to them. "Dick and Nancy, can I see you in my office please? Dick, I know you spend a lot of money here and we really like your business, but you and Nancy are drinking way too much, and my customers are complaining. We can't have that here, you can have a few, but you can't drink up the Providence River; you need to take it easy!" said the owner.

"Okay," said Big Dick. Then Dick drove Nancy to his place to have sex all night. They overslept because Dick forgot to set the alarm, and they didn't wake up until after 11am.

"11:02am! Dick is that the right time?"

"Oh! Shit! I forgot to set the alarm last night! I'll get dressed quick and take you to work."

"I'm fucked! I might lose my job. We slept the weekend away and today's Wednesday." Nancy cried.

"Don't worry Nancy I will take care of you, if you lose your job."

Big Dick dropped her off to work and he went back home to eat breakfast; he had a Western and Bloody Marys.

Nancy staggered into work and she said to her boss. "I am sorry I showed up so late for work today after missing Monday."

"It's lunchtime!" said her boss.

"I will get help for my drinking, please don't let me lose my job."

"Go see the project manager in his office, he would like to see you," said her boss.

When she showed up at the manager's office, she puked on his desk and all over his computer! She said." I am so sorry; I need to get help!"

"Nancy, punch the clock and get the fuck out of here!" said the manager. She left work and she called the sugar daddy to come pick her up.

When he picked her up, she cried, "I lost my job!"

"No shit Nancy. Now it's plan B! Let's take a break from drinking and do other things. We'll go out to eat, go bowling, go see a movie, or just go for some long rides."

"Okay!" She said.

The sugar daddy and the young lady stayed dry for a couple of weeks doing different things then it was right back to Nick-A-Nees starting all over again!

"Big Dick, you know what I would like to do, let's go to Twin River Casino and play some slots," said Nancy while drinking at Nick-A-Nees.

"Let's have a few drinks and when the bar closes we'll go!

We'll watch the MMA fight on TV before we leave. Bartender, may I have a shot and a beer, another shot and a beer, and another shot and a beer! Give me another shot and a beer before the fight starts." He joked!

"When's this fight going to start?" asked the new bartender.

"As soon as I don't have enough money to pay for the drinks," Big Dick joked.

"I'll break a beer bottle over your fuckin head old man!" said the bartender.

"Just kidding with you. Big Dick paid the tab and tip and he and Nancy left and went to Twin River Casino. Big Dick hit it big on the craps table then he had a heart attack and died. Nancy was hysterical.

SECTION 16

DRUNKEN TRIP TO MEMPHIS

'A popular blues and punk rock band was playing in a downtown Providence Rhode Island bar.'

My name is Richard Duke, the lead singer. We are from New Bedford, Massachusetts. Sit back and enjoy!" Later, the band was singing the song *Kansas City*: "We're going to Kansas City, Kansas City, here I come. We're going to Kansas City: Kansas City, here I come, there's cute little ladies here, and here I come! SING, SING, AND SING!!!" Richard Duke, the band leader, was singing and downing shots, drinking beers! He sang another song, *Going to Memphis*: "I am going to Memphis when I leave here tonight!" Big Dick is gone, but Nancy Name, from the last section, was here tonight!

The band leader was wrapping up his set at the end of the night, but through his drunken haze, he started calling airports to arrange flights to Memphis, Tennessee. It was 1:02 a.m. when he looked at his watch. Then, he booked a 3:00 a.m. trip to Memphis out of Logan Airport in Boston.

Richard Duke was in a drunken fog—he didn't realize what he was doing because he was so drunk! The band members took his sax home, and he drove like a bat out of hell in his BMW to

Logan to catch his flight! Music City Airlines had a private jet leaving in the wee hours, and Richard was boarding.

"May I have your name?" said the airline clerk at the check in counter.

"My name is: Richard Duke. Are we going to Memphis?"

"Yes, we are! Do you play for the Music City Outlaws?" asked the clerk.

"No ma'am, I play for the Red Headed Sluts."

"Oh, my goodness, where are they from?" asked the clerk.

"We're from New Bedford."

"Oh, that's nice Richard, welcome aboard! This flight is a one-way direct flight to Memphis, Tennessee. You will be responsible for your return trip back to Boston," said the airline clerk.

"Okay," said Richard. The plane left Boston on time at 3am. The plane landed at Memphis International Airport just before 6:30am on a dark, rainy morning.

"All passengers please report to the Music City buses to take you to the Grand View Music Hotel after leaving baggage claim," said airline officials.

At 7:30 a.m. the drunken Richard Duke arrived and checked into the hotel. He was in bed by 8 a.m. Around 1:30 p.m. he woke up and he went down to the hotel lobby. "Excuse me, do you know where I can get some breakfast?" Richard asked the hotel clerk.

"Yes, just walk down here on Music Way Street, and you will find The Music Brunch Cafe, a block down the road on the left-hand side," said the hotel clerk.

"Is it walking distance?" asked Richard Duke.

"Yes, sir, it's right down on the left," said the clerk.

Richard found the restaurant, went in, and sat down. A waitress came over to him to take his order.

"Hi, my name is Rachel Jones, and I'll be your server. Can I help you all?"

"Can you help me all? It's only me! I'm not here with a crowd, I'm by myself," said Richard.

"Where are you from?" asked Rachel.

"I'm from New Bedford."

"Where's New Bedford?" she asked.

"It's near Fall River! Do I have to go into great detail here?" asked Richard.

"Where's Fall River?" she asked.

"You don't know! Fall River is near New Bedford in Massachusetts."

"You all are a long way from Massachusetts. You're in Memphis, Tennessee—The Music City!"

"Memphis!" Richard said, looking around at all the cars' license plates, all reading "Tennessee" on them. He was shitting his pants, so to speak. He went back into the restaurant to finish his meal, then he called his wife.

"Hi, Debbie. I made a big mistake last night with my drinking." "Richard where the fuck are you!?"

"I am in Memphis—Music City. I don't know where the fuck I am! I must have accidentally booked a trip here, but I do not remember what I did last night after I got through playing in Providence. All I remember is waking up in a fancy hotel room, meeting strange people, and finding a restaurant. Now, I'm here at the Music City Cafe eating a Western brunch, orange juice, and coffee. All my cash is gone, and my credit card is maxed out. I don't know how the fuck I'm getting home! I feel like I'm in another world!" said Richard.

"Richard, listen to me. You need to go to Western Union and wire some money to get you back home."

"Debbie, how the fuck do I do that!"

"Go back to the hotel, make arrangements there, and get your ass home before we get a divorce!"

Richard finished eating.

"Can I help you with anything?" said the waitress.

"Yes, just give me the check, please."

"The bill is $19.82. You all have a nice day now."

"I only have a twenty-dollar bill, sorry I can't give you much of a tip." said Richard Duke, and he went back to the hotel.

"Hi, miss. I'm in trouble. I need to go to Western Union to get money to get back home to New Bedford, Massachusetts." said Richard.

"Yes, you have to go online and follow the instructions, and Western Union will send you money using the barcode on your phone app." she said.

Richard used one of the computers at the hotel, but the computer kept shutting down on him, and now he's getting pissed!

"Excuse me, miss, can you help me? The computers keep shutting down."

"I can't help you right now, I have too many customers."

"Can you call the manager for me, please?" said Richard.

"He's not here today. Let me get through these customers, and I will help you in a bit." said the hotel receptionist. Forty-five minutes later, she's still talking on the phone, doing check-ins/check-outs, etc. Richard called his wife while sitting at the computers in the lobby, waiting for help.

"Debbie, no one here is helping me, the computers are all down, and I've been sitting in the lobby for more than two hours waiting to get some fucking help!! Can you drive down here to the Music City Hotel and pick me up?!"

"No! I am not driving to Memphis! Are you out of your fucking mind?! You're the one who made the dumb mistake! That's your problem!" said Richard's wife, Debbie, and she hung up the phone.

Two hours and seventeen minutes later, the hotel manager came over to help Richard with the computer to contact Western Union.

"Hi, are you Richard Duke?"

"Yes, sir."

"My name is Larry Demino, the hotel manager. Western Union is on strike right now in Memphis, Tennessee, but I can help you. First of all, I will get you a shuttle to the airport and get you on a plane to Boston, Massachusetts. Music City Airlines will send you a bill plus a $215 wiring fee from Western Union in Boston. For the one-way trip, you will be billed about six hundred dollars total, and it will be sent to your home. You will be responsible for yourself once you arrive in Boston."

"Thank you so much, Larry."

The shuttle took Richard to the airport, where he gave the airport receptionist the paperwork from the hotel, and he was off to Boston. He got his boarding pass, and he was on his way. Debbie got a debit bill for $815 from the Music City Hotel on her phone.

When the plane landed in Boston, Richard called his wife.

"Hi Debbie, I'm here at Logan Airport. Can you come and pick me up?"

"No! You find your own ride; I am not driving to Boston in this storm! When you get home, you have a bill to pay—over eight hundred dollars."

"Eight hundred dollars! Debbie! I'll see you when I get home." Richard went to a Western Union to wire money to get home. He said, "I have no money or credit card to get back home to New Bedford."

"Western Union will help you get an Uber to take you home. The cost will be $349 for the Uber from Logan to New Bedford and $289 for the Western Union charge, and it will be billed to your home."

Later, Richard got home. Debbie was not there. He called Debbie on her phone, but she did not answer. He went looking for cash in the house and found only one dollar. He wasn't going to a bar tonight, but he did find a beer in the refrigerator and drank it. Then he went in to take a shower and put on clean clothes, then fixed himself something to eat. Afterward, he took the dog out for a walk, fed the dog, and cat later. He tried calling Debbie again, but she wasn't answering her phone. He sat down in his recliner to watch TV until Debbie got home.

Around midnight, Debbie arrived home and Richard was passed out on the recliner with a football game playing on the TV. Richard had left his dinner plate in the sink, and Debbie washed it. Debbie was drinking a cup of coffee, and the glass slipped out of her hands and broke on the floor, which woke Richard up.

He went into the kitchen and Debbie was sweeping up the glass.

He asked. "Is this the way to get back at me by coming home after midnight and not answering your phone all day long?

"Richard, fuck you! You were gone all weekend and you're worried about me coming home late, go fuck yourself! You have a serious drinking problem and you need to get help before we get a divorce!"

THE CHIMPANZEE AT EAST PROVIDENCE LANES

A man brought a chimpanzee into a bowling alley at East Providence Lanes to bowl with him. This is a true story that happened in the early 1970s.

A truck pulled up outside East Providence Lanes around 10 o'clock in the morning, and out came a man and his chimp, heading into the bowling alley. The manager at the desk said, "Hey buddy! You can't bring a chimp in here! What's the matter with you?" The man gave the manager a twenty-dollar bill and said, "My name is Charley, and my male companion chimpanzee's name is Chi-Chi. He's a good bowler, and if you don't believe me, just give me a pair of lanes in front of the desk and see for yourself."

"Lanes twenty-five and twenty-six," said the manager. Charley bowled a strike on lane twenty-five, and the chimp bowled a strike on lane twenty-six. Charley bowled another strike, and the chimp bowled another strike. Charley bowled his third strike in a row—a turkey—and so did the chimp! Then Charley left a seven-pin on his next frame, missed the spare, and got a gutter ball. The chimp did the same! They both had an identical score of 201. Every time Charley got a strike, the chimp would look at him and make noises and screams because he had to throw a strike!

After a few games, Charley bowled five strikes in a row, and the chimp did too, screaming and making chimp noises. Charley bowled a two-hundred-and-twenty-five score that game, and the chimp rolled a two-hundred-and-twenty-four. Chi-Chi was pissed because he missed one! Charley bowled straight up the gutter like Earl Anthony, and the chimp wound up like a baseball pitcher, firing the ball down the lane for his strikes! The manager at the desk shook his head in disbelief and went into his office to do some paperwork.

"Chi-Chi, do you have to go to the restroom?" Charley asked. The chimp spoke in chimp language. They both went together to the men's room. Charley stood over the urinal to pee, and the chimp followed in the same way—what a man does, peeing together! Then the chimp ran out of the men's room and into the ladies' room. Two girls coming out screamed hysterically! The girls managed to get into the toilet stalls, and the chimp was banging on the stall doors, trying to get in. The manager heard the screams and went to the ladies' room. The chimp came running out and pushed the manager out of the way, yelling and screaming chimp noises. Chi-Chi was getting out of control and was now owning the bowling alley! Charley kept calling and trying to control Chi-Chi, but the chimp had other ideas! Then the chimp ran down the aisles, chasing screaming people out of the bowling alley, making all kinds of chimp noises.

Chi-Chi then leaped off his back legs, jumped over the food counter, and helped himself to the food, throwing it around, splattering food up against the wall, and throwing drinks!

The cook, Mike, said, "Oh my fuckin God! Get this wild animal out of here!" He had to find a way to hide in the kitchen and the chimp came in knocking pots, pans, dishes and glasses over, breaking things all over the place, then the chimp came out into the food court and shit on the floor.

The cops came and started shooting at the chimp. The chimp leaped back over the counter and ran down a bowling lane, sliding like a bear in the snow all the way to the pin deck, knocking all the pins down and then he got stuck there!

Only the 10 pin was left standing; The chimp missed one again! The police ran down lane fifty-six with their guns drawn waiting for the chimp to come back out. A cop threw a pepper spray grenade in the pin deck to choke the chimp! The animal rescue league arrived to tranquilize the animal and remove it. The bowling alley was a mess and the kitchen was damaged. The man who brought the chimpanzee in was arrested for bringing a wild animal into a bowling alley. The front page of the newspaper read. MAN BRINGS CHIMPANZEE INTO EAST PROVIDENCE LANES CAUSING SERIOUS DAMAGE.

NEW YORK CRACK HEADS

CHAPTER 1

New York City was under attack, and everyone was going crazy. A gang group called the New York Crack Heads added to the threat! First of all, the NYPD and the NYC Fire Department heard about the threat and held a meeting for all areas of the city. The meeting was held at Yankee Stadium.

"Good evening, officers and firemen of New York City. My name is Captain Joseph Morehead, head of military police, coast guard officials, and military vessels. I received a warning from the Middle East about a possible attack on New York City in the near future, and we have to be ready. I don't know who's responsible, but we have to find out what's going on. Look for suspicious activity and anything that seems out of the ordinary. The report the coast guard received said to expect an attack from the sky! We don't know what it is, but we're under attack!"

"Everyone, listen up. If any suspicious activity occurs, we need to evacuate all of New York City," said the NYPD. The NY Crack Heads gang received emails about the report, and they stayed underground, in the subways, at a place called "The

Underground." It is a nightclub, strip joint, and drug factory hidden away from the general public. Only invited guests and gang leaders come here.

It was a rainy Monday, and New York City was having a normal day. There were people walking in the streets with umbrellas, yellow cabs, buses, and the subways. Then, around the 5 p.m. rush hour, the sky began to clear, and a weather balloon—a white, ball-like substance—was spotted in the sky over the Hudson River, causing people to panic. "Look up there!"

The NYPD notified the Coast Guard. Later, fighter jets started flying over New York City and the Hudson River for hours until dark. The NYPD drove around with loudspeakers in the streets and subways. "Ladies and gentlemen, please evacuate all of Greenwich Village and Lower Manhattan at this time," they announced over and over for about two hours. All transportation stopped, and people went uptown toward Harlem as sirens and attack warnings were issued by the police and fire departments.

Fighter jets fired missiles at the balloon, and an EMP bomb fell out, striking the Freedom Tower, breaking thousands of windows, bouncing off the building, and landing in the Hudson River.

It just missed a cargo ship that struck a humpback whale right in the head and sank! The bomb did not go off when it sank, and a bomb squad was called in to defuse the bomb at the bottom of the Hudson River, sparking a massive evacuation later! Before the evacuation, military divers dove in to defuse the weapon. The NYPD got the message about what it was.

"NYPD, this is Erick Richie from the U.S. Coast Guard bomb squad. The United States Air Force shot down a weather balloon with fighter jets, and an EMP bomb fell from the balloon, striking buildings before landing in the Hudson River. The bomb did not detonate—that's a good thing. If we hadn't gotten to it in time to defuse its energy, the results would have been catastrophic! The weapon is an EMP bomb, worse than a nuclear bomb. We do not know who's responsible, but we did defuse the weapon, and we're no longer in danger. However, we do not know what could be coming next. China has been responsible for the so-called UFO balloons, and Russia may be involved as well. Just to be on the safe side, I would issue a warning and call for a massive evacuation of all of Manhattan. More of these balloons/weapons could be on the way!" said Erick Richie from the Coast Guard Bomb Squad unit.

Police and fire had a meeting about the failed EMP attack in New York City.

"Good evening, my name is Randy Vincent, head of the NYPD Investigation Unit. We are under attack, and we need to evacuate all of New York City for about a week. The U.S. Air Force shot down a balloon over the Hudson River, and an EMP bomb fell out of the balloon, striking the Freedom Tower and breaking several windows before landing in the Hudson River and sinking to the seafloor, avoiding a catastrophic blast! The bomb was defused in time by the Coast Guard, thank God! Had this bomb exploded, there would be no electricity for most of the United States. Cars would not run, no cell phones would work, computers, iPads, etc. Anything that runs on electricity would not work. The only way to survive an attack like this is on plain dry cereal or grains. All liquids and water would be contaminated. The world would have to live on roadkill. This is bad!" said Randy Vincent.

After the meeting the next day, the NYPD and the fire department evacuated New York City with loudspeakers suspended from helicopters. Coast Guard boats evacuated the coastline along the Hudson River.

"May I have your attention, please. All of New York City must evacuate immediately due to a possible attack. A bomb has been detected by the U.S. Military, and an evacuation is being requested in case of further attacks until further notice. Buses and subways will be open to get everyone out of the city. For your own safety, evacuate now!"

CHAPTER 2
THE CRACK HEADS TAKES OVER

Everyone was in a panic, overcrowding buses and subways and packing yellow cabs. People were leaving work early and the city was closing down.

A gang called the "New York Crack Heads" stayed behind in an underground, unknown strip club hidden from police and the general public. The gang has free access to alcohol, drugs, prostitution, guns, assault weapons, etc..... By evening, all of Manhattan was quiet and dark making it a perfect time for the gang to start looting! People who knew the gang members were invited to the Underground Strip Joint for a fee of three hundred dollars. Everything goes here! There's NYPD, firemen, doctors, lawyers and businessmen, even the NYC Mafia belong to this gang.

"Ladies, gentlemen, and guests, welcome to the Underground; you can have anything you want here, but we do not want any violence! You want to drink, do dope, get laid, dance to techno music naked, screw anybody you want and have an all-out orgy! You're all welcome! You must do it peacefully please! We have no rules here.

Once you enter the Underground: We have Martial Law here! You fuck up, we shoot; and your body will be burned in our new incinerator. My name is: 'Hakeem Abdul Shytts Shabazz'. Just call me Shytts, for short. I am the head mentor, crime lord, or whatever you want to fuckin call it for this gang. Every word or action in this club stays here, or you will be fed to the fuckin rats! Right now, enjoy your evening, but tomorrow night we go haywire, breaking into expensive stores to see what goodies we can get and bring the loot back here to the Underground. For all my guests, if you don't like my rules get the fuck out now, while you have a chance! The door is always open if you want to leave, just see anyone in a white New York City t-shirt and they will show you the door. We have bars, dance floors, a spa, gambling machines, table games, nap rooms with prostitutes, a sauna and shower rooms.

Men, you will be checked for diseases before you fuck our women. If you have something you will be asked to leave. We have a full restaurant kitchen, order what you want, cash only. We also have roadkill, that's right! We grill New York City subway rats here in an Italian grinder bun served with curly fries and peppers. Let's all get naked and have an orgy before we go out at midnight. Eat what you want, drink, do drugs, get laid or whatever! Just enjoy the Underground. Before the fun we have to wait until all the evacuations are over.

I also got a report that we are under an EMP attack; that failed, but we're not out of the woods yet. Fighter jets shot down a balloon over the Hudson River, and a bomb fell out of the balloon, striking the Freedom Tower, breaking thousands of windows before landing in the Hudson. A Coast Guard bomb squad defused what was identified as an EMP bomb—"Electromagnetic Pulse." Had this bomb gone off, it would have ended the world as we know it. Everything would have stopped working, and we'd slowly rot away! But it didn't happen, so don't worry. "Thanks to our US Military," said Shytts. Later, the club was ready to roar all night long and all day the following day until the midnight looting departure!

First, drinks were coming around then food was served, then more drinks and drugs. The music was playing techno, then the lights lit up the club. Clothes were coming off and everyone was dancing, fucking, and sucking. It was all happening so fast! The guests were being tested for diseases before they could enter the all-out all-night orgy! Everyone was naked and partying all night! Prostitutes were free because of the three-hundred-dollar cover charge. Every mouth, bush or ass got fed! The wild orgy slept then came alive for about thirty hours strait. Breakfast, lunch, dinner and snacks, shots and drugs were served to everyone before the gang and guests go out at midnight. Everyone in the club took advantage of all the festivities, then it was time to rob Manhattan.

At midnight, the music stopped, and everyone got dressed and climbed up a ladder and through a manhole to get out of the Underground. Hundreds of gang members and guests exited the club into a wooded, forested area in Central Park, unknown to the public. Shytts, the gang leader, was the last one out and locked the club with a combination. The door to get out and enter the Underground resembled a bank vault. Then they climbed up a forty-foot ladder and out of the manhole to get to street level. Everyone was given heavy, thick construction bags for the loot and carried them like Santa Claus. Some gang members carried AK-47s. The looting began, and the gangs smashed windows like a tornado had struck! It was pure smash-and-grab chaos. Jewelry stores were the first to be hit; millions in gold and diamonds were stolen, and cash was taken during the smash-and-grab.

Clothing stores were hit next—televisions, stereo equipment, even cars and trucks were stolen. Yellow cabs were broken into, and restaurants were robbed. Sirens were heard, and the police were coming. Many of the gang members made it back to the Underground with the loot; others had to battle with law enforcement and the National Guard armed with shotguns and AK-47s. Military grenades were thrown at the police, and the National Guard ground troops were called in to help the NYPD and firefighters control the gang. Surviving gang members escaped down manhole covers to reach the Underground. Most of the manhole covers connected below street level and under subways to the Underground.

While the war was going on in the dark streets of Manhattan, the NYPD and the military began winning the battle, leaving dead gang members lying in the streets. "FOOD FOR THE GODS," someone shouted. "THE BIG SUBWAY RATS WILL BE COMING FOR DINNER WHEN DAYBREAKS!"

The gang members who made it back to the club, including gang boss Shytts, had plenty of loot. "Listen up, everyone," Shytts said. "We lost about thirteen people who were shot by law enforcement, maybe as many as thirty. We did manage to steal a lot of stuff, and it will be spread out for everyone when the looting is over a week from now! For the next few nights, only a skeleton crew will be going out to raid Manhattan, from dusk to dawn! You risk getting killed by martial law agents or getting arrested. Steal cabs and buses for transportation to carry the loot, and make sure you have guns and grenades with you. That way, you can keep military agents and police away. If you get arrested or have guns pointed at your heads, just leave the loot and surrender.

Right now, let's start splitting the loot. You can't bring cars, trucks, trains, and buses down here, but we can share what we have while pot, drugs, food, and screwdrivers are passed around."

By 6:30 a.m., the sun was coming up, and the streets of Manhattan were a ghost town. The NYPD, firefighters, and military ground troops patrolled with shotguns. The Crackheads Gang was partying in the Underground, sleeping off their loot grabs, and waiting for nightfall.

The next night, the gang spread out, coming up from manhole covers all over the city. Two men emerged from a manhole when a cop threw a stick of dynamite into it. The two men were launched like rockets! One man landed on a picket fence, and the spikes impaled his body. The second person, a man or woman, was blown through a window and killed instantly.

A cop was pistol-whipped by a gang member, who then shot and killed him with his own gun. The same gang member killed another police officer and stole his gun. Now, the gang member was armed with three guns and a bag full of grenades. He escaped without loot into a manhole swarming with rats below street level.

The area where the dead officers were found was quickly surrounded by cops, firefighters, and National Guard ground troops. The NYPD dynamited the manhole to seal it off.

SECTION 19

IHOP RADIO

IHOP RADIO is a hotline radio station for singles to meet people. "This is IHOP RADIO with Hot Rod Dick Pole, 100.3 FM on your radio dial. The singles line runs nightly for new people to meet. Call in and just call me Hot Rod Dick. I have David Springs on the phone right now. Hello, David. Tell me about yourself."

"Hi, Hot Rod Dick. I am five feet, eight inches tall, weigh one hundred sixty-eight pounds, and I like horny women, kinky sex, oral sex, and anal sex. I like to stick it in any hole I find!"

The radio station hung up on David.

"Next, we have Vivian Hope from Glennville, New York. Hello, Vivian. Tell me about yourself," said Hot Rod Dick.

"I am a computer programmer, and I like the beach, malls, movies, horseback riding, sports, and bowling. I am looking for a man with the same interests, between the ages of thirty-five and forty-five. I have an athletic build, and I am forty-two years old."

"Very good, Vivian. I hope you find the person you're looking for. Good luck," said Hot Rod Dick.

"Thank you," she said.

"Next, we have Adam Richi. Good evening, Adam. Tell me about yourself."

"I'm a mold maker from out of town, and I make fifty thousand dollars a month. I do drug counseling, work sixty hours a week, do painting on the side, and read books. I am thirty-three years old and looking for someone about my age who likes basketball and tennis."

"Very good, Adam. Good luck finding the woman you like, and thank you for calling the Hotline on IHOP Radio."

"I work a lot of hours," said Adam.

"Next, we have Wicked Good Witch on IHOP Radio. Good evening, Ms. Wicked. Tell me about yourself."

"I do witchcraft, art, and some sacrifices on small animals such as mice, rats, snakes, bats, and cockroaches. I cook them for roadkill."

IHOP Radio hung up on the witch.

"Next, we have Billy Lake. Hi, Billy. Tell me about yourself."

"I am six feet, two inches tall, weigh one hundred ninety-nine pounds, and I play football and hockey at a semi-pro level. I am thirty-nine years old and looking for a girl between the ages of eighteen and forty-seven who likes sports."

"Wow, Billy, you have a wide range of age preferences. I hope you find a nice young chick to fill your needs. Good luck! Next, we have John Thomas from Bangor, Maine, on IHOP Radio."

"Hi there, Hot Rod Dick. I have a big one!"

IHOP Radio hung up on him.

Vivian Hope met a sugar daddy. Adam Richi met a prostitute. Billy Lake met the girl he wants.

"Next, we have Zoey Hoey on IHOP Radio."

"Hi, Big Dick. I am five foot two, weigh two hundred ninety-three pounds, and I am looking for a bodybuilder. I like skiing, doing jumping jacks, bowling, playing tennis, golf, and someday I would like to run a marathon!"

"Well, Zoey, I hope you meet the right man, and thanks for

calling IHOP Radio. Next, we have Walter Wallet. Welcome to IHOP Radio."

"Hi, Hot Rod Dick. I want to meet women with lots of money because I blow money like it's going out of style! I like the casino, and I love to smoke my pot!"

"Well, Walter, I hope you meet the right girl. Next, we have Harry Ho on IHOP Radio."

"Hi, Hot Rod Dick. I am six feet, three inches tall, weigh two hundred pounds, and I play hockey and football. I go to the gym or the YMCA, and I want to find a lady to share my interests with me."

"Well, Harry, I hope you find that nice girl. Next, we have Erick Shirley on IHOP Radio. Hello, Erick."

"Hi, Big Dick. I like hunting, camping, deep-sea fishing, bowling, golfing, playing cards, going on cruises, traveling, going to vacation resorts, and gambling once in a while. I play craps, blackjack, poker, and slot machines, and I buy lottery tickets."

"You have a lot of interests, Erick, and I hope you find the lady you're looking for. We will be right back after a few minutes. You're listening to Hot Rod Dick on IHOP Radio."

Zoey Hoey met another fat pig like herself, and they just go golfing once in a while! Walter Wallet met his girl at the casino. She sold him down the river, taking his money because she was a big gambler too! Harry Ho met the girl he wants, and she's a real HO! Erick Shirley met a casino host named "Maria Honey" at the casino, and she took him to the cleaners.

Erick called IHOP Radio and said, "Hi, Big Dick! It's me, Erick Shirley! What kind of people do you have on this singles hotline? They're all prostitutes, and they all want your money!"

"Well, sir, that's the chance you take calling the hotline on the radio. Sometimes you meet someone nice, but sometimes they're not so nice. You're listening to Hot Rod Dick on IHOP Radio."

SECTION 20

THE CHRISTMAS CHURCH SERVICE

December 24, the night before Christmas, a service was held at "PEOPLES ASSEMBLY CHURCH." A pastor led the sermon, and Santa Claus was there giving gifts to children.

Before the service started, Santa Claus was sitting in his car, drinking shots of Jack Daniels and smoking a couple of joints. He got out of his car, puking his guts up, then slipped and fell on his ass in the snow on the way to the church. When Santa got in the church, he sat next to the candles and fell off his chair and had to be helped up. Santa was burping and farting before the service started. Santa was so drunk that the church was spinning in circles! Then he fell asleep sitting in his chair.

When the service started, everyone was singing Christmas carols, accompanied by a band. The band had drums, a keyboard, three guitars, horns, trumpets, saxophones, a bass, and electronic equipment, singing: *Rockin' Around the Christmas Tree*, *Jingle Bells*, *Jingle Bell Rock*, *Santa Claus Is Coming to Town*, *The Christmas Song*, *Oh Holy Night*, *Silent Night*, *Rudolph the Red-Nosed Reindeer*, and many more Christmas carols before the sermon.

"Good evening and Merry Christmas. My name is Pastor Peter Stynx, and I will be leading the sermon tonight. Christmas is the birth of Jesus Christ, born in Bethlehem on Christmas Day, December 25th. We celebrate this holiday with lighting trees, and Santa Claus giving gifts, toys, etc. Christmas brings joy, happy times, and sad times. But there's a dark side. We have snow, ice, and cold weather outside, and everyone is in a rush to get last-minute gifts, have family get-togethers, dinner, kids playing in the snow, and playing with their toys."

"In today's sermon, I want to talk about the second coming of our Lord Jesus Christ. We are now on the brink of World War Three, the war in Israel. Bethlehem is gone, blown to pieces! Three hundred thousand dead! In the war in Ukraine, that country was wiped off the map, and an estimated one million people were killed. Most of Japan was washed away from several earthquakes and tsunamis, another one million people dead, and Covid-19/24 killed more than ten million people across the globe! Lake Michigan is contaminated with human waste, thirty feet deep! Twenty-six hundred volcanoes erupted across the globe during 2023 and 2024. The country of Iceland was blown off the map, killing millions of people. My dear brothers and sisters, all these volcanoes erupting at the same time raise the fear that hell is coming from under the ground, and the devil is rising to take over. Look at the 2023 fires that burned away three-quarters of the Canadian woodlands, killing more than ten million animals/wildlife, etc. About two million homes burned down in Canada, and it's still not known how many people died in the Canadian fires! All this is coming from under the ground, burning the Earth from global erupting volcanoes.

Brothers and sisters, we are in the end times, and I believe these disasters are happening because the devil is coming from deep within the center of the Earth to burn the rest of our planet and kill all life on Earth, and we have to be ready! Then that's when Jesus returns and raises the new Earth into Heaven. Don't worry about the devil killing you. God will raise you into Heaven, just believe in Him: AMEN!"

More Christmas songs were sung, and then the pastor spoke again.

"My brothers and sisters, let's all come to the altar and praise God." Everyone came up for prayer and the blessing with the oil and holy water. Meanwhile, Santa Claus was in his chair, still burping and farting and passing out gifts and toys. One parent put her crying child on Santa's lap to receive her gift, and Santa puked all over the little girl, in her face and all down her beautiful Christmas outfit. The little girl fell from Santa's lap and onto the floor, crying her eyes out!

The parent said, "Santa, you're disgusting! Look what you did to my poor child!" Santa Claus got up from his chair, puking like a waterfall, and he fell into the candles behind where he was sitting. He burned his ass and set the church on fire when the candles burned all the drapes! Everyone ran out of the church like a bat out of hell, and the church burned to the ground! Santa ran out of the church, and he jumped in the snow to cool his ass from burning!

McCALL HIGH SCHOOL AND FULLER HIGH BASKETBALL BRAWL!

The McCall High School Black Marlins and the Fuller High School Stingrays played a basketball game that got out of control—players, coaches, referees, and fans went haywire! The coach was preparing his team for the game.

"Boys, my name is Allen David, the new head coach here at McCall Senior High School. Tonight we play arch-rivals Fuller High. According to Ken Wilford, the former head coach here at McCall, the history of these two teams has not been very good. In the last forty-seven years, we have lost seventy games to Fuller High, and tonight I plan to change the game plan, being a new coach. We both play fast, but tonight we will find a way to slow them down by playing a half-court game and using a killer press the whole game. My plan is to force as many turnovers as possible.

On offense, we will spread the floor, using the clock and driving to the basket, drawing as many fouls as possible. I don't want you guys to fire up three-pointers all day and miss shots like a bunch of idiots—that's why we keep losing to the Fuller Stingrays. If you shoot a three-pointer, you better make your shot. On defense, we will set up in a 2-3 zone and switch to a 3-2 zone press going toward the basket. We will begin the game with a 2-2-1 full-court press. Before we switch defenses, we need to make it hard for them to inbound the basketball. We're a little taller than they are. I think my plan will work. We lost thirty-six games in a row to this team, and we need to change that tonight! Are you with me?" said the coach.

"YES, SIR!" The players replied. The team stormed out onto the court, ready to play basketball.

The announcers said, "Welcome to McCall High School for tonight's game against Fuller High School, with new coach Allen David."

The McCall band played the national anthem, and then the game started. The jump ball was tipped to McCall, with a drive right to the basket, and the kid dunked it and was fouled! The Fuller player bowled the shooter out of bounds! The McCall boy got up, and they went at it, pushing and shoving each other, but the refs broke it up before a fight broke out.

The McCall player made the free throw, 3-0 McCall. The Fuller kid who fouled him said, "Hey buddy! You drive to the basket on me again, I will kick your ass!" Then the two of them started exchanging punches, leading to a double technical foul, and they were both thrown out of the game.

The game continued, and the zone press was working, building an eleven-to-zero lead with 4:50 to play in the first quarter, until a jump ball. Then a Fuller player threw the McCall player down on the floor. Suddenly, a bench-clearing brawl erupted, and players on both teams were ejected, leading to technical fouls! The possession arrow went to McCall, and they drove to the basket again, drawing a foul. The Fuller player pushed the kid out of bounds, sparking another brawl. Players started punching, kicking, throwing one another to the floor, and stepping on each other. Several players were thrown out of the game again, leading to several technical fouls before the refs could get control of the game.

The Fuller kid said to the ref, "Hey! That's not a flagrant foul. I pushed him out of bounds to stop him from scoring a basket!"

"Flagrant foul and technical, and you're out!"

"Oh ref, go fuck yourself!" said the kid before being escorted off the floor by coaches.

The McCall boy sank the free throw and technical foul shot, and he was thrown out of the game.

"Ref, why is he getting thrown out?" said the McCall coach.

"Retaliation!" said the ref.

The McCall coach was shaking his head over the call. The McCall kid decked the Fuller kid after the play. It's halfway through the first eight-minute quarter, and the game is already getting out of control! Then a jump ball, and the refs were deciding who has the position arrow as they were confused.

"Hey ref! Do you need glasses! It's McCall's ball! Open your fuckin' eyes!" said a spectator.

Then another technical was called. Both coaches were arguing on the sidelines about players being thrown out of the game during the brawl! The position arrow went to McCall, and Fuller led twenty-six to sixteen after the first quarter.

The McCall coach gathered his team together before the start of the second quarter. "We are down by ten points! Let's stop the fighting and play basketball, God damn it! Now let's go!"

The players came out on the floor, but Fuller was still dominating the game, up fifteen points before halftime. The Fuller coach yelled out on the floor, "Hey ref, that's not a foul, he didn't touch him!"

"Coach, that's a foul!" The Fuller coach threw his clipboard on the floor, and it went out onto the court. The ref called a technical foul on him. Fuller was up eighteen points with 2:50 to go, and the McCall coach called a timeout.

"Do you boys want to play basketball, or do you want to go home at halftime! We're down eighteen points! Get your fucking heads out of your assholes and start playing defense! You're standing around waiting for something to happen, they're running past us, and we look like a bunch of idiots out there!"

"Time's up, coach," said the ref, and the half resumed. Then another fight broke out between two boys, one from each team.

"Hey buddy, stop pushing me!" said the Fuller boy.

The McCall boy said, "Fuck you!"

Then the two boys started shoving each other until punches were thrown and technical fouls were called. Both boys were thrown out of the game. Then it was halftime, and Fuller was leading by ten points, forty-one to thirty-one. The McCall players and coaches went to the locker rooms to prepare for the second half.

"Boys, we're making a comeback. Down ten, keep playing good defense and hit your shots. We are having trouble getting the ball inside with their 3-2 zone press, and we need to hit our perimeter shots. They have had four starters thrown out of this game, and we have three starters still playing. We have a shot to win if you boys stop fucking up, fighting, and throwing the ball away! Let's go out there and turn things around."

The scene was chaotic as the game continued. Both teams came out shooting baskets before the start of the second half, but the tension in the gym was palpable. In the third quarter, McCall made a strong push, cutting Fuller's lead to just five points. They broke through Fuller's 3-2 zone press, but the game remained heated and physical. By the end of the third quarter, the score was 59-54, Fuller still leading.

At the start of the fourth quarter, Fuller quickly scored a basket and a foul, extending their lead to eight points. But then, as if the game had been waiting for the right moment, another brawl broke out. Players from both teams were throwing punches, shoving each other, and more players were ejected. The situation escalated quickly as some of the ejected players began pushing and shoving the referees, and parents jumped out onto the court, challenging the officials. The coaches jumped in to try and break up the fight, throwing a few punches themselves, which led to even more ejections. Both head coaches, as well as assistant coaches, were thrown out of the game, and technical fouls piled up.

The McCall principal, Darrel Sparks, had seen enough. He made an announcement over the loudspeaker to calm things down. "Ladies and gentlemen, you must stop fighting and finish this game or we will forfeit and we will not go to the playoffs!" His voice echoed through the gym, but the tension was still thick.

Meanwhile, the referees huddled together, trying to figure out how the game would continue with so many ejections and chaos erupting both on the court and in the stands. The situation was getting worse. The police arrived to remove the rowdy fans from both sides, and the situation took another dangerous turn when one parent pulled out a gun and pointed it at the police. The police reacted quickly, shooting out a net to trap the gunman, and using a taser to subdue him. He was dragged out of the gym, his body flailing like a sack of potatoes as the police escorted him out.

The refs gathered the remaining players from both teams on the court, trying to bring some order to the madness.

"Okay, here's what's going on," one of the referees said, holding up his hands for attention. "Fuller has three players left, and McCall has four. No coaches are involved from here on out, so we need to decide how the rest of this game will be played. Fuller is leading 62-54 with 7:56 to play. We will be going three-on-three for the rest of the game. If one player fouls out, we go two-on-two, and one-on-one if necessary. Patrick Marks for McCall has four fouls, so he must sit until another McCall player fouls out. If there's one more fight, this game is a forfeit and both teams will not make the playoffs. Understood?"

The gym was filled with nervous energy, and both teams, now missing several key players, were left to finish the game with whatever they had left.

"Yes!" said the players.

"Okay, let's finish the game!" said the refs.

The game had been a roller coaster of emotion, violence, and confusion, but it all came down to the final moments. McCall had staged a fierce comeback and took the lead, 74-73, with just 29 seconds left. The crowd was on their feet, screaming for their team to hold on. Fuller had the ball, and in a desperate final play, they drove to the basket, scoring a layup and drawing a foul in the process. The Fuller player stepped to the free-throw line and made the shot, putting Fuller ahead 76-74 with only seconds remaining.

McCall had no timeouts left and their player fouled out in the process. Patrick Marks, who had been sitting out with four fouls, re-entered the game for McCall with the clock ticking down. With no time to waste, Marks launched a three-pointer at the buzzer, and the ball seemed to hang in the air forever as the gym held its collective breath.

The ball went through the hoop just as the buzzer sounded, but the refs immediately waved it off. No basket. The shot didn't count. The crowd went wild, with McCall fans screaming in anger and frustration.

"Fuck you, Fuller! Fuck you, Fuller! Fuck you, Fuller!!!" The McCall cheerleaders, dance team, and spectators yelled, sticking up their middle fingers in defiance. The scene quickly descended into chaos as McCall fans fought among themselves, and tensions escalated. The police, who had already been involved in previous incidents that night, returned to the scene to escort everyone off school property.

Outside the gym, the animosity boiled over into another brawl between the players. McCall and Fuller players, unable to control their emotions, clashed again in the parking lot, a mirror of the chaos on the court.

The coaches, now furious and bitter, exchanged insults as they made their way toward the locker rooms.

"Did you go to church to win this fucking game tonight, you bunch of cheaters?" one of the McCall coaches shouted at the Fuller staff.

Fuller's coach, not missing a beat, responded, "F-U-C-K! Y-O-U!"

The game was officially over, but neither team would be going to the playoffs, thanks to the out-of-control behavior that marred the entire evening. The brawls, the ejections, and the complete breakdown of sportsmanship meant that both teams would face severe consequences. The officials, the coaches, and the players had all failed in their responsibility to keep the game under control.

The night ended in disappointment and rage, but also a reminder of just how ugly things can get when passion for the game goes unchecked.

SECTION 22

THE GREAT 300 GAME!

The Marlboro Seniors were off to a blazing start, with the score-board reflecting their explosive strategy under the new ABA 3D rule. The players had clearly bought into their coach's bold plan to break the record for the most points in an ABA game. With the added bonus of the 3D rule—where steals in the backcourt could earn an extra point, a layup or jump shot was worth three, a regular three-pointer counted for four, and a half-court shot netted five—the Marlboro Seniors were on a fast track to score big.

"Good evening, you're listening to the play-by-play for tonight's game between the Marlboro Seniors and the Baytown Bombardiers on WMRL radio here in Marlboro, Massachusetts," the announcer said, as the action unfolded.

Marlboro won the opening tip-off, and within seconds, Ronny Newbury sank a three-pointer from the perimeter. "Three to zero," the announcer called out. A few moments later, the Bombardiers failed to make an entry pass, and Newbury picked it off on the baseline, converting an easy layup and drawing the foul. He hit the free throw for a quick 7-0 lead.

It wasn't long before Bob Eyello stole another pass at mid-court and, with perfect timing, launched a three-pointer from deep. Thanks to the 3D rule, it counted for four points, pushing the lead to 11-0. The crowd was already buzzing with excitement as Marlboro's fast-paced defense and long-range shooting turned the game into a one-sided affair.

Ronny Newbury was everywhere, making steals and scoring in transition. He snatched another pass under the basket, laid it in, and Marlboro's lead ballooned to 14-0. The Baytown Bombardiers couldn't keep up, and their frustration began to show.

By now, it was clear—Marlboro wasn't just playing to win; they were playing to make history. The 300-point game seemed more and more likely with each passing minute, as their defense stifled the Bombardiers and their offense fired on all cylinders. The combination of steals, fast breaks, and long-range shots yielded an unrelenting barrage of points.

"Folks, this is turning into something special tonight," the announcer said, almost in disbelief. "The Marlboro Seniors are on pace to do something no one has ever seen before in ABA history."

The Bombardiers could do little more than watch as the Seniors continued to rack up points. The game had barely begun, but the record books were already being rewritten.

With each pass intercepted, each steal converted into an easy layup or a deep shot, the Marlboro Seniors were living up to their coach's lofty expectations. Could they really score 300 points tonight? Only time would tell, but the way things were going, the record seemed within reach.

It was going to be a long, painful night for Baytown as the Marlboro Seniors set their sights on a historic achievement.

Another pass was picked off by Steve Jefferson for Marlboro, and he fired up a three-point shot for four points and was fouled. "Eighteen to zero, Marlboro!" He made the free throw, and now it's nineteen to zero. A technical foul was called against Baytown during a timeout. Ronny Newbury will be shooting two shots for the technical. He dips, shoots, and it's good! The second shot is good as well, and Marlboro leads twenty-one to zero with 11:30 to play here in the first quarter.

The Seniors just put up five shots in thirty seconds, scoring twenty-one straight points from 3D turnovers. If this rally keeps up, Marlboro could score one hundred points before the end of the first quarter! The radio play-by-play went dead before the quarter was over because the Marlboro Seniors were scoring too many points! It was eighty-eight to eight at the end of the first quarter!

Before the start of the second quarter, the coach said to his players, "Boys, you want three hundred tonight! We're heading in the right direction, just keep playing the way you're playing, keep stealing the ball and making 3D baskets. Eighty-eight points in twelve minutes is amazing!"

The Marlboro Seniors put up seventy-eight more points by halftime, but they did miss a few five-pointer field goals from half court! Marlboro went into the locker room with a one hundred sixty-six to twenty-two lead. The coach was giving the Marlboro Seniors instructions during halftime in the locker room.

"We're looking good out there, gang. We're in striking range to break the ABA record, but we cannot be throwing up five-pointers from half court."

Keep stealing the ball, going on the 3D attack like in the first half and go to the basket. We should put up at least three shots a minute!" said the coach.

The Marlboro Seniors responded, scoring eighty-five points in the third quarter; they put up a couple of six-pointers from half court and were winning two hundred fifty-one to thirty-one after three quarters! Marlboro kept pressing in the backcourt and getting 3D baskets for three-, four-, and five-point field goals for the rest of the game, trying to push the score up to three hundred.

"We just tied the ABA record with two hundred fifty-one points after the third quarter, guys. Just keep up the good work!"

The team went wild in the fourth quarter, stealing the ball

and scoring twelve points a minute until they hit three hundred with time left to play. Marlboro hit a six-point 3D shot from half court for the three-hundredth point, and Marlboro won the game three hundred thirty-three to forty-four. The Baytown coach said to the Marlboro coach. "You are the most ignorant mother fucker to run up a score like that!

What good did it do? The Marlboro Seniors lost to the Providence Pirates in the playoffs!

SECTION 23

ICE ROAD ACCIDENTS

A trip to New Hampshire during a snowstorm with a tour bus full of skiers going up Mt. Washington. "Good afternoon, ladies and gentlemen, welcome aboard Mt. Washington Tours. My name is Rex Flonase, like the nose spray. We may all need Flonase with the cold weather and snow we've been having lately! We're leaving TD Bank Station here in Boston, going over the Tobin Bridge, up Route 93 North to New Hampshire, but we will be delayed because of accidents on the Tobin Bridge. The weather calls for snow here in Boston, and the snow will be getting heavy when we get to the White Mountains in New Hampshire. Once again, my name is Rex Flonase, and we will get to Mt. Washington in a few hours. Just sit back and relax."

The bus was going over the Tobin Bridge and had to squeeze through tight spaces between crashed cars, trucks, and buses on the bridge, but the Mt. Washington bus made it through before a big accident happened on the bridge! A few minutes later, a big rig with twenty-two tires rammed a bus from behind, sliding on ice and snow on the Tobin Bridge, and the bus rammed seven cars, causing a big pile-up on the bridge. One car went off the bridge, bounced off a tanker ship below, and landed in the

Charles River! Another car was hanging over the edge, on fire. A man and a woman from the burning car jumped into the Charles River below and disappeared! A third car was tossed up into the rafters on top of the Tobin Bridge, hanging and dangling, then the car fell back onto the bridge and was run over by another big truck and flattened! Then a tank truck entering the Tobin Bridge, going kind of fast, slid on ice, rammed the wreck ahead, and burst into flames! Then, minutes later, another tank truck struck the first tank truck that was on fire and exploded like a bomb! Finally, the Massachusetts State Police closed the bridge at both ends. The second exploding truck bowled several vehicles off the bridge and landed in the Charles River on fire!

The Mt. Washington bus was cruising up New Hampshire Route 16 in a foot of snow, plowing down the highway like a snowplow all the way to Mt. Washington. The bus driver heard about the bad accident on the Tobin Bridge on the radio and told the passengers what had happened. "Ladies and gentlemen, more accidents just occurred on the Tobin Bridge, and it was bad. Several trucks and buses crashed into each other and exploded, pushing cars and other vehicles off the bridge. Many people are feared dead, and the Tobin Bridge is on fire. We got through the first accident in time, and just minutes later another one happened! We have heavy snow falling right now, and we should be arriving at the Mt. Washington Hotel within an hour. We're making good time, and tomorrow morning we will be going up the mountain. When we get to the hotel, our rooms will have a view of Mt. Washington," said the bus driver.

A few minutes later, the bus skidded in the snow, doing a 360 spin on the highway going down a hill before coming to a stop; all the passengers were screaming! The bus driver gained control and made it to the hotel. He said, "Welcome to the Mt. Washington Hotel. All our rooms will be on the fourth floor, facing Mt. Washington. After checking in, dinner will be served in the hotel restaurant, followed by entertainment and dancing. Tomorrow morning, we get up at 7 a.m., and a continental breakfast will be served, and the bus will leave at 8:30 for Mt. Washington. Everyone had family chicken for dinner, and a band was playing." The next morning, breakfast was served, then the bus ride to Mt. Washington.

When the bus got to the mountain, the bus driver spoke. "Ladies and gentlemen, welcome to Mt. Washington. We will be going up the mountain to the summit, 6,288 feet, over a mile high, and the temperature is -32 degrees, so you better be dressed quite warmly when we get to the observatory. The wind is blowing 111 mph. If the bus makes it to the summit or not, you may start skiing down the mountain. The temperature here at the bottom of the mountain is 23 degrees, but it's 32 below on top of Mt. Washington, and 6 feet of snow on the ground. I hope the road has been plowed; I don't want to get stuck up there!" said the bus driver.

The bus went up the mountain, and it got stuck halfway to the summit. Stuck in the snow, and the bus cannot turn around because there are no railings on either side of the road. You cannot see on either side below the mountain because there's so much snow and fog!

"Ladies and gentlemen, we have a problem, we're stuck up here halfway up the mountain! You will have to get out here and ski down the mountain; this bus is not going anywhere! If you want to hike to the summit, good luck! There's 8 feet of snow up there!" said the bus driver.

"Bus driver, what are you going to do? You have no skis?" asked a passenger.

"Well, son, I have to stay with the bus!"

A few minutes later, a plow was pushing snow down the mountain with an armored vehicle, a huge plow that pushes a lot of snow, coming toward the stranded bus. A security guard at base camp at the bottom of the mountain was notified by other mountain security.

"Harry, a big bus went up the auto road and it's stuck up there! How the hell did you let that happen?!"

"I was unaware because I was either on my break or I was in the restroom having a shit!" said the base camp security guard.

When the plow got close to the bus, the driver said to the bus driver, "Hey! What the hell are you doing!? You can't drive a bus up the auto road during a snowstorm. What the hell are you thinking!? I need to plow the road! I have to push your bus off the road down the mountain! How many people do you have aboard?"

"No one is on the bus; all the passengers skied down the mountain."

"Well, buddy, move out of the way! I am plowing your bus off the mountain!"

"Hold on, pal! Are you serious about that!?"

"Get out of the way because here I come!"

"Wait, let me pull over to the side and let you pass!"

The plow truck came full speed ahead, pushing the bus off the road down the mountain, and continued plowing the auto road to the bottom. The bus slid down the mountain in the snow and was wrapped up in a giant snowball rolling down the mountain until it hit a row of trees and burst into flames, just missing a moose having a shit!

A second plow came down the road, and the bus driver was waving his arms so he could be seen in the snow. The second plow stopped to rescue him.

"What the hell are you doing hiking up here in all this snow!?" said the second plow driver.

"I had a ski team I was bringing up to the summit to reach all the ski trails on top of Mt. Washington, but my bus got stuck, and one of your friends plowed my bus down the mountain!"

"You drove a bus up the auto road with a bunch of skiers? You gotta be freakin' kidding!"

"No, I am not kidding! I am here waiting to be rescued, my bus is gone, and all my skiers skied down the mountain."

The second plow driver laughed, and he rescued the bus driver down to base camp, where the police were waiting. They handcuffed him and held him until the skiers arrived.

"Hey Rex, where's the bus?" one of the passengers said.

"The bus was plowed down the mountain and disappeared!"

"What!?" said the passenger.

The rest of the skiers arrived at base camp at the bottom of Mt. Washington by 10 p.m., but there's no bus, and the passengers had to go back to the hotel in shuttles from Mt. Washington. They were shocked to hear what happened to the bus. The bus driver, Rex Flonase, had to call for another bus from Boston to pick up the passengers at the Mt. Washington Hotel. While waiting for a new bus, the crew watched the news on TV about the accidents on the Tobin Bridge. The old bus is buried in snow somewhere along Mt. Washington and may never be found until spring.

NEWS:

"Good evening, this is a Fox News Update: 73 people have died from the Tobin Bridge accidents, and about 159 vehicles were involved, piled up and burned out, closing the bridge for weeks until all the burnt vehicles are removed. This was the worst accident ever in New England due to a coating layer of ice on the bridge. All travelers will have to find alternate routes going into and out of Boston; you may have to drive off 93 South into Somerville. Jack Russel reporting on Fox News New England."

"Ladies and gentlemen, get your credit cards out, or whatever cash you have, because we'll be here for a while until another bus gets here to bring us back to Boston," said Rex, the bus driver and tour guide.

Helicopters flew over Mt. Washington looking for the bus that was plowed off the auto road and found nothing! About a week later, the skiers went home. The National Guard and the New Hampshire park rangers went looking for the damaged bus but found nothing! The bus is still buried in snow somewhere!

In Providence, Rhode Island, work was being done on the Washington Bridge during a rainstorm, and accidents were happening, stalling traffic. Then sleet and snow began to fall. A car struck another car, then a Ryder truck struck the first car, then a school bus struck the Ryder truck, then a cement truck struck the school bus, and then a dump truck skidded and slammed into the cement truck. The cement chute popped loose, pouring cement on the dump truck when it struck the cement truck! What a mess on the Washington Bridge, tying up traffic for hours. One man said to a worker, "I just crashed my car on the bridge, and I love it!"

THE 9 FOOT BIGFOOT BASKETBALL PLAYER AT BROWN

A humanoid Bigfoot creature from the Andes Mountains of India was a human. He was named Cobra Amps. Basketball scouts from all over the world were scouting this big, 9-foot, 600-pound human Bigfoot, but no school accepted this huge gem. Finally, Brown University accepted the giant creature. A meeting took place at the Prizzatola Center on the Brown University campus. The scouts and the Bigfoot met with the Brown coaching staff, the athletic department, and the media.

CHAPTER 1
MEETING

"Good morning, Brown University coaches, staff, and media. My name is Eli Lyon. I am a worldwide scout for basketball players all over the world. My hometown is located in Constantinople,

India, and my main office is in Manning, Indiana. Please meet Cobra Richard Amps. He's 9 feet tall and weighs 601 pounds. He has 12 years of high school, two years in prep school, and four years in college, including two years here at Brown University. Mr. Cobra Amps was a Bigfoot Yeti creature shot by the Indian military in the Andes Mountains. He is covered in white and brown hair and was deformed into a freak human being. He was first schooled in the Andes jungle, speaks good English, and was raised in Constantinople. He went to Babcock Middle School, Cost Cook Regional High School, and Constantinople Prep for two years before serving two years at Bangcock Community College here in Constantinople. He then completed his online education here at Brown University. He was hidden in the Delta Tau Fraternity sub-basement shelter, serving his two-year online services until he finished, away from the general public.

Cobra's race is Indian and he was declared human according to several doctors across the globe. He has all his shots, including COVID-19 shots. Mr. Amps was in hiding with bodyguards until he was ready to interact with the general public and Brown students. According to NCAA rules, he can play two years of basketball here at Brown through the injury/COVID-19 rule. Cobra is 24 years old. He is a virgin and has had no physical contact with a woman or many people, as his life has been focused on schooling ever since he was declared human at 8 years old when he was held in an Indian jungle camp."

But it's unknown if Cobra ever had sexual activity when he was an animal at age 8. He can begin playing basketball right now. He's a very social young man, and he's ready to mingle with the general public. Next, he will meet the students, and in two days, he can begin practicing with the team and play in the next game. Mr. Amps has played in many basketball leagues around the globe, and he played for his high school, prep school, and in college. He averages 47 points per game, grabs more than 35 rebounds per game, and blocks more than 30 shots—and you can't stop him! Cobra's that good!

Cobra had all his animal hair shaved off, and the medications he takes are designed to protect him from turning back into an animal. He is 100% human, and he can play this weekend against Princeton. "Are there any questions?" said Eli Lyon, Sports Scout.

The media, staff, pro scouts, and coaches asked several questions before Cobra met the team. The 9-foot-tall Cobra had a tour through Brown University and the East Side of Providence, meeting the students, and he will be living with the Delta Tau fraternity. The students from Delta Tau made good friends with Cobra-Bigfoot-Amps and took him downtown to Providence to show him around. He went to bars, restaurants, and strip clubs. Then, it was Saturday night at the Prizzatola Center, and the crowd was going crazy—it was a sold-out game! It was mid-January 2027, and all the students were back from winter vacation. It was game time. Brown had 5 wins and 10 losses, 1-1 in Ivy League play, and Princeton was 16-0, 2-0 in Ivy play.

Brown won the tip-off and scored, then got fouled, making the free throw for a 3-0 lead. Cobra blocked a Princeton shot and grabbed the ball, firing up the court. But he threw it out of bounds. He blocked several Princeton shots, grabbing all the rebounds, but he kept turning the ball over because he tossed the ball so fast downcourt with his speed that the Brown players couldn't keep up, and the ball was thrown out of bounds a few times. The coach called a timeout to have a talk with him. The crowd booed when Bigfoot Cobra was taken out of the game. Princeton was leading 10-3 before he came back into the game.

During the timeout, the Brown coach said: "Cobra, you have to slow down when you throw the ball to your teammates."

"When you grab rebounds and block shots, just set yourself and throw the ball easy to your players; you're throwing the ball too hard, and the players can't catch it, and it's going out of play. We went over this in practice. You're striking your teammates like High Tower throwing a football in *Police Academy*. Slow down and time yourself so the players can catch the ball during the fast break. You're doing a great job blocking shots and getting rebounds. Now get back in there and keep up the good work," said the coach.

Cobra Amps went back in the game—and he went off! Princeton came down the court and threw up a rainbow three-point shot from 30 feet. Cobra leaped up high to grab the ball out of midair, passing it to a Brown teammate for a dunk. Then, Cobra grabbed the ball from a Princeton player for a jump ball, and the ball went to Princeton. Cobra, the Bigfoot, blocked the shot, setting up the fast break for another Brown dunk! Then, Cobra forced a 5-second violation because Princeton couldn't inbound the ball. Next, he grabbed a rebound from a missed Princeton shot. Then, Cobra threw a Princeton player out of bounds with so much force that he was charged with a flagrant foul and a technical foul, giving him two personal fouls. He swarmed a group of Princeton players, picking up his third personal foul. The coach removed him from the game until the second half.

Princeton made a comeback, spreading the floor and making shots, cutting the Brown lead to 10 points by halftime. The score was 34-24, with Brown leading at halftime.

The Princeton coach said to his players in the locker room, "Fellas, we need to get this 9-foot, 600-pound Bigfoot humanoid out of the game as soon as possible, or we do not have a chance! He has four fouls, and one more, he's out. We have to get this animal off the court!"

In the Brown locker room, the Brown coach was trying to calm Cobra down, knowing he was in foul trouble.

At the start of the second half, Brown kept missing shots, and

Cobra Amps kept getting the rebounds. Princeton kept boxing him out until he picked up his fourth foul, throwing Princeton players around like a pack of lions trying to take down a wildebeest! He was taken out of the game until the last three minutes, when Brown had the game won, up by 25 points—75 to 50.

Cobra went back into the game, and he drove to the basket for a slam dunk, ripping the rim, the backboard, and the pipes down. The basket glass shattered into pieces. He stood up, beating his chest like a Bigfoot/Yeti, growling and roaring like a grizzly bear! Everyone ran out of the gym in fright!

The Brown coach said, "He needs anger management counseling!" Cobra was charged with his second flagrant foul, and he would miss the next game. Later, the Brown coach was screaming at him for causing all this damage! With 2:59 left to play, Cobra was removed from the game, and the rest of the game had to be played from midcourt toward the Princeton basket. Brown won 78-56.

"Cobra, you can't be dunking basketballs and breaking backboards! You have to remember that you were a Bigfoot animal before crossing over to a human, with so much strength. You're 9 feet tall and weigh over 600 pounds. It's not the first time you've broken backboards in city parks and other games, but you can't be doing this at Brown University! Now, it's going to cost thousands of dollars to fix the damage you've done, and it's going to come out of your tuition to pay for this damage. I can't have you playing for Brown anymore if you continue to act the way you did tonight. You have to control yourself in games. You did good in practice, but you need to calm down and play together with your teammates. I know you hate Princeton, but you have to control yourself.

From now on, I don't want you dunking basketballs anymore. I need you to block shots and grab rebounds. If you want to fire three-pointers from half-court, that's fine with me! You cannot play against Penn tomorrow night due to two technical fouls and two flagrant fouls, and you have to spend a week in anger management counseling before you can play next week against Harvard. If you do okay in anger management, then you can play. I believe we can win the NCAA championship with a player like you, but you have to control yourself.

One more thing: you need to limit your fouls. All I want you to do is block shots and get rebounds. Stay away from the opposing team's basket to avoid goaltending calls. Pick off mid-air passes to set up the fast break and stop turning the ball over!" said the Brown coach.

Then Cobra left the meeting.

CHAPTER 2
THE REAL DEAL

Cobra the Bigfoot Amps and the Brown Basketball Team

Cobra Amps needed more than a week of anger management training and would miss the Harvard game the following week. Brown finished the season 7-7 and in fourth place in the Ivy League tournament. They were set to play the #1 seed, Princeton, at Princeton when Cobra returned.

The game started with Cobra winning the tip-off, and Brown scored on a layup. Princeton quickly responded, firing the ball downcourt ahead of Cobra to tie the game. Brown inbounds the ball, passes it to Cobra to set up the fast break, and gets fouled. Brown made the free throw for a 5-2 lead.

The bigfoot ran down the court like a roaring bear, getting into position to block a shot or grab a rebound from a missed attempt. Cobra knocked the ball loose, and Princeton regained possession, driving to the basket. Cobra blocked the shot, sending all the ball to a Brown player who worked the clock. Cobra then stood in the paint and laid the ball in the basket, making it 7-2 Brown.

Cobra guided the sidelines, and Princeton couldn't get the ball inbounds several times. Brown led 19-3, and Princeton was looking for answers, but the bigfoot kept getting in their way! Cobra was picking off passes and passing to teammates to set up three-pointers. When Brown missed, Cobra was there to lay it in. Brown led 50-7 at halftime.

Cobra Amps had no fouls at halftime and was playing a much smarter game. The Princeton coach was at a loss for what to do, telling his players, "We're done! Every time we try to get the bigfoot to foul, we get called for offensive fouls because he's so big, you can't get around him! We can't avoid him! We have to play the best we can, because if he stays in the game, we may lose by 100 points!"

Brown led 73-13 with ten minutes left when the bigfoot was removed from the game with only two fouls. He had played a great game, showing both strength and strategy. Brown won the Ivy League semifinal game against Princeton 89-35.

After the game, the Brown coach said, "Cobra, you played a great game: 19 points, 32 rebounds, 40 blocked shots, 33 assists, and 14 steals. A quintuple-double! That's unheard of! If you play like this, there's no chance anyone is going to catch us!"

The next night, Penn was getting ready to play Brown for the Ivy League Championship. The Penn coach said to his players before the game, "Guys, I have a plan: We have to stay away from the bigfoot, get to the basket before he does, and get him into foul trouble as soon as possible."

The plan worked for Penn, but Cobra still won the battle, getting rebounds and throwing up long three-pointers. He got into early foul trouble and didn't play much, but when he did, he did enough to help Brown win 85-75.

The papers the next day read:

"BIGFOOT COBRA AMPS SCORES 25 POINTS AND 25
REBOUNDS IN 25 MINUTES, GIVING BROWN ITS FIRST IVY
LEAGUE CHAMPIONSHIP SINCE 1986. BROWN WILL PLAY
NORTH CAROLINA IN THE FIRST ROUND OF THE NCAA
TOURNAMENT."

The next day was a pep rally on the Brown campus, where
the bigfoot met more students. Then it was time for March Madness at Chapel Hill, North Carolina. Brown took the floor, being
booed by the crowd. The bigfoot took care of North Carolina,
causing traveling violations and five-second turnovers every time
North Carolina in-bounded the ball, blocking shots and grabbing every rebound. When a player drove to the basket, Cobra
trapped the ball, causing turnovers until he fouled out of the
game. Brown won 67-33.

The announcers couldn't believe how well the humanoid
was performing. The next game, Brown played Duke University,
and the bigfoot went at it again with his killer defense! Duke,
the higher seed in the NCAA tournament, was playing at North
Carolina.

Late in the second half, Cobra fouled out with 6:30 left in the
game, and Brown was ahead 60-40. But after Cobra fouled out,
Duke took control, hitting a three-pointer and getting fouled
on the play, followed by a technical foul, which resulted in six
quick points. They hit two quick steals, and the game became a
ten-point game, 60-50.

Cobra, now on the sidelines, started swearing, beating his
chest, and growling like a grizzly, pumping up the Brown basketball team. A technical foul was called, and Cobra was escorted
to the locker room by North Carolina Arena security, where he
started punching and kicking them.

Brown ended up losing 70-67. The bigfoot was shot by police
and taken into custody, then locked up in the North Carolina Zoo

SECTION 25

TWO LAWERS BRAWLING IN A COURT ROOM

Greenland Court House in South Carolina

Two lawyers, Michael Fixpatrick and Patrick Fixmichael, are working on a case against one company, but they do not get along with each other while working on the case.

"Good morning. Welcome to Greenland County Court House. Please rise for Judge Leo Bartley," said the receptionist. Then the judge sat in his chair.

"Everyone, please be seated. The first case this morning: 'Brass & Steel Construction,' versus Michael Fixpatrick/Patrick Fixmichael," said the receptionist.

"Excuse me, Your Honor, but how can two lawyers be working on the same case? Who is Patrick Fixmichael?"

"All we're here for is to try to settle this case. It does not matter who's handling this case."

"Your Honor, Brass & Steel stole millions of dollars' worth of gold, silver, copper, brass, steel, glass, pictures, and many metals from Mount Furman Properties while they have been closed for the last 10 months due to storm damage. I have been handling this case since day one. Who the hell is this fruitcake, Patrick Fixmichael?" said Michael.

"I don't know who you are, sir, but I am the lawyer working on this case."

"Oh, is that right! I am the front runner so you can go fuck yourself!" said Michael.

"Order! Order in the court right now!" said the judge banging his gavel on the bench.

The two lawyers went at it; going through each other's files/paperwork etc... until papers, books and case files were thrown all over the court room leading to a brawl when the two lawyers started pushing each other until punches were thrown! Michael punched Patrick in the mouth, Patrick kneed Michael in the balls and punched him in the face! Michael grabbed Patrick in a head lock taking him to the floor, Patrick hit Michael with an upper cut and the two of them kept exchanging punches and blows to the head!

Finally, Michael picked up Patrick and threw him down on a table breaking the table in half before the jury, police officers, and court officials broke up the fight between them. A police officer fired his gun in the air while the judge kept trying to restore order! Then Patrick got one more punch in before they were both taken down by the police, hand cuffed, and put in strait jackets!

Michael spit in Patrick's face then they were separated.

"Order! Order! Order! Order in this court room right now!" said the judge. Michael and Patrick got away with a few words while the judge was calling for order.

Michael said to Patrick, "You're an asshole!"

Patrick said. "You're a fuckin jerk!"

"Eat shit!" said Michael.

"Fuck you!" said Patrick.

The judge was reading off the brawling lawyers chargers and

Michael said, "Judge! Why don't you go fuck yourself!" The back and forth was so bad the two lawyers had to be removed from the court room after the judge read their charges.

"Mr. Michael Fixpatrick and Mr. Patrick Fixmichael, you will serve thirty years in prison for brawling in the court room and property damage, no respect for the judge, court officials, or police officers."

"Judge, the damage is done! Why don't you go fuck yourself!" said Michael.

"Fuck you!" said Patrick.

Then the judge said, "Now you two will serve life in prison."

"Fuck You!" said Michael and Patrick!

Then Patrick and Michael were taken to jail in strait jackets and tied up in their cells. The prison guards said to one another. "What do we have here! Two Irish gays!? Michael Fixpatrick and Patrick Fixmichael!"

"I don't know Ron, but they're pretty good brawlers in a court room! We have to split them up. Michael Fixpatrick will be going to cell block E026, and Patrick Fixmichael will be going to cell block E215."

"That sounds good Gary. Let's hope they calm down before letting them mingle with the general population. They will be two Irish gays for sure staying here for the rest of their lives once the prisoners get a hold of them!" said Ron.

Gary and the rest of the prison guards had a good laugh! All Michael and Patrick can say is: "Fuck You!"

A prison guard was putting Michael in his cell, and he was acting like Michael Myers, grabbing his keys to stab the prison guard! The prison guard punched Michael, and pepper sprayed him in the face. The guards gang tackled the two lawyers, beating them and spraying them with pepper spray. They were then stripped down, put in jail jumpers, and locked up.

SECTION 26

PERVERTED ICE SCULPTURES

Toronto, Ontario, Canada

A bunch of X-rated ice sculptures lay across the city, Viagra Park. College students and visitors arrived at Viagra Park to view the X-rated ice sculptures paying a fee to get in. Shuttle carts took visitors around the park. This event happened in late February. A tour guide was explaining the ice figures.

"Good morning, ladies and gentlemen. Welcome to Viagra Park here in downtown Toronto. My name is Rocky Tito, and I am your tour guide on the Viagra Express. Please brace yourself because most of these ice sculptures may offend most people. Be prepared for what you are going to see. The first ice figure is a penis spraying water freezing on contact that is coming out the head of this penis, dripping down on the ground. It looks like sperm coming out. Red, green, yellow, and blue lights inside the ice make this man's genitals colorful. The balls under this sculpture are the testicles and are covered in snow that looks like cum from the spraying water from of the head of the penis. It is freezing around the sculpture and lights coloring the testicles, and a strobe light inside making the penis vibrate like a dildo!"

"Our next sculpture of ice is butt cheeks with a hole. And a tree log coming out of it looks like it's having a shit and there is brown frozen mud that looks like diarrhea at the bottom of the tree log. Brown and yellow lights on each cheek make it look like the butt is having a big shit. This figure also farts so we can't get too close to it. We can get out and take pictures of this famous Toronto Asshole and Penis, called the Viagra frozen ice dick!"

"Our third sculpture is a pair of a women's breast with big red nipples! The breast has white and blue lights and has water dripping out of the nipples freezing on contact that looks like breast milk in a yellow color. The boobs vibrate moving up and down. Stay clear and don't get between them so you don't get hurt."

"Next, we have a women's vagina that is all pink inside with black cubic hair around the edges and water pouring out freezing on contact making it look like it's having an orgasm with sperm dripping out of it. And above this vagina is the clitoris located in a dark red color. The surroundings around this vagina light up in pink and blue all around the cubic hairs, all pink inside, with a bright red color deep inside this vagina. I will stop the shuttle and you can get out and take pictures. Don't get too close to this beast because it will spit at you or grab you. It will try to pull you into this thing and suck you into a snowbank at the back end. Keep your distance! Next, we have a belly button in yellow lighting and frozen brown and green mud coming out of it looking like it has gangrene! Pretty gross ha!"

"Next, we will go to the frozen body parts exhibit. Here we have an ear with brown frozen mud dripping out and looking like an ear is full of wax. The ear has pink and yellow lights glowing inside it. Then we have a light brown colored nose dripping frozen water with a yellow and green color that looks like a runny nose with frozen boogers coming out; that's gross! Next, we have eyeballs looking at all of us with blue, aqua, and light green lights, and a strobe light inside the eyes' pupils. Next, we have a mouth full of yellow teeth that looks like it needs a good brushing, and the teeth have cavities and silver fillings all over them with a little blood dripping from some of the mouth's rotten teeth. The teeth light up in a white and yellow color. The mouth inside lights up with a gray and dark red color all the way back to the throat and the mouth talks and sings to you. Next, we have the human stomach that lights up in yellow and brown. Some of these body parts have black pubic hair on them and some do not have any hair at all. Next, we have the human head and the brain. The heads have blond and dark hair frozen in blocks lighting up yellow and brown. The brain is a frozen structure of ice with white and blue strobe lights inside the brain that looks like electrical chargers of lightning bolts flashing inside and makes sounds of thunder."

"This includes our tour. Thank you for visiting Viagra Park Perverted Ice Sculptures!" said the tour guide, Rocky Tito. Later, the people were walking through the park when a bunch of teenagers having fun started throwing snowballs and ice into the vagina and the vagina threw it back at them. One boy went inside this giant vagina and he disappeared! He was sucked inside and fired out the back end like a jet engine landing in a snowbank. And he broke his back!

50 SHADES OF LINCOLN WOODS

CHAPTER 1

LINCOLN, RHODE ISLAND: Lincoln Woods State Park is a beautiful place to walk, view nature, and enjoy the beach for swimming. There are many walking trails, hiking spots, and camping areas. It's the place to be during the summer. But things get a little strange at night in Lincoln Woods. At 9 p.m., the park closes, but people have been found camping in the woods and having sex parties. Yes, orgies in Lincoln Woods State Park. The police are constantly throwing people out and making arrests, even well after 9 p.m.

A black man was engaging in sexual activity with a white girl with big breasts up against a tree, and a deer was watching them! A park ranger arrived and caught them in the act, prompting the deer to run off!

"Hey, you two! You can't be doing this in public. The park is closed, and it's well after 1 a.m. You have to leave!" the park ranger said.

People camping and swimming in restricted areas were also thrown out that night. The next day, similar activities were reported on the beach during the daytime. A group of boys and girls were reportedly taking turns having sex in a tent when park police and the beach manager arrived. "Excuse me, boys and girls, you can't be having sex parties on the beach. We have kids here. Take down this tent and leave," said park police, arresting them one by one. The beach manager said to them, "I don't want to see you boys and girls in Lincoln Woods again. You're banned from coming here! You have no class or respect for others. You ought to be ashamed of yourselves! You're a bunch of pigs, and you're all being arrested for indecent exposure! Now pack up and get out."

The boys and girls were handcuffed and taken away by park police one at a time. Some of them managed to get dressed, and others remained naked. Beachgoers got a good laugh out of the situation, and the tent was destroyed and removed by park rangers.

A man on a motorcycle was helping a handicapped woman in her late 80s who was trying to get in her car in a parking lot at the other end of the park. The woman thanked him, saying, "Thank you very much. You're a gentleman."

The man stood by his motorcycle, **unzipped his pants, pulled out his penis—**about a foot long—and waved it in front of her!

The woman pointed a lipstick pencil that looked like a gun and said, "You better get out of here before you see something!"

The motorcyclist quickly put his penis back in his pants, zipped up, and drove away!

The woman called her husband to report the incident. Her husband notified the park police. Police began driving through the park looking for him. Park rangers joined the search.

Park rangers will need to walk the woods after dark until daybreak, removing people still hanging around. Anyone who comes in before 9 p.m. has the right to enter, but they must leave when the park closes," said park police.

Later, the incidents continued, keeping police and park rangers busy late at night in Lincoln Woods State Park.

At 11:02 p.m., a group of people were fishing in the designated fishing area before being removed by park rangers. One man had an attitude and was arrested.

At 12:02 a.m., a group of women, men, boys, and girls were jumping off a rock and swimming in the water. Tents had been set up for sex orgies, and park rangers arrived, removing them. Police arrested about 20 skinny-dippers engaged in sexual activities near the fishing area.

At 1:02 a.m., two gay men were arrested for having oral sex on the beach.

At 2:02 a.m., a couple was caught smoking pot while sitting on a bench in the park. Police arrested them, searched their car for drugs, and towed the vehicle. The couple was placed in the police car and taken away.

At 3:02 a.m., a man shot a deer and was dragging the carcass, a large buck with big antlers, to the street. He was arrested by police as he tried to load the deer into the trunk of his car, which was wide open.

At 4:02 a.m., a naked man was swinging his genitals at a woman jogging on the street. The woman kicked him in the groin, and when he crouched down in pain, she kicked him in the head, threw him into the woods, and pushed him down a hill. He landed against a tree with a bloody face. The woman called police on her cell phone, and a deer was seen watching the injured man moan in pain.

At 5:02 a.m., a group of joggers was running through the park and asked to leave by park rangers and police until the park reopened at 6 a.m.

At 6:02 a.m., a bald eagle flew down, dove into the water, grabbed a fish, and disappeared into the trees.

At 7:02 a.m., a group of people were on the beach before the lifeguards arrived.

At 8:02 a.m., kids were swimming with floating devices. Lifeguards asked them to remove the devices, and one kid shouted, "F--- you!" He swam out to the ropes and hung on. Park police retrieved the child using a police boat and removed him from the beach. The kid shouted, "F--- you!" again, and the officer replied, "Get out of here before you get arrested!" The kid left, pointing his middle finger at the officers. However, he was tackled, handcuffed, and taken away.

At 9:02 a.m., a group of boys in the men's restroom was standing at the urinals, reading a sign: "Hey Diddle Diddle, aim for the Middle!" Meanwhile, a man using a toilet read graffiti on the stall that said, "Please remain seated until the performance is over!"

At 10:02 a.m., police were called to handle a fight at a campsite.

At 11:02 a.m., a dust devil formed on the beach, lifting blankets, towels, and clothing into the air before tossing them into the water. It ended a minute later. Beachgoers laughed, though some were frightened.

At 12:02 p.m., police responded to a call about men and women having sex in the woods behind a vacant building. Camp kids nearby had complained.

At 1:02 p.m., a brush fire broke out in the woods, prompting firefighters, police, and rangers to respond.

At 2:02 p.m., a group of deer blocked traffic entering Lincoln Woods State Park.

At 3:02 p.m., a group of girls walked through the park topless and were arrested.

At 4:02 p.m., storm clouds formed, thunder rumbled, and lifeguards cleared the water.

At 5:02 p.m., heavy rain sent people running to their cars or hiding under trees.

At 6:02 p.m., the weather improved, and a girl rode a white horse through the park naked. She was arrested by park police.

At 7:02 p.m., kids were drinking alcohol and having sex in a camping area.

At 8:02 p.m., police arrested people skinny-dipping in restricted areas near a party boat.

At 9:02 p.m., the park closed, and police and rangers began clearing people out, locking gates to prevent cars from entering at night.

At 10:02 p.m., four people were arrested for engaging in sexual acts around a campfire.

At 11:02 p.m., park rangers and police patrolled the area to ensure everyone was gone.

Every two minutes, for 24 hours, something unusual occurred in Lincoln Woods State Park on the first day of summer. Later in the summer, the sex parties and strange incidents continued.

CHAPTER 2

The park police and park rangers met at the beach manager's office for a meeting.

"Good morning. There has been a lot of activity at Lincoln Woods in the last 24 hours. Several arrests have been made for sex parties and drinking in the park. My name is Officer David Leo, head of park police. We've talked before, but for the new park employees, we need to look more closely at the activity in the woods and campsites. Many people enter the park on foot to have these parties, and we need to put a stop to it.

The beach manager, Ms. Apardo Angel Anchor, controls the beach area. For the new team members who haven't met her yet, she's responsible for this section. The rest of the park rangers and police will handle the other areas of the park. Please stay vigilant and be ready for the unexpected, 24 hours a day, to ensure the park remains safe. Thank you."

At around 8 p.m., the beach closed, but people were still lingering. A park police officer was parked nearby, watching the beach to ensure everyone left.

Later, a park police officer driving through the park stopped a speeding car.

"Good evening, miss. The speed limit in the park is 20 miles per hour, and you were going 35," said the officer.

"Sorry, sir, but I didn't see any speed limit signs," replied the driver.

"Well, slow down," the cop said, letting the driver—a pretty girl—go.

At dusk, just after 8:30 p.m., another officer saw a car rocking back and forth and stopped behind it. Inside, a naked couple was having sex. The officer approached the car and saw a Black man with a white woman with large breasts. The man was thrusting, causing the car—a 1979 Stingray—to rock.

"Excuse me, sir, but you two can't be having sex in a car in a public place. Can I see your license, registration, and proof of insurance?" the officer asked.

"Yes, sir, after I cum!" replied the man.

The woman's large breasts were bouncing against the passenger-side window while the man finished. The cop waited, watching, until the couple stopped and began getting dressed.

The officer took the man's information and arrested both individuals.

A second cop pulled up behind the first and asked, "What's going on here?"

"Another couple screwing in a car," the first officer replied.

The second cop drew his gun while the first officer continued processing the arrest.

"Mr. Eric Magnum and Ms. Mary Connors, you're being arrested for indecent exposure. You'll receive a summons to appear in court. The park is closed, and you must leave," said the first officer.

Later that night, after closing time, the police were locking the road gates when a female officer heard loud noises:

The officer investigated the noise and saw a treehouse with a light on and a ladder leading up to it. She climbed the ladder and found a couple having sex inside, surprising them.

"Excuse me. The park is closed, and you two can't be having sex in a public place. Get dressed and meet me at the bottom of the ladder," she said.

The couple took a long time getting dressed. Frustrated, the officer fired a warning shot. The man climbed halfway down the ladder, jumped off, and fled.

"Hey! Come back here!" the officer shouted as she radioed for backup.

Before backup arrived, the woman climbed down, punched the officer in the face, and fled as well. Both individuals disappeared into the woods.

The next day, park rangers tore down the treehouse. The couple was never found.

The following night, after closing, police were following a motorcycle near a gate. Flashing their lights, they attempted to pull the rider over.

"Pull over, buddy!" the cop yelled.

"Fuck you!" shouted the rider, speeding up. He performed a wheelie, burned rubber, and jumped over the closed gate on his motorcycle, escaping onto Route 123 toward Cumberland.

Park police contacted Lincoln Police, who alerted Cumberland Police.

"Hi, this is Ryan Roxy from Lincoln Police. A motorcycle with Rhode Island plate U2PU20 escaped from Lincoln Woods and may be heading toward Cumberland. We haven't seen the vehicle since it left the park."

"10-4, Lincoln Police. I'll put out an alert," replied Cumberland Police.

The motorcycle sped down Route 123, taking a hard left onto Lonsdale Avenue in Cumberland.

The motorcycle took a hard left near the Dollar Tree in Cumberland, close to the bike path, and hid behind the Stop & Shop for the rest of the night, concealing the motorcycle in the woods. The man joined the deer in the woods for a late-night nap. Lincoln and Cumberland Police searched throughout the night for this reckless motorcyclist.

At around 8 a.m., the man woke up near his hidden motorcycle and saw two young girls walking behind the Stop & Shop. He walked up to them and said, "Hi, girls!" Then he unzipped his pants, pulled out his penis, and started swinging it at them.

The girls quickly ran off. The man zipped up his pants, got on his motorcycle, and drove away. The girls called the police on their cell phones.

When the motorcycle passed in front of the Stop & Shop, a police officer was parked outside but did not notice the man as he exited the parking lot and headed north on Mendon Road in Cumberland, aiming for Route 295 to leave town. The officer was shopping inside the Stop & Shop.

An Amber Alert was issued on street signs across Rhode Island and Massachusetts. The alert read: "Amber Alert: Rhode Island license plate U2PU20."

The motorcycle was later spotted by the Massachusetts State Police on the Mass Pike heading toward Springfield. Officers activated their lights and began pursuing the motorcycle. The man sped up, reaching 110 miles per hour, before finally crashing into a construction site.

He was boxed in by several Massachusetts State Police vehicles and arrested.

"Hey, you dick swinger! We finally got you!" one officer said.

The man was taken to a hospital with injuries, and the motorcycle was destroyed.

Massachusetts State Police contacted Lincoln Police:

"Massachusetts State Police to Lincoln Police. This is Officer Adam Rockford. We've caught the dick-swinging motorcyclist on the Mass Pike near Springfield. He's in Mohegan General Hospital in Springfield with injuries. I believe he lost his penis in the crash. All we saw was blood between his legs when the rescue arrived. Massachusetts State Police, over."

"10-4, Officer Rockford. Thank you," replied Lincoln Police.

When the crash occurred, the motorcyclist struck a row of construction pillars at a high rate of speed while being chased by police. He slid off his motorcycle on the wet pavement and hit a sharp object in the road, which severed his penis and caused a severe injury to his right leg.

The motorcycle struck a guardrail, flipped over, crashed into a ditch, and burst into flames.

The man is lucky to be alive.

(PHRASE: This accident provides the quickest path for him to become a transvestite, should he recover from his injuries.)

The next day at Lincoln Woods Beach, another incident added to the string of unusual activities. A young boy approached a lifeguard, clearly uncomfortable.

"Miss, a man and a woman are having sex in the water," he reported.

"Where?" the lifeguard asked.

"Over there!" the boy said, pointing toward the water.

The lifeguard called over to the beach manager, who quickly intervened.

"Excuse me, you two! Get out of the water!" she shouted.

The man, who bore a striking resemblance to Santa Claus with his bushy beard, pointed to himself in mock surprise.

"Are you talking to me?"

"Yes, you! And the lady too. Out of the water now!" the manager demanded.

The couple emerged from the water. The man was clad in an overly tight Speedo, while the woman wore ragged shorts with holes and a ripped t-shirt. Their disheveled appearance added to the spectacle.

A park police officer arrived at the scene and addressed them.

"A young boy reported that you two were engaging in inappropriate activities in the water. This is a public beach, with children present. We cannot allow this behavior. You are under arrest."

He continued reading them their Miranda rights:

"You have the right to remain silent. Anything you say can and will be used against you in a court of law. You have the right to an attorney. If you cannot afford one, one will be provided for you. Do you understand these rights?"

"Yes, sir," they replied reluctantly.

Another officer requested their identification.

"Mr. Robert Cardie and Ms. Mary Mudslide," the beach manager said sternly, "you are hereby banned from this beach and from all of Lincoln Woods. You are no longer welcome here. You have no class or respect for this community."

The couple was handcuffed and escorted to a police cruiser as beachgoers looked on.

Later that evening, as the beach was closing, park rangers began locking up the facilities. They inspected the men's restroom, which was clear, and then moved to the women's restroom.

A ranger called out, "Anyone in here?"

There was no response, so he locked the door and left.

However, unknown to the ranger, a man and a woman were in the shower inside the women's restroom, engaging in inappropriate activities. They left behind several used condoms and managed to climb out through a window to escape into the night.

Their departure triggered a security alarm, alerting police. Upon investigating, officers found the broken window and the discarded condoms in the shower area. The incident added yet another bizarre chapter to the increasingly notorious summer at Lincoln Woods.

SECTION 28

SERIAL KILLER BOWLER

At *Treasure Lanes Bowling Center* in Port Charlotte, Florida, Mark Fingernail, a respected and talented bowler, was known for his exceptional skill and competitive spirit. With a 235 average, he was a regular in tournaments and leagues, but his friendly demeanor hid a dangerous obsession: winning at all costs.

Mark met his nemesis, Richard Baldhead, in the finals of the Treasure Lanes monthly semi-pro scratch tournament. Their matches became legendary. The first time, Richard edged Mark by a single pin, 200–199. The loss infuriated Mark, who stormed off without a handshake.

The following month, Richard crushed Mark 279–168. The next encounter was just as decisive: 245–235. Each defeat chipped away at Mark's composure. After their third clash, when Richard extended his hand in good sportsmanship, Mark snarled, "Fuck you! Get lost!" The outburst shocked onlookers who had always known Mark as a well-liked and humble competitor.

Behind the scenes, Mark's frustrations brewed into something far darker.

One night, after a chance meeting at a bar in Punta Gorda, Mark followed Richard to a secluded park. In a fit of rage, Mark pulled out a .44 caliber handgun and shot Richard in the head, splattering his brains against the windshield. Mark sped away into the night, leaving no witnesses.

Despite his crime, Mark maintained his public persona. As a politician and community figure, he hosted fundraisers and events, all while hiding the truth about his double life.

The next month, Mark entered the Treasure Lanes tournament again. This time, his semifinal opponent was Peter Strings, a professional bowler from Las Vegas. Determined not to lose, Mark visited Peter's hotel room the night before their match.

Mark introduced himself, feigning friendliness, before pulling out a silenced handgun and shooting Peter in the head. Blood and brain matter coated the walls as Peter's lifeless body slumped against a chair. Mark locked the door and left, confident that his path to victory was secure.

The next day at Treasure Lanes, Peter's absence caused a stir.

"Peter Strings has 30 minutes to arrive, or he will forfeit," announced tournament director David Loserwind.

When Peter failed to appear, Mark advanced by default. In the finals, Mark bowled with ruthless precision, striking 11 times in a row. As he prepared for the 12th shot—a perfect 300 game—the automatic pinsetter malfunctioned, dropping the gate mid-throw. The crowd groaned as Mark was forced to re-roll. He left the 4-7 standing, his perfect game ruined.

Mark's frustration boiled over. Two days later, he visited David Loserwind's home, where the tournament director was working on his car.

"Hi Mark, how are you? Sorry about that 300," David said cheerfully.

Without a word, Mark pulled out his silenced gun and shot David in the head. Then he calmly drove away.

Mark Fingernail's descent into madness turned a celebrated

bowler into a cold-blooded killer. His charm and skill masked the darkness within, leaving a trail of bodies and unanswered questions behind him. Whether driven by obsession, ego, or a twisted sense of justice, Mark proved one thing: some rivalries are better left unresolved.

SECTION 29

ALDI'S NUTS

During the COVID-19 pandemic in 2020, the Pawtucket Red Sox Triple-A baseball team left Rhode Island for Worcester to play at Polar Park. In 2023, the new Aldi's supermarket brought a new Double-A baseball team called the Aldi's Nuts, playing their games at the East Providence High School baseball stadium. Coaches Robert Polton and Chuck Bentley talk about this team. Players range from local colleges, high schools, and other talented baseball players trying out for the team. The games are played on a synthetic field. Players on this team range in age from 18 to 60.

"Good afternoon and welcome to East Providence High School here in Rhode Island. My name is Robert Polton, the coach and owner of the team, and this is Chuck Bentley, the assistant coach and team manager. We are called the Aldi's Nuts! Aldi's Supermarket owner, Donna Sylvia, from East Providence, founded this team. We will play a 100-game schedule, playing almost every day, and we open up the 2027 season against the Bridgeport River Rats in a four-game series here at EP Stadium in mid-April. The season ends on Labor Day. The reason we are called the Aldi's Nuts relates to our speed and our high batting average. My plans are to utilize the hit-and-run style of play. Our mascot will be a cheetah! The games will be aired on WPAW Radio in Pawtucket, Rhode Island. Now we have three weeks to practice before our games begin," said the coach.

Then let the games begin.

After the National Anthem, Bridgeport came up to bat, with play aired on WPAW radio. A good crowd was watching.

"Ladies and gentlemen, now batting for the Bridgeport River Rats, #38, Arthur Andrews!"

Arthur fouled off several pitches. People waited in line for food and drinks for 30 minutes, and the same batter was still up, fouling off pitches!

"Arthur Andrews is still batting, fouling off pitches! He has fouled off 65 straight pitches, and he's been at bat for 45 minutes! Now we have a ball, ball two, and now he's fouling off more pitches—now ball three! You can't get this first batter out! A 3-2 count and another foul ball. This game will go on for hours if this guy keeps fouling off pitches! He's fouled off 83 pitches and he's still batting! Ball four, and he finally takes first base! Arthur has been at bat for 56 minutes. Aldi's pitcher has already thrown 87 pitches to the very first batter! This has to be an all-time baseball record!" said the announcer on WPAW radio.

The next batter got a base hit, putting runners on first and second base, then another hit: 1-0 Bridgeport, runners on first and third base. The next batter popped out to third base. Groundout, two outs! Then a lineout to third, bottom of the first!

"Now batting for the Aldi's Nuts, #3, David Duck," said the announcer in the press box. Play-by-play continued over the radio.

"David Duck lines a double to start off for the Aldi's Nuts! Next batter, Ricky Rox, draws a walk. Next batter, Joel Pro, was hit by a pitch, loading the bases. Next up we have Robert Hamster, the designated hitter! He lines a shot to third base, caught by the third baseman, Kevin Hell, and he throws to second base, James Cookie, completing the unthinkable triple play! Not a good way to finish the bottom of the first inning for the Nuts! Bases loaded! After one inning of play, the Bridgeport River Rats lead by a score of 1 to 0," said the announcer on WPAW Radio.

In the third inning, Arthur Andrews was up with two men on base. People in the stands got up to go to the food court and restrooms while he was fouling off pitches again—about seven of them—before he popped up and was out!

Then in the 5th inning, the Aldi's Nuts had the bases loaded with one out. The next batter flied out to right field, and the right fielder relayed a perfect throw to home plate for the third out! The Bridgeport catcher tagged the runner coming in from third, slamming him down on the ground. The Aldi's runner got up, punched the Bridgeport catcher in the head, knocked off his mask, then punched him in the face. A brawl broke out!

Both benches emptied! Both teams fought—throwing punches and kicks. Coaches, umpires, and trainers tried to break up the brawl for 30 minutes until police came with pepper spray to stop it!

The Aldi's baseball team is living up to its name: Nuts!!!!!!!!

The game announcer said over the loudspeakers: "Please stop fighting, or we will forfeit the game and the rest of the season! You must stop, shake hands, and finish the game!"

The two teams shook hands, then finished the game.

WPAW Radio was going crazy announcing the big brawl. "There's a fly ball to right and it's caught, and the throw to home plate; here comes Reggie White coming in to score the tying run, and he's out at home plate, and a fight has broken out, and both benches have cleared! Now it's an all-out brawl! Oh! My bleeping God! It's the first game of the season, and it's not good for it to end this way. After 5 innings, the Bridgeport River Rats lead 1 to 0." A few minutes later, WPAW went off the air because their equipment was damaged during the brawl. After everything settled, the game resumed.

Then, in the bottom of the 7th inning with two outs, Bridgeport was still winning 1-0. Aldi's Nuts were at bat. The batter had a 0-2 count with nobody on base. The Bridgeport pitcher hit the Aldi's batter in the head. The Aldi's batter threw the bat at the pitcher, striking him in the head and knocking him down on the ground! The pitcher charged after the batter, and the batter tackled the pitcher, throwing punches, and the benches emptied again, and it was an all-out brawl! Spectators poured out on the field fighting! The umps and game officials left the field and let the East Providence Police deal with the mess. The Bridgeport team was escorted to their locker rooms in the school and escorted back to their hotel by police presence. The crowd was arrested and removed from the stadium. The game will be resumed the next day as part of a doubleheader! The coaches and league officials had a meeting with the players. "My name is David Aldi, the owner of this team. You guys looked like a bunch of assholes out there! Worse than a street gang drug deal gone wrong fight! We can't have this kind of behavior in Professional Sports! We're lucky the game and the series did not end up in a forfeit. The only reason why this game was not a forfeit is because it's our first game ever in this new double-A league. Tomorrow evening at 6 p.m., we will finish the last two innings and start the next game 15 minutes later. If we have one more fight, I will personally pull you off the field, forfeit the remainder of the season, sell the team, and there will be no more Aldi's Nuts! There will be no spectators entering the stadium for the rest of the four-game series. See your coach because several players have been suspended from the league. Now get your ass out there and play like professionals!" said the team owner.

The next day, the game resumed at the top of the eighth inning. When the game ended, the Aldi's Nuts lost 1-0. Both coaches got thrown out of the game arguing about calls by the home plate umpire. The Nuts hit into a double play, ending the game. The stadium was guarded by police and the National Guard, stopping people from going into the stadium. People had to watch from behind the fence, wall, etc... The umpires had to switch positions because of arguments during the last game. The second game was clean: a few arguments with the umpires but no fights!

In the second game, the Aldi's Nuts won 3-2. The next game of the series, the Aldi's Nuts won 6-5 in 13 innings. In the final game, the Aldi's Nuts lost 4-3 when a player was thrown out at home plate, ending the game in another brawl, splitting the series at two games apiece! Top of the 9th inning, the Aldi's Nuts were winning 3 to 1, with two outs, and Bridgeport had two runners on base. During a pitcher's mound visit, the coach said to his pitcher, "Bubba Boots is at bat with a 3-2 count. Whatever pitch you throw, please don't let this big fat prick hit another one! He's already hit two freakin' home runs already!" The coach went back to the dugout. Then the Aldi's pitcher's next pitch, Bubba Boots blasted a three-run homer, giving Bridgeport the lead!

The coach said, "I don't believe it! This big fat cocksucker did it again!"

Then a pitcher's change! The radio announcer said, "Bubba Boots for the River Rats is at bat with a 3-2 count. He's hit two home runs already in this game: The payoff pitch! Well hit! Deep to center field, far away, and it's gone! The ball is still going high into the stratosphere, high enough to reach St. Peter's Gate! And Bridgeport leads 4 to 3!" The next play was a ground out.

In the bottom of the ninth, Aldi's got a hit, the next batter bunted the runner to second base. A passed ball moved the runner to third base. Then a fly ball to left field, two outs! Then the runner came in to score, bowling the Bridgeport catcher over, and the runner was out! Bridgeport won the game! The catcher got up and started throwing punches at the Aldi's runner, then took off his mask, striking the Aldi's player in the face. Then a brawl broke out, and both teams started hitting one another with baseball bats!

SHADES OF PRIESTS AND NUNS

St. Michael's Church and rectory have a dark side.

THE PRIESTS: Father Michael, Father Patrick, Father In, and Father Donald. Monsignor Joseph.

THE NUNS ARE: Sister Jacky, Sister Colleen, Sister Claire, and Sister Margaret. Mother Superior Fitzgerald. At 11 p.m., everyone is home at the church convent. At 12 midnight, they're all in bed. By 1 a.m., the convent is quiet. By 2 a.m., the Mother Superior's job is to make sure doors are locked and check on the priests and nuns to make sure everyone is here before she goes to bed by 2 a.m. Monsignor Joseph is the boss who runs the church. The Mother Superior runs the convent. The Mother Superior was in bed sleeping when suddenly she heard noises in the restroom, waking her up! She looked at the alarm clock, and the time was 3:02 a.m. She got up and went to the restroom, where she heard moaning noises in the shower.

She pulled back the shower curtain and she saw Monsignor Joseph and Sister Margret having sex. The Monsignor had Sister Margret up against the wall, standing up in the shower stall and he was giving it to her! The Mother Superior said. "Monsignor, you Dog! What are you doing? You're a devil! Bless my heart and bless my soul! I never saw a high priest and a nun having sex in the shower, naked!"

Then she made the sign of the cross and said the rosary! "Mother Superior, we will talk about this tomorrow morning after breakfast in my office," said Monsignor Joseph.

The Mother Superior stormed out of the restroom, and she went back to bed saying her prayers! By 4am the Monsignor and Sister Margret was still having sex in the shower, finishing with a double header, before it was over! At 5:02am, Father Michael and Sister Jacky were getting it on! At 6:02am Father Patrick and Sister Colleen were screwing around! At 7:02am Sister Claire was giving Father Donald oral sex while Father In was screwing Sister Claire from behind, doggy style!!!

At 8:02am everyone's getting out of bed to get ready for breakfast! At 9:02am breakfast was served and all the priests and nuns enjoyed leaving all the sex from last night behind!

Monsignor said. "Mother Fitzgerald, we will have a meeting at 10am in my office after breakfast." She gave the Monsignor a dirty look. Breakfast was served: Muffins, bagels, donuts, sweet bread, scrambled eggs, cereal of all kinds, pancakes, breakfast sausage, orange juice and coffee. After all the priests and nuns finished eating, the meeting with the Monsignor was held at 10:02am.

"Mother Superior Senior Sister: Delores Marie Fitzgerald. I know you're new here at St. Michael's Parish. But what went on last night with Sister Margret has been happening here for the last six months. All the nuns work for me except you, but you can join the action with us or just do your job. You see, we're in the process of losing this church. We lost two thirds of the people attending St. Michael's. The only way we can get the money to keep this church open is for the parish to do devilish things! All the priests and nuns are having sex just like living in a whore house! The nuns and priests do it among themselves and go both ways! I realize this is not what God wants, but to keep the church, I have to do what it takes to get money! I am the pimp for all the nuns and women who visits the church. The nuns are sent out to find men for prostitution, drug dealing and gambling where it's legal in some private camps here in Montreal."

"Monsignor, what is a pimp?"

"A pimp is a man that hires women or gay men to prostitute and get money to split half between them and me, just like collecting a 50/50 raffle."

"Monsignor! I think you're going to hell when you die!" The Mother Superior walked out of the meeting.

At 11:02am Monsignor was writing up a report in his office about the meeting, then around noon, lunch was served— soups, salads and sandwiches, milk, coffee and yogurt etc..... At 1:02pm, Monsignor Joseph was giving the nuns and priests instructions.

"Mother Fitzgerald. I want you to go food shopping for the convent this afternoon. Then come back and finish cleaning the kitchen and restrooms, dusting and vacuuming. The rest of you nuns and priests, clean your rooms and write up church reports. The nuns will cook dinner tonight. 2:02pm, Monsignor Joseph picked up a black prostitute on a Montreal street corner next to the McGill Hotel and he was arrested by police.

He said. "Hey there honey. What are you doing today, standing in the street?" "I am looking for someone to keep me company in the hotel."

"You got it! Let me find a parking space and we can hook up!" said Monsignor Joseph.

The so-called black prostitute was a cop, trapping criminals on the streets. He was arrested and taken into custody. The Monsignor called the rectory and Mother Superior Fitzgerald answered the phone.

"Mother Fitzgerald, I was arrested for prostitution, I will not be coming home tonight! Just do what you have to do, I will be going to church in jail this weekend."

The Mother Superior hung up!

Father Patrick was at a speak easy looking for a quick fix! He looked at his watch and the time was 3:02pm. One hour later, Father Michael was driving around the city streets looking for prostitutes. Father Donald was at a strip joint in downtown Montreal getting a lap dance. He looked at his watch and the time was 5:02pm. The girl was naked and sat across Father Donald's lap and rode him like a raging bull!

At 6:02pm, dinner was served at the convent/rectory. The nuns cooked and served dinner before the ladies go out to have their fun before going to church tomorrow morning. Ham, mashed potatoes, corn, a green salad, and pea soup were served for dinner. Carrot cake tea and coffee were served later.

At 7:02pm Sister Jacky went to a strip joint to go dancing and pick up a man for money. Sister Colleen was hanging outside the convent dressed like a prostitute, showing her sexy legs and hoping for a quick fix. She looked at her watch, and the time was 8:02pm.

One hour later, Sister Claire was on a downtown street posing as a prostitute. She looked at her watch and the time was 9:02pm. A car stopped and a man picked her up and took her to a hotel for sex. In the room, she said to the man. "$150 dollars, before we start!"

"Fuck you, you cunt!" said the man.

Sister Claire pulled out a gun and she said, "We're already naked and you are wasting my time."

The man paid the $150 and he got laid then he left the room. Sister Claire got a cab to go back to the convent. She gave the cab driver $10, and she went into the nun's house about an hour later. The cab driver gave her a funny look when she got out.

At 10:02pm, the Mother Superior was fingering herself in the shower. At 11:02pm all the priests and nuns made their money for the day before going to bed for the night.

The next day was Sunday and they're all went to church. "Good morning, and welcome to St. Michael's Church. My name is Father Richard In, taking over for Monsignor Joseph. He was arrested for prostitution yesterday at the Mc Gill Hotel. I understand that's not the news you want to hear in the house of God. The city of Montreal is the sex capitol of the world, 80% of the restaurants and night clubs are all strip joints with naked waitress and bar tenders running around in public, dancing and looking for sex.

Prostitutes rule every street corner, subway, hotel, even at the airport. You can get sex for $50 here in Montreal but most hookers charge $100 and up! We lost more than 75% of the population here at St. Michael's because of sex. Prostitution is getting into our church, you would never believe our high priest would get arrested for prostitution, but it happens! When you leave this church. Go downstairs to the gift shop. If you go down another flight, you will end up in a strip joint! The Bible says that Hell is under the church.

SEX! My dear brothers and sisters, the Devil is ruling Montreal coming up from the sub-basement to the high towers of the skyscrapers, and we have no control over it. If you come to Montreal, you have to have sex or find sex! That' my sermon for today!"

When the priest left the church he went downstairs to the Cameron's Strip Joint Restaurant for lunch, a few bears and then he hid behind a curtain with a little honey for SEX!

When evening comes after supper the Canadian Mounted Police came to St. Michael's Rectory to investigate the prostitution going on there. They all got arrested and will have to go to court at a later time. Now things will have to change before the court date. The priests had sex among themselves at the rectory and the nuns had to be dikes at the convent.

IN COURT. "Everyone please rise in honor of Judge: Joseph Robert Pesci.' Please be seated. Case #123 St. Michael's Church verses the Canadian Mounted Police," said the receptionist. "As of today July 17th, 2027, I order St. Michael's Church closed due to illegal prostitution arrests there and on public city streets. Prostitution is against the law in Montreal," said the judge.

OFF STREET ROAD KILL

CHAPTER 1

A roadkill restaurant opens up in Tiverton, Rhode Island.

Tiverton Casino: A southerner at the casino was looking to open up a restaurant inside a vacant spot. The man was playing blackjack and asked the dealer for the casino manager. The dealer directed the man to the front desk.

"Are you the owner of this casino?" said the man.

"I am the general manager of Bally's Tiverton Casino, and my name is Michael St. Patrick."

"Pleased to meet you, Michael. My name is Roy Lewis Mercer from Mow Southern Oklahoma. I am a restaurant owner, and I noticed you have an open space and are looking to open up a new restaurant. My restaurant is called 'Off Street Roadkill,' and I would like my new restaurant to be in a casino because of the foot traffic here."

"What do you serve in this restaurant?" said the manager.

"You kill it! We grill it! That's what we do in Southern Oklahoma!"

"I'm sorry, sir, but I am not looking for a restaurant like that," said the casino manager.

The roadkill man left the casino, and he found a spot in an open field on Eagleville Road in Tiverton. He called a phone number he saw on a sign to make arrangements to meet. Phone call from a cell phone:

"Good afternoon. My name is Roy Lewis Mercer from Mow Southern Oklahoma. I noticed a sign while I was driving on Eagleville Road about a restaurant opening. I am a restaurant owner, and I am looking to open one here in Tiverton. Can we meet and talk about it?"

"Yes, sir. Meet me at the property in about an hour."

One hour later, the property owner pulled up in a GMC pickup truck.

"Are you the property owner of this building?"

"Yes, sir. My name is Russel Roberts."

"Russel, pleased to meet you. Roy Lewis Mercer. I am interested in opening a Roadkill Restaurant here: Southern Hospitality. I think it will go well here in Rhode Island, not far from the casino down the road. My restaurant was hit by a tornado twice back home. I recently moved to the old city in Massachusetts next door, Fall River! I moved here because we don't get tornadoes here very often."

"Mister Mercer, what kind of restaurant is roadkill?"

"You kill it! We grill it!"

The property owner laughed and said, "Come inside, and I will show you what we have here. This building has been vacant for about 5 years. This property was supposed to be a crematorium for cremations, but the town of Tiverton did not allow it, and it's been in the courts for years. I decided to open up an upscale restaurant in the works, but I have to remove these ovens first." said the property owner.

"Don't do that, Russel, because I can use them to cook my animals!"

"Do me a favor? Please don't cook any humans in here!" the property owner joked.

"Oh! No, sir, I will not do that!"

The property owner gave Roy, the man from Southern Oklahoma, some instructions before he could open his new restaurant. "These ovens get very hot. Only burn no more than two at a time because I don't want you to burn the place down! Good luck." Then the owner left.

Two weeks later, the new restaurant was ready to open: 'OFF STREET ROADKILL.' Help wanted signs were posted outside, and people were coming in looking for work.

"Good afternoon. Please fill out job applications on the tables, and you will get an interview in a group," said Roy.

"Come, let's take a journey through this restaurant. We have big freezers and big ovens. This property was supposed to be a crematorium where bodies came here to be cremated, but it was denied by the town of Tiverton. My name is Roy Lewis Mercer, and I am from Mow Southern Oklahoma. I bought this building from Russel Roberts. Now called 'Off Street Roadkill.' It doesn't look like a restaurant in here, it's more like a fire-burning factory, but I have trucks coming from Oklahoma to give this place a nice fixer-upper and bring in frozen roadkill to get started. We will have cooks, waitresses, waiters, bartenders, and hunters. If you applied for a hunter position, you must have a gun permit and a clean record. When the trucks arrive, the hunters are responsible for unloading and loading the trucks. Then you will be given shotguns and a company vehicle, and you will be going out killing animals, birds, fish, etc. Do not shoot and kill people!" Roy joked.

Then he continued the interviews.

"The hunters will drive through Tiverton killing wild animals, such as deer, raccoons, rats, snakes, birds, and even fish. Roadkill is illegal in Rhode Island. Don't get caught by the cops! This is why you're being paid big money to go out killing animals. If you get caught, you will be fired! You will be driving everywhere looking for animals to kill."

You may have to travel to Maine and New Hampshire if needed. You will have to go deep-sea fishing on a vessel, and when a big fish gets away, you are allowed to shoot it as long as the vessel is in international waters. If you have any questions, email me at: roylewismercer@offstreetroadkill.com.

The next day, Roy and the former property owner went over a catalog about what animals are listed in Tiverton.

"Roy, the biggest kill here in Tiverton that is legal is: deer and snakes. We are the rattlesnake capital of the world. Our woods are loaded with them! Then we have bobcats, fisher cats, foxes, rats, coyotes, possums, etc... We have all kinds of rodents running around here in Tiverton. Good luck with your new restaurant," said Russel Roberts, the former owner.

An electric truck loaded with roadkill left Oklahoma with no driver on its way to Tiverton. It made it to a truck stop in upstate New York, and the battery died in an unpopulated, closed-off truck stop. It was a hot day, and all the roadkill rotted away. The truck was never heard from again!

CHAPTER 2
ROAD KILL!

The hunters are out on the job. The roadkill hunters were out driving cars, trucks, walking through wooded areas with big guns, and in boats fishing and gunning down big fish to bring back to the restaurant to cook, serve, and freeze. Weeks later, a sign was put up on the building called: Off Street Roadkill Cuisine.

The hunters were shooting deer and loading them on flat-beds, about 20 of them, and bringing them to the restaurant to be chopped up, cooked, and frozen into 10,000,000 hamburgers by the cooks. Others trapped snakes using animal traps; thousands of them! They brought them to Roadkill. The snake keepers were cleaning up the Tiverton woods. A boat was out of Fog Land Beach in Tiverton catching fish from a fishing vessel. One man shot a great white with a bazooka, blasting the shark into pieces, and the fishermen were scooping up the shredded pieces in the water and loading them onto the boat, then placing them in freezers. The same man shot a whale with the same weapon, blasting the whale into three pieces! The water was covered in blood, attracting hundreds of sharks, and many more were shot with big guns and loaded onto boats. The job was done late at night. The boats pulled up to the beach and unloaded, placing the fish in freezer trucks that were then taken to the Roadkill Restaurant in Tiverton. There was so much fish kill that the freezers were filling up; the rest was left in the freezer trucks. The trucks parked behind the restaurant out of view before daybreak. While the trucks were unloading, a hungry buck watched! A man pulled out a gun and shot the big deer! The giant buck ran away but had a bullet in its head! The buck was shot again in the ass, but it got away! Now the sun is rising, and the shooting is over!

The Navy had a lot of shooting: pop, pop! Bang, bang, on radar, and the Coast Guard was called in to investigate the bloody waters off Fog Land Beach. No one was caught. Gunmen shot so many deer and wildlife to be served at the Roadkill! One man shot three raccoons, he shot a German shepherd, and a crow, and carried them to his car to bring the kill to Roadkill. One man shot a bald-headed eagle! Another man shot a horse! Foxes, bobcats, and coyotes by the dozens were loaded onto a truck late at night and brought to Roadkill.

A Tiverton cop was parked at the restaurant while the man was unloading the dead animals. He said, "Excuse me, pal, but do you have a hunting permit?"

"Yes, I do, officer."

"Can I see it, please!?" The man showed the cop his hunting license. Then the police left before he unloaded the dead animals. Other hunters caught insects for dishes and pies, emptying beehives, going into wet places, collecting cockroaches, flies, maggots, and all kinds of bugs for dishes to eat.

The Tiverton Police sent emails to town residents, warning them to watch their animals because we have a roadkill restaurant located on Eagleville Road, and hunters are killing the wildlife. The Roadkill is open for business, and lean burgers were cooked from deer and steaks, horse meat, etc... Any dogs or cats that were shot in the neighborhood were ground up with deer and horse meat. Bugs were mixed in! Other roadkill coming in was kept frozen. Deer meat was served with mashed potatoes, green beans, and corn. For dessert: chocolate-covered cockroaches and black flies were served until a full menu was completed. The cooks were preparing food, working on the menu. The hunters are still out killing animals.

CHAPTER 3
THE ROADKILL MENU

Item 1: Baked steak horse meat. $39.95, served with sweet potato fries, onions, and peas.

Item 2: Baked stuffed raccoon, with fried cockroaches, maggots, and black flies. $29.95.

Item 3: Broiled bobcat, served with garlic mashed potatoes covered with fried maggots. $32.

Item 4: Open-faced wild turkey, served with black flies and fish kill blood soup. $34.95.

Item 5: Baked fisher cat, served with blood stuffing, brown bread, and liver balls. $38.95.

Item 6: Stuffed duck with brown blood gravy, served with carrots and black beans. $31.99.

Item 7: Baked possum with liver balls, coleslaw, fried maggots, peas, and corn. $30.95.

Item 8: Sliced open muskrat stuffed with bread stuffing, blood pudding, and corn. $44.00

Item 9: Fried cockroaches, maggots, black flies, carrots, and greens with mixed meats. $38.00

Item 10: All-you-can-eat Off Street Roadkill, served with soup and salad of choice. $38.00

Item 11: Horse meat penis sliced open like a hot dog, served with maggots and fries. $49.00

Item 12: 3 field rats served with crawfish, boiled oven potatoes, and salad. $36.99.

Item 13: Baked stuffed twin foxes, served with oven potatoes or fries and mixed greens. $44.00

Item 14: Open Tiverton Pig Roast family meal, served with fried bees and honey sauce. $90.00

Item 15: Broiled rat and mice, served with a vegetable casserole and fried bees. $44.95.

Item 16: Roadkill all-animal mix bowl with broccoli cheese, covered with fried black flies and maggots. Family dish feeds up to 8 people. $300.00.

Kids' Meal:
Two hot dogs served with fries. $9.95.
Hamburger plate with mac and cheese. $10.95.
Chicken fingers/tenders with fries/flies. $10.95.
Vegetables and pasta. $10.95. All-you-can-eat.

American Grill:
Filet Mignon: Jr. cut $30.95, Medium cut $39.95, and King cut

$59.95, served with choice of potatoes, rice, fries, flies, and mixed vegetables.

New York Sirloin with the same choice of fixings: $33.95.

Open flat iron steak with egg on top covered with fried bees in honey sauce and a green salad. $35.00.

T-bone steak with shrimp, choice of potatoes, vegetable or salad, and maggot or black fly soup. $50.00.

All steaks are served with choice of fixings, vegetables, or green salad.

Steak tips served in a bowl of cockroaches, flies, maggots, mice, and shrimp—family of four dish. $195.95.

Chicken Dinners:

Broiled, fried, steamed, or raw, served with choice of potatoes, fries/flies, and vegetable or green salad. $29.95.

Add roadkill fixings: $49.95.

Turkey dinners with the same fixings.

Fish: market price.

Ham Dinners:

Served with potatoes, vegetables of choice, or salad. $19.95. Add roadkill: $39.95.

Sandwiches:

All served with fries, salad, or roadkill.

Ham & cheese: $10.95

Chicken: $10.95

Roast beef: $11.95

Philly steak: $16.95

Hamster & mice wrap: $15.95.

Roadkill wrap: $22.95.

Add $10 for roadkill fixings.

Steak wraps with roadkill and fish kill blood: $34.95.

Ham, chicken, and beef wraps: $12.95.

Squirrel stew served with fried mice, cockroaches, black flies, and maggots: $24.95.

With roadkill, add $10.00.

Baked squirrel in an open torpedo roll, sliced open like a hot dog, served with a side salad.

Seafood Menu:

Swordfish, served with choice of potato, vegetable, or salad: $39.95.

With roadkill fixings, add $10.00.

Fish & chips with fries and vegetable.

Tuna fish and Tuna cat served with fries and vegetable: $29.95.

Marlin with roadkill: market price.

Appetizers:

Chopped snake: $13.50.

Baked stuffed rabbit: $13.95.

Broiled open coyote: $22.95.

Maggot pie: $13.95

Bowl of fried cockroaches: $13.95

Rice bowl with black flies: $13.95

Open hamster in a hot dog bun: $12.95

Baked ferret in a bun, served like a hot dog: $16.95.

Komodo dragon ears, served with roadkill: $129.95.

Side Items:

Side of fries: $6.95

Sweet fries: $8.95

Side of cockroaches: $7.95

Side of fried black flies: $7.95

Side of fried maggots: $6.95

Two hot dogs with roadkill fixings: $29.95

Salads:

Snake salad: $15.95.

Green salad: $8.95

Meat salad: $19.95

Roadkill salad: $27.95

Fish salad: $27.95.

Cockroach salad: $9.95

Maggot salad: $7.95

Black fly salad: $9.95

Soups:

Cockroach soup: $11.95

Maggot soup: $10.95

Black fly soup: $10.95

Roadkill soup, served with animal body parts: $35.00

All other meat soups: $15.95

Drinks:

Bottomless Coffee, tea, regular and decaf, $4.95. Milk $3.99.

Alcoholic drinks: Top shelf: $19.95. Bar drinks $14.95. All domestic beers $7.95. And premium beers, $10.95.

MARIJUANA CIGERETTES: $29.95 a joint, $395.99 for an ounce. Roadkill animal body parts with cockroaches, flies and maggots, pot seeds and marijuana sprinkled and boiled in Vodka and Hennessy in a large bowl, served with a green salad, $159.95.

Desserts:

Check out road kill's famous chocolate covered cockroaches, $17.95.

Maggots pie $11.95.

Black flies pudding, $9.95

Road kill ice cream $13.95.

Muffins Cakes and pastry, $8.88 With roadkill, add $10.00.
THANK YOU FOR COMING TO THE OFF STREET ROADKILL.

CHAPTER 4
ROADKILL CUSTOMERS

Finally, this restaurant is fully open for business. The hunters are still out killing animals. A group of eight coming from the casino came in for dinner. "Welcome to Off Street Roadkill. My name is Cammy Headneck, your waitress. Can I help you all?"

"Yes, my name is Ricky Lowell. This is my wife, Paula. Next is my brother Tom and his wife, Claire. Next, this is my brother Glenn and his wife, Colleen, and finally, my youngest brother, Jay, and his wife, Charlene. We know the owner: Roy Mercer. We're from Oklahoma visiting Tiverton, Rhode Island, and enjoying the casino here."

"Welcome! Take a look at today's specials. The broiled lobster served with fried scorpions is on sale for $49.95; add roadkill for $10 more. I will take your drink order first."

The group looked over the specials while the waitress was ordering the drinks.

"I will order a vodka roadkill martini, and my wife will have a glass of white wine," said Ricky Lowell.

"I will order a Sam Adams Summer Ale, and Claire will have a Sex on the Beach," said Tom.

"I will have the Roadkill Martini and a big fat joint! My wife will have a Tito's Vodka Martini," said Glenn.

"I will have a Coors Light, and my wife would like a red bottle of wine and a big fat joint!" said Jay.

The waitress finished the drink orders while the group looked over the specials menu.

Specials for Today:

Broiled lobster served with fried scorpions, $49.95.

Scorpion salad with roadkill, $29.95.

Lobster Roll served with fried black flies, $29.95.

Cow meat roadkill with corn, $29.95

Cow Balls and roadkill fixings, $39.95.

Open roadkill fixings all you can eat, $49.95.

Steak Tips, served with roadkill and animal blood soup, 69.95.

Pasta with roadkill and animal blood soup, $33.00

Hamster& Ferret Salad and roadkill fixings and blood soup, $59.95.

Steak ham chicken pork and turkey tips served with roadkill and cockroach, black flies and maggots in a salad. All you can eat. $79.95.

Chinese Specials:

ALL SERVED WITH ROADKILL FIXINGS: COCKROACHES FRIED BLACK FLIES AND WHITE AND YELLO MAGGOTS AND PASTA.

Suc me wang, $139.95.

Fuc you man $100.00

Chicken & Pork Chow Mein. $95.95.

Pussy bow wow! $239.95 with steak tips.

Pee you platter, $129.95.

Chow wang hotdog, $119.95.

Open poo poo platter, $189.95.

Twat Sum Soup, $33.95.

Please see more online or mobile Phone.

"Are we ready to order?" said the waitress.

"I will have the Awesome Possum meal, and Paula will have the Pee-You Platter. Thank you," said Ricky.

"I will have the Lobster Fried Scorpion Special, and Claire will have the Roadkill Pig Roast," said Tom.

"I will have the horse's cock hotdog!" said Glenn.

"Can you be more specific, Glenn?"

"Yeah! I want the horse's dick hotdog meal!"

"Glenn, please have more respect."

"I will have the horse's penis meal, the thing!"

"That's better, Glenn."

"My wife will have the broiled raccoon," said Glenn.

"I will have the cow's meat cow balls, and my wife will have the Open Broiled Coyote Meal," said Jay.

"All meals are served with coffee, tea, or soft beverages. We also offer chocolate-covered cockroaches for dessert!" said the waitress.

By the time the party of eight finished eating, the bill was about $1,000 with the tip included.

Meanwhile, more people came in to order food; the restaurant was busy. The hunters were shooting dogs and cats with bows and arrows in Tiverton neighborhoods, and these animals were grilled at the restaurant. Neighbors were calling the police, reporting missing cats and dogs.

Days later, the health department went to Off Street Roadkill to investigate what was cooking.

"Good afternoon. My name is Harry Lacy from the Rhode Island Department of Health. May I speak to Mr. Roy Lewis Mercer, the owner here?"

"Yes, sir. I will go get him," answered one of the workers.

"Roy Mercer speaking. How are you today?"

"Sir, we have several complaints about your menu here at Off Street Roadkill. Hundreds of cats and dogs in the Tiverton and Fall River area have been reported missing."

"Well, whatever runs in the road, we kill it and grill it!" said Roy.

The Department of Health looked over the menu and ordered the restaurant to close.

SECTION 32

HE CHEATED ON MY WIFE

CHAPTER 1

A cop was dating a married woman. The woman's husband was a contractor, and the man dating her was a cop.

Police stopped the contractor's wife for speeding in Tampa, Florida.

"Good evening, ma'am. Are you racing to a fire?"

"No, sir. I'm going to a dance club! I didn't realize I was driving so fast!"

"Can I see your license, registration, and proof of insurance, please? The speed limit on I-75 is 70 miles per hour in Tampa, and you were clocked at 91 miles per hour."

"I'm sorry, officer."

"Miss Karen Foster, you nearly caused a serious accident from your speeding. You have a very heavy foot. This isn't the first time you've been stopped for speeding in Florida."

"Again, I am sorry, officer. I was trying to pass some cars while driving behind a big truck to get to open road."

"Karen, you almost hit those cars, and you nearly ran me off the road! You have to slow down. Where are you going?" asked the cop.

"I am going to 'The Black Gate' night club in downtown Tampa."

"Karen, you have several driving violations in both cars and motorcycles along with unpaid summonses totaling $956.

You can do two things, pay the fine, or give me free sex at the Black Gate whenever I want."

"Officer, that's sexual harassment!"

"It's my word against yours! How would you like it if I arrest you for prostitution right now, plus dealing with drugs; that's a nice marijuana bong you have on the driver's side floor. Take the deal or we go to court and you end up in jail for the next 10 years!"

"I'll take the deal."

"Good Karen meet me at the Black Gate. We can be friends. My name is: Officer Glenn Joel. I will see you in about an hour. Please slow down."

"Can you meet me after midnight, I have to stop somewhere first."

"You got it!" said the cop. At 1:02am Officer Joel arrived in his police car at the Black Gate strip joint to meet Karen for a piece of ass! One hour later he got a blowjob from another girl before going back to the police station.

A week later, Karen met her husband at a restaurant. "The Rose Garden" was the name of the restaurant.

"Karen, I know we've just been married for six weeks, and we bought a nice house here in Florida, but I need to question your work schedule. We don't see each other much because I work days, and you work crazy nighttime hours. What's the Black Gate?"

"Well, Frank, you know I am a bartender there, and some nights I work until 2 a.m. On weekend nights, I go in late, work all night, and I don't get home until 8 a.m., depending on what band is playing. I am new at the Black Gate, and I have to work 60 hours a week. With your construction job, we need to keep our house, especially since we will have a baby soon. Little Frankie will be born in five months, and we need to pull together and work long hours to keep our lives together. I know it's hard, but we have to go through this."

"Karen, where is the Black Gate?"

"It's in downtown Tampa."

Weeks later, Karen fell in love with the policeman. Her husband looked online while Karen was at work, searching for the Black Gate. One night, he decided to pay Karen a visit while she was tending bar.

When the husband arrived, he read the sign before going into the bar: "The Black Gate Gentlemen's Club."

"Good evening, Karen. I came to see you for a surprise visit. You never told me you were working in a strip joint! What's going on here!?"

"You never asked me what kind of place this was. All I do is tend bar and waitress once in a while, that's it! I am not a stripper or dancer. We have strippers here and also a restaurant. I work the bar or waitress in the restaurant, and I make good money with great tips. That's why I picked this place to work. You came to see me, and now you found what I do: fix and mix drinks. You need to trust me, I don't do anything else in here! What are you drinking?" asked Karen.

"I'll have the usual: 'Sex on the Beach.'"

"Who the hell are you!?" shouted Karen's pimp.

"I'm Frank, Karen's husband. Who the hell are you!? Do you have a problem!?"

"Yes, I have a problem. I'm the manager here, and the Black Gate is a private club. You can't come here unless you're invited or call first."

"I came to see my wife, so go screw yourself! You touch her, and I will tear your head off! So, screw you!"

The pimp threw beer in Frank's face. Frank grabbed the pimp's beer glass, smashed it over his head, cut him with the broken glass, and then punched him in the face. Frank kicked him in the nuts, and when he fell, Frank kicked him in the head and smashed a chair over the pimp's head, knocking him out.

He said to his wife, "Karen, if I catch you with anyone here, you're gonna get what he got! He's bigger than me and look what I did to him!"

The bouncers arrived and escorted Frank out of the club. Frank drove out of the parking lot, parked on the street facing the club, and waited until Karen left.

At 3:02 a.m., Karen left the club alone, got in her car, and drove home. Frank took off before she got in her car.

CHAPTER 2
KAREN'S DOUBLE LIFE!

At 4:02 a.m., Officer Glenn Joel arrived at the club looking for Karen, and one of the bouncers/pimps told him she went home. Whether the cop got laid or not, he left a half hour later.

Two days later, Karen was at work tending bar, and she said to the pimp that her husband had kicked his ass.

"I am so sorry for what Frank did to you. I didn't think he was going to act like that! What I need you to do is ban my husband from coming here and watch the cameras to see if he's coming around. When you provoked him, he snapped!" said Karen.

The bouncers and pimps were watching around the property when Karen was dancing, giving lap dances naked, and engaging in prostitution in the club. She was hired to travel to homes and vehicles for sex in exchange for money. Officer Glenn Joel was involved.

About a week later, Karen was shopping at Walmart, kissing another man, when suddenly her husband caught her. Workers at the Black Gate were watching Frank's whereabouts, at his home and following him when he was near the club.

Frank walked up to her and said, "Is this why you work at the Black Gate!?"

"Frank, it's not what you think. This is my brother, Bob. He just came from his best friend's funeral."

"Pleased to meet you, sir. My name is Bob Manning. Your wife is my best sister. She's the only family member I can talk to when things go wrong."

They talked in Walmart while Karen was shopping, and then Frank went back home.

When Karen went home, she said, "What do you think of my brother Bob? He's from Boston, Massachusetts. You've never met him before; he's visiting us here in Florida and staying in Orlando."

"I think he's a nice guy. He was nice to talk to," said Frank.

Days later, Karen was at a restaurant in Tampa, talking to a police officer, Glenn Joel. Just before they kissed, Frank walked in and saw them together. Frank sat down with them and said, "My name is Frank, and this is my wife, Karen."

"Pleased to meet you. Officer Glenn Joel, TPD. Your wife is a nice lady."

They had brunch and coffee together.

Two days later, Frank saw Karen talking to the same police officer while sitting in his police cruiser near a strip mall in Tampa, where Frank was working. Karen had tight shorts on with a noticeable split up the back. Frank drove by in his cement truck and pulled over to the side of the road. He got out and said to her, "What's going on!?"

"We're just chatting before I go to Walmart," Karen replied.

Frank jumped back in his cement truck with its 8 giant wheels and drove off.

Later, Frank saw Karen talking with the same police officer multiple times: in the street outside the police station and near the Black Gate, where she worked. Frank called the Black Gate, and confirmed she was there.

Frank staked out the club late at night with a fellow worker in different cars to see who she was leaving with. However, she always came out alone, going to her car between 2 and 4 in the morning and leaving by herself.

Two days later, Frank was pouring cement from his truck into a foundation while talking to one of his workers.

"Arthur, would you like to get a couple of hours' break every day for a week or two from work? I need you to do me a favor from 11 a.m. to 1 p.m., five days a week. I need you to check up on my wife. I think she has something going on with a police officer.

"The policeman's name is Glenn Joel. The license plate number on his police car is TPD123, and his badge number is 45. I've seen them talking outside her workplace, the Black Gate. I've also seen them talking at the police station, Walmart, the Tampa Boat Yard, a bowling alley, and even under a bridge at an exit ramp to Route 75.

"I haven't seen any sexual contact or kissing, but she's always wearing shorts with a crack showing every time she's talking to him. She's working in a strip joint, and I haven't caught anything inappropriate when I've shown up at her work, but I still think something's going on with this cop.

"I've met him before, and he told me she's just a chat partner, and that she's a nice lady. Here's a photo of her; her name is Karen Foster. Here are the places she frequents."

Follow this police officer and be careful. Keep a safe distance and take pictures. Don't confront him. Come to my car and I have a camera to give you and here's $100. Go get a nice meal and Thank You," said Frank.

CHAPTER 3
YES KAREN'S A SLUT!

Frank's co-worker, Arthur, went to work spying on his wife. Arthur was driving on I-75 and had to slow down in traffic due to an accident. He saw the police car and Karen was standing up against the car half naked. The police officer was at the accident scene. Karen had shorts on so tight you could see her pussy hairs! Arthur started snapping pictures!

After driving through the accident scene about an hour and a half later. Officer Joel arrived at the Tampa Police Station with Karen in his car. He took more pictures. The cop and Karen split up and she went home. The cop went into the police station. Arthur took more pictures and drove off.

The next day at work, Arthur met with Frank showing him the pictures he took yesterday. "Arthur, go to my house and stalk where Karen is going. She said she's going to lunch with her girlfriend at the Google Coffee House. Follow her there and find out who's she's going with," said Frank.

At 10:56am Arthur showed up and he parked near the Foster's home and at 11:02am Karen came out of the house, and she jumped into a car. Arthur took pictures then followed the car to a house a few miles away. Arthur was taking pictures of the car and license plate the whole time. Officer Glenn Joel, the cop, gets out and he's arm and arm with Karen, Hugs and kisses! Then they went into the house—Officer Glenn Joel's House!

Arthur took pictures, then he drove off. Arthur was parked under a tree out of view from being seen. He went to McDonald's for lunch, and he sent pictures from his phone to Frank. Arthur used the camera, taking pictures and videos from his I-phone. Frank called him.

"Arthur, after you finish lunch go back to Officer Joel's house and see if she's still there. If she's still there, stay out of sight and follow her to where she's going. Do not leave until they leave the house. Don't bother coming back to work just keep monitoring my wife, That fuckin cunt.

Arthur went back to officer Joel's house and he was still there. He looked at his phone and the time was 1:49pm. At 2:02pm, Officer Joel comes out of the house with Karen hugging her and grabbing her crotch as Arthur was taking pictures. Karen was home by 3:02pm. Arthur showed all the pictures and video from his phone to Frank. 4:02pm Frank was still pouring cement at his workplace. He called Arthur.

"Tomorrow morning I want you to go by my house about 9:30 and watch when she leaves the house. Follow her and take pictures. If she's going with the police officer, he's going to get his surprise tomorrow night!"

The next day was Friday. Arthur went to the Foster's home and he parked his car and waited. At 10:02am Karen came out of the house alone and she got in her car. Arthur followed, taking pictures. Karen drove to officer Glenn Joel's house and she went inside. By 11:02am, they must have been fucking! 11:30am they came out of the house and the cop got in her car and they went to the beach together. Arthur followed, taking pictures. 12:02pm they were at the beach having a picnic lunch as Arthur watched taking pictures and video of them. Eating, drinking, sunbathing and going swimming. Then Karen was home by 3pm. When Frank got home from work yesterday and today; He asked Karen. "Where did you go today, while I was at work?" Her response was: "I went out to lunch with my friend Jean." Friday afternoon. "I went to the beach today."

Later Friday night, Karen went to work at the Black Gate. Arthur was there watching her giving lap dancers and dancing on stage. Arthur, who she did not know, said "Hi" and put a $5 bill in her G-string. He waited until she left at 11:02pm. Karen left the Black Gate and went to officer Glenn Joel's house. Fucky! Fucky From midnight till 3am!

Arthur followed and waited. Frank went to officer Joel's house in his cement truck around 2 in the morning. The cop and Karen were sound to sleep. Frank pulled up to officer Joel's car smashing the windshield and poured cement from his truck, covering the inside and outside of his car then he left.

SECTION 33

BEAR BREAK INS!

CHAPTER 1

A couple moved into a home in Vancouver, British Columbia, Canada, in the high mountains of the Metro District mountain range, near Tish Columbia Mountain.

"Good afternoon. Welcome to Vancouver, Tish Village. My name is Nancy Nana, from Seattle Realtors."

"Frank and Elsie Cooper."

"Pleased to meet you. Where are you from?" said Nancy, the realtor.

"We're from Gunside Ranch, New Mexico," said Frank.

"Come inside, and I'll show you the house. This is the kitchen, which you enter through the front door. You have a stainless-steel refrigerator and stove, a microwave oven, and a double sink. You have a center cooking block in the middle of the kitchen and lots of cabinet space. The living room has three windows, a fireplace, and the dining room is separate from the living room with a large chandelier and wall lights. Here in the foyer, you have a staircase going up to the second floor with three bedrooms and a bath. You have a big porch with wall lights overlooking the mountains. You have a pretty big yard at the back of this house with a long driveway leading to a barn and tool shed behind the trees. We'll look at that later. Come downstairs, and I'll show you the basement. Here, you have your washer and dryer hookups, a laundry room, a workbench, and a bar. There's a bulkhead leading out to the backyard, and this door leads to the garage. Come outside, and I'll show you the barn and tool shed. Years ago, this property used to be a farm," said the realtor.

"Are there a lot of bears in this area?" said Frank.

"There are a lot of animals here. We have big brown grizzlies, black bears, and even polar bears high in the mountains around mountain lakes. We have mountain lions, bobcats, and all kinds of wildlife!" said the realtor.

"Have there been any bears breaking into homes here?" said Elsie.

"No, I've never heard about any bear break-in issues here, but you will see them walking around out here with their cubs once in a while. Just keep your distance, and they will not bother you. Right now, the bears are going into hibernation because winter is coming. I have not seen a bear around here in over a year. The bears are high in the mountains in mid-November. Do not leave food outside, and make sure your trash is covered because the bears will get into your trash at night. Bears rarely come into residential areas. You may never see them. Let's go inside and sign the mortgage agreement so you can enjoy your new home."

Frank and Elsie signed the papers and began moving in.

About a week later, just before Thanksgiving, Frank and Elsie were all moved in and settled. Thanksgiving, celebrated in late November in the U.S., is held on October 10th in Canada.

The night before Thanksgiving in the U.S., Elsie cooked a turkey for the next day's meal and left it in the oven heating on low before she went to bed so the turkey could simmer overnight.

Elsie and Frank were sleeping when suddenly they heard a big crash! A big brown grizzly bear broke into their home, smashing down the front door. It entered the kitchen, knocking over a table and chairs, opened the oven door, and grabbed the turkey, eating it in one bite!

Then the bear opened the refrigerator, tearing the door off. It started eating all the Thanksgiving fixings and throwing food, milk, and juice out of the refrigerator, making a big mess!

When Frank heard the crash, he grabbed his shotgun and slowly made his way downstairs. He saw the bear going through the refrigerator and shot the bear in the head! The bear ran out of the house, and Frank shot the bear in the rear as it ran away. Frank chased the bear and shot it again in the rear.

Elsie came downstairs with a baseball bat, and she cried, "Oh my God! Did a bear break into our house!?"

"Yes, it did—a big brown grizzly!" said Frank.

"Look at this place! It looks like a tornado struck!" Elsie cried.

The front door, picture window, and a big wall were broken through where the bear broke in! The oven door and refrigerator door were torn off, and all the food was eaten, with milk and juice spilled all over the floor. The kitchen table and chairs were busted into pieces!

"Elsie, we need to call the realtor, and they have to put us up in a hotel until this house gets fixed. The realtor will have to give us another home, or we'll go back to New Mexico."

Then Frank called the police to report the damage, and the realtor came over. The Coopers later went to a hotel.

CHAPTER 2
THANKSGIVING BEARS!

Bears know it's Thanksgiving in the US or Canada and it's time to break in homes and restaurants and eat plenty of food before going into hibernation for the winter and come out on Easter to get the salmon in the rivers!

At 11:02pm the night before Thanksgiving, a big brown grizzly broke into a dumpster behind a restaurant in Seattle eating what was inside and making a big mess breaking into boxes! A cop was riding by and saw the bear and he got out of his car and pulled his gun out of his holster and shot the bear in the ass three times, and the big brown bear ran away into the woods! Lucky this restaurant was closed for the evening.

12:02am a bear broke into a car, smashing the driver's side window to get in. The car was parked in a parking lot.

At 1:02am, a big brown bear broke into a closed bakery crashing through a door eating all the cakes, muffins, donuts etc... The bear set off the alarm and the Seattle Police arrived and shot the bear in the ass with his gun! The bear ran out carrying a box of donuts and ran away! The bakery was left in a big mess!

One hour later a bear broke into a farmhouse/barn attacking a horse, the time was 2:02am Pacific Time. The horse was found dead a half hour later and the barn was damaged and the rest of the animals in there ran away!

At 3:02am is when Frank and Elsie Cooper's home was broken into.

At 4:02am a bear broke into an ice cream parlor jumping through a window and ate all the ice cream opening freezers and emptying all the containers and eating all the cones then the bear exited the same window it broke into leaving the place a mess!

At 5:02am a big brown grizzly and 4 cubs broke into a farm attacking farm animals while farm workers were feeding them! The bears attacked pigs, cows, chickens, wild turkeys for, THANKSGIVING, horses, goats, birds and several other farm animals! The Farm workers with shotguns were shooting the bears; killing the cubs and mama, bear was shot dead in the head! The bears were torched over a fire pit for a meal later!

At 6:02am a black bear broke into a Starbucks Coffee Shop, smashing down the front door and jumped over the counter smashing down all the coffee tanks and drinking the coffee in all flavors! Then the bear was sucking up its coffee mess! People were in there screamed hysterically when the bear crashed into the coffee shop!

"AHH!" When the bear jumped over the counter, the customers were able to run out! The manager struck the bear in the head with a heavy bowl and ran out the back door! Then the bear exited the coffee shop. Two girls were coming in, saw the bear run out the exit it smashed through, and the girls screamed and ran back to their cars!

At 7:02am, a big brown grizzly broke into a school and made a big mess knocking things over, setting off the alarm. The police arrived, and one cop said to another, "Someone broke into Charles Bentley High School at 7am on Thanksgiving morning!" The police saw a door busted at the main entrance; the other policeman said, "It looks like a bear, or a moose broke into the school!" The alarms were ringing, and the police drew their guns and went in looking for the intruder! The bear broke into classrooms but found nothing it wanted, knocking over desks and chairs. Then it crashed into the library, but bears don't like books; it just made a mess throwing books around like a madman! Then it broke into the gym, shooting basketballs and kicking them like soccer balls! The police found the bear in the gym, throwing up half-court shots, and gunned the bear down dead! The Seattle Animal Rescue League arrived to remove the dead bear. The damage was so bad, the school looked like a tornado went through inside, and the school would need to be knocked down!

At 8:02am, a big brown grizzly broke into the Vancouver International Airport and ran into a storage area, tearing open bags leaving the baggage claim area before being loaded onto the plane. The airport ground traffic workers went into the storage area to load baggage into carts and saw the bear ripping open bags and making a catastrophic mess! The workers chased the bear out, throwing things at it! The bear ran into the baggage compartment area inside the plane, and the baggage workers closed and locked the door, trapping the bear inside.

The Animal Rescue League from Canada arrived to tranquilize the bear when the baggage shoot opened. When the bear ran out, it was shot and removed.

"Good morning and happy holidays! Flight 212, departing from Vancouver International Airport to Montreal, has been canceled because a bear broke into the baggage area. Several bags were damaged. Please stand by and wait for your name to be called before proceeding to baggage claim. Sorry for the inconvenience," said the airport staff.

"How did a freakin' bear break into an airport?!" said the airport officials.

At 9:02am, a bear broke into a closed bowling alley, setting off the alarms. The bear grabbed bowling balls and threw them down the lanes across the bowling alley. Some balls were rolled, and some were tossed like missiles! The bear threw a few strikes before the police arrived and shot the bear dead! While the police started shooting, the bear ran down the lane, sliding into the pin pit and knocking them over for a strike. The police opened fire at the bear for a double strike!

At 10:02am on Thanksgiving Day, a big brown grizzly broke into a high school football game with two cubs in Seattle. A banner was placed in front of the scoreboard for the home team football players to crash through to celebrate the Thanksgiving football game. The banner read: "Covid Regional High School vs. Seattle Metro High School in the Thanksgiving D2 Playoff Semi-Final Game." The large crowd was cheering, waiting for the team celebration, when suddenly, a big brown grizzly and her two cute little cubs crashed through the banner before the football players! The unexpected surprise shocked the crowd, and screaming spectators ran out of the stadium in all directions! The bears jumped into the stadium and ran for the exits, chasing people. The bears jumped into the concession stands, helping themselves to the food. The football team came out, and the coaches said, "Get back into the school. Bears broke into the stadium!" After the bears cleaned up all the food, they ran away, taking down the scoreboard before running back into the woods, leaving a big mess behind.

At 11:02am, a bear broke into a church while a service was going on. People screamed and ran out of the church! The church pastor struck the black bear in the head with a brick, and it ran out of the church! The bear regained consciousness and ran up to the altar, knocking things over, drinking all the wine, and eating the communion! The bear was so drunk that it passed out, laying on the altar. The pastor cried, "Close all doors and close them quick! The bear is still inside the church!" The bear regained consciousness and started playing the piano, sitting on the organ until it broke in two, then it pooped and peed on the altar before exiting the church, crashing through a side door, and getting away!

At 12:02pm on Thanksgiving Day, a big brown grizzly broke into a pizza joint while the owner was baking and making pizzas and grinders. The big brown bear could smell the good cooking and crashed into Vancouver House of Pizza right through a window in the kitchen. The cook said, "Oh my freakin' God!" and ran out the back door. The bear ate all the freshly made pizzas and sandwiches, making a mess out of the joint before running into the main restaurant. Customers in the restaurant saw the bear behind the counter, knocking over pans, dishes, and boxes looking for more food to eat! The customers ran out of the pizza joint like bats out of hell! The bear jumped over the counter into the restaurant area, breaking down tables and chairs and eating food left behind. Finally, the big brown grizzly stood up on its hind feet, beating its chest and roaring away after it got enough food to eat! The owner came back into the pizza joint with a shotgun and opened fire at the bear until the beast was dead! The owner fired several bullets at the bear, splattering its guts all over the place!

At 1:02pm, a bear broke into a restaurant in Seattle—another grizzly, and a big one too! A Thanksgiving meal was being served at the Boat Gate Restaurant, located at a seaport away from bear country. But this huge brown grizzly had other ideas! The restaurant was packed with customers when suddenly, the giant bear ran across the parking lot like a freight train and barreled its way through the front door with no warning into the restaurant! The customers had no time to react!

The very hungry brown grizzly crashed into tables, eating food and people! The bear ate all the food on the tables, biting people while they fled, trying to get out, and the bear bit arms and legs off of people, but it does not taste as good as all the turkey dinners. The owner shot the bear with a pistol gun from behind the counter, making the hungry bear even madder! A little pistol is not going to kill a mega grizzly! The bear jumped over the counter while being shot with several bullets and had the owner for a meal, biting off his head and eating his body! Then the bear opened oven doors while turkeys were cooking, stealing the turkeys until it gets its belly full! Survivors called police on their cell phones. A mob squad arrived with big guns to kill the fuckin thing!

At 2:02pm, a bear broke into a mall, chasing people and running to the food court because it wants some food to eat! A mall cop shot the bear. The bear ran under a row of Christmas trees to hide, but the mall police trapped the bear and shot it dead!

At 3:02pm, a bear broke into a movie theater, crashing

through the front door and running to the concession stand for a quick meal! The people there screamed and ran out of the theater! The bear ransacked the concession stand, eating the food. Suddenly, police came into the theater shooting the bear. The bear ran into the movie theater while a movie was playing; It was a kids' movie. The bear ran down the aisles and the police were chasing the bear, and the poor little children ran out of the theater like a bat out of hell, screaming and crying! The bear jumped through the movie screen, and the police trapped the bear and killed it!

At 4:02pm, a bear and her cubs broke into a laundromat, chasing screaming people out. The bear got into people's laundry, making a big mess! One of the cubs opened a dryer door, drying clothes, and the cub jumped inside! The manager chased the bear out, striking it in the ass with a baseball bat, and closed the dryer door, and the cub was spinning inside the dryer. The owner struck the other cubs with a baseball bat! He said, "Now get out!" The cub inside the dryer fell out and was trying to get its balance, and the owner smacked the cub with the baseball bat, knocking the little young fella out! Then he dragged the wobbling cub out of the laundromat and closed and locked the door. Then the battered bears ran off!

At 5:02pm, a big brown grizzly broke into a fish market. The manager said, "Oh my fuckin God! Here comes a big brown bear!" The bear smashed down the front door and it started eating the fish and tearing the place apart! The bear knocked over fish tanks, eating the fish and spilling water all over the floor. The store clerk opened the freezer, and the bear ran into the freezer; The clerk closed the freezer door, trapping the bear inside. The bear helped itself to the frozen fish, eating as much as it could until its belly was filled! The manager called for help to get the bear out of the fish market. The bear smashed open the freezer door and ran out of the fish market.

At 6:02pm, a bear broke into a campsite, breaking into cabins looking for food. A turkey was cooking in an oil cooker, and the bear knocked it over, spilling the oil, and it grabbed the turkey and ate it whole with one bite! Then it went to its business out in the woods.

At 7:02pm, a bear broke into a hockey rink, smashing concession stands down looking for food; It had plenty of candy to eat because there's no game tonight!

At 8:02pm, a bear running like a freight train smashed through a side window of a McDonald's and jumped over the food counter, eating all the burgers, chicken, and fries. The bear was eating the fries and chicken out of a boiling violator. People ran out of the McDonald's like a bat out of hell! The kitchen workers threw a hot pan of oil in the bear's face, then ran out a back door to safety, but it doesn't faze the bear, it's going to eat! Eat! And eat! Until all the food is gone.

At 9:02pm, a bear broke into a bar and everyone there ran for cover to get away! The bear jumped over the counter, knocking down bottles and binge-drinking just like people do! The bear chugged down 14 bottles of liquor and threw the bottles, smashing them up against a wall, and ran out of the bar. The bar owner shot the bear in the head with a shotgun! The drunken bear still managed to get away!

At 10:02pm, Thanksgiving night, bears know food's running out! A bear broke into a police and fire station because it smelled of food, big mistake! The bear was gunned down!

At 11:02pm, police and the military with big guns are ready to go to war, chasing the bears back up into the mountains.

Finally, at two minutes after twelve, on Black Friday morning, the bears are returning to hibernation! The grizzlies don't celebrate Christmas!

SECTION 34

50 SHADES OF THE BIGFOOT

Warning: There's a lot of bad language in this story.

Bigfoot creatures are the biggest mother fuckers in the world, and they mate with the Italian Yeti. All monkeys from small to giant fuck more than any living human or creature that moves on the ground. All monkeys are the mother fuckers of the world! If you think that there's no sex high up in the Andes Mountains, you better think again! Here's why. The yetis live in the snow peaked mountains just like polar bears live in the arctic. The yetis come down from the high mountain snow peaks to mate with the bigfoot at the bottom of the snow line into the green forest. If no bigfoots are around, they return to the high peaks and fuck each other! It doesn't matter if they're male or female, yetis go both ways!

A bigfoot giant monkey was roaming around in the Red Wood Forest in a Vancouver Park and met a mega big brown grizzly bear face to face! The bear went after the bigfoot, swiping its front claw and striking the bigfoot in the face. The bigfoot kicked the bear in the head with a very powerful blow! The bear went down realizing it's not the only king of the forest. The grizzly got up and grabbed the bigfoot and pinned the giant monkey on the ground, ready for a meal later. The bear was slapping the bigfoot with its claws but the bigfoot broke free and head-butted the big brown bear and punched the bear in the head with one blow after another until the bear was knocked out!

The bigfoot dragged the unconscious grizzly and threw it up against a rock and fucked the shit out of it! The bear was busted wide open because it was a male. Had it been a female, the bigfoot would have slid in like a Vaseline boat slipping into the Virgin Islands!

Two bigfoot giant monkeys are roaming these redwoods and they're both males. They were friends looking for mates in the forest; They mate each other occasionally! Later another grizzly arrived to challenge the bigfoot.

The bear charged at the bigfoot and the bigfoot picked up a big bolder and threw it at the charging grizzly then it kicked and punched the big brown bear and fucked it until it was dead! The two bigfoot creatures began torturing other animals, fucking them and tearing them open including grizzly bears then eating them and drinking their blood! The giant monkeys tear animals open eating its guts and sucking out the blood for a meat and blood-filled meal.

A tour bus from Seattle came to explore the redwoods in Vancouver. The bus pulled up to a pavilion, and a lady came out. "Hi, my name is David Timberwolf from Seaside Tours from Seattle. I am the bus driver, and we just passed customs."

"Pleased to meet you, Tammy Thomas. I need to see everyone's passport before you get a pass to enter the park. Welcome to B.C. Wildlife Park." The lady went on the bus checking passports, then the bus went on its tour. The bus was going through the park to see all the wildlife here, and when the bus rode up the mountain, the passengers saw terror. Cows, bears, moose, deer, willow beasts, buffalo, wolves, and all kinds of animals torn open, lying dead in the bloody snow, and the mountain vultures from above were feeding on the dead. The passengers started screaming and taking pictures of the dead animals, some got sick!

The bus driver said, "Ladies and gentlemen, we need to cut our tour short because something is happening in these mountains. I'm sorry for the inconvenience." The bus came back down from its tour, stopping at the B.C. pavilion. The driver got out and he went inside.

"Hi, Tammy, you have something attacking your animals up in the mountains. Even bears and buffalo are torn open and the insides torn out, with blood filling the snow, and vultures feeding on the dead. Whatever is doing this is much bigger than a grizzly bear!" said the bus driver.

"Oh! My God!" said Tammy, the park manager. Seaside Tours went back to Seattle. The park rangers closed the park.

"Tom, Paul, and Rex, close the park! Something is killing the animals. We might have a Bigfoot or something from the heavens that's not from Earth!" said Tammy. The park rangers went up the mountain toward the mountain peaks and saw the dead! Rex went with Tammy.

"Oh! My God! Did a chupacabra do this!?" said Rex.

"No, we don't have chupacabra's here, they're in the south," said Tammy. Then they saw a white snowy giant yeti fucking a bigfoot in the ass!

SECTION 35

MESSY MARVIN, THE BEACH BUM

Messy Marvin was a special needs student in school with no high school education, and he dropped out of school at age 16. He was a loner, and he always hung out on beaches in the Los Angeles area, Santa Monica most of the time. He hung on street corners, begging for money to buy drugs and booze. This kid is a freaking bum! He'd hang with gangs who treated him once in a while, and he would eat out of trash cans. He stayed at homeless shelters because he's homeless with no family and no one to go to but gets into trouble. Marvin made some money from friends on the beach, and he went into a restaurant in town to get something to eat. He ordered liver and onions, and he drank a glass of Coke. He started burping and farting in the restaurant while he was eating. A lady sitting next to him said, "Where's your manners!" Marvin just looked at her and he was still burping and farting. Then he laid out a loud burp and everyone was looking at him. Marvin finished his food, and he paid the bill with no tip, and he left the restaurant. The people in the restaurant were talking about him.

The same lady said, "What a sick man he was! He has no class! We have some crazy people here in Santa Monica." Everyone was laughing.

Later, Marvin was drinking a bottle of Jack Daniels on a street corner, and the bottle slipped out of his hands and broke on the sidewalk. Then he threw up, and the puke was all over him! Then he went back to the beach, and he went swimming with his clothes on to wash off his puke. Then he went under a loading dock to have a shit, then he laid down on the sand to go to sleep. When the sun rose, he got up and hit the streets again. Marvin wore a Lakers t-shirt, bell-bottom jeans, and beach sandals; he did not wear underwear. He's a typical California beach bum! Later, he met a homeless woman on the beach, and she saw him crying.

"Are you okay?" she said.

"I need a quick fix!"

"What's your name?" said the woman.

"My name is Messy Marvin."

"Mary Harding, baby."

"Pleased to meet you, Mr. Marvin. I have a joint with me; we can smoke it together," said the woman.

Later, Messy Marvin found a sandwich in the trash on the beach. "Ah! Steak and cheese!" he said to himself. He started eating the sandwich; the pigeons and seagulls fed on it first! Flies were buzzing around the sandwich while he was eating it. Then he threw up! Then he went back to the beach to lay down.

Messy Marvin met this big black girl with big tits walking on the beach and they had sex by the ocean at sunset! Later Messy Marvin went for a walk on the beach after the black girl he was fucking had left! He met the girl he had met earlier on the beach, and they met up with a gang to drink some beers and do drugs. He went to sleep under a boat ramp near the beach for the night.

A man walking by untying his boat at 6 a.m. saw him. He

said, "Hey buddy, you can't be sleeping under there, you have to leave!" Messy Marvin gave him the finger, then he got up and left from under the boat ramp. He was carrying his cut-off jeans, and his t-shirt was covering his private area. He went for an early morning swim, then he put his pants on, and he went into town. He went for a walk in the forest and found some mushrooms. He started eating the mushrooms, pulling them out of the ground. Minutes later, he started tripping! First, he sat down near a big tree, and he saw what looked like the trees coming alive, and the ground started moving. It was because an earthquake was happening! Then he saw all kinds of colors and blurry vision. He saw a deer looking at him, and he screamed, spooking the deer, and it ran off! Then he got up and got lost in the forest. Then it started raining, with thunder and lightning flashes, and the trees and rocks in the woods looked like monsters coming after him as he screamed and cried the night away, stuck in the forest for the rest of the night because he was so high, tripping on the mushrooms! When the sun came up, he managed to find his way out of the forest and back into downtown Santa Monica. He walked into a liquor store and grabbed a bottle of Jack Daniels.

As he started walking out of the liquor store, the cashier yelled at him, "Hey pal, you have to pay for that! It's not Christmas time, you know!" Messy Marvin walked out of the liquor store, and the owner ran out and grabbed the bottle of Jack Daniels off of him.

Messy Marvin ran off! Then he went into a bar and ordered a few beers. He said to the bartender, "Can I run a tab, Miss Greenville?"

"Yes, you may!" she said.

After 9, 16-ounce beers, Messy Marvin passed out because he was pretty drunk. The beer cost $4.50 each, and Messy Marvin saw a bill resting in front of him when he woke up four hours later! $40.50.

"Miss Greenville, I only have $19.53. Can I pay the rest later?"

"Yes, you may," she said. Then Messy left to find out what other trouble he could get into. He went looking for food to eat, going through trash cans, dumpsters, etc.

He was in the back of a restaurant fishing through a dumpster when the owner came out of a back door and said, "Get out of there! And get lost!" Messy did just that! Then he went into a McDonald's and stole someone's order. He walked out and went to the beach to eat his wonderful snack! He had two Big Macs, two McDoubles, two fries, and two strawberry shakes. A $35 value, and he ate it all, not even leaving a crumb for the seagulls as the birds watched him stuff his face! The man waiting for his order at McDonald's was caught sleeping/not paying attention when his order was stolen.

"Hey! Where's order #13? I have been waiting here for half an hour!"

"Order #13 was called a long time ago, sir," said the take-out worker.

"What! Someone stole my fing*** food!"

The man was pissed, and the manager came out. He said, "What did you have?" "I had two Big Macs, two McDoubles, two fries, and two strawberry shakes for my family. You did not see someone steal my fing*** order! What's wrong with this place?!?!?"

"Sir, take it easy. I will make you a new order," said the manager. He was nice, and the man was able to feed his family. McDonald's had to eat the stolen order to help the man, as he wasn't paying attention when the order was left behind. Messy Marvin had enough to eat for a couple of days. Then he went into the same liquor store where he tried stealing a bottle of Jack Daniels the other day. While the clerk had her back turned, Messy tried the trick again, and this time he got away with it! He tucked the Jack Daniels up his shirt, and he calmly walked out, hiding behind a dumpster before making a run to the beach. When Messy walked out of the liquor store, the buzzer went ding-dong, alerting the clerk, but Messy Marvin was long gone! He hid under a big rock to drink the whole bottle of Jack Daniels, and he was drunk for two days. Three days later, Messy Marvin had not finished paying his bar tab at the local bar in town.

"Excuse me, Harry. Did you ever see this weird-looking, wiry-haired man, about 25 years old, who wears a Los Angeles Lakers t-shirt, bell-bottom ripped jeans, and beach sandals? He's a strange character?" said Miss Greenville, the bartender.

"I know who this person is! His name is Messy Marvin, the Con-Artist of Santa Monica! Did you have a problem with him?" said Harry.

"Yes, he hasn't finished paying a $40.50 beer tab. And he owes $20.97," said the bartender.

Don't worry Mary, I will find this dickhead! He hangs around the beach area," said Harry.

Later in the evening, the bar owner Harry was walking on Santa Monica beach, and he saw Messy Marvin sleeping on the beach. Harry kicked him in the ribs, waking him up!

He said, "Mr. Marvin, my name is Henry Hopkins, the owner of Monica Tap, a bar you visited a couple of days ago. You ordered nine beers, and you paid for half of them but I'm here to collect the other half."

"I don't have any money right now, but I will pay the rest of the beer when I get my money," said Messy Marvin.

"I will give you two days to pay the rest of the beer tab, or I will split your fuckin head open!" Then Harry walked away.

Messy went into town, hanging on a street corner posing as a homeless man, and he made $21.00 for the day in tips. He went back to the bar and paid for the rest of the tab. Then he left.

The next day, Messy found a credit card on the ground and he started using it until the card was stopped. He went to a restaurant and ordered a steak and cheese sandwich, then a couple of beers. Then he went to a strip mall to buy some clothes, shoes, and a Los Angeles Lakers hat. He bought shorts, underwear, socks, and some t-shirts with the credit card, spending more than $150. Finally, he went back to the Monica Tap to order more beer, and Harry was behind the bar that night.

"Hi, mister, I paid my tab yesterday. Do you take credit cards?" said Messy.

"No! Cash only! Thank you for paying for the rest of your tab, but I don't want to serve you here anymore! Please leave." Messy left the bar, then he went to the liquor store to buy a big bottle of Jack Daniels.

"Excuse me, sir. This credit card is no good. And your name is not Mary Whitewater," said the clerk.

"She's my girlfriend!"

A girl waiting said, "My name is Mary Whitewater. You stole my fing*** card!" Messy Marvin got arrested and taken to jail.

SECTION 36

THE MISERICORDIA HOUSE

Great Barrington, Massachusetts

The Misericordia House is a mansion with a ghost haunting it late at night. Visitors come to visit and stay here hoping to see this ghost.

A tour bus pulled up from Vermont to visit the bed and breakfast mansion.

"Good morning, ladies and gentlemen. Welcome aboard Vacation Tours Vermont, weekend getaway. First, we will be going on a ferry across Lake Champlain to visit Upstate New York and then a bus trip to Great Barrington, Massachusetts to visit the Misericordia House Mansion where we will stay one night before returning to Poultney, Vermont. My name is Mary Mudham, your tour guide. We will have lunch on the ferry, and dinner tonight at the Misericordia House. Enjoy your trip."

Before evening the bus pulled up to the Misericordia House. "Welcome to the Misericordia House. Come inside and meet the Mother Misericordia. My name is Marie Martha Madonna. Or call me the triple M!"

Before dinner I will take you on a tour through the mansion.

First of all, the Misericordia is gold and silver, and we have a ghost here! This is the living facility with an 18-foot-high Christmas Tree with 20,000 lights. The tree is artificial. We have a natural wood burning fireplace 8 feet wide and 6 feet high. This room is 23 feet high from floor to ceiling with velvet furniture. The Misericordia House has 18 rooms, 6 on each floor, and two restrooms on each floor. This building has 4 floors, the 4th floor is the meeting room, special events etc... There are two restrooms on the 4th floor. We are a bed and breakfast facility, and we serve snacks for lunch, a tea party from 2pm until 4pm and dinner will be served at 6pm. The dinner tonight is Lamb chops, mashed potatoes, corn and peas. Tomorrow morning you will get a full breakfast, before checking out. Check out time is at 11:30am. Before everybody checks in let's finish our tour.

On the top floor is the meeting room and restrooms. We have extra bedding in this room for large crowds. Now the third floor here in room 305. You have two Queen Beds and a bath. All the rooms are the same on each floor throughout the facility. 4 people can sleep in each room, but if you open the sleep sofa, you can sleep 6 in each room. "Whoever sleeps in this room has a good chance of seeing the Mother Misericordia ghost. There is no guarantee that you will see the ghost, but she haunts this room most of the time. She's also been seen by the fireplace at 5 minutes past 3 in the morning. If you see the Mother Misericordia, she may spit at you or make her appearance."

"Mrs. Marie Madonna, will this ghost hurt us?" said a guest.

"We had people knocked out of bed, or pinned to the bed, or slapped in the head, but no serious injuries! You will have to experience her for yourself! You may never see her, or maybe you will; you'll find out when you sleep here tonight!" said the house madam, Marie Martha Madonna.

The guests had dinner, played cards, sang Christmas carols, and enjoyed a nice warm fire in front of the fireplace before going to bed for the evening. The Mother Misericordia made her appearance to this group tonight.

Room 305 sleeps 4 people. A girl woke up and looked at the alarm clock; the time was 3:02 a.m. Three minutes later, the Mother Misericordia appeared in the large French mirror as a heavy-set woman dressed like someone from the 1600s and she had enormous tits with spinning laser lights like Black & Decker lamps shining brightly at the guest in that room. The lights were coming from her nipples, then they turned red like Rudolph the red- nosed Reindeer! The guests all woke up screaming and ran out of the room telling their story.

Room 306 saw nothing. Then the Mother Misericordia appeared in room 304 minutes later, she appeared in the mirror as a bright image, then she came out of the mirror and a set of chubby legs appeared over the beds. The legs opened wide show-ing a mega vagina with shark teeth and it rained on the guests sleeping. Then she fired out a slime spitting all over them, then a bright red light shot out of her clit, then the vagina lowered down on all 4 sleeping in that room opening and closing like she was going to swallow them! When a guest turned a lamp on the ghost disappeared! The Mother Misericordia cunt pinned everyone down in their beds until she was finished! All 4 in room 304 were wet and covered with Chisholm slime and water all over them.

All the beds and the floor were wet in that room. Minutes later the guests ran out of their room to the lounge in front of the fireplace to tell their story.

Later the Mother Misericordia Ghost appeared in room 101, near the front desk. One man from the tour was sleeping in that room. He woke up hearing people talking and laughing when suddenly a pair of big tits glowing green with blue glowing nipples appeared above his bed. When he got up the tits went between his head banging back and forth until it knocked him out of bed with a hard fall! The tits kept bashing the man's head into the bed board for 10 minutes before finally throwing him out of bed! The man was knocked out! A bell rang alerting the desk clerk. The clerk heard the man screaming and she entered the room and saw the man out cold laying on the floor. The bed board was broken in half and the room was a mess. The superior of the Misericordia House called 911 to come get the injured man and guests who were injured.

The ghost appeared in room 205. A family of 6 was sleeping in that room. First, a young boy woke up and he saw lights flashing around in the room. Orb lights from a ghost! Then Mother Misericordia appeared in the French mirror with her big tits popping out! The young boy yelled, "Ma! A ghost is in the mirror!" The Mother Misericordia roared like Kathy Bates screaming at James Caan and jumped out of the mirror. She flipped both queen beds over on top of the guests sleeping in them and left the pull-out sofa untouched. The boy was in the pull-out sofa and he was okay watching the lady ghost in shock! The four victims managed to crawl out from under the flipped over beds and they all were okay. The ghost disappeared when she flipped the beds over. The boy turned a lamp on and helped his family get free from under the turned over beds and the six of them got out of that room in a hurry!

Just before 5am the Mother Misericordia appeared in front of the fireplace and she opened her legs and she pissed on the floor then a yellow slime was pouring out between her legs like a waterfall and it went into the fireplace putting the fire out, then she disappeared and never seen again by the Vermont Vacation tours staying there. Rescues, fire trucks, and police arrived at the Misericordia House to check on the injured guests.

The man in room 101 was taken to the hospital with a head injury. The victims, who were haunted by the Mother Misericordia ghost, saw her again in front of the fireplace peeing some kind of load on the floor. The fire went out, the lights flickered, and the power went out after Mother Misericordia disappeared! The witnesses screamed when the place went dark.

The House Superior, Marie Madonna, got a call in the middle of the night when help arrived to assist the injured. She saw police cars, rescues, and a fire truck there. The building was in darkness.

"Are you Marie Madonna?"

"Yes, Sir."

"Great Barrington Police, Officer Jason Brown. What's going on here?"

"We have a ghost here, and she comes and goes every once in a while! This ghost appears as the Mother Misericordia, back in the 1600s when this building was built. She's not known to hurt anyone, but tonight I heard something happened here."

"Eric Andrews, from Vacation Vermont Tours, staying in room 101, was attacked by something in that room, suffering a head injury, and he's in Hannibal Hospital in Great Mercy, Vermont. The room was damaged," said the police.

Marie and the police saw the mess in room 101.

"A ghost is not going to do damage like this!" said the police.

"Oh my God, the beds are broken, and there's a big hole in the wall. The headboard is broken in half. I wonder if a bear broke in during the night. We have a lot of bear sightings around here," said Marie.

NOW FOR BEDTIME STORIES!

"My name is John Dunbar, from Vacation Vermont Tours, staying in room 305."

We saw the Mother Misericordia Ghost and her private parts appeared coming out of a mirror and pinning all four staying in that room in our beds until I put a light on and the ghost disappeared! She appeared as a heavy-set women with a big bust with lights coming out of her. We did not get hurt but it was scary and funny." "My name is Julia Debra. Staying in room 304. We were attacked by a huge vagina with shark teeth opening and closing pinning everyone down in our beds and covered everyone in a thick yellow slime until someone put a light on. The beds and the room were flooded in this shit, and we were covered in it! We just saw the ghost having a shit in front of the fireplace putting out the fire then power was lost, and everything went dark."

My name is David Green, staying in that room. This ghost appeared like a women. She had big legs and a vagina so big came down on top of everyone sleeping in that room and it looked like it was going to swallow everyone. We had to get out of that room in a hurry! She had big tits with lights coming out of her and a giant vagina with shark teeth ready to eat everyone. Funny but very scary and fear of getting hurt."

The guest witnessed in room 304. "Hi, my name is Justin Max and she's my mom Jennifer. We were staying in room 205. I woke up and I saw lights flying around in the room, then I saw this big fat lady ghost in the mirror, and she had big boobs! I yelled, Mom! A ghost in the mirror. Then the ghost came out of the mirror, and she flipped all the beds over dumping my brothers and sisters on the floor. I got up and turned a light on and helped everyone get free from under the turned over beds. Lucky, no one was badly hurt. We got out of that room in a hurry and joined everyone in the lounge. We saw the same ghost crapping yellow in front of the fireplace. She was funny, but scary!" said the boy.

After all the stories were told. The madam of the house put hurricane lamps in the lounge until the power came back on. The fire in the fireplace re-lit by itself on some wood burning under brush. Everyone stayed clear away from the fireplace. The night person madam of the house and Marie Madonna were checking the damage in rooms 101 and 205.

The tour guide was giving instructions to the guest. "Ladies and gentlemen. Just stay here in the lounge and everyone sleep together before everyone gets up for breakfast at 8:30. It's 6:30 and you have two hours before everyone gets up. Everyone stay close together. The rest of the tour will stay in their rooms until check out at 8am." said Mary Mudham, the bus tour guide.

At Hannibal Hospital. "Jimmy Cornhole, Dr. Jeff Decosta. Do you remember what happen to you at the Misericordia House?"

"I saw a women with big boobs changing colors, blue, green and yellow above my bed and she attacked me punching me in the head with her big boobs until the bed board broke and I was thrown up against a wall and the ghostly figure threw me out of bed and that's the last thing I remember! This thing-ghost or whatever you call it, kept attacking me for a long time!"

"Mr. Cornhole, you have quite a bump on your head! You have a concussion, but you will be okay!" said the doctor.

BACK AT THE MISERICORDIA HOUSE. A few minutes after the Misericordia House power came back on shortly after the fire re-lit in the fireplace. By 7am it was getting bright. 8Am the guests were getting up and went to the cafeteria for breakfast. Waffles, pancakes, muffins, sweet bread, bagels, eggs, sausage, ham, home fries, Cheese, crackers, orange juice and coffee/tea was served for a full breakfast-brunch. The ghost victims re-told their stories during breakfast. Then everyone checked out and boarded the bus.

"Ladies and gentlemen. We had some issues here during the night with the Misericordia Ghost as you all heard. We had some injuries and lots of damage! Jimmy Cornhole will not be with us because he was hurt bad and he's in the hospital. Beds got broken, holes in the walls and wet rooms due to a mysterious slime blob and rotten flesh smells have been reported. The Misericordia Ghost showed herself several times showing her private parts to our guest during the night. We are lucky no one was killed that's how much damage she left behind. You wanted to see the

Mother Misericordia Ghost and she made her presence known," said the tour guide on the bus, Mary Madham.

One lady said. "We never saw the ghost staying in room 303. We never heard any noise next door; That's strange."

"The ghost haunts some of the rooms and moves from room to room but she does not go to every room. Some people see it, and some don't. Hope everyone is safe and let's hope Jimmy Cornhole recovers. Everyone has their gatherings, let's go back to Vermont," said the tour guide and the bus left.

BACK INSIDE THE MISERICORDIA HOUSE: "Marie Martha, we need to get a priest or some kind of paranormal investigator in here to bless this building before something really bad happens! I have worked the night shift here for 23 years and I never had a night like this! I saw the ghost a couple of times in my 23 years here,'" said the madam.

ROAD TRIP

CHAPTER 1

A man was building a race car to compete in race car events going across the country. His friend was helping him build this car. The man's dream was to race in the Daytona 500. The man's name was Tom, and his friend's name was Paul, and they were from East Greenwich, Rhode Island. Tom owned the car, and Paul was his helper. They were building an engine ready for racing.

"How fast can this car go, Tom?"

"180 miles per hour! I need to build this car to go a lot faster! I need this car to go at least 300 miles per hour!"

"Tom, that's impossible!"

"I am not going to win races going 180. We need to put jet thrusts in this car to get it to go 300 miles per hour."

"Tom, that's illegal! It's too fast! You're going to crash this car!"

"Paul, when we get through with this car, I may get it to go over 300! We'll do wheelies with this car! I will order the jet thrusts and will go to Max Race Way in New Hampshire to train for the Daytona 500!"

When the car was done, they drove to New Hampshire going 100 miles per hour up Route 495, and they were stopped in Marlboro by the Massachusetts State Police. Fire was coming out of both exhausts before the car stopped and pulled over in the breakdown lane.

The cop came up to the car and said, "May I see your license, registration, and proof of insurance, please?"

The cop took Tom's information and went back to the police car to check for violations, but Tom was clean. He gave Tom back his license, registration, and insurance papers and said, "Why were you going so fast? Are you going to a fire? Route 495 is not a racetrack, you know!"

"Officer, I did not realize I was going so fast. I just finished building this car with my friend Paul, and we're on our way to New Hampshire to train for the Daytona 500 in February."

"You have a few violations here: You were driving 35 miles per hour over the speed limit. Plus, I clocked you going 97 through a construction site, and finally, you're driving an illegal car! You can't drive on 495 with a jet car with fire coming out of the exhaust! The fines here are more than $1,000. But because you have a good driving record with no accidents or previous violations, I will give you a break and a ticket for $150. I think that's fair. Or you can go to Massachusetts State Court and fight the ticket. I would pay the fine if I were you because if you go to court with these charges, the judge may send you to jail, throw away the key, and junk your car! Read the instructions on the ticket and please slow down."

"Yes, sir Officer Richard," said Tom.

Then he made it to Max Race Way in New Hampshire. A 1999 souped-up sports car with jet engine exhaust pulled up to the main gate at Max Speedway.

"Holy shit! Is this a jet car?" said the guard at the gate.

"It's a 1999 super race car Camaro. Tom Hatchet. Do you

remember me: Tom Carol and my best friend Paul Duke, from East Greenwich, Rhode Island? I made arrangements with you about six months ago to practice here for a week and train for the Daytona 500 in February."

"Yes, I do, Mr. Carol. Come in and sign some paperwork, and you can get started. There is an $850 practice fee for one week of unlimited racing, but please, no crashes!" said the gate manager, Tom Hatchet.

Tom's race car was a gem, practicing going around the track several times at a high rate of speed, as Tom, the owner of Max Speedway, was impressed! Fire was coming out of Tom's race car, driving over 200 miles per hour!

Later, a meeting took place.

"Mr. Carol, you look good out there. I like the way you handle the track and burn rubber on your turns. I give you a 10 for sure! But you will have to wait until next year before I hire an agent for you to race the Daytona 500. However, I can get you into the Indy 500 later this summer. But before that, you have to race here at Max Speed Way on Memorial Day and finish in the top five. Before the Indy 500, you have to win one of them before you can think of racing the Daytona 500! If you win the Indy 500, you don't need a checker agent, and you qualify for the Daytona 500. If you win my race instead, you will have to pay a fee for a checker agent, and that's $1,120. What's the name of your car?" said the gate manager, Tom Hatchet.

"My car is called: 'The Road Trip Fire Engine!'" said Tom Carol, the owner.

"Okay, let's fill out the paperwork and credit card fees for the Max on Memorial Day. And good luck. Before the race, your car will get checked out and declared legal for all races. I believe you may win this race with a car like this. And if you do, you will win $50,000," said Tom Hatchet.

CHAPTER 2
TIME TO RACE!

Tom Carol was ready to race the Max New Hampshire Speedway, and his friend Paul was in the press box writing up scouting reports. Scouts from the Indy 500 and the Daytona 500 were there!

"Ladies and gentlemen, welcome to the Max Speedway for today's race. The weather is clear, and it's 64 degrees. Welcome a new member in car #1: Road Trip Fire Engine! The track is dry, and it's 100 laps before the winner takes home the checkered flag and $50,000. Start your engines! Good luck! And they're off!" said the racetrack announcer.

Tom's car took off like a bullet, rounding every lap without looking back! Fire was coming out of the exhaust, keeping the rest of the 100 cars behind him to avoid getting burned! Tom's car, Road Trip Fire Engine, owned the track, swerving, burning rubber, spreading smoke, and using his killer speed to keep the rest of the cars at bay. Behind him, no other cars had a chance to pass as he raced at 199 miles per hour, driving all over the track and going up the speed wall. Tom's car sounded like a jet, going like a bat out of hell!

He won the race easily, and all the spectators cheered! One man yelled, "Car #1 is illegal!!!!!!" The management team and checkered flag directors said, "Car #1 is legal."

The Manager, Tom Hatchet, said, "Congratulations! You are the Max Speedway Champion! Come back next year!"

Later, Tom Carol raced the Indy 500 during the summer. At a meeting at Lucas Oil Stadium in Indiana, Tom went to the main office.

"Good afternoon. My name is Tom Carol, the New Hampshire Max Raceway winner back in May. I have a meeting with Mr. Harold Spark about racing the Indy 500."

"Pleased to meet you. My name is Paula Penn. Have a seat, and I will contact him."

A man came out and introduced himself.

"Harold Spark. Mr. Tom Carol from East Greenwich, Rhode Island; the Max Speedway winner back in May."

"Pleased to meet you. I heard a lot of good things about you, and you have a wild jet car Camaro! You have what we need in this race. Let me tell you a little bit about the Indy 500. We have a big track like the Daytona 500, and you will go 500 laps, the same as the Daytona 500. Your car number will be 13, sitting in that spot, and if you finish in the top five, you will qualify for next year's Daytona 500. Your agent at the Daytona 500 will be Mr. Robert Black Senior. He will be scouting you throughout this race. Your friend Paul will be writing up reports to get you ready for the next race.

The race is not here in Lucas Oil Stadium—this building is a football stadium. You bring your car to the track the night before, and you will be shuttled to and from your hotel to the track three hours before the race. Once again, my name is Harold Spark; Indy 500 Agent. Good luck!"

Tom did some practice rounds hours before the race, then came the real deal!

"Ladies and gentlemen! Welcome to the Indy 500! Start your engines! We are on our way!" said the announcers.

The checkered flags waved, and the race was on! Tom's car, Road Trip Fire Engine, lived up to his dream. After several laps on a dry track, late afternoon thunderstorms arrived with heavy rain, blinding racing viewers. But Tom's car? No problem! He fell behind 31 cars but started getting aggressive, cutting cars off the track and hitting a few cars. Then he did a wheelie, jumping and flying in the air over six cars until he was way ahead. He finished second in the race.

"Your winner: Car #10, 'Lucas Oil 10!' Second: Car #13, 'Road

Trip Fire Engine!' Third: Car #20, 'Have Cruise.' Fourth: Car #8, 'All Eights!' And finally, fifth: Car #3, 'Juice Rider!'" said the announcer.

Everyone cheered for Car #13, "Road Trip Fire Engine." The crowd went crazy; they loved Tom's jet car!

Next, he raced the Daytona 500, and the crowd gave Tom's car a standing ovation! Tom's car was number 2 in this race.

When the race started, Tom's car, Road Trip Fire Engine, was leading most of the way until late in the race. His fiery car caused some serious issues: hitting cars, running them off the track, doing wheelies, jumping over cars, and crashing cars into the sideboards and over the railing fences into the crowd. Cars were crashing and burning.

Finally, Tom's car was bowled over by several cars crashing into him, dragging his car along the burning track, and Tom was killed in the Daytona 500.

DOGS VERSUS CATS AT THE ANIMAL SHELTER

The Bryant University Animal Shelter was bustling with activity, known for its variety of animals, especially bulldogs. A couple walked in one sunny afternoon, looking to adopt a dog.

"Welcome to the Bryant University Animal Shelter," said Eric Brown, the shelter owner.

"Hi, my name is Robin Boots, and this is my friend Mike Hunt," said Robin. "We're looking to adopt a bulldog. What exactly is a Bryant Bulldog?"

"The Bryant Bulldogs are the university's mascot," Eric explained. "Here, we have all kinds of bulldogs. Over here is a French Bulldog, though they can be a bit cheeky. We also have Boston Terrier bulldog mixes, full-breed bulldogs, and many others. And if bulldogs aren't for you, we have plenty of cats and other animals as well."

Robin smiled and pointed to a cage. "We like this dog here."

"That's a German Bulldog puppy. They can grow quite large," said Eric as he unlocked the cage.

"We'll take him," Robin said with enthusiasm.

Eric handed them the puppy, who eagerly kissed the couple and wagged its tail, already forming a bond with its new owners.

As the shelter closed for the evening, the dogs erupted in a chorus of barks: "Ruff, ruff, ruff!" The cats joined in with a cacophony of "Meow! Meow!" Puppies yelped, the German Shepherds growled and barked, stomping their paws, and the beagles and wolf dogs howled long into the night: "Ooooo-hhhh!" The shelter echoed with the sounds of restless animals.

The next morning, Mary Thunderhead, the day-shift animal keeper, arrived early to feed and clean. Just as she finished her rounds, a truck pulled into the lot, and two health inspectors stepped out.

"Good morning. We're from the New England Animal Inspection Company (NEAIC). My name is Vivian Mello, and this is my partner, Gloria Mead. We're here to ensure your shelter is clean and that the animals are well cared for."

Mary greeted them politely. "Good morning. Please, let me show you the facility."

She guided the inspectors through the shelter, showcasing the dogs, cats, and small pets like birds, hamsters, rabbits, and even white rats.

However, Vivian frowned as she heard faint noises from downstairs. "I hear other animals. May we look around further?"

Mary hesitated but relented. "Sure, follow me."

As they descended into the basement, Vivian gasped. "Mary, you have illegal animals down here! Raccoons, bobcats, foxes, fisher cats, coyotes, wolves, and even hyena puppies? And what's this? Hawks, bald eagles, and monkeys? This shelter is only licensed for dogs, cats, and small pets!"

Mary protested, "We don't have lions, tigers, or bears!"

"That's hardly comforting," Vivian snapped. "This sign— 'WILD ANIMALS TO FEED THE DOGS'—is outrageous! You have one week to remove all these wild animals, or we'll shut this place down. Everything upstairs is fine, but this basement is a disaster."

The Animal Rescue League promptly arrived to remove the wild animals, and Eric Brown came in to oversee the cleanup. By evening, the shelter was quiet again. All the animals were fed, and the staff prepared to leave.

Unfortunately, three cages were left unlocked: one holding a bulldog, another a Boston Terrier, and the last a tiger-striped cat.

Late that night, the tiger cat slipped out of its cage and began prowling the shelter. The bulldog followed, growling and ready to pounce.

A fierce fight ensued: the tiger cat slashed at the bulldog's eyes, and the bulldog retaliated with bites. The cat clawed furiously, ripping the bulldog's ears, but the bulldog refused to back down. Blood and fur flew as the two animals battled.

Meanwhile, the Boston Terrier watched the chaos from the safety of its cage, smart enough to stay put.

When the dust settled, the tiger cat limped away, victorious but battered. The bulldog lay defeated, whimpering in the corner.

It seemed that the Bryant Bulldogs had lost this round—badly.

MRS. DOUBTFIRE'S BOARDING HOUSE

CHAPTER 1

Mrs. Doubtfire's Boarding House is a mental institution for crazy people, like Messy Marvin, the Santa Monica, California, beach bum—he's here! People are looking for work here through help-wanted ads outside the building, TV ads, newspapers, walk-ins, etc. After several people filled out applications for work, a meeting and a video about the facility were held in the auditorium.

"Ladies and gentlemen, my name is Sister Mary Marie Parkinson. I am the head manager here at Mrs. Doubtfire's Boarding House, located at 1099 Pinchnerve Street, La Jolla, California, Suite #300. After all the paperwork is filled out, we will see a brief video about what we have here, and I will explain the details after the brief film. Follow me to the auditorium. Everyone grab a seat and watch the video," said Sister Parkinson.

After the movie, Sister Parkinson spoke again.

"Okay, after watching this 30-minute video, this is what we have here! Mrs. Doubtfire's Boarding House is a mental institution, and I expect a multitask work effort here! We are a hospital. We have a jail here, an isolation ward for crazy people and animals. We have psychiatric patients and animals we deal with here.

I need doctors, nurses, bounty hunters, animal control units, police officers, bouncers, lawyers, and maintenance workers for everything: plumbing, electricians, carpenters, painters, custodians, etc. If you apply for a custodian position, you'll be cleaning up puke more than once a day!

I need teachers, mental health counselors, drivers, and firemen. We're open 24 hours a day, and there are three shifts for all workers:

- The night shift starts at 11:02 PM and ends at 7:30 AM.
- The first shift starts at 6:35 AM and ends at 3:00 PM.
- The second shift starts at 3:00 PM and ends at 11:30 PM.

You have a 25-minute lunch-supper break and two 15-minute coffee-rest breaks. Anyone caught texting or on their phones during company time, unless it's an emergency, will get a warning first. If it happens a second time, you will be written up and sent home. If you are caught a third time, you will be fired.

I run a strict workforce here at Mrs. Doubtfire's Boarding House, and I expect everyone to follow the rules. We have no union to help you. It's just like playing baseball: you mess up three times, you're out!

We are working in a facility with crazy people and wild animals. We don't have lions, tigers, bears, or bigfoots here, but we do have animals from the wildlife of California.

Five years ago, the Boardman Institute in Connecticut closed and moved here to La Jolla. The Boardman Institute was the house of the devil, and now it's all here! You will deal with the workforce—it's not going to be an easy place to work. You will be paid good money to work here. If you don't think you can handle it, get out!

Yesterday morning, a groundskeeper was killed when a special-needs boy hit him in the head with a brick. These are the kinds of people and animals we deal with here. You have to pay attention, be aware of your surroundings, and be ready for the unexpected.

The animal care unit is required to carry a gun because some of the wild animals here can kill you! We have mountain lions and some very aggressive monkeys. Occasionally, animals may break loose from their cages and attack you.

Last week, a monkey killed a young boy in the playground. I suggest everyone carry a can of mace with them when they come to work in case they get attacked.

Ward 5 is the worst place to work because you have mentally unstable individuals—kids may attack, throwing everything they get their hands on, even biting you like a wild animal! Just look at what happened to the groundskeeper last week. We have kids with serious problems here.

Good luck, and I will contact those who are qualified for the open positions. Any questions?"

"My name is Gary Barry, from Worcester, Massachusetts. The Boardman Institute in Connecticut was haunted. The building had many ghosts there!"

"I don't know about that because I don't believe in ghosts. We have had many accidents here with kids getting hurt, killed, and attacked by animals, like what happened in Connecticut. I have not seen anything strange like ghost sightings here," said Mary.

"Jimmy Wood from San Francisco. You have a jail, hospital, and a mental institution with crazy people and wild animals! What else do you have here?"

"We have a school with dorm rooms in this facility. We have

a safe place here if you follow the rules and regulations," said Mary Parkinson.

CHAPTER 2
QUESTIONS AND ANSWERS, THEN ACTION

"Mary, why was this boarding house named after Mrs. Doubt-fire?" said one lady.

"The name came after a summer camp with special needs children got out of control, and the only way to control their issues was to play the movie *Mrs. Doubtfire* to calm them down when they got violent, upset, etc. A second reason is the way the movie was made—it helps children understand how to behave. By watching this movie, I want people here to learn how to follow instructions," said Mary.

11:02 PM: A boy was throwing up in the hallway, and a custodian had to clean it up!

12:02 AM: Messy Marvin, held in the homeless detention cell in the psychiatric ward, was trying to escape. He managed to pull a loose brick out of a wall in the detention room, smash the knobs and locks on the door with the brick, and break it off. He escaped! He ran down a stairwell, out of a fire door, setting off the alarms, and into the night. Messy Marvin was on his way back to Santa Monica—he's got a long escape route.

Nurses and security guards went to the staircase where the alarm sounded. Then, another team in the detention unit found the empty room, the damaged door, and broken pieces of brick on the floor.

"Jesus Christ! Messy Marvin from LA broke out! He's a dangerous homeless beach bum from the Los Angeles area, and he needs to be found and locked up again!" said a security guard.

"Look here—he scaled the brick wall in the room, loosening up a weapon to get out," said another security guard.

1:02 AM: A boy was shooting baskets in the gym, and he was caught by a nun. The nun escorted him back to his room in Ward 5.

2:02 AM: Two teens—a boy and a girl—were caught having sex in the same stairway where Messy Marvin broke out. A nun made the sign of the cross and broke them up.

The young girl managed to break free and run back to her room. The nun slapped the boy in the face, but the boy punched the nun in the mouth until she was bleeding. Then, he kicked her in the shins and said, "You f-*ing* c***!" He broke free and ran back to his room—again in Ward 5, where all the mentally unstable children are housed.

Security put the boy and girl in isolation detention rooms. The boy had to be put in a straitjacket. The young girl spat in the nun's face. The nun pushed her aside and locked her up.

"We have some crazy people here!" said a security guard.

3:02 AM: A pit bull broke out of its cage in the animal unit, surprised the animal keeper, and bit him in the leg. The keeper managed to get back to the office with the dog clinging to his leg. He grabbed his gun and shot the dog dead! He was taken to the hospital unit to be treated.

4:02 AM: A thunderstorm caused lightning to strike a propane storage unit, which exploded like a bomb! The fire department arrived to put the fires out. The blast woke everyone up in the neighborhood!

5:02 AM: A police officer was sleeping in a recliner in the lounge—he's not supposed to be sleeping! A young Ward 5 boy managed to sneak up on the cop, grab the gun out of his holster, and shoot him in the head, killing him! The boy shot the cop twice, then returned to his room with the officer's gun.

The night madam heard, *Bang! Bang!* She ran to the lounge

and saw the police officer's head blown off; his body slumped in the recliner! She screamed, "AHH!" for 45 minutes before help arrived.

"Oh, my dear God! What's happening here? There's blood everywhere!" said a nun.

"Sister Delores Marie, you couldn't hear me screaming all this time?"

"I was taking care of a sick patient on the third floor until I heard you screaming near the north staircase, Sister Madam Donna Gold."

"Officer Jayson Brown was just murdered, or he shot himself because I don't see his gun. I checked the area here, and there's no sign of a break-in," said Madam Donna Gold.

"Maybe Messy Marvin killed him! He broke out of his detention cell during the night, and there's a manhunt going on right now looking for him!" said Sister Delores Marie.

The body was removed later on. Several staff members arrived to witness the dead police officer.

6:02 AM: The body was finally removed. A group of nuns and security searched the facility for a possible intruder.

7:02 AM: Sister Mary Marie Parkinson arrived, hearing about all the problems that occurred during the night. A bee was buzzing around her head when she arrived for work.

"If Messy Marvin was able to break out of a jail and get away, he probably killed Officer Jayson Brown and has his gun!" she said.

8:02 AM: The search for Messy Marvin was called off. "He's nowhere near the facility; he's gone!"

A nun was trying to wake the children up for breakfast, but she had a difficult time with one young boy.

"Come on, Danny, get out of bed! Danny! Get up! I'm going to ask you one more time—get out of bed, or I am going to drag you out of bed!"

"Fuck you, Sister Ivan!" He pulled a gun from under his pillow and shot the nun in the head, killing her instantly! The time was 9:02am. Then he got up and he shot the nun again between her tits! Other nuns and nurses heard the gun shots and saw blood coming out of Danny's room and Danny oh! Boy! Came out like a mad man, killing a nurse and another nun before a third nun was able to knock the gun out of his hands and tackle the boy. She tied him up and put him into a detention cell until he was arrested by police!

Several rescues arrived to remove the dead bodies. Madam Sister Mary Parkinson was shocked about the shootings. "This is bad!" She cried.

"Who's this young boy?" said a police officer to Madam Parkinson.

"His name is: Daniel Oh boy." She cried.

"He killed four people including Officer Brown in here, with this same gun firing 6 shots!" said the police officer who made the arrest.

A young girl grabbed a baseball bat and hit another girl in the head, and she almost killed her! The time was 10:02am. A nun grabbed the attacker, and the injured girl was taken to the hospital. A crazy adult man broke into Sister Mary Parkinson's office and stole a set of keys and took off in a truck and drove away. The time was 11:02am.

Minutes later the crazy Ward 5 man crashed he truck into a tree and burst into flames! He managed to get out of the truck and run away! The truck was a maintenance truck. Later police found the burning truck with nobody inside. One nun said to Sister Parkinson. "Ruby Boil is missing, and a maintenance truck was stolen from the lot and your office was broken into."

"What!" said Sister Parkinson. The ward 5 kids were in the cafeteria for lunch and a brawl broke out between boys and girls throwing punches, kicking one another and throwing food around! The time was 12:02pm.

A man hunt for Ruby Boil during lunch was unsuccessful! He's long gone! Maybe he went looking for Messy Marvin! The Mrs. Doubtfire Boarding House was surrounded with police all night and all day. Two patients broke out, and four people have been dead since 11pm last night! At 1;02pm police were making an arrest from the ward 5 cafeteria brawl. Helicopters were flying around, and police cars were out looking for Ruby Boil and Messy Marvin. The time was 2:02pm.

They're hiding somewhere. Finally Ruby Boil was found hiding under a rock at La Jolla Beach one hour later. At 3:02 pm. He was hand cuffed and taken back to the boarding house and locked up in a jail cell. Messy Marvin is gone!

4:02pm, there was an earthquake, and the windows rattled at the boarding house. "Did you feel that!? Sister Parkinson."

"Earthquake!" She said.

At 5:02pm, the cafeteria was guarded by police in case more fights broke out. At 6:02pm another brawl broke out in the Ward 5 Unit. A group of kids were fighting and police and the facility workers, nuns and nurses had to break it up, but it got out of control and the national guard was called in to help at 7:02pm.

The fight was under control an hour later. Arrests were made at 8:02pm! Bad boys and girls had to be hand cuffed and put in jail at 9:02pm.

At 10:02pm The power went out and it came back on one hour later. Someone is fucking around; Maybe the Mrs. Doubtfire Boarding House is haunted from the Boardman Institute in Connecticut. A late-night meeting was held with Madam Sister Mary Parkinson with the night shift workers. "Ladies and gentlemen. The Doubtfire is getting out of control and changes will be made. First all the animals will be removed and taken to a zoo. The dogs and cats will be taken to a local California animal shelter. Then we will have around the clock police presence and the national guard on patrol, 24 hours a day. The last 24 hours were catastrophic, and I hope it doesn't continue! I am thinking of closing this facility if these bad things continue to happen. I don't believe in ghosts, but I begin to wonder about what happened two minutes after every hour since we took over the boardman Institute, because it happened there. Messy Marvin is still missing. We need prayers!" said Madam Mary Marie Parkinson.

SECTION 40

POT PLANE C-130 CRASH

A soccer game was underway at a school near an open field not far from a residential area when a four-propeller C-130 plane flew very low over the school. The plane crashed and burst into flames! The plane was loaded with bales of marijuana, and the victims and attack dogs onboard were killed!

Before the crash, the announcer at the soccer game was introducing the teams:

"Good afternoon, ladies and gentlemen, and welcome to Resurrection Regional High School and the Garden City Wildcats here in New Jersey! Please rise for the playing of the National Anthem."

Suddenly, the plane roared low over the high school, flying just above the soccer game, before disappearing behind a cluster of trees. Then: *Ba-BOOM!*

It was worse than a gasoline truck crashing into a nitroglycerin plant! The plane exploded with the force of a nuclear bomb. The smell of pot began to fill the air! Spectators at the game ran toward the burning plane, inhaling the smoke, getting high, and eventually passing out!

The game was stopped because the smell of marijuana overtook the field, causing players, coaches, and fans to pass out.

People began calling emergency services from their cell phones to report the crash.

Police, rescue units, and fire trucks arrived at the scene. Medical helicopters landed to search for survivors, but everyone onboard was already dead. The smell of marijuana had reached the school. Teachers, staff, and students opened all the windows and doors to let the strong scent in—and they too began passing out from getting too high! The scene looked apocalyptic, with people sprawled on the ground, appearing dead.

The fire department was the first to arrive, wearing respirators to approach the burning plane. However, some firefighters removed their respirators to "get a good high" before fighting the fire! Bales of marijuana were burning in the field where the plane had crashed and broken apart. Some firefighters passed out after extinguishing the flames.

Police and news reporters—**from TV stations and newspapers—**arrived next. They began taking notes and reports, only to succumb to the strong marijuana fumes and collapse like the firefighters.

Rescue workers entered the wreckage wearing respirators and using night vision, as darkness began to fall. Rain started falling, spreading the burning marijuana smoke through nearby towns and neighborhoods.

"Resurrection, New Jersey Police to Luna, Texas Airfield. Flight 1314, C-130 Hurricane Bomber full of marijuana, has crashed into a field in our town. Six people and two attack dogs are confirmed dead. Over."

"I have the message, officer. The pilot must've flown too low because he was too high. Luna, Texas Airfield. Over."

Residents noticed the green mass of smoke spreading through their neighborhood.

"What is that? Is it pollen from the trees?" asked a neighbor.

"No! That's a plume of pot smoke from a plane crash I just heard about on the news. Take a whiff!"

The strong marijuana odor filled the streets, causing car accidents as drivers became impaired. Hundreds of people ran to the crash site, forming lines like they were attending church to "get a good buzz."

A woman hanging clothes in her backyard inhaled deeply and passed out! Residents opened their windows and doors, letting the plume of marijuana smoke fill their homes. Families—adults and kids alike—lay together, passed out from the overpowering fumes.

Eventually, the rain washed the plume away. People who had raced toward the crash site were disappointed to find that the fire department had hosed everything down. The great "high" was over.

Police managed the crowd, turning people away. The fire department sprayed the wreckage with foam to suppress the marijuana fumes. Rescue workers now had to treat and revive hundreds of people who had passed out.

Cars and trucks on the highways continued crashing, as drivers were too high to control their vehicles.

SECTION 41

ARTIFICIAL INTELLIGENCE INTO YOUR BRAIN

Salisbury Air Force Base, Maryland: A military training facility was preparing the United States Air Force on artificial intelligence. A meeting was held in an airplane hangar.

"Good evening, my name is General Matthew Matt from Hartford, Connecticut. All workers stopped here at Salisbury Base due to a possible EMP attack in the United Kingdom. From London to Manchester, England has no power. Nothing is moving—no trains, air, or transportation. No lights, no cell phone use, no cooling or heat, and food's getting scarce due to food shortage. Residents are hunting for themselves on the farms and emptying the rivers and waterways to eat. They are eating insects, roadkill, such as rats, raccoons, foxes, deer, even lions, tigers, and bears, etc.... EMP = "Electromagnetic Pulse." This is a warfare weapon, worse than a nuclear bomb, and it comes from artificial intelligence (AI). AI was a dream in the late 1980s before the first Iraq War, Desert Storm. Now it's a reality! The EMP attack warnings began in 2020 during the COVID-19 pandemic. In May of 2024, the UK was threatened, and the attacks began in late

November 2024 and continued until now, in 2027. The United States has been threatened too, but it's happening in the United Kingdom right now, one town or city at a time. We do not know who's responsible for the EMP attacks. If we have an attack here, nothing will work—no electricity, no phones, computers, or lighting, nothing!!!!!! You can't even drive your car—anything computerized will not work. The world runs by computers! You will be living like the Civil War times or back 10,000 years ago. You hunt during the day and sleep at night. Amish times, etc.... Now, do you want to hear a nightmare in reality? AI is watching you: Your smart TV, phone, computer, UFOs, and street cameras. On June 27, 2024, a UFO crashed in Westport, Massachusetts, in the woods off of Route 88 near Horse Neck Beach. There was nothing on the news about what was found there. The UFO crashed around 5:30 p.m., and alien humanoids were pulled out of the burning wreckage by the United States Air Force and taken to Area 51; that's all we know. There's other life in the universe, and they're AI, maybe better than ours. We will be watching a video on Discovery+ after this meeting about UFOs. We do not know where this UFO came from that crash in Westport, Massachusetts. AI is watching! The government knows everything you're doing. Whether you are fully clothed or naked, AI is watching. You're watching TV while having sex on the couch, AI is watching! If you're talking on your phone, making a drug deal, AI is watching! If you're on your computer, watching porn, AI is watching too! If you go through a red light, a stop sign, or do something you're not supposed to do, AI is watching you! Prostitutes and drug dealers, listen up! Get off the streets! AI is watching you. You can't hide because AI is watching you! If you try to get away from law enforcement, AI is watching you. If you try to hide from Robert De Niro, AI is watching you! Let me tell you a story. Richard and Ruth Sunwater were vacationing in Florida in 1999. The hotel they were staying at had cameras in the bedroom recording every sex act for an hour and a half. About 5 years later, they went to Paris and, while watching a porno movie on TV, saw themselves having sex from Florida. The hotel chain was the same hotel they stayed at in Paris. AI is watching! Richard and Ruth were staying in a timeshare, not a hotel. Robots, drones, cameras, sunlight, and animals: AI is watching! If you are hiding something, be careful because AI has an eye out for you. Before we watch the video about UFOs and Artificial Intelligence, are there any questions?"

"General Matt, sir: Who's the next president of the United States?" said someone in the crowd.

"Artificial Intelligence!" he said.

Then the group watched the movie. {MOVIE: "Welcome to Discovery Productions. Learning about the cosmos and artificial intelligence (AI). We have been visited by other worlds with technology that may be better than ours! UFOs and USOs (Unidentified flying objects and sea objects). Of course, we do not know where they're coming from, but they're landing in the oceans, using water for energy and hydrogen power, and flying at a high rate of speed. These crafts have landed on Earth many times, and alien beings and humanoids have been found. Please watch the video."

SECTION 42

THREE DAY BARBECUE

The Attleboro Elks hold a big event every summer during the first weekend in August. There are several different bands with plenty of food and drinks, and the Elks pack it in every day, called "The Elks Three-Day Barbecue." When you enter, you buy tickets for food and drinks. When ordering beef, steaks, chicken, potatoes, you cook them yourself over fire pits on the property. Shish kebabs are cooked over the fire pits. Hotdogs are steamed and served in a bun. You can order pounds of beef/steaks and bread while buying tickets. One man ordered cheeseburgers, and he cooked them over the fire pit. He was looking at this beautiful lady cooking a chicken and a potato. The man kept stalking the lady until she sat down. Then he went to the bar to order a Jack Daniels on the rocks, and he had a few of them! Picnic tables and carnival booths/tents were set up with games and food being served. The blonde lady went to the game booths while the man watched, drinking his drinks and finishing his cheeseburgers. The man watched every move the pretty lady made. She won a teddy bear.

The man went over to her, and he said, "Congratulations! That's a nice teddy bear! What's your name?"

"Cindy," she said. Then she walked away, and the man followed her, but he kept his distance, stalking her until she sat down by herself, drinking a rum and coke. Then the man sat down next to her, and he said, "Hi Cindy, my name is David Duncan."

"Pleased to meet you," she said.

David put his arm around her, and he said, "Can I buy you a drink?"

Her husband came and pushed the man, David, away. He said, "Hey buddy! Stay the hell away from my wife!"

"Oh, I'm sorry, sir!" And he disappeared. Then he sat down next to another young girl with his legs wide open, showing a bulge in his pants, opening and closing his legs. The girl got up and walked away. Then the man went up to another girl, asking her to dance.

"No, thank you!" she said. He went up to another girl asking her to dance, and he got the same response. He kept asking girls to dance, and they all said, "No!"

The Great Escape was the name of the band playing, a Journey tribute band. He went into the woods to pee, and a police officer caught him and said, "Hey buddy, you can't be doing that, there's porta-johns in the parking lot." The man, David, is being a pain in the ass at this barbecue; he's lucky he didn't get arrested! The cop was being nice.

Later, David exposed himself to a biker girl loaded with tattoos. He unzipped his pants and pulled out his "hotdog" swinging it back and forth, then he put it back in his pants and walked away. The boyfriend biker surprised him from behind, grabbing him by the neck.

"Hey punk, you like pulling your dick out of your pants to impress all the girls? See that lady over there? She's my girlfriend. The next time you do that, I'll cut your cock off and shove it down your throat! Now you go over to her and say you're sorry.

I am letting you off easy. I could have beaten the little shit out of you! Right now. I know you're trying to have fun because you've had a few drinks, but this is not the way to have fun. That's very disrespectful."

"I am sorry, sir."

"Now go over to my girlfriend and say you're sorry." Later, the police came over to him—David.

"Sir, you're going to have to leave and don't come back!"

"Why, officer?"

"Because you're bothering the girls and making a fool out of yourself! Put the drink down! And get out!" The police escorted him off the property. Motorcycles followed. David Duncan is lucky he didn't get his ass kicked the way he acted at the barbecue!

Now another pain in the ass emerges at the Elks barbecue: A tall, red-headed Irish man! What he does, he got away with it. He's got the dough and the dope! He asked the girls to dance, and he got rejections just like David, but he got some dances too! He asked the biker girl for a dance; the same girl David showed his hotdog to! She said, "No thanks, I am with someone." And he walked away, next!

The Great Escape Band was playing the song "Faithfully." The red-headed Irish man was on the dance floor dancing with a girl. The girl had a mini skirt on and she said, "I have no underwear on." The Irish man pulled his hotdog out of his pants and put it between her buns. He burst his hotdog when the song was over! He said, "What's your name?"

"My name is Camille Underleg."

"Pleased to meet you. My name is Rory Celtic. Let's go get a drink and bullshit for a while, and maybe we can hook up sometime," said the tall red-headed Irish man.

Camille and Rory Celtic went to get a drink. The girl he was dancing with is married. Her husband was working the game booths while the redheaded Irishman was fucking her on the dance floor.

Then the Attleboro Elks Barbecue was closing up on Friday night. Rory and Camille were sitting at a picnic table having a drink at closing time and Camille's husband came over to her and he said. "What's going on here!?"

"We're just talking about the barbecue and the bands here. He bought me a drink. This is Rory."

"Pleased to meet you. My name is: Eugene Underleg, Camille's husband."

"Sorry sir: I didn't realize she was a married woman"

"That's okay," said the husband.

"It was nice meeting you sir," said Rory Celtic, the redheaded Irish man. Then he left. The redheaded Irish man got away with this one!

DAY TWO: It was pouring rain, thunder and lightning, but the redheaded Irish man is coming back for more! First, he got two drinks double fisting, Jack Daniels on the rocks and eating beef tips Shish Kabob cooking over the fire pit. Then he's on the move! Wuhan, was the name of the band playing hard rock. Cory was on the dance floor dancing with a black girl also wearing a mini skirt.

He said, "Do you have undies on?"

"No. why do you ask!?" She laughed.

"Because you have sexy legs and a nice ass! Do you like tall redheaded Irish men. I have a foot long hotdog!"

"Yeah baby!" She laughed. "Let's go to my van and we'll smoke a joint. Off they went!

Later a pregnant women was dancing and her water broke and she had the baby right there on the dance floor! The woman is Jewish and the baby's black. Help arrived to help her. It's a good thing the band was taking a break.

Later Cory Celtic, the redheaded Irish man went back to the

barbecue after he finished with the black girl he was fucking! Then he sat down next to another girl with big tits!

He said, "Good afternoon. My name is Rory Celtic."

"Linda Bulldozer."

Her husband came by with drinks, and he said, "Excuse me pal, this is my wife."

"Oh, I'm sorry."

Then the redheaded Irish man found another girl, dancing with her for a while and he said, "Thanks for the dancing. Do you want to go to my van to smoke some crack because the band's going on its break."

"Okay!" She said.

The redheaded Irish man got laid again! Later Cory went back to the barbecue to have dinner and he found another honey on the way, sharing food together and buying drinks, then they left together. He got laid three times today, eating, drinking and doing drugs with the girls.

The next day was Sunday, the last day of the Elks Barbecue. He was buying food, drinking and playing games at the booths. He won a tiger stuffed animal and a girl won a lion stuffed animal. "Congratulations, sweetheart, we're both winners! My name is: Cory Celtic."

"Pleased to meet you. My name is Jennifer Sup."

"Let's grab a table and have some drinks and play some cards. Jennifer, do you like tall redheaded Irish men? I have a foot long hotdog!"

"Yes, I do, but it's going to cost you to give me your foot long hotdog!"

"After all these drinks and dinner, you're going to charge me to fuck you!"

"I am a prostitute. I will fuck you for $200; A blowjob for $150."

"How about a trade off! We go to my van right now and smoke

crack cocaine together and you will be crawling up the walls when I give you my foot long hotdog!" said Cory Celtic, the redheaded Irish man.

"Okay! Let's go!" She said. Then they left together.

Later a fight broke out on the grounds pouring out into the parking lot. Then a food fight after that, because people are getting too drunk. The girl, the redheaded Irishman was fucking on the dance floor had a big fight with her husband, pushing and shoving, throwing food and drinks at each other! They were arrested by police and taken away.

People were cooking over the fire pits and one of the fire pits gave way swallowing up all the food, people were cooking. Fire caught on to trees and a big fire started burning tents and spreading along the ground and everyone ran for cover to their cars to get out, ending day three barbecue early.

The band stopped playing because the fire was getting too big and had to pack up in a hurry to get out! The Attleboro Fire Department arrived to fight the fire. When the fire was finally put out, police were escorting the remaining crowd to safety. Hours after it was all over. Animals came out of the woods to feed on the burnt food left behind, from the collapsed fire pit.

SECTION 43

CROSSWALK SPEEDERS IN CRANSTON

A school bus stopped on Park Avenue near Cranston East High School letting school kids off around 7:30am and a car raced through the flashing redlights on the school bus, breaking the stop sign on the bus and nearly hitting two girls. One girl almost lost her dress; Had she ran out further, she would have been killed! The bus driver yelled, "Hay! You asshole!"

A Cranston Cop parked on Rolfe Street near the former Park Cinema, saw what happened! He raced up Park Avenue like a bat out of hell chasing the speeding car! The speeding car ran a red light at Reservoir Avenue about 89 miles per hour; Two cars and a bus nearly hit him.

The speeding car continued booking down Park Avenue at speeds greater than 80 miles per hour while the police were chasing it, toward Dyer Avenue! This mother fucker is not stopping! A second Cranston Cop joined the chase. The speeding car struck and killed a dog and went through another red light at Dyer Avenue, past Cranston Street, running a third red light!

A third Cranston Cop joined the chase, and this car is not

stopping! The speeding car took a hard right turn on Atwood Avenue hitting a car and swiping another smashing the left rear quarter, picking up speed racing down Attwood Avenue into Johnston blowing through red lights and stop signs at will nearly hitting several vehicles!

Three Cranston cops and the Johnston Police have joined the chase. A second Johnston cop boxed the speeding car until it went over a curb near McDonalds before route 295. It hit a telephone pole and flipped over, resting upside down in the middle of Attwood Avenue, spinning like a top! The driver never got arrested after all that! Believe it or not! Because the driver went through the windshield when the car hit the telephone pole, and he landed in the McDonalds parking lot, and he was killed instantly!! His head was split in two and blood and guts pouring out of him! The car burst into flames, closing Attwood Avenue at both ends. Police were directing traffic.

People eating in McDonalds saw the accident and were screaming. "AAAHH!" They were shocked to see the man flying in the air landing headfirst in the parking lot! Cranston and Johnston Police identified the man. Jeffery Jackson was the name on his name tag on a work uniform. "I guess he was in a hurry to get to work this morning! I hope he goes to Heaven now!" said a Cranston cop.

A second Cranston Police Officer said. "Jeffery Robert Jackson works for FedEx. He has a long list of moving vehicles violations! He was a former race car driver and a Boxer and MMA fighter." The man's body was removed and put in a rescue and taken to the Cranston City Morgue. His guts were scooped up with a shovel and put in his body bag!

A group of people were eating at a Subway on Cranston Street when a speeding car ran a bike over and a young girl was killed! The speeding car took off like a bat out of hell! "Jesus Fuckin Christ! Did you see that! Where's the fuckin cops tonight! The crowd yelled! People ran out of the Subway to help the girl, and others went in their cars to find he hit and run car. The girl lay dead in a crosswalk with no head covered in blood! The girl's head was rolling down Cranston Street like a bowling ball resting up against a curb!

The police arrived after the damage was done! The speeding car killer ended up in Providence and got away! The driver washed his car at a do-it-yourself car wash, and he went home! An old lady in her 90's was trying to cross Reservoir Avenue with a walker and it's going to take a half hour for her to get across. Cars driving by were blaring their horns, a motorcycle almost clipped her and another one went around her, almost hitting her. Finally a cop arrived to stop the traffic so the lady can cross the street.

"Do you think, anyone would stop and let the lady cross or help her! Absolutely Not! These drivers are always in a hurry to go nowhere!" One witness said to a police officer.

One man at a crosswalk was trying to cross Park Avenue and a car speeding by almost hit him! The man gave the speeding car the finger! A car was slowing down at the intersection of Park and Warwick Avenue, and the light was yellow and then turned red. The car came to a sudden stop to avoid going through a red light. The same speeding car that almost ran a man over trying to cross Park Avenue slammed into the back of the car at the red light! A women got out of the car holding the back of her head after she was hit.

A man from the speeding car got out and he yelled, "You should have gone through when the light was yellow, you fuckin cunt!"

The road rage escalated between the man and the woman at the accident scene, until the woman pulled out a gun and shot the man in the head! The man laid dead in the middle of Park Avenue. This woman wasn't fucking around! The police arrived and the dead man's body was removed, and his car was towed away! The woman was arrested for the shooting and treated at the hospital. Her car was towed away by AAA.

A women was standing outside McShawn's Pub on Cranston Street having a smoke, when suddenly a motorcycle almost ran her over, tearing off her dress! She remained standing there in her undies, screaming! She went into the bar and told everyone what had just happened. A group of men left the bar looking for the motorcycle, but it was long gone!

Another auto accident at the intersection of Park and Reservoir Avenue ended up with a street fight between a few men until police arrived with pepper spray and made arrests.

One old lady was pointing her walking cane at cars, wanting to cross Park Avenue, and not a fuckin car stopped to let her cross for 45 minutes until police came to help her!

A women and her little boy were going to church on Sunday morning. She parked her 2024 Subaru Outback on Broad Street in front of St. Paul's Church. She got out of her car with the boy, and she was surprised by the devil! A dude pistol whipped her in the head, knocking her to the ground. He grabbed her pocketbook and car keys, stole her car, and drove off, just missed hitting several church goers crossing Broad Street and Norwood Avenue.

The stolen car ran a red light almost hitting two cars then took a hard left, pealing rubber. It raced down Norwood Avenue like a bat out of hell into Roger Williams Park heading toward Cranston! A cop at the church saw the horror show. The Cranston cop got in her car quickly and gave chase, a second Cranston cop joined the chase and then two Providence Police joined the chase!

The stolen car ran a red light almost hitting a motorcycle and turned into a parking lot at Park View Middle School not realizing he's driving to a dead end. The police boxed him in, and the stolen car backed up hitting a Cranston Police car. The stolen car turned quickly, trying to get away and struck a Providence Police car. The second Cranston Cop rammed the stolen car into a tree! Then a shootout erupted between the police and the man in the stolen car! He was shot dead on the spot! As soon as the driver got out to shoot at the cops he was gunned down in seconds!

The man's head and body were full of bullet holes! Back at the church. The women laid in the street unconscious in front of St. Paul's Church and the little boy was screaming and crying when help arrived. Police called for backup and a rescue took the injured women to the hospital.

A man cut off a car on Park Avenue causing a crash! A School bus was going to Bain Middle School full of kids when a car cut the bus off and some kids went flying over seats. The bus driver blew the horn, but the car kept going, almost causing an accident.

"Where's the fuckin cops, God Damm it!" The bus driver said.

Some of the kids were hurt. The cut-off car went down Cranston Street all the way to Providence. One man was parked in a loading zone and a Cranston cop pulled up beside him and asked him to move.

"Why officer, I park here all the time."

"You're in a loading zone, you have to move, or you will get a ticket," said the cop. Then the man drove off.

A food truck pulled in to unload, a few minutes later. A women was waiting for a bus near St. Paul's Church. The bus drove up on the curb almost hitting the women. The bus driver was drunk! A cop boxed the bus in, and the driver was arrested for DUI.

A woman driving drunk on Cranston Street crashed her car into a bus stop depot smashing the glass seating area. Meanwhile a cop pulled up behind her car. The time was 3:02am. It's a good thing no one was sitting or standing there in the wee hours of the night.

"I am so sorry officer; I fell asleep at the wheel," said the women. Then she collapsed in the street.

Two more Cranston police cars arrived at the scene. The woman was given a breathalyzer test. "3.5. She must have had 20 or 30 drinks. "That's enough to kill her!" said one of the cops. The woman was taken to the hospital and she was arrested there.

"I DON'T WANT TO DRIVE IN CRANSTON AFTER ALL THIS, ANYMORE!"

50 SHADES AT KEENE STATE

CHAPTER 1

A young girl was driving kind of fast on route 103 in Swansea, though Warren and into East Providence, where she was stopped by East Providence Police near Pawtucket Avenue.

"Good morning, miss tattoo sports girl. You were clocked going 28 miles per hour over the speed limit. Can I see your license, registration and proof of insurance please?"

The girl gave the cop what he needed.

"Where are you going?" said the cop.

"I am on my way to college in New Hampshire."

"You need to slow down, you have a long way to go! I am issuing you a ticket for $330. You have 14 days to pay it or you can fight the ticket in court. The fine doubles after 14 days. Failure to pay the fine will result in you losing your license. You have a heavy foot, slow down. The cop threw the ticket in her car. The girl gave the cop a dirty look. She pulled out and she was on her way. Traveling over the new Washington Bridge in Providence, the girl ripped up the ticket and threw it out the window!

This young girl is a bitch! So was the East Providence Cop who stopped her! Now she's on her way to Keene State.

This girl is the main initiation manager for a women's sorority. When everyone arrives at college, she's the main speaker for the house.

"Good evening, ladies. My name is Debra Ho, the head house manager of Gamma Delta Pi. Welcome back to Keene State. Welcome to Gamma Delta Pi Sorority. Fore you newcomers, you will join the rest of the girls during your initiation to belong here. If you were placed here by the college, it doesn't mean you're staying here unless you join the sorority. If you don't want to go through the sorority initiation, you have to leave. We are going to do two things: First, every girl here must strip naked and streak through the campus. Second, every girl staying in this sorority must take naked photos of their private parts, including me, with their phones, computers, iPad and show the entire campus of Keene State what we look like naked! If you can't deal with that the doors right there! We could be thrown off campus for doing this, so we have to do it on a Saturday night.

I think you got off with a deal this year! Last year, the girls had to drink a bottle of Jack Daniels, plus drink a keg of beer together and fuck every guy in the delta house next door. Six girls got pregnant, two died from alcohol poison, and 13 girls quit and were thrown off campus!

Beginning tonight, and for the rest of the week, I want you to get your phones taking pictures of your naked bodies. Show your bush, inside your vagina, opening your legs wide so everyone on campus can see what you have. Show you asshole, your buns, long/short hair, whatever you have; I want you to show it all! Me too! I'm with you.

Then Saturday afternoon, the whole sorority will streak naked and run through the campus like a cross-country track team! Saturday night after the soccer game we're going to pose naked in front of the Keene State Owl mascot with the cheer leaders, dance team and the band. Then we will run through the Delta Tau Omega men's fraternity. Before we take naked pictures of our bodies, let's wait until we go streaking Saturday Afternoon. You can do what you want but wait to show the public after Saturday.

Everyone will get itineraries with my instructions on what to do. You do not, I will tell you again, you do not show naked pictures off campus! You don't want the whole state of New Hampshire, the US, or Canada, to see your naked photos, because if you do, you will get arrested and thrown out of Keene State!

Keep your private photos on campus only! After you finish your initiation, you can do what you want! If you want to go to tonight's soccer game naked, that's up to you. Keene State is playing Rhode Island College. If you want to have sex orgies at the Delta House next door, you may, after the run through! We will be sharing some wild weekend parties with Delta Tau Omega, throughout the school year. That's right ladies, I go hardcore here at Gamma Delta Pi. The Delta House will be serving orange blossoms served from a 55-gallon trash can filled with pure grain alcohol, 190 proof stirred up with a hockey stick and served in 16-ounce cups. Here at GDP, will be serving iced tea in 20-ounce cups. Vodka, clear rum, tequila, gin, whiskey, pure grain alcohol and triple sec, splash of coke served with ice, lemon and a lime. Let's get fucked up, ladies! Once again, my name is: Debra Ho!"

CHAPTER 2
THE ACTION IS AT KEENE STATE

"Hay! You bitch! Here is where I stay, the college put me here and I am not doing what you want me to do. I joined the sorority to be with a nice group of women, not with a bunch of sluts! You're a fuckin pig!" said one girl.

"There's the door honey! Get the fuck out!"

"No, I'm not going anywhere! I am going to turn your ass in!"

Debra fought with the girl until she threw her out of the sorority house. The girl and a friend went to campus police to file a complaint. Two more girls left and went to the town police department. Four girls ended up leaving the Gamma Delta Pi Sorority.

At Campus Police:

"Hi, my name is Lisa Johnson and she's Cathy Blassie. We're students at the Gamma Delta Pi sorority for the school year. The madam or manager of the house wants to run an illegal whore house with a bunch of drunks there, and she threw us out, and we live there!" The two girls cried.

"I didn't come from Dallas, Texas to go to a nice school like Keene State to live in a whore house!" Cathy Blassie cried.

The campus police brought the two girls back to the sorority and met with Debra Ho. "Are you the leader of this Sorority?" said Campus Police.

"Yes, my name is Debra Ho."

"Whatever is going on here in this dorm, you cannot be throwing people out when they're assigned here until they can find a place to go," said campus police.

"Come on in, you fuckin bitches!"

"Hay, miss Ho! Go fuck yourself!" said the two girls.

One of the girl's shoulders whipped Debra Ho, knocking her to the ground and she walked out and stayed with her boyfriend next door at the Delta House. The second girl kicked her in the head when Miss Ho was laying on the ground. She left.

The other two girls who had left filed a report at the town of Keene Police Station. The Keene Police said. "We will take care of the issues at the sorority house; don't you worry about that!" The girls filed the town police report and then they found somewhere to go.

Then it's Saturday afternoon and the Gamma Delta Pi Sorority naked girls were streaking around campus waving the Keene State Mascot Flag with the owl. The initiation period begins. Then the girls went to the Delta House to party with the boys before going to the soccer game tonight. The girls drank, had sex with some of the boys and had a cookout at the Delta House and everyone was naked!

At the soccer game the score was 1-1 at halftime, then here comes the naked girls running across the field and the crowd went wild cheering! Rhode Island College won the game 3 to 1. The naked girls waited under a big tent with Debra Ho until the game was over, singing the school's Alma mater! Before the game was over it began to rain and it's time for the naked girls to pose with the cheerleaders, dance team and the Keene State band in front of the owl mascot in the middle of the field.

The girls ran out of the tent in the pouring rain like a football team breaking through the mascot flag while the band started playing and the naked girls were dancing with the cheer leaders and dance team. Then minutes later it was thundering and lightning forcing the streaking rally to end while a wild cheering crowd watched! Then the girls went back to the Delta House to have a sex orgy with the men and party all night!

The next day was Sunday. In the nice town of Keene, New Hampshire, everybody goes to church together, while the Gamma Delta Pi Sorority Girls are taking naked photos of themselves on the Keene State College Campus!

The following weekend, the Gamma Delta Pi had a hardcore iced tea party and a band was playing and people were drinking and dancing in the sorority lounge. The Delta House next door was having an orange blossoms pure grain alcohol party and drugs were sold there. A Disc-Jockey was playing music in their lounge.

The campus police, the Keene Police and the New Hampshire

State Police went to these parties joining the students, drinking, smoking pot, doing drugs and having sex with them! The police did nothing to help those girls earlier, they're part of the party. Delta Tau Omega men fed the cops food, drinks and drugs and they were fucking all the women next door at the sorority house!

One cop in town went back to the police station. He was so drunk when he went to the dispatcher's desk that he puked all over the paperwork, passed out, and slept in it!

The cops are always drunk and the college kids too! The four girls filed a complaint with the dean of students and the Gamma Delta Pi Sorority was thrown off campus.

SECTION 45

UFC FIGHT

A Big UFC fight was going on at Madison Square Garden in New York City. The fight was sold out and it was on pay-per-view. Spectators paid hundreds and thousands of dollars to see this fight—Jaylen Brown versus Jayson Tatum.

"Good evening ladies and gentlemen. Welcome to Madison Square Garden in New York for tonight's middle weight championship fight between Jason Tatum and Jaylen Brown on pay-per-view. We have a three-fight card tonight. Our first fight is the women's middleweight championship between Paula Pierce and Lori Bird. Your referee is Donald Biden, Jr. Please rise for the playing of the National Anthem," said the announcer at Madison Square Garden.

Pay Per View, was calling the fights. "Ladies and gentlemen, in the blue corner, she hails from Dallas, Texas, let's hear it for Lori Bird."

"Boooo! Went the crowd.

"In the red corner from New York City, Let's hear it for Paula Pierce!" said the fight announcer.

"Yeah!" Went the crowd!

Then the two women came out fighting in the octagon! Paula

and Lori are exchanging punches, there's a nice jab by Paula Pierce, Lori Bird sweeps Paula's left leg. Paula jumps back waiting for Lori to come in and Paula hit her with an uppercut, she follows that up with a jab-cross and kick and Lori Bird chases Paula with a round house. Paula kicked her in the nuts, knocking her down, I hope she has a cup on!" said the pay per view TV announcer.

A second announcer said. "This is a women's fight, they have no nuts! Before Lori Bird got up the first round was over. Then punches and kicks by both women. Then Lori Bird hit Paula Pierce with a back fist, then Paula hit her with an uppercut, then a jab-cross in the face, then a side kick and a spinning round house and kicked Lori Bird in the head knocking her out to finish her off! Lori Bird hit the canvas out cold! The crowd went wild cheering.

"Ladies and gentlemen, Your winner by knock out in the second round. Paula Pierce!" said the fight announcer.

The next fight was two heavy weights. Before the second fight starts. Lori Bird is still lying in the octagon, and she was being carried off in a stretcher and taken to the hospital.

"Ladies and gentlemen, our next fight for the evening. In the blue corner, hails from Las Vegas, Nevada, weighing 235 pounds with a 12-5 record. Let's hear it for Bubba Vincent!" said the fight announcer.

"Boooo!" Went the crowd.

"Our next fighter hails from New York City, weighing 246 pounds with a 16-1 record in the red corner. Let's hear it for Donald Bradley!"

The crowd cheered, "Yeah!"

"The referee for this fight is Daniel Crowley," said the fight announcer.

Donald Bradley charges after Bubba Vincent like a freight train punching him in the face knocking him to the canvas.

The referee is giving Bubba, the count," said he Pay Per View, announcer. "1-2-3-4-5-6-7!"

Bubba got up throwing punches at Donald Bradley! Both fighters were exchanging punches until Donald Bradley swept both feet from under Bubba Vincent knocking him down and the bell rang ending the first round. The two fighters started the second round of a five-round fight, throwing punches at each other like a boxing match, jab crosses and not connecting most of the jabs until the third round.

Then Donald Bradley went after Bubba Vincent like a mad man with a power punch, a side kick, a double round house, a karate chop, finally an uppercut blow to the head, knocking Bubba Vincent out cold!

"Your winner by knock out! Donald Bradley!" said the fight announcer.

"Ladies and gentlemen and friends around the world. The fight you have been waiting for! It's time!!!! In the blue corner with a record of 1-0 From Marietta, Africa, weighing 195 pounds, Let's hear it for Jaylen Brown!"

The crowd went "Booo!"

"In the red corner, he hails from, St. Louis, Missouri, USA! Weighing 196 pounds also with a record of 1-0. Let's hear it for Jayson Tatum!" said Bruce Buffer.

"Yeah!!" Went the crowd.

The fight was a clean fight for the two of them because they don't want to get hurt before basketball season so the Celtics can win another championship! The crowd was booing because they were throwing missed punches at one another until all five rounds were over.

"Ladies and gentlemen, after 5 UFC rounds, this fight's a draw!" said Bruce Buffer.

"Booo!" Went the crowd.

SECTION 46

VICARIOUS

A speech from a very powerful man speaking in a church.

"Good evening, ladies and gentlemen, welcome to St. Vincent's Church here in Burlington, Vermont. My name is Father John Rockets. A very powerful man is here this evening to speak about the future, in my church. Doctor Pleasure, please."

"Good evening. My name is: Dr. David Vicarious Pleasure. I am here to give a speech and pick your brains. I will be talking to you about me into you, so to speak. I will be watching you but doing things you do, and I will not do. For example, if you go bowling and bowl a 300 game, something I have never done, but if I watch you bowl I can tell before I say a word, I already know that you are capable of bowling a 300, I can tell if you have done it before or not but I feel that you will get it if you're as good a bowler as you say you are. I see through people, and I can tell what kind of life you are having. Later in my speech I will call up a few people from this church who are struggling with problems. I will call you by your name to come up on stage and I can see through you and maybe I can help you or explain where the rest of your life is going from today on, in front of 3000 people. I want to talk about AI, artificial intelligence.

Before we move on, I experience people, watching them, reading them, listening to them, doing something they will do rather than doing it myself. I may not know you but by looking at you watching the way you walk or just being a normal human being, I will get to know you by picking your brain just like AI. I will be watching you, but I will not be doing what you do. I believe and feel there are good spirits in this place. I also believe in bad spirits, such as ghosts and the devil. I can feel them everywhere I go, and I give a lot of speeches in all the United States and Canada. Stay away from the Bennington Martins Triangle; it's evil and has a history of demonic spirits! Many people have gone there but never made it out. The rest of Vermont is a good place to be.

Let's talk about artificial intelligence. AI The government has a way to alter your voice or someone you know- family member, etc... Saying they're in trouble and demanding money over the phone with their voice crying for help and it's not true. Let's say you get a phone call. "Hello this is ISIS, and I have your son Allen. You need to send $10,000 dollars or he will be killed;" The phone voice will alter his name crying for help. If this happens to you, call Allen to see if he's okay. AI has a lot of scams out there. If you get a phone call from the IRS telling you that you owe thousands of dollars in taxes, just hang up! If you owe taxes, you will get a letter in the mail. Most calls over the phone with threats are scams unless you're messing with someone's spouse," said Dr. Vicarious Pleasure as he joked.

Everyone had a good laugh! Then the doctor continued. "Look at your phone, because it's watching you! I hope you're not doing a drug deal because the Burlington Police will be coming to arrest you!" Everyone laughs!

Then the doctor continued. "Your phones, smart TV, there are cameras everywhere watching every move you make; They're on street corners, in lights hiding in the ground, they're everywhere!

Whatever you're watching; you are being watched. Artificial Intelligence is a good thing and a bad thing, it's good for the police because it's easier to find you," said the doctor. Everyone laughed!

Then the doctor continued. "AI can steal your identity, you're social security, banking information, make changes in language, analyzing data from advanced science from a robot with technology that enables computers, phones, robots, anything electronics, etc.... AI has been around for a while but it's so advanced it will try to pick your brain and turn you inside out! How many people believe in UFOs? I want a show of hands!" Very few raised their hands. The doctor continued his speech. "I don't see a lot of believers in here. But I think you better think again. We have been visited by other worlds and I have a personal story to prove it!

In July of 1970 when I was a little boy, I was in a group called "The wee blows", it's a group of cub scouts before becoming boy scouts. We were camping in Bangcock Maine at Lake Cockhead. And me and my three friends, Pat Magroin, Ricky Hurts and Peter Paderka were going fishing. Our scout master told us to be careful because it's getting dark and there's a new moon. We all got our fishing poles and bait to go night fishing out on the lake. We saw the moon rise. It looked like a full moon, but it was something else! The moon-like disk got bigger! Bigger! And Bigger! And it was so bright we had to turn away! Suddenly we smelled ether, then we passed out and found ourselves inside a spaceship just like Star Wars! We were laying all naked on carts and these strange unexplainable humanoid creatures were doing experimenting on our bodies, using acupuncture with big needles and other tools that we cannot explain. I thought this is it, we're all going to die today! The humanoids stuck a pipe, a foot long and three inches thick up my butt. Then stuck me with acupuncture needles all over my body, inside my ears, up my nose, in my eyes and in my mouth. My friend Richard Hurts had a pole shoved up his butt and coming out of his mouth. He was hanging from a hammock, swinging back and forth, and being whipped. Pat Magrin had a foot long needle driven through his head in one ear and out the other. His feet were tied up with wire and needles were sticking in his feet and a rag was shoved in his mouth and needles in his nose.

Finally my friend Peter Paderka was tortured. He was hung up with rope or wire wrapped around his penis and his legs were wired together and a rope was around his neck hanging him in the air and hundreds of foot long needles were stuck in his body all over him and a baseball like looking stick was shoved up his butt and the creatures sprayed a slime like foam all over him, that smelled like ether. The humanoids were playing with his private parts while he was being sprayed with the foam. Then we all passed out!

Later we woke up fully clothed on the beach and our boat and fishing gear rested on shore like nothing happened. We all checked ourselves to make sure we were okay," said the doctor.

"Doctor Pleasure, you just had a nightmare! Get your head on straight, will you!" said someone in the crowd.

The doctor continued. "No! This is not a dream. This really happened, I wouldn't be telling you this story if it was not true!

The scout master came down to the beach and he said, "Hey boys it's 3:30 in the morning, why are you still out here? We have to get up early tomorrow morning!"

"We told him that we were abducted by aliens, put on a space-ship and tortured! He said, "Go to bed!" "He did not believe us. Later I went to the Bangcock Town Hall, talked on radio stations, newspapers and TV shows, but no one believed me. They said I was full of bologna, and I need my head examined! This really happened, ladies and gentlemen! It's not the first time I was abducted by aliens.

In the summer of the year 2000, I was laying on a beach in Prince Edward Island, Canada and I saw what looked like a baby polar bear walking up the beach walking toward me. And it came up to me and it was a humanoid that looked like the ones that were on the spaceship during the summer of 1970 in Bangcock, Maine. The humanoid grabbed my leg and it bit me! I got away, then I kicked the creature with a karate kick, and it went flying into the water and disappointed! I mean it disappeared! No one believes this story, but it happened!" said he doctor.

Some of the people started leaving the church; They're sick of hearing Doctor Pleasure's bullshit! Then the doctor started calling up people looking for help and prayer. "Before I end this speech, I will call up five people by name for counseling. If the rest of you needing help and advice, just go to my email. doctor-vicariouspleasure@gmail.com, all lower case. Thank You."

"Miss Vivian Brown. Please come to the stage.' Hi Vivian, it's nice to meet you. According to Fr. Rockets, you're in the process of going through a divorce."

"Yes." She cried.

"I see through you right now, and it looks like it's very negative, and badly strong. What I would suggest you do is go to the police and put a restraining order against your husband and his family because if not, your husband is going to kill you! Don't answer phone calls or emails from him and see a lawyer.

Mr. Kenwood Harvard, please come to the stage. You have been scammed out of thousands of dollars. You must go see a good lawyer, check your bank statements and do not send the Brass Construction Company any more payments. Finally, do not do direct deposits anymore. You're in a big mess Kenwood. Good luck.

Mrs. Robin Parkfield, please come to the stage. According to Fr. Rockets. You have a serious gambling problem. You owe a lot of money, and you can't pay it back. You have to stop gambling and see a counselor and make some kind of arrangement with your online gambling or things are going to get worse. Good luck, Mrs. Parkfield.

Mr. Richard Duncan. Please come to the stage. According to Fr. Rockets I understand you lost your job at the University of Vermont.

"Yes sir: Dr. Pleasure."

"Do you have a union at the University of Vermont?"

"No! Not the work I do there. I do maintenance from an outside contract doing work in the university."

Mr. Duncan, I would suggest you see an outside lawyer for help, not someone from the university. Fr. Rockets said you were fired because of racist remarks. I don't think you have a chance of working there again or getting a job within the university. I understand you live close by, but you will have to find a job somewhere else. See a lawyer but I don't know if the lawyer can help. You may be looking for work under the table because racism is a very serious charge and you have a defending lawyer fighting against you. Good luck.

My last patient is Lori Nudes. Please come to the stage. You lost your home from lack of installment payments, causing you to go homeless. Go see a lawyer and try to get a reduced mortgage. And get to a homeless shelter, because the cold weather will be here soon. Try to find a way to stay with friends or family, because living on the streets in the State of Vermont is not welcomed. See if Fr. Rockets can help you in this church. Good Luck! Go to my email for help or see what the church can do for you. My counseling is brief and I can only talk with five people with the permission of your priest, Fr. Rockets.

Once again, my name is Doctor Vicarious Pleasure. doctorvicariouspleasure@gmail.com Thank you for hearing my speech this evening and I hope I was a lot of help! Thank You and God Bless you."

"Ladies and gentlemen, you just heard one of the most powerful men in the world. Dr. Vicarious Pleasure is the next Nostradamus. Thank you. God bless you and I will see you in church on Sunday," said Fr. Rockets.

Outside the church, news reporters, newspaper writers, and TV, stations were there for tonight's event at St. Vincent's Church in Vermont.

One man said to another. "What did you think of Dr. Pleasure's speech?"

"I think he's on crack! He don't make sense!"

The other man said to his wife. "What did you think of this weirdo?"

"I think he needs his head examined! He needs a counselor rather than one himself." She said.

A news reporter said to a TV camera operator. "Hay Randy, What do you think of Dr. Vicarious Pleasure's speech?"

"I think he has rocks in his head!"

The same news reporter said to lady coming out of the church. "Hi, how did you like Dr. Vicarious Pleasure's speech?"

"I think he's fake and he needs his own doctor!" said the lady.

The lady said to another lady. "Karen, how did you like the speech?"

"I think he's a big bullshitter!"

"He's a nut case!" One man said walking by.

"I think Dr. Vicarious Pleasure is on drugs!" A women told reporters.

"Hi my name is Gloria Tanning, a member of St. Vincent's Church. I came to this speech to listen to a powerful man like Nostradamus and learn something, and I found he was overrated, he didn't make sense, and his eye contact was not following his conversations. I swear he's on dope! Belonging to this church fore 39 years, I never listened to an idiot like him! If he's a powerful doctor, he does not act like one. I think he needs to see his own counselor."

"She was Gloria Tanning talking about tonight's speech, and several witnesses were disappointed saying the speaker was fake and there were many complaints. WMVT News Channel 5 in Burlington Vermont."

Later a few people were hanging around complaining to news reporters. Churches, schools and stadiums blocked future events with Dr. Pleasure's speeches.

During Sunday's mass at St. Vincent's Church, Fr. Rockets talked about the speech in his sermon. "Good morning my dear brothers and sisters, About Thursday night's speech, I was told by the pope that Dr. Vicarious Pleasure was the next Nostradamus. A very powerful man for peace and a religious man for all churches. A strong man of God and all his help with speeches and counseling. I think that this man could be fake. He's not the man who I thought he was. I believe some of his speech didn't make sense and he was more challenging and difficult to understand. Me as a priest does not like to talk down about people but this man's conversations in almost every sentence was, *I,I,I,I,I.* A person like that has a lot of suspicion or something he's hiding or something he does not want to say during his speeches. I thought some of his speech was helpful. This man had speeches all over the world. There were a lot of complaints after Thursday night's speech. Be prepared for speeches like this. He could be an Antichrist. He used me as a tool before the speech, getting information about people. In the name of the Father, the Son and the Holy Spirit, AMEN," said Fr. Rockets.

SECTION 47

TYPHOON THUNDERHEAD!

A giant storm is brewing and it looks like a mega vagina over the ocean heading for Thailand. This storm formed over the Philippines, heading straight for Thailand and passing through shipping lanes. It looks like a giant vagina, it formed as a thunderhead with high tops and a wide mass that looks like a wild bush with black pubic hair around it and a pink opening looking like the inside of a woman's vagina, and a red clitoris cloud with a bolt of lightning coming out and striking the water and wind being sucked up into this big cunt and forming waterspouts with multiple funnel clouds!

The storm picked up speed into a full deadly typhoon! A cargo ship loaded with storage containers was passing through the storm and rough waves were crashing up against the ship, rocking the ship back and forth until the storage containers were falling off the ship into the ocean. The storm spawned so many multiple vortices and big waves until the ship sank.

A cruise ship heading for Thailand was struck by the sudden storm. It was a nice smooth cruise on a hot sunny day and the water was as blue as the sky. Suddenly a giant wave hit the side of the boat coming out of nowhere knocking people over! The cruise ship almost tipped over! Then the ocean started getting rough and the ship was going up and down in the big waves as Typhoon Thunderhead was coming. Passengers on the cruise ship were getting seasick and puking all over the ship. People were sliding in the puke like sliding on ice! When the first wave hit, light fixtures started falling then dishes, chairs, and tables fell over and food and drinks were flying everywhere, hitting people in the kitchen-cafeteria. The bar was destroyed with all the bottles falling from the bar breaking on the floor. The bar flipped over and it was destroyed. The bedrooms were damaged and the lower deck was flooded, the restrooms backed up with piss and shit flowing down the hallways; the casino, nightclub and movie theater was flooded and damaged after several giant waves struck the ship. Anyone out on deck were washed overboard in 50 foot waves and disappeared! Then the ship ran aground hitting a big rock and half of it sank! A fire started in the casino sparkling like fireworks because the machines were shorting out.

Now this big cunt is ready to strike Thailand dead on! People in restaurants and bars were watching weather reports. Titty Nipple Bar was packed with customers watching weather reports and drinking IPA'S. The weather was partly cloudy, windy and it was 100 degrees and a moderate surf at the beaches packed with swimmers and sun bathers, not knowing that a freak storm is coming! Back at Titty Nipples.

"Good afternoon, A major typhoon is heading for Thailand in the coming hours and you have very little time to evacuate! Please go to higher ground and upper floors in buildings at this time. Typhoon Thunderhead with 200 mile per hours winds is coming quickly with a powerful tsunami with waves well over 100 feet high when it strikes land. Several may day calls were reported out at sea. A typhoon warning has been issued for Thailand. You must evacuate right now and get to higher ground! You're listening to World News Cable Network Satellite Channel

One in, China. This is Doctor Vicarious Pleasure world leader reporting."

A Chinese interpreter, broadcast the warning in Chinese. (DR. VICARIOUS PLEASURE WAS JUST IN VERMONT, WHAT THE FUCK IS HE DOING IN TAILAND.) The big cunt is heading for Bang Saen Beach then it going to hit the city of Bangkok dead on! The water started going out fast at Bang Saen Beach and fallowed by a mild earthquake and rumbling. The beach goers know what's coming; A tsunami. Everyone ran off the beach like a bat out of hell! The sky clouded up quickly and the wind was sucking water up into this cloud, then it went quiet, then this big cunt arrived! Lightning came out of the clitoris striking trees, Tiki bars homes and wood frame structures. Then the big black cubic haired surrounded the beach, then a strong wind came out of the pinkish red vagina looking inside this giant thunderhead with loud roars of thunder and lightning bolts flying out of this big cunt striking everything in it's path! When the pink vagina covered the beach, it was the eye of the storm before she has an orgasm!

Was the back end with the killer winds, waterspouts and tsunami waves swallowed Bang Saen Beach until nothing was left but tree stumps! Dead whales sharks and sea life littered the beach when the quick storm passed. People in downtown Bangkok were going into buildings to get away from the tsunami coming. People leaving the Titty Nipple Bar saw the big transformer mega thunderhead heading for the city.

"Look up in the sky! It looks like the inside of a women!" said the crowd.

"Let's get inside quickly! A mad ladies bottom is coming, everyone get to higher ground, Typhoon Thunderhead is coming!" said one man.

"Look up there! The Storm has a big hairy cubic black hair bush and the inside of a women and lightning is striking out of the center! Let's run for cover in a hurry!" said another man in Chinese language.

One man said in one of the buildings watching the storm coming. "This lady typhoon has something much bigger than I can handle!" Typhoon Thunderhead struck a farm after leveling Bang Saen Beach and cows, horses, pigs, goats, deer and all kind of animals were sucked up into this big cunt and disappeared in the giant thunderhead and they will rain down from the back end of the storm, later! Animals and sea life including sharks were stored in this thunderhead until the typhoon passes. Then the storm's heading for downtown Bangkok! People in buildings high up on floors were watching this big cunt overtake downtown.

"Everyone, get away from the windows and get to a closed in area and find something to cover your heads!" said security guards in the buildings high up on the upper floors. Then Typhoon Thunderhead struck downtown Bangkok! The pink slit arrived after strong gusts of wind, then it stopped and the sun started shining in the eye from the heavens inside this pink cunt. All the animals and sea life were washing high up into the thunderhead with lots of hail stones washing like a washing machine until the storm has her orgasm! Then the back end of the pink vagina started sucking debris into it before she blows her load in downtown Bangkok! Roofs of buildings, trees and loose debris were being sucked up in Typhoon Thunderhead's vagina! Then the big pink cunt exploded! Strait line winds blew out of the storm with 200 mile per hour winds blowing out windows in several buildings, sucking people out of buildings who were hiding because the strong wind blew out windows from one end of the buildings and out the other side! Some smaller buildings were blown away and disappeared! Many people have died because you can't hide from Typhoon Thunderhead! If anyone survived being sucked up into this big black, pink middle thunderhead, I hope they enjoyed it before being killed!! Anyone who died in this storm; I hope they went to heaven!

Then after the pink slit passed, the sky turned jet black like night with 200 mile per hour winds and duck pin bowling ball size hail and pouring rain driving sideways and hail smashing everything in its path! Cars trucks and buses sitting in city streets looked like a junk yard pile of metal and broken glass covered up on each other. Then the tsunami arrived with 100-foot waves and moving as fast as the wind. An oil tanker was washed in from the sea and bowled into all buildings knocking them down like domino's! The water was about 50 feet high in downtown Bangkok washing vehicles away and ship washing into the city from the sea. It looked like the movie *The Day After Tomorrow* when a tsunami washed into New York City. Then after the strong winds died down, another message was coming from the heavens, and it was not coming from God! Fish started falling from the sky, then small animals, like foxes, raccoons, coyotes, dogs, cats, the deer, bigger animals and dead people, then sharks, dolphins and whales fell from the sky! A women living in a high-rise apartment building was taking a bath after the storm past. Suddenly she heard a big crash. She got out of the tub wrapped a towel around her and she came out of the bathroom and her dog was barking up a storm! When she came out of the bathroom, she was face to face with a great white that crashed through her 47th floor window! The shark charged after her but she was able to get to her bedroom and close the door and she called 911 in Chinese.

The dog kept barking and growling at the shark, then the lady heard, *Yelp! Yelp! Yelp! Yelp! Yelp!!!!!* while she was calling for help. The shark ate her dog as she screamed, "AAAAHHHHH!" Cows, horses, pigs and other animals crashed into buildings! Vultures eagles and other birds or animals that survived were eating the dead after the storm!

SECTION 48

MANNY

I, Ricky, am the author of this book. When I was a little boy I didn't come out of my diaper until I was almost three years old, I didn't walk until I was four, and I didn't eat until I was almost five years old. I only would eat hotdogs or peanut butter and jelly sandwiches. I almost died; it was that bad. I would not eat what was on the table- I hated cube steak! Being in a military family we were taught to eat what was on the table. My father Manny had eight kids and I was the sick one, so I needed special attention. I started grinding my teeth on lead paint cabinets and acting like a wild animal! I got sick and acted cuckoo, from lead paint poisoning.

I, Ricky, am the author of this book. When I was a little boy I didn't come out of my diaper until I was almost three years old, I didn't walk until I was four, and I didn't eat until I was almost five years old. I would only eat hotdogs or peanut butter and jelly sandwiches. I almost died; it was that bad. I would not eat what was on the table- I hated cube steak! Being in a military family we were taught to eat what was on the table.

My father Manny had eight kids and I was the sick one, so I needed special attention. I started grinding my teeth on lead paint cabinets and acting like a wild animal! I got sick and acted cuckoo, from lead paint poisoning. "Emotionally disturbed" was my diagnosis. I was send to a mental hospital to calm my animalistic craziness! I was strapped to a bed to get the devil out of me! When I was four years old I was in a hospital because I would barely eat.

Before I was five, and I remember it well, during a tropical storm, Dad put me in the oven and made believe he was going to cook me for the next holiday meal. I screamed my life away inside the oven! I remember hearing my mother say: "If you turn that on, I will divorce you right now!" Dad let me out of the oven and I was traumatized! I shit my pants and peed on the floor.

I started eating better; not only better but when I got older, I ate them out of house and home! Ma and Dad had to hide the food because I ate so much. Dad turned me into a crazy mother fucker when he put me in the oven!

At six, I was eating better, at age seven, I was fascinated with light bulbs. I would put them in my mouth and stick them in my ears to see if they would light up! Then I would go through the neighborhood unscrewing and stealing everybody's light bulbs; especially my aunts' homes when we were living on Borden Road in Tiverton, Rhode Island. My Aunt Louise would come home and the house would be dark because crazy Ricky stole all her light bulbs. She would call my mother.

"Ricky stole all my light bulbs!" The next night, was Mrs. Moniz's turn, my Aunt Louise's neighbor. The next night, my Aunt Elsie called because all her light bulbs were missing. The next night was Aunt Mary's turn. Day after day, crazy Ricky went through the neighborhood robbing every home's light bulbs! I liked the blue and yellow light bulbs, I put the yellow ones in my mouth and the blue ones in my ears!

At age eight it was bleach bottles, cement trucks, airplanes helicopters and GI-Joe toys. I robbed every home just like I had with the light bulbs! With the bleach bottles, I would wait for neighbors to go out and I would break into their basements, emptying the bleach bottles into their washing machines, bring the empty bottles home, and line them up in the cellar. The house smelled like bleach all the time.!

Then it was airplanes, helicopters and toys. In the neighborhood you would hear, "Manny! Ricky's stealing my bleach bottles and toys!"

Finally, Dad had enough, and he put me in a nut house hospital to straighten my ass out! Dad brought me a green Whirlybird Chinook helicopter with double rotors to help me from getting out of control at the crazy hospital! Then I was into airplanes and helicopters. A doctor/social worker brought me a real airplane propeller while I was in this temporary nut house. One day I brought the heavy airplane propeller outside into the courtyard and I was swinging it like a helicopter rotor and hit this little girl in the head knocking her down on the ground. There was blood everywhere! The propeller was taken away from me and placed into archives. The only way I can see my propeller was by watching it in a display case. I was a fucked up little boy!

After leaving the nut house hospital, I started getting interested in sailor hats and uniforms. My sister Claire's first husband was in the navy and he took me to the Newport Navy Base and aboard his ship, Destroyer 764 Loydd Thomas. That's when the sailor hats started. Then the family moved to Stafford Road in Tiverton. Urban's Grove Beach campground on Stafford Pond had a navy festival every summer and I would go, meet the sailors and navy officers and made friends with them, and eat all kinds of food and soda pop, ice cream, etc. The sailors gave me uniforms and many sailor hats because I wanted to join the navy when I grew up. Then one of the navy officers gave me an old captain's uniform and hat. I looked like a little boy captain of the navy with bell bottom pants so long they covered my black shiny boots. I would walk through the neighborhoods in Tiverton showing off my captain's uniform. Then I started walking on the main street and the highway waving at cars going by, until the police stopped me, and asked what I was doing and I had questions to answer. The Tiverton police said, "You can't be wearing uniforms like this if you're not a captain in the navy; that's impersonating an officer, that's against the law!"

The cop took me home and told my mother what was happening. "You can wear them in your house but you can't be walking around outside." I had about 51 sailor uniforms and 131 sailor hats in all sizes! I only had one captain's uniform and hat. I guess Dad took them all to the dump when in grew out of them and started playing with my plastic bowling pins,

When I was a good boy, Dad took me bowling; Duck pins first but I liked the big balls better! He would take me for an airplane ride, but when I was bad he started getting rid of my sailor uniforms and hats. So now it's the sailor uniforms to bowling and back to airplanes again. Dad brought me a plastic bowling set so I can set them up and bowl with them in the cellar.

Then he brought me a bike and when I learned how to ride it, I was riding everywhere; all the way to Fall River some days. One day I rode my bike down Corey's Lane all the way to the bottom to Wartupper Pond and I found hundreds of real ten pin bowling pins floating in the water. I took forty of them home in bags making several trips. Dad never found them until I did something very wrong, because I hid them under bags of clothes in the basement. First I marked the cellar floor like a bowling lane, clearing the area near the washer and dryer. Then I set up ten wooden pins when mom and dad went out on Saturday nights. I split a hole open in my plastic bowling ball and I filled it up with rocks. I covered the opening with duct tape after placing a plastic piece to hold the rocks in place and prevent them from coming out of the thirty-pound bowling ball. I fired the bowling ball full of rocks down the make-shift lane, but my plan did not work! The ball never made it to the pins. When I threw the ball it split in half and all the rocks struck the washer and dryer causing major dent damage. It looked like large hail denting cars from a storm! When I told Dad about the accident, he beat the ever-living shit out of me! He took off his belt from his pants and he hit me leaving welts on my ass, then he picked me up and threw me in my bed like throwing a bag of trash in a dumpster. He threw me in the top bunk bed hitting my head on the wall. Then he got rid of all my bowling pins. (real and plastic), and he never took me bowling again!

My brother Tommy laughed his ass off when the washer and dryer were shattered with rocks! One day I grabbed the next-door-neighbor's cat and washed it in the washing machine then I put it in the dryer for a full cycle and the cat survived. I swear this wobbling cat had ninety lives for what I put it through!. Then I put the pour cockeyed cat out in the snow, and it ran away! It's a good thing my father didn't hear about that story or he would have killed me!

My brother Tommy was an instigator; he was daddy's boy. One night, Dad had just finished building a new house and it was right before we move in and I yelled. "Tommy! Dads coming!" He closed the screen door and when I ran out of the house I went right through the screen, tearing it open! Did I get my ass kicked for that!

One day I was a little lazy about taking a shower, and Mom said. "Come on Ricky, or we're going to be late for church."

Dad said. "He's probably playing with his ding dong!"

"Ma said, "Manny! That's enough!

One night Dad came home from work in a bitchy mood! Mom said, "Who went in my room and stole the cookies/candies etc."

Dad said, "I know who! Big Dick over there!"

One night we were eating supper and my brother Glenn didn't finish his spaghetti and meatballs. Dad said, "Give it to the garbage disposal he'll eat it!" Meaning me. My brother Tommy was always right and I was always wrong when I got in trouble with my father. I got the belt across my ass! One night I had an argument with my dad, and he gave me a beating and I ran out of the house and thumbed a ride. A women picked me up and I told her to take me to Newport Navy Base, and she said, "Okay!"

Instead, I asked her to drop me off at my cousin, Evelyn Rezendes' house on the other side of Tiverton. Evelyn was my bail-out partner. Anytime I was in trouble with Dad, she went to bat for me! She gave me a ride home. After getting enough beatings at home, I am surprised I'm still alive.

In 1969 The Tiverton High School was playing in the State Championship baseball game in Providence. For two dollars, I could take the bus from the school to the game. Dad said, "It's too much money, you're not going!'" Tiverton lost 6-3.

Then in the fall, Mom gave me a dollar to go see Tiverton High play football in back of Pocasset School. Mom brought me to the game, not Dad! Aunt Louise brought me home when the game was over. That's when I started liking sports; Football, basketball, and baseball in that order. I want to go see the games and Dad said, grinding his teeth, "You're going to work with me in Little Compton!"

Evelyn said, "Oh, for God's sake, Manny, let Ricky enjoy his summer and football games on Saturday afternoons."

I got friendly with all the coaches at Tiverton High School and on good behavior, Dad let me go see the games, keeping me out of trouble. I was being a good boy, when I didn't have to shovel gravel with my brother Tommy all day, with my dad being a pain in the ass! But when I did get in trouble, he would take my basketball or baseball bat away instead of beating me with his belt, because when I got older and Dad hit me with the belt,

I would grab the belt and spin away! So the only way to punish me, was to take my sports things away and stop me from going to the games.

One day I took the late bus home from a basketball game or from practice, and I was three hours late for dinner. My mother thought something happened to me! Mom and Dad called the police, but no Ricky. Here I come, off the school bus at 7:02pm, and did I get a beating from Dad!

Later in December 1972 we moved out of Tiverton to Cranston. Then I was working and I learned how to ride the city bus up and back from work and go to the games. Then I started getting into music- disco, and going to nightclubs and dancing. I worked two jobs so I could go to all the local games and nightclubs. When I was home I would play my records loudly on my stereo and dad would stomp on the floor for me to turn the music down. When I turned the music down it was still thumping and dad would stomp on the floor again when he was watching TV. I turned the music way down and dad came downstairs and he said, "Turn that God damn music down! What the hell do you think this is: A nightclub?"

I had to keep the music down so low you could barely hear it; My dad was a pain in the fuckin ass! When he was out I would blast the neighbors away. One night Dad was home and I thought he was out, so I blasted my stereo with a pounding beat from the disco group "Cerrone." Dad came downstairs, pushed the bedroom door open and punched and broke my stereo! He said, "That's the end of that!" And he went back upstairs. I ran out of the house and went to Uncle Richi's house until midnight to get away from the crazy bastard! The next day Dad tried fixing my stereo, but he couldn't : It was busted! My mom, brothers and sisters were pissed about Dad breaking my stereo. Claire whipped Dad's ass with a big stick then hit him in the head with the stick! My sister Paula punched Dad in the stomach before

Claire finished him off! All my aunts and uncles were pissed at Manny- you bastard!!! The next day I told my Dad, my stereo was old and I was going out to get a new one! A bigger one too!

"He said, "You better keep the God damn volume down or I'm going to break that one too!"

I bought the new stereo, had head phones, and Dad in a good mood, "That's a nice one!" He said.

I put the head phones on and Dad can't hear a thing! One night Dad and Ma were out and I had the stereo blasting without the head phones! My brother Jay, acting like Dad, came in the house and he said, "Ricky! Turn that God damn stereo down!" I quickly turned the volume down putting on the headphones and Jay came down joking. "Dad's not here!"

One Saturday afternoon I was watching a college basketball game on TV and Dad came downstairs complaining about why the TV was so loud. He said, "Turn the God damn TV down!"

Me and all my brothers and Tommy's friends were watching the game, anybody could turn the TV down but Dad stormed over to me as I was laying on the top bunkbed, and he threw a punch at my head. I blocked his punch, pushed him away, jumped off the bed and I swept both of his legs from under him and put him on his ass. Then I ran out of the house like a bat out of hell in zero degree cold and went over to Uncle Richi's house crying to Nana and Aunt Hilder. That was the last time Dad hit me! It got to a point where Dad couldn't hit me with the belt anymore, because I would grab the belt and hit him in the hand with the belt buckle, or he'd take my sports things away until I get to a point where I didn't care anymore and he tried to punch me but that didn't work. Then I started taking Karate and that was the end of Dad's beatings. I did a round house, and I said, "Go ahead Dad, hit me and see what you get!

PARKING FEES AND THIS GOD DAMN TRAFFIC!

A bus was on its way to Fenway Park with a tour group to see the Boston Red Sox. The bus driver was bitching about the traffic and crazy drivers.

"Good morning, ladies and gentlemen welcome aboard Church Tours from the Diocese of Fall River. After everyone has finished boarding, we're off to Fenway Park to see a Red Sox and the New York Yankees Baseball Doubleheader. The first game starts at 1:30pm and the second game will start about 5pm. How many Red Sox fans do we have on this bus?"

"Yeah!" The crowd cheered!

"How many Yankee fans do we have on this bus?"

"BOO!" Went the crowd!

"My name is David Leo, your bus driver and tour guide. After leaving the bus station we will be traveling up Route 24 North to Route 128 into Boston. Sit back and enjoy the trip. Go Red Sox!"

The bus left Fall River and as soon as the bus entered Route 24, it was stuck in parking lot traffic!

"Oh, you've got to be kidding! What the hell is going on!

Ladies and gentlemen, it's a good thing we left early, we're stuck in traffic for a while!"

The traffic did not move for two hours due to an overturned truck at the Bridgewater exit. The truck spilled food, water and soda all over the road. Deer came out of the woods on to Route 24 to feed and get a drink before retreating back into the woods.

The bus driver is getting angry! "Ladies and gentlemen, it looks like we're going to miss part of the first game because this God damn traffic is not moving!"

One man yelled from a car. "Come on you mother fuckers! Move!"

Another man was driving in the breakdown lane and over the grass on the side of the road only to be stuck behind a parked Massachusetts State Trooper. The man got a ticket. Horns were blaring the whole time! One man got out of his car to walk up and see how far the traffic's backed up. His car ran out of gas causing another problem.

The mess was being cleaned up and a tow truck arrived to move the turned over food truck to the side and open up the traffic. For two hours all you can hear is the bus driver swearing and bitching!

"Come on God Damm it! This is getting out of control! Are we going to be stuck here all day! I have no way we can turn around and go another way! We're stuck here. Come on! Let's move!"

Finally, the traffic moved slowly, inch by inch, before reaching full speed, only to be stuck again in parking lot traffic for another two hours at the Brockton exit due to a bad accident! "Jesus, Mary and Joseph! Not again! Ladies and gentlemen, it looks like we're going to miss the first game."

At 11:02am the bus left Fall River, at 12:02pm the bus is stuck in traffic in Bridgewater. At 1:02pm the bus was still stuck in traffic, not moving. At 2:02pm the bus is stuck in traffic again in Brockton. At 3:02pm the bus is still stuck at the Route 24 Brockton exit!

"Ladies and gentlemen, we'll be lucky to see the second game, this traffic is fucking ridiculous!" Said the bus driver. Finally, the accident scene was cleared and by 4:02pm the traffic moved slowly toward Route 128. It was a slow ride going into Boston. "The Red Sox won the first game, ladies and gentlemen, 1-0!" Said the bus driver.

"Yeah!" The bus passengers cheered.

At 5:02pm the bus made it to Route 128 only to be stuck again in traffic going to Boston. At 6:02pm it started raining and the second game was in a rain delay in the second inning until 7:02pm. The bus driver was going berserk, swearing F- bombs! F-this and F-that!

"Ladies and gentlemen, it looks like we're going to miss the second game too! Stuck in traffic again in Boston in the rain! We will go to the ballpark and try to refund our tickets and trip package and head back to Fall River. Sorry for the inconvenience." Said the bus driver.

The bus finally made it to Fenway Park. The time was 8:02pm. The second game was still being played 3-3 in the fourth inning. The bus parked on Lansdown Street at 8:13pm letting passengers off. A police security guard said to the bus driver. "Sir: you can't park here; you're in a fire lane. You have to park in the bus lot up the street, there's no street parking in and around Fenway Park."

"Yes sir, officer. The bus drove up entering the bus lot, meeting the guard.

"Hi, welcome to Fenway Park. It's $110 to park your bus." Said the guard.

"$110, are you out of your fuckin mind! Fuck you! I'll park in the street!"

"You can't park anywhere in the street or you will get towed, and it will cost you a lot more than $110." Said the guard. He had to pay the parking fee!

You can't strand 55 passengers if their bus gets towed. It was 9:02pm before the bus driver got to his passengers at the gate. The game was in the bottom of the 7th inning tied at 4-4. The bus driver said to a ticket selling agent. "Hi, my name is David Leo from Church Tours in Fall River, Massachusetts. My bus passengers had a game package for today's doubleheader, and we were stuck in traffic all day on Route 24 and getting into Boston. We were stuck in traffic for more than eight hours, and we would like to get our promotion packages refunded.

"Sure Mr. Leo, go to the press box upstairs and they will take care of you." Said the ticket agent. The bus driver met the promotion package manager in the press box. The name tag on his shirt showed his name was Jeffery James Thomas. At 10:02pm the game was still tied, 4-4 in another rain delay in the 11th inning. Finally, the game ended before 11pm and the Red Sox lost in 13 innings. Some of the passengers watched part of the second game for free. The managers and ticket agents were very helpful.

The Passengers followed the bus driver to the bus depot. The time was 11:02pm and it took two hours to get back to the highway trying to get out of Fenway Park. At 12:02am, stuck in traffic again at Fenway Park. 1:02am, still stuck there! The bus driver started pulling his hair out of his head because he was so mad! He doesn't have a wig either! At 2:02 am, they are stuck in traffic again on Route 128 heading for Route 24.

"Ladies and Gentlemen try to be patient, I think we're going to be stuck in Boston all night. Try to get some sleep and I'll get you back to Fall River as soon as I can!" Said the bus driver. At 3:02am the bus is stuck in traffic again on Route 24 because of an accident. At 4:02am the bus is still traveling in slow moving traffic on Route 24 because of another accident. The bus finally made it back to Fall River at 5:02am.

At 6:02am there was another accident on route 195 heading for downtown Fall River and drivers were stuck for another two hours! Three cars crashed, three people died, and all three cars involved caught fire!. A helicopter and rescue vehicles arrived. The time was 7:02am. The accident was cleared by 8:02am. The passengers from the bus tour that got stuck in this, were bullshit! A truck jackknifed on the Washington Bridge in Providence at 9:02am, closing the highway. A man pulled into a parking lot in downtown Providence and the parking attendant came over to the man's car. He said, "Excuse me sir, it's $10 to park here, $20 for the day." The time was 10:02am.

The man left, and he said, "I'm not paying to park; fuck that!" He stormed out of the parking lot.

A car from Massachusetts pulled into a parking lot at Narragansett Town Beach, with 5 people inside. The parking attendant said, "The parking fee is $30 for out-of-state cars."

"What! To go to the beach! You've got to be fuckin kidding!" Said the driver.

"You're not from Rhode Island and this is a town beach. It's $20 each person to get into the beach. Or you can drive down the road for a mile and go to Scarborough State Beach and the parking is much cheaper." The car peeled out of the parking lot and drove to Scarborough Beach! The time was 11:02am.

"$130 to go to the beach at Narragansett Town Beach, those price-gouging mother fuckers!" Said the driver. They paid $12.00 to park at Scarborough Beach.

The five Massachusetts residents went to get something to eat. "$19.50 for a cheeseburger, fries and a small drink. This cheeseburger is from McDonald's, look how small this thing is. The fries taste like rubber, and my drink is watered down! I'm not going to the beach in Rhode Island anymore! This place is a fucking rip-off!" Said the Massachusetts driver.

Another passenger said. "Maybe we should have stayed at the

other beach, before we get out of here, we're going to pay $100 anyway!" The time of the argument was 12:02pm, an hour later they were done eating and by 2:02pm they were in swimming and calming their tempers down.

A month later it was football season and a car with five people was driving from New Bedford to watch the New England Patriots game against the New York Jets. The group left home at 9am for a 1pm game in Foxboro hoping for a tail gate party in the parking lot outside the stadium. It was a smooth ride through Fall River until they got in traffic at the Washington Bridge in Providence for an hour because of a broken-down car.

"Come ON! Are we going to be stuck all fuckin day?" Said the driver.

When they got to the parking gate at the Patriots game, the parking attendant said, "$65 to park sir." The road rage begins. The car rammed down the gate almost running the parking attendant over!

SECTION 50

RUNNING RED LIGHTS

A motorcycle gang formed in North Attleborough, Massachusetts, staying in a vacant building. They named themselves, "The Truth or Dare," motorcycle gang. One motorcycle raced toward a red light, peeled rubber, then went right through the red light when no cars were coming. It picked up speed and was doing wheelies while racing down Washington Street during the early-morning rush hour. A cop parked nearby, gave chase. The motorcycle went through another red light and turned right, nearly hitting a parked car into the Emerald Mall parking lot.

He was doing tricks with his bike then two more North Attleborough cops gave chase! The motorcycle took off and the police tried trapping the motorcycle, but it got away and crashed through the front door of JC Penney's, driving through the store, knocking over clothes, nearly hitting customers, and crashing into signs.

There were ladies' panties wrapped around the motorcycle's exhaust pipes as the motorcycle drove through the mall into Macy's like a bat out of hell! People were screaming. The motorcycle drove a zigzag through Macy's, crashed through a glass window into the parking lot, and got away! The entire North Attleborough Police Force arrived at the mall.

"What happened?" One cop said to another.

"A motorcycle with jet speed crashed into the JC Penny and disappeared somewhere in the mall while being chase by police. Macy's gave their report on the damage the motorcycle had caused when it flew through a plate glass window and sped away.

The police were going through every street and neighborhood in North Attleborough looking for the motorcycle. The motorcycle was hiding in a wooden area waiting for the sirens to quiet down. Wooooo! Wooooo! Wooooo!

Then the motorcycle went through side streets because Attleboro Police had been notified of his location.

The Motorcycle hid behind Market Basket then it went into Pawtucket, Rhode Island. The motorcycle parked behind Spumoni's restaurant and the driver went in for lunch. The driver was a man with a broken nose. He had a pizza for lunch and a beer. Then he drove down Newport Avenue in Pawtucket toward East Providence. *I wonder where he's going for dinner tonight? In Jail I guess!*

A Pawtucket cop followed the motorcycle to the East Providence town line, going the speed limit. The Pawtucket Police got a call from the North Attleborough Police.

"North Attleborough Police, notifying Pawtucket Police. Look for a speeding motorcycle with Massachusetts Plate. UpU2."

"North Attleborough Police, this is Officer Steven Brad from Pawtucket Police. I followed this motorcycle from Spumoni's Restaurant to the East Providence line. He was driving the speed limit when I was following him. His bike had women's panties covering his exhaust. I will notify East Providence Police. Steven Brad, Pawtucket Police over!"

"!0-4, thank you, North Attleborough Police over."

The motorcyclist was hiding behind a dumpster at East Providence Bowling Alley, snorting cocaine and smoking a joint. A worker came out to empty trash into the dumpster. The motorcycle peeled out and took off! The worker was scared and stunned. The motorcycle continued driving down Newport Avenue, heading straight onto Pawtucket Avenue. The East Providence Police officer was following and turned on its lights, then a second and third cop joined, following the motorcycle.

"North Attleborough Police, This is officer, David Mello, from East Providence Police. I am following the motorcycle you're looking for with MASS plate UpU2 with ladies' panties hanging over the bike's exhaust. I have back up following me as well. As soon as he picks up speed or does something wrong, we will pull him over. Right now, he's driving the speed limit heading into a school zone near East Providence High School. We can't stop him until he does something wrong. He's heading for Route 195 West."

"10-4, Officer David Mello. He's a very dangerous person causing major property damage. I will send a helicopter out. Meanwhile, contact the Massachusetts and Rhode Island State police if he exits onto 195 West. North Attleborough Police Over."

Another East Providence cop blocked the exit ramp to route 195 West. The motorcycle booked past the 195 ramp and headed for Route 44. He didn't stop at the red light and made a hard right turn at a high rate of speed, running over a girl's foot as she was trying to cross the street The bike made an illegal U-turn to get to Route 44.

The Motorcycle was heading toward Seekonk, being chased by five East Providence Police cars. One East Providence cop boxed him in and the Motorcycle made a wheelie, riding over the cop's car and getting away!

Seekonk Police joined the chase, then Rehoboth Police closed the highway. The motorcycle pulled into the parking lot of the Alive Restaurant and police trapping the motorcycle by blocking the entrance to the restaurant. There were 20 police cars involved from East Providence, Seekonk and Rehoboth Police.

The man jumped off his motorcycle and ran into the woods and the Rehoboth K-9 team sent in dogs to catch the mother fucker! A dog found him and bit him in the leg: The man pulled out a gun and shot the dog in the head! A second dog went for the man's throat. A third dog joined the attack, finally taking the mother fucker down! A fourth dog bit the man's ears off! Police cuffed his arms and legs and he was taken to Rhode Island Hospital before being sent to jail.

One night, a big rig was uploading motorcycles at the Truth or Dare camp in North Attleborough. A bunch of men and women also went in the back of the truck. The truck drove to downtown Providence and parked at the bottom of College Hill and a bunch of motorcycles with naked men and women road out of the back of the truck, went up College Hill by RISD, rode down Waterman Street on the East Side of Providence and through the Brown University Campus.

The Brown University Police said, "Oh, My goodness! Do you see what I see?"

Students on campus got a good laugh and cheered all the motorcycles riding by with the naked people on them. Then the naked bike riders went through red lights and stop signs, riding through the East Side. Then the Providence Police were chasing them and boxing them in and making arrests!

"Headquarters, this is Officer Reynolds from car#12. I need some serious back up on Angell Street on the East Side. Providence and Brown University Police have stopped forty motorcycles with naked men and women riding them, going through stop signs and red lights, causing a major disturbance to the public!"

"What! 10-4, I will contact the Rhode Island State Police headquarters, over."

At 11:02pm, all fifty-two naked riders were handed a summons to appear in court for indecent exposure, and running red lights and stop signs on forty motorcycles! Police followed the motorcycles back to the truck where they came from. The truck went back to North Attleborough.

Days later the Massachusetts State Police followed the forty naked motorcycle riders through Boston and up the MASS Pike, cross country. *Wow! I guess it's legal to ride naked in Massachusetts!*

A man was riding a motorcycle in downtown Providence, going through red lights and stop signs and two Providence police cars gave chase. The motorcycle had a good path in front of him before police closed him in. Before he was boxed in, the motorcycle did a wheelie, jumped up onto a pedestrian bridge, landed in the Providence River, and disappeared!

For weeks, the Truth or Dare motorcycle gang was constantly getting into trouble, running lights and going through stop signs. A motorcycle ran a stop sign in a school zone hitting a bunch of kids and knocking them down like bowling pins, in North Attleborough. The group got into fist fights and gun and knife attacks with Hell's Angels and many motorcycle gangs going cross country on summer trips.

A meeting was held at the North Attleborough Police Department. "Ladies and Gentlemen, friends, my name is Captain Roy Hoyer, just sworn in last week. We have a very dangerous road kill, new world order motorcycle gang breaking all the laws of the United States here in our town. The name of this gang is, 'The truth or Dare,' motorcycle gang. People are getting killed and they are running out the rules of the road. They are called, 'Red Light Runners'. We need to find this group and kick them out! They got here illegally, and they're staying somewhere! We need to travel through town and find this gang, or a lot of people may die. I fear there could be more than three-hundred members!

North Attleborough has been on the news and is known as the town of evil. We need to change that."

Later, the North Attleborough Police found the vacant building where they were staying. A task force was called in to get them out, and the vacant building was fire bombed.

SECTION 51

AREA 51

Let's see what's here! A bowling alley: String pin bowling at ding dong lanes.

I'm going bowling with my twin brother Al Broker.

The end.

Me and Al Roker have the same birthday, August 20th, and we are the same age, 71.

ABOUT THE AUTHOR

Richard Rezendes worked at Brown University and the East Greenwich, Rhode Island school department before retiring at age of sixty-two. He likes sports, football, basketball, and baseball, in that order. He is a bowler tenpins and currently holds a 220 average. His dream was to one day publish a book, and he has since published eight—*Ground of the Devil: Book One, Ground of the Devil: Book Two, Ground of the Devil: Book Three, The Revelation of Emma Grace, A Haunting in Mattapoisett, Hell Under the United States, Windy Outbreaks,* and *A Little Bit of Everything.*

www.richardrezendes.com
rezendes_richard@yahoo.com

Made in the USA
Middletown, DE
29 June 2025

77637510R00189